Mackinac Maze

Jerry Prescott

Proctor Publications of Ann Arbor • Michigan • USA

© 1997 by Jerry Prescott, First Edition

Published in the USA by
Proctor Publications
PO Box 2498
Ann Arbor, MI 48106

Library of Congress Catalog Number: 97–75369

Publisher's Cataloging-in-Publication Data
(Provided by Quality Books, Inc.)

Prescott, Jerry J.
     Mackinac maze / Jerry Prescott. -- 1st ed.
     p. cm.
     ISBN 1–882792–55–6

     1. Mackinac (Mich.)--Fiction. 2. Detective and mystery fiction.
     I. Title

PS3566.R56M33 1997   813'.54
                                QBI97-41222

*This novel is derived from the imagination of the author. The characters portrayed are ficti-
tious and none of the events described actually occurred. Though readers may be familiar
. with the settings and locales mentioned, the author in several instances has taken the liberty
of changing their descriptions and locations. The novel's purpose is solely to entertain the
reader.*

Dedication and Acknowledgments

I was first captivated by the charm of Mackinac Island when a fellow freshman in high school, Jim Wills, invited me to come spend the summer there with him and his parents. We were the island tennis pros, impressive titles for the two boys responsible for getting and keeping the clay courts in shape for the season. This richly rewarding experience continued for several summers. While we were attending the University of Michigan, Jim, Bob Weinbaum, and I co-founded a weekly summer newspaper, *The Mackinac Island Town Crier*. This book is dedicated to these two friends and in memory of all our parents who were so supportive in our launching of this venture.

As the three of us were completing Law School, we sold the newspaper to Wes Mauer, then the Dean of the Journalism School. The paper served as a summer intern program for several of his students. Members of the Mauer family have continued to publish the paper for nearly forty years.

There are so many people to thank for this book. I'm grateful for those of you who enjoyed my first novel, *Deadly Sweet In Ann Arbor*, and who enthusiastically encouraged me to write a sequel. I especially wish to express my thanks and appreciation to Linda Flanery for her dedication and long hours of hard work. Her proofing, editing, and perceptive suggestions were invaluable. Thanks also to Kandi Simmons who worked closely with Linda, proposing changes she thought would enhance the story. Working with my publisher, Hazel Proctor, has been a joy as she committed herself to orchestrating the best quality book possible. I was blessed once again to be able to utilize the artistic talents of Milt Kemnitz. He's a true gentleman with a wonderful sense of humor.

Friends and my entire family have been undaunting in their support, raising my spirits during the discouraging times. My hope is that readers will experience just a fraction of the fun and enjoyment as they read this novel as I did writing it.

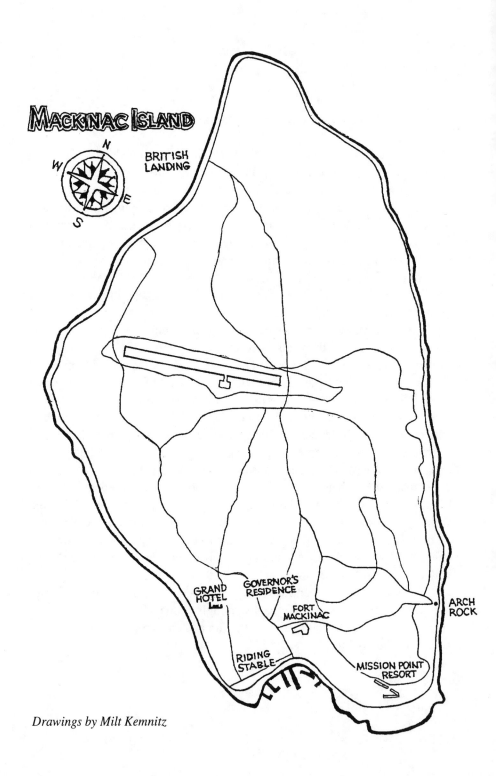

Drawings by Milt Kemnitz

Mackinac
Maze

Chapter 1

The six people were seated in the rear of the restaurant, clustered around a circular table, speaking in hushed tones.

"Damn it! Quit interrupting. Give him a chance to finish," one of the men said, raising his voice. The woman in the group raised her index finger to her lips to caution the man as two of the other men glanced over their shoulders at the nearby tables to see if his outburst had attracted attention. That didn't appear to have been the case. The din of other conversations, the sounds of lunches being served and tables being cleared, seemed to be muffling their hushed discussion.

"You're certain of this?" one of the men asked the young man, thirty-something, who'd been briefing them.

Nodding his head, he whispered, "Yes. Gallatin has always been a reliable source for us. He's connected to the top echelon, very wired in. The details he provided lead me to believe it's a done deal and not just an idea being discussed. The dates are set, arrival Saturday afternoon with the initial meeting scheduled for nine o'clock that night, following cocktails and dinner. Additional meetings are on tap over the course of the day on Sunday with a final meeting tentatively planned for Monday morning. Did I already mention approximately thirty people are involved, only twenty of whom will actually be sitting in on the meetings? The participants are being encouraged to bring their spouses with them, to give the appearance they're just regular tourists. They've also asked everyone to arrive wearing casual attire, to bring tennis racquets and golf clubs, even though it's unlikely they'll be used. Portions of the two top floors on the west end of the hotel are being sectioned off for the group. They're using the Grand, the major hotel on the island, quite famous, actually."

Several heads nodded, indicating they were familiar with Mackinac Island's Grand Hotel, as the young man continued.

"People will be flying into—," he hesitated a moment, referring to his notes, "the small town of Pellston. It's approximately fifty miles south of the Straits. They'll be taking regularly scheduled boats to the island from Mackinaw City. There's a small landing strip on the island, but the decision was made to forego use of it. As you can see, a number of steps are being taken to keep everything low-key so the local residents and other island visitors won't be alerted to the fact the meetings are taking place. Security will be minimal. No VIP treatment, which might prompt rumors or talk."

"But won't several of these people be recognized?" the man to his left asked. "Most of them have to have been seen on television or had their pictures in newspaper or magazines."

The young man shook his head. "I think you're right in that regard, but Gallatin has indicated the people attending won't be the high-profile politicians people might recognize. Though they're all key decision makers, they usually work behind the scenes. Their names might be familiar, but not their faces. Gallatin indicated this was by design, another attempt at maintaining secrecy."

The man who appeared to be the senior member of the group, at least in terms of age, spoke up, his face flushed. "I can't believe this. All this secrecy, the audacity to leave us totally out of the picture, entirely out of the loop."

A slight smile formed on the face of the man sitting to the right of the older man. "I can. The political fall-out if they were able to hammer out an agreement without our involvement would be devastating to us. It could lead to our downfall. I have to compliment whoever's orchestrating this though on their success thus far, in keeping us in the dark. What is it? Four days from now they'll be meeting and we're just learning about it. I wonder who's coordinating this, how many prior meetings there have been."

"I question whether everyone has been apprised of the fact that we're being excluded," the woman in the group said. "I can understand in terms

2

of the French and the Brits, but our southern neighbors? Do you think they've bought into leaving us out of the picture?"

The man across from her who'd spoken earlier smiled again. "Not only would I guess they're aware, I wouldn't be surprised if they weren't the ones who suggested it, or demanded it. Our exclusion and total secrecy."

"Damn!" the older man exclaimed. "What right do they have to meddle? Apply pressure? This is a Canadian issue. We need to prevent those meetings from taking place."

"Agreed," replied the woman. "But how? Should we leak details of the meetings to the media? What would that accomplish? It might just discredit us, publicize the fact we're being frozen out of the meetings, and raising questions as to why. If we're attributed as the source of the leak, it could backfire. Having us portrayed by the media as a major source of the problem, rather than part of the solution. Picturing us as interested in maintaining the status quo, the turmoil and uncertainty, rather than serious about finding a solution."

"What about just demanding that we be represented?" one of the other men suggested.

"Who do we approach to make the demand?" the woman replied. "The media? I just outlined some of the risks."

The senior member of the group had been holding his head in his hands. He looked up, shaking his head. "I can just visualize the media being notified on Monday of a major breakthrough. Picture those bastards on the steps of the Grand Hotel with cameras humming. And where will that leave us, not having been a party to the agreement? It could finish us as any kind of political force for years, make us the laughing stock of Canada. There has to be a way to stop the meetings, at least until we're brought into the negotiations. To prevent a sellout, a forced settlement. To offset the leverage being applied by . . . those foreigners, outsiders dictating Canada's future."

There was a moment or two of silence around the table, bewildered looks being exchanged as the six of them contemplated their dilemma, before the young man who'd been briefing them spoke again.

"What if we were to threaten to disrupt the meetings? Maybe go so far as to intimidate the people who plan to attend. Frighten them into thinking they might be harmed or injured. That in going forward with the meetings, they'd be placing everyone's welfare in jeopardy."

The man who'd made the previous sarcastic comments smiled again. "That would do wonders for our image, our credibility. From worry over damage control, we'd end up talking survival."

"Hear me out," the young man responded. "I wasn't suggesting we take responsibility for the threats. The onus could be put on another group, one of those radical fringe organizations that's only known by name, that no one really knows if they actually exist or not or who's behind them. Better yet, we could invent one. I was envisioning totally distancing ourselves."

The previous speaker smiled again. "Aren't we getting into a fairly risky area? Can we be totally certain things wouldn't be traced back to us? If they are, we're goners. We're assuming that they're going to succeed in coming up with some type of agreement. That's far from certain. They could also reach an agreement, some division of Canada, which would play into our hands, actually serve to strengthen us, win support for our goals. Chances are . . ."

"Bullshit!" the one man who'd been sitting back, to this point, just listening to the others, said. He was a muscular, thick-necked, dark-complected man who appeared to be in his mid-forties. He had an angry expression on his face as he lowered his voice and spoke.

"Too much is at stake for us to just sit twiddling our thumbs while we're becoming history. Hell! If we truly believe in our cause, we should be willing to fight for it, literally go to war if that's what it takes. I think this young man's right, I think those sons-of-bitches can be intimidated. With the right plan, we can distance ourselves from any negative repercussions. In case something goes haywire, in case people were to be injured or killed."

The woman was vigorously shaking her head. "I don't like the tone of this, the direction we appear to be headed in." One of the other men was nodding his head in agreement as the woman continued. "Good heavens, we're not a bunch of terrorists. What are you proposing? That we blow up the Grand Hotel, kill or injure a number of innocent people?"

"Oh, get real, Marie," the man who'd just proposed the immediate course of action said. "It's shit or get off the pot time!"

Marie recoiled in her chair as he continued. "All I'm saying is we have to act, that there are risks involved. We have to be willing to take them. And yes, I think our first priority has to be to protect ourselves. If it comes to a question of our survival, a question of us being exposed, versus some innocent bystander or someone who poses a threat being injured or killed in the process, I'd opt for the latter. Too much is at stake to think differently."

After pausing a moment for the others to digest that comment, the man continued. "I propose we get some professionals involved, allocate up to a hundred thousand dollars, maybe as much as two hundred thousand dollars from our coffers, our war chest at this stage, and put a plan of action in place. I think we can accomplish our goal, a cancellation of the meetings or at least a postponement, with a minimal risk."

No one said anything for a couple seconds. It was the senior member of the group who finally spoke. "As you all know, sometimes John and I don't see eye to eye on some issues. We've had some major differences of opinion. But this time, I think he's right. Our options are very limited. I'm going to make this a formal proposal. First, that we authorize John to proceed ahead post haste, empowering him to do what needs to be done. Second, I propose we supply him with two hundred thousand dollars cash. And third . . ." he hesitated for a moment, "that we offer a prayer that we'll be successful in preventing the meetings being held without us and that no one will be seriously hurt in the process. I'm convinced this has to be done. I see no other alternative. We can discuss this till doomsday. The problem is, that could be next Monday for us. What do you say? Are you all in agreement?"

Marie opened her mouth and started to say something and then changed her mind. One of the other men did the same. The older man glanced around the table.

"Okay then. Everyone in agreement with my proposal join hands." It was an awkward moment, the peer pressure was intense. They exchanged stares. Marie pulled away her hand initially as the man sitting next to her reached over to take it. A moment later, shaking her head, she reached out her hands to clasp the hands of the two men at her sides, completing the joining of hands around the table.

"Excellent! It's decided then." The older man bent his head and the others followed his lead.

A man sitting at the next table reached over and nudged his female companion, probably his wife. He nodded in the direction of the group at the circular table behind them who had joined hands, and now with heads bowed appeared to be engaged in prayer.

He whispered, "Not your typical Sunday school group. I'd love to be eavesdropping, to know what that's all about."

Observing the group the woman answered, also in a hushed voice, "Maybe they've just learned a friend is critically ill."

"Maybe," the man replied. "You're probably right."

Chapter 2

Kelly hunched her shoulders, shivering as she dug her hands deeper into the pockets of her windbreaker.

"Brrr! It's freezing. The wind chill must be in the thirties. I warned you the weather could be this iffy," she said to Mike.

His face broke into a grin, nodding his head in agreement as he pulled up his collar. There was a look of excitement on Kelly's face as she reached her hands out to grab the boat rail to balance herself in the stiff breeze. The island was gradually coming into clearer focus.

Kelly had talked nearly non-stop during the drive up from Ann Arbor, delighting Mike with tales of her summers spent working on Mackinac Island while in college. They'd made the five-thirty boat from Mackinaw City with only ten minutes to spare.

"I still find it hard to believe this will be your first visit, Mike. I assumed everyone who'd grown up in Michigan had been here at least once. I think you'll love it. Let's hope it warms up for the weekend."

Kelly Travis and Mike Cummings had become engaged three weeks ago, May 26th to be exact. They'd begun dating last November, following a major murder investigation they'd worked on together. The two were employed by the Ann Arbor Police Department. Mike was Kelly's immediate superior, heading up the Investigative Division. How their current relationship and pending marriage would impact their employment was still a question. Their mutual desire to have children, at least two, could provide the answer. Though Kelly was only twenty-eight, Mike was nearing forty. They were in agreement that they shouldn't wait long before attempting to have a child. This would be Mike's second marriage. One of the underlying reasons for his divorce had been his wife's refusal to consider children.

The trip to Mackinac Island had a dual purpose, a long weekend together to celebrate their engagement and a scouting expedition to explore whether the island would be a good site for a late summer or early fall wedding. They'd booked a room at the Grand Hotel for three nights and would be driving back to Ann Arbor Monday afternoon.

Mike stepped forward and placed his arm around Kelly's waist, leaning down and kissing her cheek as he hugged her.

"You notice we're the only ones brave enough to come up on deck," he said.

She turned toward him, her blue eyes twinkling as she answered. "Or dumb enough."

Mike laughed as he turned and gazed into the distance. "Let's see, that building has to be the Grand Hotel," he said, pointing, "with the world's longest porch. And that has to be the fort, to the right, where the flags of three countries have flown."

Kelly giggled as she replied, "So you were paying attention this afternoon after all. You're right! And the building we're just beginning to see down below the Grand along the shore is the Iroquois On the Beach. That's where I waitressed my first summer."

Overhearing conversation, Kelly and Mike turned to see another couple who'd come up to join them on deck. They appeared to be in their mid-fifties, both substantially overweight. That added insulation will come in handy up here, Kelly thought, sensing Mike was having the same thought.

"See, what did I tell you, Martha," the man said. "I said we wouldn't be the only ones up here. Wow! It's even chillier than I thought it would be."

The man smiled as he came toward Mike with his arm extended. "Hope we aren't interrupting anything. My name's Roy Miller and this is my wife, Martha. We're from Canton, Ohio."

Mike grasped Mr. Miller's hand saying, "Not at all, we're glad to have company, we were getting lonesome up here. My name is Mike Cummings and this is my fiancée, Kelly Travis. We're from Ann Arbor."

"Pleased to meet you," Mrs. Miller said, shaking both their hands. "Have you set a wedding date yet?"

"Late this summer or maybe early fall," Kelly answered. "We're actually thinking of getting married here on the island if we can arrange it."

Mrs. Miller beamed. "Oh, how romantic. Right, Roy?"

Her husband nodded. "We're about to celebrate our thirty-fifth. Of course, Martha was a child bride," he said with a laugh. "Our generation married much sooner, younger than yours. Things change. For the better, I think." He winked at Kelly and Mike as he added, "Martha and I would have loved the opportunity to have been able to go off and explore potential wedding or honeymoon spots. Wouldn't we have, Martha?"

Martha blushed. "Please ignore him," she said as she turned to her husband with a glare.

"Roy's the Chevrolet dealer in Canton," Mrs. Miller said, changing the subject. "Miller's Auto Mall. I bet they'd like to know how many cars you delivered last month, Roy."

It was Mr. Miller's turn to blush as he held up his hands. "Oh heavens,

Martha, I'm sure they couldn't care less." But he quickly turned to Kelly and Mike and said, "One hundred and ninety-seven. Our goal this month is two hundred. Not many dealers reach that level."

Kelly smiled. "Sounds impressive to me."

"Me too," Mike said. "But quite frankly, I don't know that much about the car business, how many cars an average Chevrolet dealer would sell."

"Well, Roy's not average," Martha quickly answered. "If you lived within a hundred miles of Canton you'd know your best deal is with Miller."

Mike smiled. "I'm sure that's the case."

"Even though you hail from Ann Arbor, I would give you a good deal, too," Mr. Miller said, handing Mike his business card. "As you might expect, we're Buckeye fans ourselves. We really get fired up over the Michigan-Ohio State game, don't we Martha?"

Beaming again, Mrs. Miller said, "Roy won ten bucks last fall from a U of M alum who's a neighbor. Remember, Roy?"

"We remember the game," Kelly said. "That goal line fumble kept us from going to the Rose Bowl."

"Well, you've won your share over the years, that's for sure," Mr. Miller said. "It's a great rivalry."

"Do you subscribe to Travel Tips Galore?" Mrs. Miller asked. Kelly and Mike shook their heads no. "Well, we do and a couple years ago they had an article on the top fifty places to visit in the United States. Mackinac Island will be the thirty-seventh one we've been to. We're trying to hit them all. Initially, the magazine was going to give a prize to any reader who visited all fifty. Proof, in addition to your word, would be a postcard from each place. The prize was quite nice. Do you remember what it was Roy?" Her husband shook his head no.

"Well, anyway, they had to back off. Seems some college student got a list of the magazine's subscribers and offered to sell them a set of the fifty postcards for a fraction of the value of the prize. So now we're just collecting the set of postcards for the fun of it. By the way, is this your first visit to the island?"

"It is for me," Mike replied. "But Kelly worked on the island for three summers during college. She can answer all your questions."

"Oh, great!" Mrs. Miller replied. "I bet those were fun summers. Where did you attend college?"

"I actually started out at Miami of Ohio," Kelly replied. "I transferred to Michigan State my junior year because of its program in law enforcement. Mike and I both work for the Ann Arbor Police Department. He's in charge of the Investigative Division."

"Oh, really, how exciting," Mrs. Miller said.

"Martha's a real nut for all those police shows on TV. There must be one every night. And the O.J. case, I don't think she turned off the set for six months."

Glancing over the Millers' shoulders, Kelly and Mike observed another brave soul had joined them on deck. A tall man, possibly six-foot-three or -four, attired in a light-weight, dark-colored business suit, not ideal for the current weather. His white hair gave him the appearance of one nearing his sixties, slender and looking physically fit. He flashed a warm smile and nodded his head in greeting as the Millers turned to see what had distracted Kelly and Mike. He walked past them to the end of the deck and stood by the railing looking out toward the island.

•

For the past several minutes, Kelly and Mike had been standing next to the boat rail with the Millers. Kelly identified many of the island's landmarks as they came closer into focus. Mr. Miller had an impressive-looking camera and was taking numerous photos. He was extremely proud of his new toy and delighted in showing Kelly and Mike the powerful telescopic lens feature.

"You can even identify people on the porch of the Grand," Mr. Miller boasted. "We're staying there, how about you?"

Mike explained they'd also be at the Grand and Mr. Miller turned to his wife. "Hear that, Martha? They're also staying at the Grand. How about having dinner together? We've heard they put on quite a spread."

Kelly was relieved as Mike quickly answered, "Thanks for the invite, but we thought we'd just have a quiet dinner by ourselves tonight."

"I understand, a heck of a lot more romantic than having dinner with a couple of old fogies."

Kelly and Mike smiled as Mike grabbed Kelly's hand. "Nothing personal," Mike said.

"Maybe tomorrow night, at least for a cocktail," Mrs. Miller suggested. "That is, if you're starting to get bored with one another by then," she added with a giggle. "Somehow I don't think that's going to be the case."

"Maybe we can talk Mike into taking a photo of us with the island as a backdrop, Martha."

"I'd be glad to," Mike said as Mr. Miller handed him the camera, explaining how everything was automatic.

"Just find us in the view finder there and push this button," Mr. Miller said.

After Mike had taken a couple photos, Mr. Miller took the camera back and suggested he get one of Kelly and Mike. "I'm sure there's a twenty-four-hour photo service somewhere on the island. It'll be a souvenir for you to take home to Ann Arbor."

As Kelly and Mike walked to the side of the boat to pose for a photo, she whispered in his ear. "They're something else, aren't they? I'm glad you turned down the dinner invitation." Mike smiled and winked at her as they turned to face the camera.

"Martha, see if you can make a few faces so we get a big smile out of them, okay? Hey, that's good! One more. Okay, I have two shots left on this roll. How about one of the four of us?" Looking over his shoulder, he called out to the man at the opposite end of the deck. "Suppose you could give us a hand, buddy? Take a shot of the four of us?"

The man smiled and nodded, and started toward them as the boat's horn blasted, startling everyone.

"Oh, my Lordy," Martha said. "That scared me half to death!"

Kelly smiled. "I should have warned everyone. That means we'll be docking in about five minutes."

"I better hurry then," the tall, white-haired man said as he took the camera from Mr. Miller. The four of them proceeded to arrange themselves along the rail.

"Ready . . . one, two, three," the man said before taking their photo.

"There's just one shot left on the roll, might as well finish it up," Mr. Miller said to the man. The man had been eyeing the crowd of people on the dock as their boat approached and appeared not to have heard Mr. Miller. An excited look appeared on his face. Turning to Mr. Miller, he said, "I heard you describing the telescopic lens feature earlier. If you could instruct me on it, I'd like to take that last shot. I think I recognize someone on the dock. Would that be all right with you? I'll buy you a new roll of film."

Taken aback, Mr. Miller stammered, "I—I guess so. Sure, go ahead. Here's how it works," he said as he showed the man the focus button for the telescopic lens.

As the man focused the camera and took the last photo, Kelly stared at the crowd of people gathered on the dock to see if she could determine whose picture he was taking. As she did so, two men standing next to one another appeared to sense their photo was being taken and looked up. Both quickly turned their heads to the side and raised a hand to hide their faces. The two then stared up at the man who was now lowering the camera. Turning quickly, the two men pushed their way through the crowd in the opposite direction from where the boat was now docking.

"Thank you," the man was saying to Mr. Miller. "I'll take the roll of film and have it developed. I heard you say you're staying at the Grand. I'll leave your prints at the desk with a new roll of film by noon tomorrow. Which film speed do you use?"

"Wait a minute, hold on," Miller replied. "Why don't I get the photos developed? I'll leave the print of the one you took at the Grand Hotel desk in your name. I don't know you."

The man smiled in understanding. "I could leave my watch with you. Maybe some money. No, you're right. Could you please get the film processed as quickly as possible, though? Hopefully, a one-hour photo service if it's available." The man handed Miller two twenty-dollar bills. "Two prints of the photo I took. Leave them at the desk in my name. Here, I'll write my name down and give you a number to call as soon as you have them."

The man removed his billfold and fished around for a blank card. "Ah, here we are, this will work." He ripped off the lower half of a memo note he'd removed from his billfold. "Just leave the message the photos are ready. You don't even need to take time to identify yourself. If I'm not there, the person answering will know what you're referring to. I can't tell you how much I appreciate this. Thank you in advance."

The man turned and quickly headed down the stairwell. When the Millers and Kelly and Mike had reached the main deck, the boat had already docked and the man had disappeared. He must have been one of the first ones off the boat, Kelly thought. She glanced at Mike and shrugged her shoulders. "Strange, huh?"

Mike smiled. "Remember, we're on vacation. You're right, though, that was very unusual. Did you get a look at the name he gave Mr. Miller?"

Kelly nodded. "Black. R. Black. I think I saw whose photo he took, too. Two men, mid-thirties. Dark-haired and dressed in jeans and windbreakers. I doubt if I'd recognize them if I saw them again, though."

"Well, let's get our luggage. I see the Grand Hotel dock porter over there. The vacation begins starting now."

Chapter 3

Kelly and Mike climbed into the Grand Hotel carriage. There were two other couples already inside in addition to the Millers.

"Isn't this exciting?" Mrs. Miller said. "I just love the way the driver's dressed, his top hat and red tails. And those plumes on the horses' heads. I can already see why you liked it here, Kelly. So quaint, all the flowers."

"Me too," Mike said, squeezing Kelly's hand and smiling at her.

"You didn't have to tip the dock porter, Mike," Mr. Miller said. "Luggage handling and tipping is included in the cost of the package. At least ours is. I would think yours is, too."

Mike nodded and smiled. "I realized that. Thanks for the reminder, though. In fairness to the boy, he also told me a tip wasn't necessary. He's a junior at Hope College and I'm sure he can use a few extra dollars for next fall."

Kelly had been about to say something to Mike about the tipping and was now relieved she'd kept her mouth shut. Mike was very generous with his tips, she'd observed during their dating. It wasn't at all for show, to impress. Mike genuinely liked people and empathized with them. No pretensions, he treated everyone the same. It was one of the many things she loved about him.

"Did you get your room number?" Mrs. Miller asked. "We're going to be in 337. The boy said they'd have our luggage in our room in less than an hour. I certainly hope so. We'll need a few minutes to dress for dinner. We're cutting it pretty close, aren't we Roy?"

Mr. Miller laughed. "I'm sure they're not going to close down the kitchen before we get there, Martha. They're expecting us."

"In answer to your question," Kelly said, "no, we don't know our room number yet. We know the room we wanted to have. I called over three weeks ago to specifically request it and they assured me there wouldn't be a problem. They actually confirmed it in writing, the Mackinac Suite. The room has a spectacular view of the Straits and is beautifully decorated. It was one of the first group of rooms they upgraded way back when I was working for the Grand. The dock porter told Mike there was a question mark beside our names under room number. He thinks the prior occupants may have delayed their check-out or something. He told us not to worry."

"Well, I certainly hope it works out for you. Sounds as if it's a lovely room, a very romantic setting," Mrs. Miller said, smiling and nudging her husband with her elbow. He'd been glancing out the windows of the carriage and suddenly lunged up out of his seat and started pounding on the roof of the carriage.

"Can you stop for a minute?" he shouted up to the driver. As the carriage continued on, Mr. Miller grabbed the door handle and opened the door. "Can you hear me, driver? Can you stop for a minute while I drop off a roll of film?"

Looking out the window, Kelly and Mike saw the Island Photo Store which had prompted Mr. Miller's reaction. The message under the sign with the store's name stated "Three-Hour Processing."

Mr. Miller apologized to the other two couples. "Sorry, this will only take a few seconds. I need this roll developed right away. Right?" he added, glancing at Kelly and Mike.

While they were waiting, Mrs. Miller, Kelly and Mike introduced themselves to the other two couples. One couple, who appeared to be in their early twenties, explained they were honeymooners who'd be living in one of the Detroit suburbs. The second couple came from Chicago. They were celebrating their twenty-fifth wedding anniversary.

True to his word, Mr. Miller had taken only a couple minutes. The driver held the door open for him as he climbed in, breathing heavily. "That was lucky," he said. "They were just closing up. In fact, he had the key in the door. I can have the prints by noon tomorrow."

The carriage started up once again. "Don't you love the clip-clop sound of the horses' hooves?" Mrs. Miller said. As the carriage turned off of Main Street, Kelly pointed and said, "That's the Iroquois Hotel over there, where I worked my first summer. This hotel is the Lakeview and the Windemere is behind it. My parents stayed there a couple of times when they came up to visit me."

Mike and the Millers sensed Kelly's excitement as she described all of her old familiar haunts as the carriage continued.

"She is one gorgeous girl, Mike," Roy whispered in his ear. "She has a look of Princess Di."

Chapter 4

"I know, I'm sorry. It sounds trite, I realize, but it's really something out of our control. Something very out of the ordinary came up."

Kelly and Mike were in the assistant manager's office. They'd been told at the registration desk that they could only have the room they'd planned on for one night. They would have to move to a far less desirable room after tonight. They were asked if they wanted to spend the one night in the Mackinac Suite, knowing they'd have to move. One consolation was the fact one of the nights was being complimented because of the problem. Kelly had still said she wanted to speak with Mr. Woodbridge, who was not only the manager, but also the major owner of the Grand Hotel. Kelly knew him from the time she'd worked for the Grand. Mr. Woodbridge had left for the day and hence, they were in the assistant manager's office, hearing him out. He was new since Kelly's days on the island.

"We apologize. We know we're in the wrong. That's why we're complimenting you one night. That's a major concession. Please try to understand."

Kelly debated over whether she should ask for Mr. Woodbridge's home number. She'd been dreaming about staying in the Mackinac Suite with Mike for the past couple weeks. A definite disappointment, but she guessed they could live with it. She smiled to herself, thinking of the amount of money they'd be saving with the free night as well. Steve Richards, the assistant manager, was still talking as these thoughts passed through Kelly's mind.

"We've given you one of the nicest rooms available. I realize it's not the one you wanted, but I think you'll be pleased."

"Why couldn't you move us to one of the other nearby suites?" Kelly asked.

"I'm sorry. They're all spoken for as well. All part of the same situation. Frankly, it's been a nightmare for us."

Kelly and Mike exchanged looks. "Well, we'd like to spend at least one night in the suite," Kelly said.

"Fine," Richards said, his face beaming. "Just give me about five minutes. I'll call and arrange for your luggage to be taken up at once. Thank you for being so understanding."

Mike smiled at Kelly after Richards had left the office. "So understanding?" he said, laughing. "I'd hate to see you in action when you weren't so understanding. This will work out."

Kelly smiled. "Oh, I know it will. It's just that I wanted this weekend to be so perfect."

"It still will be," Mike said, embracing her in his arms and sharing a long kiss with her.

14

•

The bellman who had escorted the two of them up to the suite stepped back after opening the door and held it open for them. The room was even nicer than Kelly remembered. The view was spectacular. It was decorated in a lilac theme, very light and airy. The floral patterns in the wall coverings and furniture, the drapes and valance around the huge four-poster bed, all were beautifully coordinated. There was a huge, spring flower arrangement on the circular coffee table, and a bottle of wine chilling in a bucket on a small table in front of the expanse of windows facing west.

"Pretty special, isn't it?" the young bellman said, a huge grin on his face. "The weather is supposed to clear and warm up tomorrow. The view of the sunset from this room is awesome."

Kelly and Mike were standing in the middle of the room, holding hands, soaking up the beauty of the room as they glanced around.

"I see why Richards delayed us a few minutes downstairs," Mike said, pointing to the bouquet and bottle of wine. "I bet those arrived just ahead of us."

Kelly nodded as she observed that their luggage was already in the room as well.

"The last dinner seating is in about forty-five minutes," the bellman said. "I hope that gives you enough time. If not, room service is available until midnight. Can I answer any questions for you or get you anything further? The cable TV program guide is there right next to the set. You have two controls, on the end tables on both sides of the bed."

"I think we're fine, thank you," Mike told him. "Anything else you can think of, Kelly?"

"No, I can't think of anything," she answered. "Thank you."

As the young man turned to leave, Kelly thought of something. "One question. While we'd love to watch the sunset tomorrow from this vantage point, we're having to move to another room. Would you have any idea as to the time they'd like us out, what time you want to move us? We have an appointment at the Little Stone Church at eleven o'clock tomorrow morn-ing. We—"

"Oh, that's too bad," the bellman said. He grinned. "Having to move, not the appointment. Check out time is normally noon with check-ins at four. They're generally pretty liberal about extending check-out a couple hours. I'll ask and let you know." He hesitated a minute. "Why don't you plan on two o'clock unless you hear from me. Would that work out for you?"

"That would be perfect, if you could arrange it," Kelly replied. "We'll plan to switch rooms at two, unless we hear differently."

Chapter 5

Their dinners had been delicious. Both had ordered the whitefish with the special Grand Hotel salad, which featured watercress and Michigan dried cherries. They'd both quickly showered and dressed for dinner following the bellman's departure and arrived at the dining room with a few minutes to spare. Mike had topped his dinner off with fresh Michigan cherry pie a la mode. Kelly had a single scoop of Mackinac fudge ice cream.

"I feel so relaxed," Mike said as they sipped their coffee. "My initiation to Mackinac Island has been a delight, thus far. I particularly enjoy the tour guide," he said as he reached across the table and squeezed Kelly's free hand.

"Would you like to take a stroll on the porch?" Kelly asked.

Mike smiled. "The world's longest. Sure, I'm game for that. It might be a little chilly, though. Do you want me to go up to the room and bring down a sweater for you?"

"That would be nice, if you would. The white one, it's in the bottom drawer. I think I'll visit the ladies room while I'm waiting."

"Nature calls for me, too. I'll use our bathroom while I'm getting your sweater."

They strolled out of the dining room, nodding to the young honeymooners they'd met during the carriage ride to the Grand earlier. They were seated at a table near the entrance.

"It's a shame they put them there," Kelly said to Mike as they entered the hallway. "They should have given them a more private table, one of the dark corners."

"They don't seem to mind," Mike replied. "They're so wrapped up with one another, it won't make any difference where they're sitting."

Kelly laughed. "I think you've got that right. Why don't I meet you at the front door in about ten minutes. Maybe on the porch—I'll check the temperature. The wind usually dies down in the evening."

Mike put the index finger of his right hand to his lips and blew Kelly a kiss before turning and heading to their room. As Kelly walked through the lobby, heading for the ladies room, she glanced around the lobby. A small concert for the earlier diners had just finished and the lobby was quite crowded. Looking toward the front entrance, she saw the tall man they'd seen on the boat, the one who'd taken the group photo of Mike and her with the Millers. His back was to her as he headed toward the door. He turned and looked over his shoulder. Kelly was too far away for him to notice her, but something caught her eye.

A man half-way between where she was standing and the front door had seemed to freeze in his tracks and quickly kneeled down, turning his head away from the entrance as he tied his shoe. As the tall man went out the door, the man who'd been kneeling quickly stood up and hurried out the door behind him.

Just my imagination, Kelly thought. The tall man was still wearing the same dark suit he'd worn during the boat ride. She was certain he was being followed. Strange, she thought. The incident on the boat had been odd also. The man asking Mr. Miller's permission to take a photo of someone he'd recognized on the dock. What do I do? Kelly said to herself. Let it be, I guess, she concluded as she turned and headed once again to the restroom.

Chapter 6

Kelly was elated as she came out the door onto the porch. The bellman had been right—the weather was clearing. Several stars were visible and there was hardly any sign of a breeze. The air had warmed, she really didn't even need a sweater. She and Mike should have checked before he headed upstairs.

She turned to her right and headed down the porch. It's beautiful, she thought, amazed there weren't more people outside enjoying the lovely evening. She turned her head from time to time to see if Mike had come out on the porch yet. He mentioned he had to use the facilities. I hope he doesn't have a problem, she thought.

She was all alone as she neared the end of the porch. She'd passed a few couples coming back towards the entrance during her walk. She looked back again. No sign of Mike. She gazed in wonder off into the distance at the bridge connecting Michigan's upper and lower peninsulas, outlined by lights which appeared to twinkle. There were several viewers mounted at this end of the porch, through which hotel guests could get a magnified look at the bridge. Kelly did so for a minute or two, but concluded they were best used in the daytime.

She looked to her left, down the hill in front of the Hotel, at the lighted grounds and the swimming pool Esther Williams had made famous in the forties or fifties, in a movie with Jimmy Durante. They still showed it at the island's local movie house every summer she'd worked here, along with other movies which had been filmed on the island. "Somewhere In Time" had been her favorite.

Kelly gasped. Was that a body floating in the pool? The dark shape appeared to be a man floating on his stomach, with his arms and legs stretched out. She stepped back to the viewfinder and crouched down, tilting the viewer towards the pool and twisting the knob to bring the image into clearer focus. She gasped again. It was a man's body! Not only that, it also appeared to be the body of the tall man she'd seen earlier, the man they'd met on the boat, with the dark suit and white hair.

She let loose of the viewer and started running towards the hotel entrance. "Damn," she said, looking down at her shoes. She bent down and removed them from her feet and quickly started down the porch again. Mike came out the door and immediately spotted her racing towards him with her shoes in her hand. She was breathing heavily as she flew into his arms.

"Are you okay? What's wrong?" he asked, wide-eyed.

Kelly whispered in his ear. "I think I saw a body floating in the swimming pool. The same man who was on the boat with us. I need to tell Richards or whoever's on duty."

Mike's eyes opened even wider. "Are you sure?" he asked in a hushed tone. "I shouldn't have asked that," he said as he grabbed her hand and they entered the Hotel, hurrying towards the concierge desk.

"Is Steve Richards available?" Mike asked the woman at the desk.

"I'll check for you," she said, sensing Mike's need for urgency and viewing the shoes in Kelly's hand. "Who should I say is asking?"

"Mike Cummings and Kelly Travis. We spoke with him earlier today."

She related the message to Richards or whoever she was talking to on the phone and hung up. "He says he'll be with you in about five minutes or so. You could just wait or come—"

"We need to see him right away," Mike said, raising his voice. "Let me talk to him."

Taken aback, the woman picked up the phone and dialed the extension again.

"Sorry to bother you again, but they say it's an emergency. Can I put Mr. Cummings on the line?"

"I'll take you back now," she said to them as she hung up. "Just follow me."

•

Richards was just rising from the chair behind his desk as Kelly and Mike entered his office. He smiled as he asked, "How can I help you? Is there something wrong with the room?" He was having difficulty concealing his annoyance over being harassed again by this couple, a somewhat disgusted look on his face as he noticed Kelly's shoes in her hand.

Mike glanced at Kelly, who blurted out, "There's a man's body floating in your swimming pool. I just saw it from the porch. I'm not mistaken, I took a closer look through one of the viewers."

Richards' expression changed to one of shock and concern. "Damn it! Probably a prank by one of those college boys. Is he wearing a swimsuit?"

"No!" Kelly replied, shaking her head. "I mean it's the body of a man dressed in a dark business suit. I think it's the same man Mike and I met on the boat coming over today. I—"

"Who else have you told?" Richards asked, now wide-eyed with a confused expression, clearly having difficulty assimilating what he was being told.

The question angered Mike. Richards' first concern appeared to be the impact this would have on the hotel.

"We came right to you," Kelly answered. "I don't think anyone else is aware of the body yet. I don't think it's an accident, I think he may have been murdered."

Richards grabbed his phone and pressed a button. "Hello Mac, Steve here. We may have a major problem. There's a woman in my office who says she just saw a man's body floating in our pool." Richards listened for a moment before saying, "She was on the porch. She used one of the viewers. Five minutes ago. We'll just sit tight here in my office while you take a look. We'll wait here until we hear from you."

As he hung up, Richards said, "That was Ian McKenzie, in charge of hotel security. He and one of his men are heading down to the pool now. We should hear back from him in a couple of minutes. I can't believe this." Richards was shaking his head. "Sorry, can I get you a coffee or something? A glass of water?" he offered.

Kelly and Mike shook their heads no.

"You said you thought you recognized the body, the man in the pool?"

"That's right," Kelly replied. "Besides seeing him on the boat, I also saw him in the lobby twenty minutes ago. He was heading out the front door. I think he was being followed."

"Wait, let me get this straight," Richards said. "You saw the man whose body you think you saw in the pool less than half an hour ago? What makes you think he was being followed?"

Kelly explained what she'd observed. Mike was also hearing these details for the first time and was as absorbed in Kelly's explanation as Richards was. They both pressed her for a description of the man who'd knelt down to seemingly tie his shoelace. Kelly shook her head, closing her eyes, attempting to recall what she'd seen.

"I'm not sure I'd recognize him if I saw him again," she said. "I'm not even sure what he was wearing. A blue blazer, I think. Maybe tan pants. I couldn't even verify if he was wearing shoes with laces. Maybe in his thirties, light brown hair, no facial hair, no glasses."

"If he's responsible, he must want to make a statement of some kind," Mike suggested. "The body could have been left in the bushes. Maybe he has a grudge against the hotel."

"I've had the same thought," Richards said. "Excuse me for a second. I'm going to make a call and have the west end of the porch roped off."

•

No sooner had Richards hung up than his phone rang. Picking up the receiver, he answered, "Yes." After listening for a moment he mouthed, "It's Mac" to Kelly and Mike. He listened for the next few minutes, asking questions from time to time. "How about any trace of blood? It doesn't appear anyone's broken into the office, the locker rooms? You've checked the fence?"

He finally concluded the conversation by saying, "We'll just wait for you here in my office then."

The man was telling Richards something further as he listened for another moment or two before replying, "I understand."

Richards hung up. Mike thought he was seeing a slight trace of a smile on Richards' face as he began to relate the conversation to them.

"To begin with, they haven't found a body, in the pool or anywhere else." Kelly and Mike exchanged surprised looks. "You heard some of my questions. No sign of blood. No water splashed around the pool deck. No signs of a break-in, through the office or the fence. Nothing out of place. No debris or footprints. They'll be having another look in the daylight tomorrow morning. McKenzie is on his way up, just checking something out first."

Kelly stared at Richards in amazement. "I didn't make this up. I know what I saw."

Richards looked down at his desktop as Mike reached for Kelly's hand.

"You aren't attempting a cover-up, are you?" Kelly asked.

Richards looked up in surprise. "What are you suggesting? Heavens no! Would publicity about a body being discovered in our pool, possible foul play, hurt the Grand? You better believe it! But would we, would McKenzie or I, be a party to a cover-up? No way! That's a low blow." Richards' face was flushed.

Kelly nodded. "I'm sorry. I was trying to think of an explanation. Maybe he was alive, trying to give the impression he was dead, floating in the pool. But why?"

"I was going to wait for Mac, but I think it's only fair to warn you— caution you," Richards said, addressing Kelly. "McKenzie reminded me of something just now. A couple of years ago a handful of kids, college students, girls as well as boys, climbed the fence and had a pool party. It was about eleven o'clock. The pool was still lit and they went skinny dipping. Swan dives off the diving board, all sorts of things. Some guests were on the porch and arguments began as they vied to use those viewers at the end of the porch. Comical now, but it turned into a brawl, a couple of fist-fights. What's the point in my telling you? Following that, Mr. Woodbridge made arrangements to adjust the viewers so that they could only be used to view the Straits and the bridge."

Mike nearly lunged from his chair. "What are you suggesting? That Kelly's lying?"

"Hold on," Richards said, holding up his hands. "Mac is checking out the viewers now, on his way up. I just wanted you to be prepared. I'm certain Mac will find one of the viewers has been tampered with, so—"

"If you're so damn certain, why in the hell did you accuse Kelly of lying?"

"I'm sorry," Richards stammered. "I apologize, Mrs. Cummings. I–"

"I'm not Mrs. Cummings," Kelly said. "At least not yet, we're just engaged. My name's Kelly Travis. I'm not some kook. I'm a detective with the Ann Arbor Police Department. Mike is, too. He heads up the division."

Richards was holding his hands up. He was relieved to hear a knock at the door, and a man stuck his head inside the room as the door opened.

"Come in, Mac. Perfect timing. I'd like to introduce you to Kelly Travis and her fiancé, Mike Cummings. This is Ian McKenzie."

"Just call me Mac," McKenzie said as he shook their hands. Wasting no time, he said, "One of the viewers has been tampered with, no problem seeing the pool through it. It actually wasn't too difficult for whoever did it, a Phillips screwdriver and a couple minutes' time."

Mike patted Kelly's knee. He'd known that would be the case. Why was he feeling relieved? Kelly glared at him as if she was reading his mind.

"Steve's probably told you," McKenzie continued, "we didn't find a body. Someone would have had to move pretty fast to get a body out of the pool before our arrival without leaving a trace. We were there in less than five minutes after you called, Steve. Very mysterious."

"Miss Travis—Kelly—has raised the possibility of the man simulating he was dead, floating in the pool," Richards explained to McKenzie. "He could have climbed out and disappeared before you got there—jumped the fence without leaving a trace."

McKenzie nodded. "I hear you, but it sounds pretty farfetched to me. Why would he do it? I guess anything's possible, though. It's better than anything I've been able—"

Richards interrupted McKenzie. "I'd like Kelly to brief you on some other details, Mac. She saw the man whose body she thinks she saw in the pool, in the lobby just a few minutes before she spotted him in the pool. Go ahead, Kelly. Fill him in."

Chapter 7

Mike removed the key from the open door to their room as Kelly stepped inside. The room looked very inviting, the bed had been turned down and two of the lamps were on. Mike glanced at his watch. It was nearly twelve-thirty. Kelly collapsed in one of the room's comfortable easy chairs, removing her shoes and lifting her legs onto the hassock in front of the chair. She appeared to wilt as she exhaled a breath of air and began to unwind.

"Would you like a glass of wine?" Mike asked.

Kelly nodded, a smile appearing on her face. "Thanks for being so supportive, Mike. I'm sorry I was upset with you for a moment or two there. It's all so confusing."

Mike smiled as he handed her the glass of wine and bent down and kissed her gently on the lips. "No apologies needed. I only wish there was a simple explanation. McKenzie's going to notify the local authorities. You heard Richards, though. The police department on Mackinac is virtually a one-man show. They bring in three or four part-timers for about ten weeks over the summer months, but still—"

"They were hesitant when you suggested notifying the State Police," Kelly said. "Said they'd mull it over. In fairness to them, I can understand where they're coming from. No body, no evidence of a crime being committed, just my story. I think they both want to believe me and I think they do— even Richards. But they're right in being concerned about damage control, wanting to limit communications until there's more to go on."

Mike nodded. "Do you want to take McKenzie up on his offer? Meet him and his people in the morning for a look at the pool area?"

Kelly shrugged her shoulders. "I guess so. I'm so exhausted now I'm having trouble thinking."

Mike nodded again. They sat for a few moments, sipping the wine, rehashing the day's events in their minds.

"This evening started out so well," Kelly finally said. She sighed. "So romantic. I was wondering how our honeymoon could top it. And then . . ."

Mike couldn't help but smile. "I understand. Why don't we just try to get some sleep. Maybe everything will sort itself out tomorrow. Let's hope so."

•

Kelly woke with a start. Mike was also awake. "What on earth was that?" Kelly asked. "I don't think it was thunder."

Mike threw back the covers and sat up on the side of the bed. "No, more like an explosion. Off in the distance rather than near or in the hotel."

They both strained their ears, listening for additional sounds, possibly a siren. Mike stood up and walked to the door leading out to their small balcony. Opening it, he walked out and gazed around.

"It's quiet now," he said, coming back inside. "It's a lovely evening, stars galore. There's not any unusual activity, no lights coming on. And there's no sound of cars."

Kelly laughed. "Remember where we are, Mike. I think there's only three or four vehicles on the island—maybe two fire trucks, an ambulance and a police car."

Mike smiled. "Well, I didn't hear or see any of them."

"What time is it?" Kelly asked.

Mike walked back to the window and with the aid of the moonlight, looked at the watch he was now holding in his hand. "Half past four."

"Why don't you call down and see if anyone can tell us what happened," Kelly suggested.

Mike walked back to the bedside table next to his side of the bed, picked up the phone and dialed the operator.

"A busy signal," he explained to Kelly.

"Probably means we weren't the only ones to hear whatever it was," Kelly said. "That it wasn't just our imaginations."

Mike grinned, knowing what Kelly was thinking. While she'd been the only one who'd seen the body in the pool, others—including Mike—had probably heard the explosion.

Over the course of the next ten minutes, Mike tried to reach the hotel operator and the front desk again, continuing to get a busy signal.

"I could get dressed and go downstairs, I suppose," Mike suggested, stifling a yawn.

"I'll come with you," Kelly said as she saw Mike yawn again. "But there's probably a simple explanation. We'll know soon enough. Maybe we should try to catch a couple more hours of shut-eye."

Mike nodded and slipped back under the covers, falling into a deep slumber in a matter of minutes.

Kelly envied him and the sound of his snoring as she continued to toss and turn. It was over an hour before she was finally able to drift off to sleep.

Chapter 8

Kelly's eyes blinked open. Light was streaming into the room. She saw Mike was already up and fully dressed. She reached over to her bedside table and picked up her watch. Ten of seven. They'd planned to meet Ian McKenzie at the pool at seven.

"I see you're awake," Mike said. "I was just about to leave you a note. Why don't you just relax. I'll go down and meet McKenzie. I'll also see if I can learn something about the noise that woke us up last night—this morning. Maybe I can get a paper, too. I started the coffee."

Kelly smiled and nodded, smelling the aroma.

"Maybe we can have breakfast here in the room," Mike continued. "I shouldn't be long. You can go ahead and order if you like. One egg over light and toast and orange juice will take care of me."

Kelly nodded again as Mike stepped around to her side of the bed, leaning down and giving her a kiss. "I'll see you in a few," he said as he turned towards the door.

"I'll be waiting," Kelly replied, a teasing smile on her face. "I'm sorry I overslept. Thanks for meeting McKenzie on your own."

"No problem," Mike said as he opened the door.

Kelly leaned back in the bed, stretching her body. She felt reinvigorated, ready to tackle a new day. There was a knock at the door. Mike must have forgotten something. She flung the covers back and leaped up, grabbing her robe and putting it on as she moved towards the door.

"Just a minute, I hear you."

She opened the door and was surprised to see it wasn't Mike, rather a handsome, blonde-haired young man, perhaps a few years her senior. He was dressed in a sport shirt, a dark blue windbreaker and blue jeans. She noticed the Nike logo on his sport shoes. She was glad she'd taken time to slip into her robe.

"I'm sorry to disturb you at such an early hour. My name's Brett Anderson. Steve Richards suggested I speak with you about last night's events as soon as I could." He had his billfold flipped open in his left hand as he further explained, "I'm with the FBI."

Kelly quickly glanced at his identification. "You just missed my fiancé." She leaned her head out the doorway over the man's shoulder to see if she could spot Mike in the hallway. "He just left a minute ago. He went down to the pool area to meet with Ian McKenzie."

The young man nodded in understanding. "Maybe just the two of us could talk for a few minutes. Could I come in?" he asked as he replaced his billfold in his hip pocket.

Flustered because she hadn't already invited him in, Kelly apologized. "Sorry, certainly. I just thought if we could catch Mike you could talk with him, too."

"I'll want to," the man who'd introduced himself as Brett Anderson said as he came in the room. "This shouldn't take long. Again, let me apologize for the early hour."

Kelly shook her head, indicating that was no problem as she asked if he'd like a cup of coffee.

"That sounds good, if it's not much trouble."

"Not at all, the pot just finished brewing," Kelly said, reaching for a cup as she gestured him toward one of the chairs Mike and she had been sitting in the previous night.

"Let me begin by saying we owe you an apology," Anderson began as Kelly handed him the cup. "We're sorry about the anguish we put you through last night. We were the ones who removed the body from the pool. That's why the hotel security people didn't find it. The man was a fellow agent. We're not sure what happened. Another agent spotted his body floating in the pool, probably about the same time you did."

The young man paused for a minute, taking a sip of the coffee, giving Kelly a moment to digest what he'd just said.

"I'm going to be speaking to you in strict confidence now, for your ears only. I think we owe it to you after what we've put you through. We're here because of some top secret meetings which will be taking place starting this evening, here at the Grand. Around thirty people are involved; half from Canada, the others from Paris, London, and Washington. Top-level decision makers, here to discuss, hopefully to reach some type of agreement on some of the critical questions now facing Canada. The discussions are at a very delicate stage. As you're probably aware, there are extremists on both ends of the spectrum. Groups which would probably feel threatened if they knew the talks were taking place."

Kelly nodded. Headline stories had dealt with Canada's problems for the past several months, detailing how close the country was to possible civil war due to the influence of extremists on both sides.

"One of these groups learned of the meetings," Anderson continued.

"They mailed threats to the Grand Hotel in an attempt to get the meetings cancelled. We still haven't been able to pinpoint the specific group, the ones actually involved. Only minimal security was planned for this weekend, part of the attempt to maintain secrecy about the meetings. However, when the threats surfaced, the decision was made to bring us into the picture. As a matter of fact, some of our group aren't here yet. I myself just arrived late yesterday."

"We met the man whose body was in the pool coming over on the boat yesterday," Kelly volunteered.

Anderson arched his eyebrows in surprise. "You did? I wasn't aware of that. I'll want to get back to that in a minute or two. But where was I? Oh yes, I was just explaining to you we'd just recently become involved.

"The agent whose body you saw in the pool, the man you've said you met, was murdered. His neck was broken. We still don't know if he was killed to lend credence to the threats, or if he might have discovered something. Seen something which prompted those involved to act to protect themselves. Regardless, placing his body in the pool was a further attempt to intimidate the Grand. Get the hotel to cancel the meetings."

Kelly was nodding in understanding as Anderson went on to ask, "Did you hear the sound of an explosion last night? Early this morning, actually?"

Kelly again nodded as thoughts raced through her mind. This was all becoming clear now—why there had been the request to transfer rooms, why Kelly had the feeling Richards and McKenzie were hiding something last night.

"That was another attempt to intimidate the Grand, and the attendees. Some explosives were set off a few hundred yards from Arch Rock, on the eastern side of the island. The message was clear. One of the scenic treasures of Mackinac could have just as easily been destroyed. Carrying it one step further, the next explosion could easily be set off in the Grand Hotel."

Kelly was shaking her head. Terrorism was a sign of the times. It was terrible how a handful of people could have such an impact on world events. The problem was no longer just one other countries had to face. It was now close to home.

"The people who've put this meeting together have already been apprised of what's been happening; the death—the murder last night—and the explosion. They still want to proceed ahead, however. They think it might be one of the last opportunities for a peaceful solution. Up until last night—

this morning—many believed this group was making empty threats. When all the attendees are informed, the decision to go ahead with the meetings might be vetoed. Quite frankly, if I were you and, is it your fiancé?" Kelly nodded. "I'd move to another hotel on the island. There's no sense in exposing yourselves to needless risk. I actually think the Grand has an obligation to warn all their guests of the potential danger. That's just my personal opinion.

"Well, that's my story. Not a pretty one, is it? If you have questions, I'll try to answer them. If not, I have a few for you."

"Why don't you go ahead," Kelly suggested. "You might cover some of the same questions I have in the process."

The young agent nodded, agreeing that might be the best approach. "First, let's get back to you and your fiancé meeting the agent who was murdered. You were on the same boat yesterday? Did you have any conversation with him?"

"No, not really. We were up on deck together. It was pretty chilly and there was only one other couple up there with us. They had a camera and the husband asked," Kelly hesitated a second, "—the man who was murdered if he'd take a photo of them with us. He politely agreed to and was about to take a second shot of us when he noticed someone on the dock. He asked Mr. Miller, he's the man whose camera it was, if he could use it to take a photograph of whoever he'd recognized on the dock. Mr. Miller agreed. I glanced to see if I could tell who he was going to photograph. I saw two men, seeming to sense their photo was being taken, turning and shielding their faces. That may have just been my imagination, though. I'm not sure they were the ones he was trying to photograph. He could have been taking a shot of someone else. I know I'd be hard-pressed to identify the two whose photo I think he took."

"But he actually took someone's photo?"

"That's right," Kelly replied.

"Did he ask—what did you say his name was—for the roll of film?"

"Miller, Roy and Martha Miller, from Canton, Ohio," Kelly said, smiling. "Yes, he asked for the roll, but Mr. Miller told him he wanted to get it processed on his own. Mr. Miller said he'd leave two prints of the photo your fellow agent took under his name at the hotel desk."

"Did our man give him his name?"

"Yes. He wrote it down on a blank slip of paper."

"This might be expecting too much, but do you recall the name he wrote down?"

Kelly thought for a moment. "I'm pretty sure it was Black. Yes, I'm certain, with the initial R." Kelly was about to ask if that was the name of the man who was murdered, but before she could, Anderson had continued on.

"Changing subjects, and I'm sorry I'll have to speed this up," he said, glancing at his watch. "Can you describe what you saw last night? Did you see anything in addition to the body in the pool?"

Kelly shook her head. "Not around the pool, no. But did Richards tell you I saw the man you say was murdered in the lobby just a few minutes before I saw his body in the pool? That I thought he was being followed?"

Anderson's face registered surprise once again. "No. He didn't mention that to me. What makes you think he was being followed?"

Kelly described what she'd observed, explaining she'd have difficulty identifying the other man she'd seen.

"Could it have been one of the same men you saw on the dock, one of the two our agent may have photographed?"

"I just don't know," Kelly replied. "Maybe if I saw the print of the photo that was taken, it might jog my memory. Otherwise . . ." Kelly shrugged her shoulders.

The phone rang and Kelly stood up to answer it. "It's probably Mike, my fiancé. Help yourself to more coffee if you'd like."

"I'm sorry, I really have to leave now. Tell him I don't think there's any need to bother him. I think you've answered all of my questions."

Kelly had lifted the receiver as the agent spoke. It was the front desk. She was told the hotel wanted to transfer them to the other room by ten o'clock if at all possible.

"But we thought arrangements had been made for two o'clock," Kelly said.

Anderson was holding up his hand. "Thank you," he mouthed. Then in a normal tone he said, "Remember, I'd advise that you change hotels. You've been very helpful, thank you." He let himself out the door as Kelly continued her conversation.

"I understand, it's just that we planned on a later move. There's also a possibility we might be checking out. I'll call you in just a few minutes when my fiancé gets back to the room. No, everything's fine. We've been pleased with the room, the service. Give me your name, I'll call you back."

As Kelly hung up, it dawned on her she still hadn't ordered breakfast.

Mike would be expecting it. As she was reaching for the phone, it rang again.

"Hello."

It was Mike. "I'm on my way up," he explained. "I just wanted to call ahead and tell you I'm bringing someone with me, a man who has a few questions for us. Okay?"

"I guess so, I'm still not dressed. I haven't even ordered breakfast."

"Why don't we give you a few minutes then. You must have fallen back to sleep. Good, you needed that. See you in about ten minutes."

Kelly hung up the phone. Where do I start, she mused, smiling to herself. Too much was happening. She'd forgotten to tell . . . what was his name? Brett Anderson. She'd failed to tell him Mr. Miller wouldn't be picking up the photos until noon today. She'd also failed to tell him she'd spent a couple of years working for the FBI herself. Oh, well. She slipped off her robe and headed to the bathroom. I wonder who Mike has with him? Maybe it's the local police chief, she surmised. She was eager to tell Mike what she'd just learned from Anderson. If I hurry, I'll also have time to order breakfast before Mike gets here, she thought as she reached for her toothbrush.

Chapter 9

Kelly had just hung up after calling in the order for breakfast, when there was a knock at the door.

"Hi Kelly, it's me," Mike called out from the hallway.

"Just a second," she called back. As she opened the door, she saw Mike with a tall, muscular man standing next to him. He was dressed in a beige-colored suit and a red tie, his professional air contrasting with Mike's warm-up.

"This is Stuart Kreicheff, Kelly. He needs about five minutes of your time. I've already briefed him on the basics. He's with the FBI."

Mike noted the look of surprise on Kelly's face and said, "The man we met on the boat, the man whose body you saw in the pool last night, was also with the FBI. They're the ones who removed the body from the pool. Stuart will fill you in. Would you care for a cup of coffee?" Mike asked, turning to the man beside him, who nodded yes. "Can we fix him up, Kelly?"

Kelly smiled as she turned to walk over to the coffee pot. "Sure can.

Just black?"

The man nodded again. Kelly wondered if he was aware she'd just spent the last half-hour talking to his fellow agent, Brett Anderson. Mike interrupted her just as she was starting to say something.

"I've learned what that explosion, the noise we heard, was all about, too. Someone—they suspect a group of teenagers—detonated a bomb of some sort. On the east side of the island, not far from Arch Rock. Everyone thinks whoever did it had no idea how powerful it would be. It probably scared the daylights out of them, too. No serious damage, and it doesn't appear anyone was injured."

Kelly studied Kreicheff's reaction as Mike briefed her. He was nodding his head, endorsing Mike's version of what had occurred.

"Ready with your questions, Stuart?" Mike asked.

Kelly again started to say something about her earlier visitor, but then had a second thought.

"Can I see your identification first, Mr. Kreicheff?"

Mike stared at Kelly with an incredulous look on his face. "I've already seen it, Kelly. I was introduced to him downstairs in Mr. Woodbridge's office. He sends his regards, by the way. He's looking forward to meeting with us."

"Oh, good. You've met him, then. A wonderful man. He's the one who hired me when I worked here."

Mike nodded, acknowledging he remembered her telling him that.

"I'd still like to see some identification, though," Kelly said, turning her head to face Kreicheff. She realized Mike thought she was being obstinate as she caught a glimpse of his frown. Attempting to cast her request in a less confrontational light, Kelly said, "I want to see if there's been any changes since I worked for the department, a few years ago."

As Kreicheff reached into his pocket, he said, "Mike made me aware of that fact, Mrs. Cummings."

"He should have also told you that it's not Mrs. Cummings yet. We're just engaged," Kelly said as Kreicheff handed her his billfold, having flipped it open to show his photo ID and badge. "Let's use first names, okay? It's

Kelly."

She caught the expression of puzzlement and hurt on Mike's face. This isn't going well, Kelly thought. He'll understand my behavior though, when I tell him about Anderson. Bear with me, Mike. As she removed the ID and examined it, she fired a series of questions at Kreicheff.

"Why haven't you leveled with Mike on the true significance of the explosion? Is he aware of the meetings, the reason we're having to change rooms? The tie-in with Canada? What's the name of the agent who was murdered?"

Kreicheff recoiled back in his chair, his face flushing in embarrassment. Bypassing Kelly's initial questions, he answered, "I'm sorry, Kelly, I can't give you his name until his next of kin have been notified."

"We have to talk, Kelly," Mike interrupted. "Just stay where you are, Stuart, no need to leave. Help yourself to some more coffee, we'll use the bathroom."

•

"What in the hell is going on?" Mike asked as he shut the door behind them. She started forward to embrace him, but he stepped back, his body rigid.

"I'm sorry, Mike. I was holding back in front of him," she said, gesturing to the other room.

She quickly proceeded to tell Mike about her earlier visitor, the highlights of what he'd told her. He listened intently, nodding his head, more clearly understanding where Kelly had been coming from.

"I started to tell you both when you arrived," Kelly said, reaching for his hand. "But then you explained about the explosion and I just got sidetracked. I don't think Kreicheff's leveled with you."

Mike nodded his head as he responded. "Maybe the agent you spoke with is more senior; felt more comfortable sharing sensitive information with you. As to Stuart's lack of knowledge you'd already been questioned by one of his associates, it wouldn't be the first time . . . the right hand wasn't aware of what the left hand was doing. It happens in our department. I think you've overreacted. You've really been quite rude to the man—hardly giving him a chance."

Mike was probably right, but Kelly tensed as he criticized her. "The other agent even advises us to switch to another hotel. The hotel wants us out of this room by ten this morning."

"Let's get back in there," Mike said, reaching for the door knob. "We'll tell him what you were told. Maybe we'll learn more."

Kelly nodded as she preceded Mike out of the door.

•

"You say he identified himself as Brett Anderson?" Stuart asked, a look of alarm on his face.

Kelly nodded as Mike asked, "His name's not familiar? Could he have been brought in and you've just not been advised yet?"

Kreicheff was shaking his head. "No. That can happen, of course, but that's not the case here. Worse than that. That's the name of the agent who was killed. The one whose body was in the pool."

Kelly and Mike looked at one another in shock. "Did he show you a photo ID?" Kreicheff asked.

Kelly shrugged her shoulders. "I'm not sure. You'd just left. I only took a quick glance and then tried to see if I could still catch you."

"Let me make a quick call," Kreicheff said. "Make certain there aren't two Brett Andersons."

As Kreicheff made the call, Kelly and Mike talked in hushed tones. "He did most of the talking," she explained. "I'm trying to remember everything I told him. I guess I was challenging the identity of the wrong man."

Kreicheff was just ending his conversation. "Yes. I'll call you right away. She hasn't even provided me with a description yet."

"You heard?" Kreicheff said, coming back to the chair. "It definitely appears he was an impostor. I'll need a complete description, physical traits, how he was dressed."

Reaching into his pocket for a note pad and a pen, he continued. "I'll also need to know everything that was said. By both of you. Everything. Regardless of how inconsequential you might think it was. Take your time."

Kelly nodded. "I remember at the time thinking it was strange he never took a note. We talked for nearly half an hour. I remember the agency used to be almost paranoid about that—detailed notes on interviews. That should have alerted me."

The two men didn't offer a comment as Kelly began by giving Stuart a complete description of the man who'd posed as an agent.

•

Midway through Kelly's narration, room service arrived with their breakfast.

"I'll get it," Mike offered. "Just continue."

Kelly couldn't contain a slight smile as she remembered her conversation with Mike earlier that morning, both looking forward to a relaxed breakfast with the gorgeous view from their window. The three of them moved to the table in front of the window. Kreicheff continued to make notes as Kelly answered additional questions between bites of her breakfast. During one pause, as she bit into a blueberry muffin, Kreicheff volunteered that virtually everything the bogus agent had told her was true.

"Everything jives with the facts I've been privy to. And he's right about us not knowing at this stage who's involved, who's responsible."

As Kelly was relating what she'd told the man who'd identified himself as Brett Anderson about meeting the murdered agent on the boat, and the photo he'd taken of someone—possibly two men—on the dock, Kreicheff gave them some additional information.

"We've all been given photographs of people the agency thinks might be involved. Anderson might have recognized someone, maybe more than one person, he'd seen in those photographs. That may have prompted his murder."

Kelly had Kreicheff's complete attention as she explained that Mr. Miller had dropped the roll of film off at the photo shop on Main Street. "I didn't get around to telling him that this morning, though. Thank heavens! Nor the fact the film was supposed to be developed by noon today. I only told him about the arrangement to pick up the prints at the hotel desk. Miller was planning on leaving them there under the name the man had given him— R. Black."

As Stuart digested this information, he commented, "As you know, Kelly, we often utilize fictitious names."

She nodded, remembering she'd actually been assigned some alias names to use when she'd been at the Bureau.

"Miller's first name is Roy?" Kreicheff asked, verifying the name in his notes.

"Yes," Mike answered. "An auto dealer from Canton, Ohio," he added, giving Kelly a wink.

"We'll contact him immediately. I'll be anxious to see the print. Anything else you can recall, Kelly?"

She shook her head. "I think I've covered everything. I told you about his advice to move to another hotel." Glancing at her watch, she saw it was already nearly ten. "They wanted us out of this room by ten. I said I'd call them back."

"Don't worry about the timing. I'll make arrangements for a delay," Kreicheff said. "As far as my opinion on whether or not you should switch hotels, I don't know how to advise you. From what you've told me, Kelly, I don't think you, either of you, are in direct danger. He knows, they'll know, you'd have difficulty identifying the man you saw in the lobby following Anderson, or whoever he took the photo of from the boat. Of course, you'd be able to identify the man himself—the one who posed as an agent. But he realized that in advance. It doesn't appear he made any attempt to disguise his features—that must not be a concern. If he thought you posed a threat, he probably would have . . . maybe taken action when you were alone in this room with him."

Kelly glanced over at Mike, reading each other's minds. She was relieved she hadn't said anything—been able to tell him anything—which would have placed her in danger.

Mike pointed to his watch. "Remember, we've also scheduled a meeting at the Little Stone Church at eleven."

Kelly nodded.

"Why don't I see if I can arrange for—let's say—a one o'clock room transfer or checkout," Kreicheff said. Will that give you time enough?"

Kelly and Mike both nodded.

"Before you leave for your meetings, I'd like to have you stop by downstairs, the office next to Mr. Woodbridge's, to take a look at the photographs I mentioned earlier—the ones of people who may be involved. Maybe they'll jog your memory, Kelly. You might spot someone who looks familiar. The added time—'til one p.m.—will also give you the opportunity to decide whether you want to switch to another hotel. I should tell the two of you that the Bureau has actually made the suggestion—the recommendation—the meetings be canceled or postponed. We think now, more than ever, there's a high risk of someone being injured—even killed. I should say an additional someone. But we aren't the ones making that decision. Currently, as far as I know, they're still planning on going ahead with the meetings.

"I'll see you downstairs in a few minutes. I'm going to be making some calls. Thank you. You've both been of enormous help. One request—

please keep everything to yourselves, at least for now. I'll try to keep you apprised. Be sure to leave word at the front desk for me if you decide to move to another hotel.

"And finally," he said, handing each of them a card, "here's a number where you can reach me, twenty-four hours a day. If I'm not there, I'll be paged. I'll see you downstairs in a few minutes with those photos. Don't hesitate to call, for any reason, at any time. You might just want an update."

●

As Kelly and Mike headed across the lobby, they saw Roy Miller standing near the front desk. He spotted them as well and came toward them.

"Can you believe it? My camera was stolen while we were down having breakfast. We slept in this morning, but wanted to have the full buffet, rather than just room service. Guess that was a mistake."

Kelly and Mike exchanged glances.

"There's someone we'd like you to meet," Mike said. "Could you come with us, back into the office area?"

Mr. Miller gave them a questioning look. "You mean someone's found it—found a camera?"

"Not exactly," Mike replied. "But someone was planning to contact you. What he wants to discuss may be related to your missing camera."

Confused, Mr. Miller followed them.

"We're expected," Mike explained to the woman standing behind the information counter. The woman smiled, seeming to have been apprised of that fact.

●

Mike introduced Stuart Kreicheff to Roy Miller and the two of them headed to another office, while Kelly and Mike sat with another agent pouring over photographs. There were three pages, each containing about a dozen faces. A binder contained 8 x 11 enlargements of all the individuals pictured, to be referred to if any of the smaller photos triggered a reaction. The agent with them was interrupted frequently during the less than ten minutes' time spent studying the photos, twice by phone calls and three times by people who Kelly and Mike assumed were other agents, sticking their heads in the doorway to ask questions.

The photos proved no help. There were maybe five men who could have been the man Kelly had seen in the lobby. Even more could fit the vague description Kelly remembered of the two men she'd observed on the dock. Kreicheff returned just as they were about to leave.

He asked if they'd had any luck and they both shook their heads. He asked if they could stop by again after their meeting at the church to take a look at the photo the murdered agent had taken. Kreicheff explained he'd just called the Island Photo Shop. The prints were ready, and an agent had been sent to pick them up. He was hopeful there would be a match with two of the men whose photos Kelly and Mike had been studying. In case that wasn't true, he wanted the two of them to check back.

He smiled as he told them they'd also be able to pick up enlargements of the photos of them, with and without the Millers. Kreicheff said he'd like to take credit for thinking of that, but Roy Miller had been the one to negotiate it before agreeing to turn over the claim check.

Chapter 10

A colorful sight greeted Kelly and Mike as they headed out of the Grand Hotel's main entrance. The hotel's carriage and several horse-drawn taxis were waiting in line at the bottom of the red-carpeted stairs. A young man dressed in a white uniform and wearing a Panama hat, shovel in hand and pushing a small cart, was busily occupied policing up after the horses. It was a gorgeous day. Not a cloud in the sky, with the temperature in the sixties. Mike took Kelly's hand as they started down the sidewalk, which was bordered by huge planters containing red geraniums and white petunias. They glanced over the hedge on their right to view the gardens below.

"Tea and sweets are available down there in the late afternoon, usually with some musicians," Kelly informed Mike.

"I can easily see why you loved it here," Mike said. "Let's hope we have a day like this for our wedding. The air's so crisp and clear. Of course, the aroma of the horses takes a little getting used to."

Kelly laughed as they continued along the sidewalk and began their descent down the steep hill which led up to the Grand. Pointing across the street, she explained, "That's the snack bar where I waitressed when I first started working for the Grand. Great fringe benefits! Their specialties were Pecan Balls and Snow Balls, huge scoops of vanilla ice cream with gobs of fudge, covered with pecans or shredded coconut. I think I had one or the other two or three times a week."

Mike smiled, seeing she was savoring the memory as she talked.

"I was lucky to be on the late shift most of the time, from four p.m. until about two a.m. It gave me a chance to get out in the sunshine during my off-time, for tennis and horseback riding."

Mike smiled at Kelly again. "That's right, you threatened to get me on a horse while we're here. To give me a tennis lesson, too. I hope we can still work it in."

Kelly realized he was teasing her. Mike was very athletic. He'd teamed up with a friend to win several handball and paddle tennis tournaments. He claimed he was a novice at tennis. But he was such a perfectionist, that probably meant he was far above average.

"You can see the courts over there," Kelly said, pointing to their right.

Mike nodded. The colorful flower beds bordering them and the gorgeous weather made them very appealing.

"Maybe we can get out later this afternoon," Mike suggested. "Can we still use them, even if we're not Grand Hotel guests? In case we decide to change hotels."

"Sure can. This area is actually a public park, even though everyone refers to the courts as the Grand Hotel's. There's a charge, of course, for the Grand's guests as well."

The Congregational Little Stone Church was just ahead, across the street on their left. They waited for a carriage to pass before crossing the roadway. Some of the passengers waved and smiled, relaxed and happy, enjoying their visit to Mackinac Island. A sharp contrast to the tense atmosphere they'd just experienced at the Grand.

Chapter 11

A woman's bicycle was parked in the rack next to the main entrance on the south side of the church. It was definitely not a rental bike. Bright-colored carrying baskets were attached to both sides of the rear wheel and a single red geranium in a pot was mounted on the rear fender.

"It looks as if Mrs. Taylor is here ahead of us," Kelly said.

Entering the church, they saw a woman standing on one of the pews, holding a long-handled feather duster. She was reaching up towards a cobweb in the corner of the one of the stained-glass windows. Sensing their presence, the woman turned, looking over her shoulder. Smiling, she greeted them.

"You must be Kelly and Mike. Welcome to the Little Stone Church. I'm Irene, Irene Taylor."

After shaking hands, Kelly explained she'd often attended services here, during the summers she'd worked on the island.

"As a matter of fact, one of the boys I dated one summer was responsible for keeping the church cleaned and ringing the bell." She pointed out to Mike the rope leading down from the ceiling, attached to a hook on the side wall. "A half-hour before the morning and evening services and just before the services started."

"That's still the way it's done," Irene said, smiling. "The young man they have this year isn't too reliable. Your boyfriend was probably more conscientious. Our pastor has had to ring it himself, the first bell, a couple of times already this summer. And it's just June. His name's Terry Noonan, by the way. Our pastor, not the boy who's supposed to ring the bell," she said with a laugh. "It's his third summer with us. I think you'll like him. He says he'll be available after the morning service tomorrow in case you'd want to meet with him. I've penciled in the two dates you mentioned in your letter, Kelly. They're both still available. I should remind you . . . Oh, heavens, having worked here, you're already aware, I'm sure, that there's a substantial drop in the hotel rates after the Labor Day Weekend. I don't know how many guests you expect, how many will be in the wedding party, but you might be able to negotiate a special discount for a block of rooms with nearly any hotel. That's true for either date, but especially true for after Labor Day.

"Here's a list of questions most people have," Irene said, handing a sheet of paper to Kelly. "From the seating capacity to the sources for flowers. I also have an album of photographs from other weddings. They might give you some ideas. I'll give the two of you a few minutes and then I'm open for questions. Isn't this a pretty little church? Today would have been a gorgeous day for a wedding. There are some photos in the album of decorated carriages, too. The island is really a picturesque, romantic spot for a wedding."

•

It was nearly noon before their discussion with Irene concluded. They were both excited. It was left that they'd be consulting with the Grand, Mr. Woodbridge, on the availability of its facilities and a possible discount on rooms, before making a final decision on the date. They were leaning toward the August date, knowing the chance for nice weather would be better. They'd decided they also wanted to give people another option or two on hotels. Even with a discount, the Grand would be expensive.

As they crossed the street to head back up to the hotel, Kelly said, "Wouldn't it be wonderful to have a day like today?" She grinned as she continued. "For a couple minutes there this morning, I thought you might be having second thoughts. I'm sorry."

Mike laughed. "No apologies needed. I should have realized there was a reason for . . ." he laughed again, ". . . a side of you I hadn't seen before."

"Hopefully, you won't see it many times in the future," she said, grabbing his hand. "About changing hotels. I'm thinking we should just stay at the Grand. There's still a chance the meetings might be cancelled. If not, they've indicated our new room will be on the opposite end of the hotel from where they're taking place, if there is trouble." Kelly smiled. "We also have a complimentary night. It doesn't mean we can't change our minds later, depending on what happens."

"We're in sync," Mike answered. "I was going to suggest the same thing. Our minds seem to be meeting on all fronts today."

Kelly nodded, realizing how smoothly things had just gone with the decisions about the wedding.

As another carriage came down the hill past them, Kelly said, "I'm taking a second look at everyone I see, hoping to see one of the faces we saw in those photographs. Maybe spot the man who came to my room this morning. Or the one I saw in the lobby, or the men on the dock. I'm getting paranoid." She grinned as she added, "My mother always kept telling me, 'Kelly, it's not polite to stare.' I'm glad she's not watching me now."

Two boys on bikes raced past them, flying down the hill. "That could be dangerous," Mike said. "I wonder if they use this hill for sledding in the winter."

"See all those caution signs?" Kelly asked, pointing. "There have been several accidents over the years. They banned skateboards when I was here. Years ago, they used to have bicycles with basket chairs in front in which

two or three people could sit. An exciting, one-way trip downtown. You'll see some photographs of them downstairs at the hotel."

Mike bent down and picked up a newspaper someone had dropped or discarded. "The Mackinac Island Town Crier," he said, reading the masthead. "Parade Planned For Fourth of July Weekend."

"Let's keep it," Kelly said. "We'll be able to find out what's happening this weekend. Besides what we already know about," she added, smiling. "Wouldn't the paper love to have that story? The Town Crier was part of a summer internship program for University of Michigan School of Journalism students when I was here. It probably still is. Three University of Michigan college classmates started the paper from scratch back in the fifties. They continued publishing it for several years, all having gone on to Law School. Then they sold it to the retiring dean of the U of M Journalism School. Neat story, huh?"

"You are a walking encyclopedia," Mike said, laughing. "What don't you know about Mackinac?"

"Plenty, that's for sure. But there's lots more I do know that I haven't told you yet." She smiled. "I'm just getting warmed up. Just wait 'til we go horseback riding."

Mike laughed again.

They entered the Grand through the eastern entrance, down a long, wide corridor which was beneath the Grand's massive dining room on the main floor. Kelly stopped a few times, pointing out specific photographs and framed reprints of newspaper and magazine articles having to do with the Grand Hotel and Mackinac Island.

"See, Mike, here's a photograph of those bicycles with the basket chairs." Next to it was a news story covering President Harry Truman's visit to the island.

"I'm impressed," Mike said as he scanned some of the other articles and pictures adorning the walls. "Look here, the Republican National Committee met here just last summer. This is fascinating. Lots of historic happenings, that's for sure."

"Maybe another chapter in the island's history is being written this weekend, Mike. Who knows?"

Glancing at his watch, Mike replied, "You may be right. We need to stop by and see Kreicheff again before we head up to our room. They're probably anxious to get us out of there, to know whether we'll be changing hotels or just changing rooms."

Hand in hand, they hurried along the corridor past a series of gift shops and an ice cream parlor. As they started up the staircase which led to the main lobby, they saw the beaming faces of the Millers, who were coming down the stairway toward them.

"We've been looking for you," Roy said. "I just called your room, as a matter of fact. Two reasons. First, we're just heading across the way to the Jockey Club at the golf course for lunch and wondered if the two of you would like to join us. And second, you're in for a little surprise. That man you introduced me to this morning has a couple of photos for you."

Martha, her face still beaming, said, "I think you'll be pleased. Should we give them a preview, Roy? I'd love to see their expressions."

Roy nodded his head, indicating he would too, as he reached into the brown manila folder in his hand. He slipped out an 8 x 11 size print of Kelly and Mike and the Millers posing together.

"That fellow did a pretty good job of catching us all smiling and looking at the camera, don't you think?" Martha asked Kelly and Mike. They nodded as Roy joked, "Especially with what he had to work with."

As he laughed at his joke, he removed a second print of just the Millers. Martha's eyes were closed.

"That's my doing, my fault," Mike said. "I wish for your sakes it was reversed, that your eyes were open in the photo I took."

"No problem, never you mind," Martha assured Mike as her husband nodded in agreement. "It just means the photo of the four of us is the one that will make our scrapbook. And that's best anyway, we've plenty of shots with just the two of us."

"The one of the two of you is great, though. That fella wanted to give the two prints I had him get for you to you himself, though. Said he was going to be seeing you in a few minutes. What the hell's going on, anyway? That Krieshaft, or whatever his name is, was pretty tight-lipped with me, ignoring my questions and not volunteering why that last photo the fellow on the boat took was so damned important. He did agree it might be related to the theft of my camera. He's optimistic my camera will eventually show up, minus the film. The good news is he says if it doesn't, he'll give me money for a new one. Now that's strange too, isn't it?"

"Roy, we can talk more at lunch," Martha interrupted. "Are you going to be able to join us?"

"We'd love to," Kelly said with a smile. "But we have to change rooms. They wanted to move us by one o'clock and it's nearly that time now. I'm not sure how long it will take."

"What's that all about?" Roy asked. "Nothing you initiated? They've made you change? As I recall, you had your room booked, a particular one, for over a month. Doesn't sound right you having to move."

"The good news is that they're complimenting us for one night because of the mix-up," Mike volunteered.

"Hear that?" Martha said, nudging her husband in the stomach. "We should be so lucky. Why don't we get a table for four and if you catch up, fine. If not, you have a rain-check. We won't wait to order."

"That sounds good," Mike replied. "We'll try our best. Lunch outside under one of those umbrellas is what we were planning on ourselves."

Chapter 12

A few minutes later, Kelly and Mike were seated across from Stuart Kreicheff, studying the photo he'd handed them.

"We weren't able to match up those two men with any of the photos I had you look at earlier. You can see the two seem to be aware someone had a camera focused on them. They're both just starting to turn their heads and raise their hands to shield their faces. There doesn't appear to be any doubt that they were the two who prompted Anderson to snap the photo."

Kelly nodded in agreement. "They're the same two I remember seeing, sensing they were trying to avoid being photographed." After studying the photo for a few additional seconds, Kelly continued. "I can't be sure if either one is the man I saw in the lobby last night."

"Another agent of ours thinks those men look familiar. The problem is, he doesn't know why. I'm hoping something will jog his memory.

"What I'd like the two of you to do is to keep an eye out for these two men. Also the man who came to your room this morning, Kelly. Or anyone who resembles the man you saw in the lobby."

Mike winked at Kelly with a twinkle in his eye, wondering if she was going to tell Stuart she was way ahead of him. He didn't seem to notice.

"If you do or if either of you should notice something suspicious, please let me know. Immediately. Use the number I gave you earlier."

•

"Let's check to see if Mr. Woodbridge is in while we're here," Kelly suggested. "We can tell him where we stand with our wedding plans and see if we can schedule a meeting to review some of our options and get an idea as to costs."

"Good idea. We also need to see if there's a problem with either of those dates due to a major convention or something."

Kelly nodded in agreement as they walked down the corridor towards Mr. Woodbridge's office. His secretary told them that while Woodbridge was around the hotel somewhere, she wasn't quite sure where, or when he'd be back in his office. She cheerfully offered to page him, but Kelly said that wasn't necessary.

"I think I'll just leave him a note," Kelly said to Mike.

"Do you need a pen or some paper?" the secretary asked. "I'll put it on his desk and also remind him it's there. I'm not sure how quickly he'll get back to you. I know he's swamped today."

"We're hoping we can schedule a meeting sometime before we leave on Monday morning," Kelly explained as she wrote the note to Woodbridge. "We're making wedding plans."

The woman beamed as she congratulated them. "I'll tell him, and either he or I will call your room or leave a message, probably later this afternoon." She smiled again. "I don't mean a meeting for this afternoon, I don't see that happening. But we'll get back with a couple of options as to a time for tomorrow or Monday."

•

"That didn't take long," Mike said to Kelly as they headed up to their room. "If we can make the room switch as quickly as that, we should be able to catch up to the Millers after all."

"I'm thinking that's not a good idea, Mike. You know he's just dying to ask us a bunch of questions."

Mike smiled. "I'm sure that's the case. But you know they're just going to keep bugging us to join them for something. This seems to be as good a time as any. I'm sure we'll be able to dodge their questions. Besides, you were just saying we should get to the Jockey Club sometime during our stay."

"I know. But I was thinking this evening or tomorrow night. There's a piano bar. We could have dessert. It's a real romantic setting."

Mike smiled. "You don't have to sell me. Sounds great! We'll skip the Millers, then."

"I have the feeling I'm coming across as a long-time married, bossy wife. I hope you don't think my true personality is beginning to surface. I like the Millers. I'm certainly not interested in cultivating a life-long friendship, though. I usually go out of my way to be nice to people. No excuses, but maybe the events of last night and this morning have had more of an impact on me than I thought."

Mike smiled. "You're doing just fine. We're doing just fine. And I love you."

"Did you happen to bring your service revolver with you?" Kelly asked as she squeezed Mike's hand, thanking him for his patience and understanding.

He shook his head. "That didn't figure into any of the plans we had. But the same thought crossed my mind. I'm thinking we should stay together until this affair sorts itself out, though. And I suppose we could approach Kreicheff if your—if our—concerns mount," he said as he leaned down and kissed her on the forehead.

Chapter 13

Mike thanked the bellman as he handed him a five dollar bill. Rather than reaching for it, the young man pulled his arm back.

"That's not necessary, Mr. Cummings. We're the ones who put you to the inconvenience of having to change rooms."

"But that wasn't your doing," Mike replied with a smile. "Still in school?"

The young man nodded as he answered. "I'll be starting my senior year at Ferris this fall."

"Well, you can probably put every dollar you make this summer to good use," Mike said, pressing the money into the young man's palm. "And thanks for getting the ice for us, too."

The young man grinned. "Remember, my name's Jim. Anything I can do to make the remainder of your stay more enjoyable, you just let me know. And thank you!"

Kelly was standing at the window as the door closed. She swung around, extending her arms. "This room's far nicer than I anticipated. We'd be thrilled if we hadn't been spoiled by the suite. I love the decorating and it's so large and airy. I'm excited!"

Mike smiled. "Me, too. What's your pleasure? Should we unpack now or grab a bite of lunch first?"

"I can almost hear your tummy growling," Kelly replied with a laugh. "If we're not going to join the Millers, we should probably head downtown rather than eat at the hotel. We could use the stairs down to the gardens so that we don't run the risk of the Millers spotting us. There's a path through the woods that comes out by the tennis courts."

"Whatever you say," Mike answered. "Maybe the Iroquois. That'll bring back some memories for you."

Kelly grinned. "What do they say, a woman's prerogative? Seeing the Jockey Club from our window makes me realize that's really the perfect choice with today's weather. What do you say we join the Millers?"

Mike laughed as he walked over and embraced her. They kissed for several minutes, before Kelly pushed him away.

"We're going to miss lunch if we're not careful," she said with a wink. "I can hardly wait until this evening, though."

Chapter 14

"Hasn't this been fun?" Martha Miller said. "The weather couldn't be nicer. And no mosquitoes or flies. At least I haven't seen any. I love eating outdoors. These umbrellas are so colorful."

"It's been enjoyable for us, too," Kelly answered, smiling at Mike. She was sorry about having originally fought the idea of joining the Millers for lunch. It was a gorgeous day. The food and service had been excellent. Even the conversation was good. The Millers had lots of questions, but to Kelly's surprise, nearly all had been directed to her. Questions concerning what the Millers should be seeing and doing during their island stay. Mike had smirked as Kelly enthusiastically fielded all of their questions.

"Are you sure we can't convince you to change your minds?" Kelly asked. "I'm certain they could find some gentle horses for you."

While they'd been waiting for their food, Kelly had called and reserved horses for her and Mike. She'd booked for two hours starting at four o'clock.

"No, I think we'll still pass," Roy said with a chuckle. "I know the horses will appreciate our decision. Two hours with Martha and me aboard would tucker any horse."

"I've got concerns about the two hours, too," Mike said with a twinkle in his eye. "In my case, I'm more worried whether my fanny can handle it. Remember, Kelly, I'm just a novice."

"You won't have a problem," Kelly told him. "You'll be amazed how quickly the time will pass. It takes a good ten minutes just to get up the hill to here and another ten minutes before we get off the main road, onto the trails and the back roads. That's when it starts to be fun."

•

Kelly and Mike arrived at the stable on Market Street at about ten to four, a few minutes ahead of schedule. A man in his sixties, dressed in cowboy attire, spotted them as they stepped inside the office. His face lit up.

"Kelly! I'm so pleased to see you." He wrapped her in a bear hug. Stepping back, holding her by the shoulders, he said, "Darned, if you haven't grown even more prettier. I hadn't thought that would be possible."

He looked over at Mike and Kelly introduced them. "Mr. Chamberlain is the owner, Mike. Mike's my fiancé."

"What's this Mr. Chamberlain bit? It's Ray," he said, grabbing Mike's hand. "Congratulations, son. You've found yourself a hell of a girl. A hell of a woman, I should say." Turning to Kelly, he asked, "How long has it been, young lady?"

Before she could answer, he turned to Mike. "She used to come riding two or three times a week, all through the summer. I think she must have spent the bulk of what she was getting paid here with us, even with the special discount we worked out for her. By the way," he said, lowering his voice, "the same deal applies today—half price for both of you."

"You don't need to do that, Ray," Kelly said. "We're—"

"Now, don't you go telling me what I can do and can't do, Kelly. I'm so glad to see you I should be letting you ride for free," he said, laughing. "This really brings back the memories. You rode Blaze, didn't you? I'm afraid she's long gone. I'll try to find Betty to see if you can borrow her horse this afternoon. She's new since you were here. Her horse, Patch, will remind you of Blaze. You'll enjoy her."

Looking Mike over, Chamberlain said, "How about you, Mike. Ridden much?"

Mike shook his head as Kelly said, "He's very athletic, though. He'll be a fast learner."

"You're pretty fair-sized, too. I think Big Buck is available. Don't let the name scare you. He's a great horse."

Glancing over his shoulder, Chamberlain motioned to a young lady, perhaps in her early twenties.

"There you are, Betty. Come over here. There are some people I want you to meet."

•

As they stood outside waiting for the horses to be brought up, Mike glanced around, observing the bustle of activity. Business appeared to be good, with a constant stream of riders entering the yard, returning, as another group of would-be riders prepared to depart.

Betty had been enthused over Kelly taking Patch out for an airing, commenting that the horse was eager for a workout. As Kelly mounted up, Chamberlain related a few instructions to Mike.

"All our horses are trained to neck rein, Mike. Know what I mean by that?"

Mike nodded.

"The only time you'll need to use the bit is to stop him. Old Big Buck here can almost read a rider's mind—just a slight tug should do. Two tugs for reverse," he added with a laugh. "I know Kelly can help you if you have questions or run into a problem."

•

They were only a block or two from the stable when Big Buck stopped in the middle of the street. Mike kicked him gently with his heels, talking to the horse, removing one of his hands from the reins and slapping Big Buck's hind quarters.

Kelly was circling back toward him on Patch. She'd quickly moved out ahead of Mike, her frisky horse almost prancing. She grinned as she approached.

"I see what the problem is," Mike said, hearing the plopping sound of horse droppings. A couple with a young child, a boy of maybe four or five years of age, was strolling down the sidewalk on their left. He was tugging on his mother's skirt, pointing and giggling, as he stared in fascination. A couple passing on the right on a tandem bike smiled up at Mike, identifying with his predicament. Mike's face flushed.

"A really auspicious start, eh?" he said to Kelly. It must be a humongous pile, Mike thought, his patience being tested as Big Buck continued his doings. Finally the horse snorted and started forward at a fast trot. Mike grabbed the saddle horn with one hand, gripping tightly on the reins with his other.

"That's better," Kelly said, laughing. "Ride 'em, cowboy." She turned her horse around and cantered past Mike, quickly slowing down after she'd done so and guiding Patch closer to the curb. Glancing back at Mike, she giggled.

•

Both horses appeared to handle the steep hill with ease. Mike spotted the table on their right where they'd just lunched as they continued on, first past the hotel and then its carriage barn. After proceeding another hundred yards or so, Kelly circled back again and directed Patch abreast of Mike and Big Buck.

"We have some options now," she explained. "We can go off to the right, past the Governor's Summer Home and the fort. Maybe go on as far as Arch Rock, possibly see the hole, the damage the explosion must have caused."

Kelly had pointed out the Governor's Summer Home to the Millers and Mike during lunch, explaining the flag at full mast meant the Governor was there for the weekend. It was on the other side of the Grand Hotel's golf course, the opposite side from the restaurant.

"Or we could go off to the left. See the backs of some of those magnificent homes on the West Bluff and some charming cottages in the Annex. There's also a hotel overlooking the Straits called Stone Cliff we could stop by and see. What interests you?"

"Why don't you make the decision," Mike replied. "But out of curiosity, what's straight ahead?"

Kelly smiled. "Good question. I suppose that's an option, too. The town of Harrisonville. A number of year-round residents live there. Years ago it was referred to as the Indian Village—most of the residents being Native Americans. Back then it consisted of a cluster of fairly dilapidated houses, almost shacks. As the island prospered through its tourist trade, the area has been upgraded. There are some fairly nice homes out there now, even some multi-family units where some of the summer employees stay. It's still not what you'd call one of the scenic highlights of the island, though. There's really not much to see.

"The road continues on to the north end of the island and British Landing. I think it was during the War of 1812 when the British troops landed there. The Americans thought they had the fort well defended, heavily fortified, expecting an attack from the harbor. The British surprised them coming in from the rear, capturing the fort without a shot being fired. Part of the island lore. I think Skull Cave's out in that direction, too."

Mike smiled, sitting astride Big Buck, happy to have a moment or two to rest. Big Buck had trotted during most of their brief ride. It was already taking a toll on Mike's rear-end. He also enjoyed hearing Kelly's stories about Mackinac. Her enthusiasm was contagious; it was fun to see.

"I think heading left is probably best," Kelly suggested. "Hopefully, we'll have a chance to walk over to the fort sometime tomorrow and spend a few minutes there."

"Sounds fine with me," Mike said. "Lead the way, I'll try to keep up."

Patch broke into an easy, gentle canter. Wonder of wonders, Big Buck started to canter as well. Mike was delighted in the difference it made. This made riding fun.

•

It would be hard to imagine a more delightful day to be out on horseback, exploring the island. Rays of sunshine poked through gaps in the foliage. It was so quiet and peaceful, with only the musical chirping of birds marring the silence. They'd seen only a handful of people; one or two carriages. Many of the homes they'd passed didn't appear to have been opened up for the summer season yet.

Big Buck's canter hadn't lasted for long. They'd walked the horses for the most part. When Kelly's horse pranced ahead from time to time, Mike's would break into a fast trot to catch up.

"Why don't you go on ahead and air out Patch," Mike suggested. "She still appears raring to go."

Kelly smiled and nodded, very willing to act on Mike's suggestion. "I'll double back," she said. "Just continue on and veer to the right when you reach a fork in the road, okay?"

She cantered off. Chamberlain had been accurate in his description of Kelly as a skilled rider. She was so graceful, her movements blending in with those of her horse. Mike smiled, thinking of how clumsy he felt aboard Big Buck by comparison.

•

It doesn't get much better than this, Kelly thought to herself as she cantered along, passing several houses as she entered the Annex area. She noticed that many of them appeared to be unoccupied. She slowed Patch down, patting the horse's neck. What a great horse, she thought. Chamberlain was right in thinking she'd remind me of Blaze.

The house coming up on her right didn't appear to have been lived in for several years. The grounds looked as if they hadn't been tended to in some time; the windows were all boarded up. Kelly noticed the side door open and a man step out. She was surprised in that the house had appeared abandoned. She did a double-take. Yes, it was one of the men she'd seen earlier today in the photo taken from the boat.

The man caught sight of her, perhaps sensing her stare. He quickly turned and appeared to push a person following him, back inside the house. He disappeared through the door, pulling it shut behind him.

Kelly's mind was racing. He—they—might be observing me through one of the windows, she thought. Behave as if you haven't been alerted, aren't concerned, she reminded herself, patting Patch's neck again. I need to get back and tell Mike. We need to notify the FBI, call Stuart. I can double-back along that parallel road over there, she thought.

•

Mike saw Kelly galloping up the road towards him and smiled. As she approached closer, however, he could see the look of alarm on her face.

"What's wrong?" he asked as she pulled her reins, halting in front of him. She blurted out the story of what she'd seen.

"They must be hiding out there," Mike suggested. "We need to notify Stuart. I just saw a woman in her yard a few houses back, working in her garden. Maybe we can use her phone." Kelly nodded.

Mike maneuvered Big Buck around in the roadway. By the time he'd accomplished that feat, Kelly was already at the house where Mike had seen the woman, climbing off Patch and looking for a place to tie her reins. Mike's horse trotted after her.

He was just preparing to dismount when Kelly came back, having just spoken to the woman. "Stay up there," she instructed him. "She doesn't have a phone. This is a hide-away retreat for her and her husband and he's refused to install a phone. She suggests the Swanson cottage, three doors down. She thinks they're home."

As they trotted toward the Swanson's, Mike removed his billfold and removed the card Stuart had given him on which he'd written his phone number. Once again, Kelly had been able to move faster than Mike. She was already at the front door as Mike was climbing off Big Buck. The Swansons had a hitching post on which Kelly had tied her reins, and Mike followed her lead.

Kelly was talking to a very attractive woman who was standing in the doorway. She was probably in her thirties, Mike guessed, wearing blue jeans and a colorful sweatshirt. Hand-painted, Mike thought, an array of spring flowers. She opened the door for them to enter as Kelly quickly introduced Mike.

"Sydney is the Swanson's daughter-in-law," Kelly explained. "The phone was just switched on day before yesterday, so we're in luck."

"Here's Stuart's number," Mike said, handing Kelly the card. "Why don't you call? You're the one who saw him. You'll also be able to give him directions." He smiled. "I'm not sure where we are."

"The phone's back there in the library," Sydney explained, pointing out the room. "You can't miss it, on the desk."

Three young children had entered the room, staring wide-eyed at their mother's visitors. They appeared to range in age from about nine down to four, two girls and the youngest a boy. Sydney introduced them to Mike. Kelly was already in the library.

•

As Kelly came out of the library, she saw the three children clustered around Mike. He'd just removed a coin from one of the little girl's ears and the other two were giggling. The thought flashed through Kelly's mind that Mike would be a great father. Looking up and seeing her, Mike asked, "Did you get through to him?"

Kelly nodded. "I left a message. Told the man I spoke to . . ." Kelly glanced over at Sydney, hesitating. "I told him what my call was about and left this number. He says he'll be having Stuart call us back momentarily."

"Would you like a cup of coffee, maybe an iced tea, while you're waiting?" Sydney offered.

"Iced tea sounds great," Kelly answered, flashing a smile. "How about you, Mike?"

"Sounds good to me, too," Mike said. "If you're sure it's not too much trouble."

"Not at all. Do you take lemon?"

Kelly and Mike both nodded. "Why don't I give you a hand," Kelly volunteered, following Sydney into the kitchen as she heard Mike in the background saying, "Knock, knock."

•

The phone rang. "Why don't you answer it, Kelly?" Sydney said. "It's probably the call you've been waiting for."

It had been over ten minutes since Kelly had made the initial call. A minute or two ago, Sydney had asked her children to give Mike some respite, suggesting they go out in the yard to play. Delightful and well-behaved, the three had trucked out the front door with a minimum of protest.

The call was from Stuart Kreicheff. He apologized to Kelly for the delay in getting back to her. He asked her to repeat what she'd told the man she'd spoken to earlier, and then verified the location of the house where she'd seen the man in the photograph. He promised that he and others would be there as quickly as they could. He then asked where she was now.

"I don't want to place you or Mike at risk," Stuart said. "But if you could, from a distance, observe and see if anyone leaves the house, it could really help us. We'll move as quickly as possible. But you realize it's going to take us a minimum of ten minutes, maybe longer. We don't want to alert or alarm anyone by using the island's police car. We can probably get there just as quickly by carriage anyway. I already have some agents lining one up out front now.

"A word of caution, Kelly. If you see someone leave, don't even attempt to follow them. The risk of exposing yourselves is too great. Just try to get descriptions of who you see. Remember, they've already killed one agent. Be careful. I'm coming, too. I should be seeing you soon."

•

Kelly motioned for Mike to join her in the library. In hushed tones, she briefed him on her conversation with Stuart.

"Sorry I didn't think ahead," he said, shaking his head. "I could have just as easily gone on to watch the house while you were notifying him. That would have been so logical."

"I didn't think of it either," Kelly replied. "Even if I had, I would have been hesitant. Remember—neither of us is armed. Stuart cautions us on keeping a safe distance."

Mike nodded. "Let's hope the mistake doesn't hurt the chances of their being apprehended. How far's the house? Within walking distance?"

"Yes. It's a ways, but I think the horses might be in our way."

"You could wait here," Mike suggested. "I could—"

Kelly's angry expression cut him off in mid-sentence. Smiling, he said, "Sorry I asked."

•

Sydney assured them it would be all right for them to leave the horses where they were for a few minutes.

"They're both good horses," Kelly said. "But you might want to make sure your children keep their distance. They shouldn't attempt to feed them."

"Or ride them," Mike said with a twinkle in his eye.

Leaving the house, they first checked to see if the horses' reins were secure. The two gave verbal assurances to Patch and Big Buck that they'd be back shortly as they patted them. They quickly broke into a jog as they headed up the road.

The three children merrily scampered after them for a hundred feet or so, finally stopping and waving goodbye. The oldest of the little girls shouted, "We'll be waiting for you."

Kelly looked over at Mike, smiling. "Do you have any more tricks or jokes up your sleeve? You made a hit with them."

Chapter 15

Kelly was crouched down in the shrubbery bordering the house next door to the one she was observing. From her vantage point, she could see the front and east side of the house under surveillance, approximately fifty to sixty yards away. There was no sign of activity. The house in the yard she was in had the appearance of having been opened for the season, but there was no sign of the occupants. Mike had circled around through the woods behind the house where she'd seen the man, to position himself so he would have a view of its rear and the opposite side. Kelly checked her watch. Stuart and the other agents should be arriving any minute. She glanced over her shoulder again to see if there was any sign of them.

A moment or two later Kelly noticed a young couple coming down the road in her direction. They were dressed in tennis attire and the man was carrying a small duffel bag from which the handles of two tennis racquets protruded. She wondered if perhaps they were the occupants of the house whose yard she was in. Sensing some movement behind her, she quickly turned and saw two men approaching, thirty or forty feet from her. One, dressed in jeans and a plaid summer shirt, had placed his finger to his lips. The younger man, behind him, appeared dressed for a round of golf. Kelly could identify the Ralph Lauren logo on his shirt. The first man extended his hand as he approached Kelly, saying, "I'm Rick Sobelinski, FBI."

As if reading her mind, he pointed. "Those two coming up the road are agents, too."

The second man had joined them. Dark-haired, good looking, with an athletic look, he appeared to be about the same age as Kelly. The first man appeared to be in his late forties, shorter and slimmer than the younger agent.

"Where's your boyfriend?" the younger man asked. Taken aback by the abruptness of his question and the tone of his voice, Kelly nonetheless quickly explained to the two where she thought Mike had positioned himself.

"Stu's right behind us, at least he was," the younger man said following Kelly's answer. The way he said it was somewhat demeaning, suggesting Stuart might have lost them. Kelly recalled her initial reaction to Kreicheff had also been negative, and that had now changed. Maybe it's me, she thought.

"Have you sighted him again, seen anything?" the agent who'd introduced himself as Rick asked.

Kelly shook her head.

"Damn it, where's Stu?" the other agent said, having turned in the direction they'd come from.

"That's the door you saw him start to exit from?" Rick asked.

Kelly nodded. "I think there was another person behind him. I only saw the one man, though."

"Finally," the agent who Kelly had taken a dislike to said. Kelly and

Rick looked back to see Stuart Kreicheff and another man, possibly in his late thirties, approaching through the trees.

•

Stuart greeted Kelly warmly, thanking her for notifying them and congratulating her for having spotted one of the men in the photograph.

Kelly was relieved to see he was the one who appeared to be in charge. He'd immediately sent the agent who'd arrived with Rick off to locate Mike and inform him of their arrival. He then quickly filled her in on what was planned.

Pointing out the tiny listening device in his ear, he explained, "As soon as we hear from Mike and Fritz, the agent I sent to inform him we're here, I'll give those two the go-ahead." He'd gestured toward the couple in tennis attire, who were now in front of the house next door. The man was kneeling, appearing to be tying his shoelace, the bag containing the racquets resting on the road next to him.

"There's a small megaphone in the tennis bag. Jim will be taking it and rushing towards the house, taking a position under one of those windows near the door, while Mary's taking cover. He'll announce we're here and for those inside to come out with their hands on their heads. Hopefully, that will work. One of our goals is to keep a low profile, not alert the neighbors if we can avoid it. If they don't respond, we'll have to force our way in. I'll want you to just stay here where you are. Understood?"

Kelly nodded.

Glancing at his watch, Stuart continued. "We should be hearing from Fritz any minute. By the way, Charles Woodbridge was trying to contact you. Something about setting up a meeting to discuss your wedding plans. He indicated he has some suggestions and costs for you. He's quite a man— definitely from the old school. The meetings are still on, only one no-show and she might have arrived by the time we get back. Mr. Woodbridge and the Grand Hotel are accepting a huge risk in this affair. In his mind, it's a patriotic risk. If there's an attempt to sabotage the meetings, if someone, possibly a hotel guest, is injured or killed, maybe more than one, the hotel could have a massive liability suit on its hands. I don't know if I'd be as brave as Mr. Woodbridge, if I was in his shoes. He could have stopped the meetings. I suppose he still . . ."

Stuart hesitated in mid-sentence. "That was Fritz," he said, turning towards Rick Sobelinski with a thumbs-up sign. Rick placed two fingers in his mouth and whistled.

If she hadn't been watching him, Kelly was sure she'd have assumed the high-pitched sound was the shriek of a bird. The man who'd been kneeling in the road was dashing into the front yard next door, the tennis bag clutched in his left hand.

Chapter 16

Stuart, Rick, and the agent who'd used the megaphone were now in the house. The woman Stuart had referred to as Mary was standing just south of the door they'd entered, her gun drawn and back pressed against the siding of the house. The attempt to get the occupants to come out had failed. From Kelly's vantage point, it had appeared the door had been unlocked when Stuart and the other agents went in.

They'd moved quickly, guns in a ready position. Kelly was relieved to have heard no sounds of gunfire. They'd already been inside for several minutes.

Stuart was the first to come out. He said something to the woman before looking over in Kelly's direction and waving, motioning to her to join them.

As Kelly approached, Mike and the agent Stuart had sent to contact him, came around the corner of the rear of the house.

"Someone, looks as if there were several, maybe three or four, camped out here," Stuart explained. "They're gone now, but the beds have been slept in, and there are dirty dishes. They cleaned up after themselves, though. Nothing of value left behind that we could see."

The other two agents had also come out the door. "I'll call and get a team out here to check for prints," Rick said.

Stuart nodded. "Necessary, but I'm doubtful if they'll find any. The glasses on the kitchen counter had smudges, but no signs of prints. I think we're dealing with pros. They probably wore surgical gloves."

"One of us should have stayed here while the other contacted you," Kelly said to Stuart. "We goofed—"

Stuart interrupted her. "None of that. Without you, we wouldn't have known the man was still on the island. But he—they—might be aware we're on to them. From what you saw, it appears they were ready to leave when you sighted him. They probably gave you a minute or two to move on and then left as they'd planned to."

"There's also a good chance she was recognized," the agent who'd been with Mike suggested, "as the woman who was standing next to Anderson when he took the photo. The man who came to her room this morning might have been here, too. He may have seen her from one of the windows. That's probably what prompted them to clear out."

"Regardless," Stuart responded. "We've been forewarned. Some of them are still here on the island. We need to get back to the hotel."

Mike had walked over to Kelly's side and had his arm around her shoulder. "We need to get those horses back, too," he said to her.

Kelly nodded as she replied, "We're already going to be late. We'll call from the Swanson's."

•

The children had been disappointed they couldn't stay. Betty answered the phone when Kelly called the stable. She told Kelly not to worry, that their horses weren't scheduled out again. "We'll just see you when we see you," she said. "We're here until about eight."

•

The horses appeared delighted to see them. Big Buck in particular seemed to sense he was headed back to the stable as Mike mounted him. He broke into a fast trot before starting to canter. Mike laughed as Kelly and Patch came up alongside of him.

"Maybe we'll have them back in the barn on time after all," he joked.

Chapter 17

Shortly after six-thirty, Kelly and Mike arrived back at the stable and were just in the process of dismounting as Chamberlain came out of the office. He waved off their attempts to apologize for being late and to pay him for the extra time.

"Forget it, I'm just glad you had such a lovely day to show off the island to Mike, Kelly. Where did you go?"

Kelly explained in general terms where they'd ridden and Mike commented on how much fun they'd had and how impressed he was with the beauty and tranquillity of the island.

"What did you think of Stone Cliff, Mike?" Chamberlain asked. "Did you get a look at the Jewel, the Grand's new golf course?"

Mike and Kelly both shook their heads. "We didn't get a chance to," she said. "We didn't get quite that far."

"Where did you get held up?" Chamberlain asked, surprised she hadn't shown Mike those spots. His face suddenly flushed. "Sorry to pry," he said with a chuckle and a knowing look. "The point is, you had fun."

Kelly blushed and glanced at Mike. It was an awkward moment. They really couldn't say anything to correct Chamberlain's assumption of how they'd spent their time without complicating matters.

Attempting to change subjects, Chamberlain asked if they'd heard about Mr. Woodbridge's accident.

"Just an hour or so ago. He was walking home from the hotel down the sidewalk near the bottom of the hill from the Grand, the same route he takes several times a day. Seems a man lost control of his bicycle as he was coming down the hill. The bike jumped the curb and slammed into Mr. Woodbridge."

"Was he badly injured?" Kelly asked, knowing Mr. Woodbridge was now in his early seventies and that recovering from injuries, especially if any bones were broken, wouldn't be as swift as it would be for a younger person.

"He was lucky," Chamberlain replied. "A doctor was there who'd been walking behind him down the hill, or heading up to the Grand. One of our riders who saw the accident says the doctor was kneeling down next to Mr. Woodbridge in a matter of seconds. It didn't appear he was badly injured at first. He was struggling to sit up and locate his glasses. Then he suddenly appeared to pass out. The doctor caught him as he collapsed. The young man who described all this to us said he overheard the doctor saying something about a slight concussion.

"They used the island's EMS vehicle to take him home. It's good that other doctor was there. Doc Solomon, the island's only doctor, was out in Harrisonville making a house call."

Kelly nodded, remembering there'd been only one physician on the island the summers she'd been here.

"I'm sure he'll be stopping by this evening to check in on Mr.

Woodbridge," Chamberlain continued.

"Well, I suppose it gives the tourists who saw the accident something to write about on their postcards. As you well know, Kelly, Mr. Woodbridge is revered as almost the patron saint of the island. Sure hope he hasn't been seriously hurt."

"How about the man on the bike?" Mike asked. "Was he injured, too?"

"Don't rightly know, son. Wasn't told and didn't think to ask."

Kelly and Mike proceeded to thank Chamberlain profusely for their ride. "Sure brought back memories," Kelly said.

Chamberlain smiled, shaking Mike's hand as he said, "For me, too, Kelly. I'll have horses available if you want to give it another go while you're here. Remember, I'd like to be included on the guest list for the wedding."

Chapter 18

The message light was blinking when Kelly and Mike entered their room a little past seven. Mike walked over to the phone, lifted the receiver and pushed the button for messages. He arched his eyebrows and smiled at Kelly as he listened to the message.

"That was Charles Woodbridge, inviting us down to his house for cocktails. He says he has a proposal together for us to review. He indicated he'd tried to contact us earlier this afternoon. The message was left at five-twenty."

"Must have been just prior to when he left to go home, just before the accident," Kelly said.

Mike nodded. "The timing for the invite was six-thirty. He said he'd have to be back up to the hotel by seven-thirty."

"Probably to formally greet the people who've come for those meetings," Kelly said. "I think I'll call him and let him know we just got his message. Check to see how he's feeling."

"Good idea," Mike said. "Hopefully, his injuries aren't too serious and we'll be able to re-schedule a meeting with him, sometime tomorrow or Monday, before we leave."

"It's too bad today didn't work out," Kelly said. "It would have been nice to have seen him and fix the date before we meet with Terry Noonan tomorrow after church. Maybe he can tell me enough over the phone now, so that we can decide on the date.

"You might want to jump in the shower now, Mike, while I'm calling. Looks as if we'll be rushing to make the last seating for dinner again tonight."

"A shower sounds good," Mike said, breaking into a grin. "You can come join me if you're so inclined."

Kelly shook her head, laughing. "My mother warned me to be careful when I told her we were coming up for the weekend. I don't think she was referring to slipping on a bar of soap, though. We'll see how long I'm on the phone."

•

Kelly recognized the voice that answered, "Mr. Woodbridge's residence." It was the Asian man Mr. Woodbridge had employed for years. She'd met him when she'd worked for the Grand. What was his name?

"Is that you, Chan? This is Kelly, Kelly Travis. I spent a couple of summers employed by Mr. Woodbridge, a few years back. I met you then."

"But of course, Miss Travis. I remember. It is nice to hear your voice again."

"I'm calling to see how Mr. Woodbridge is. I heard about the accident. Is he up to taking phone calls?"

"I'm sorry, Miss Travis. He is resting now. He asked not to be disturbed."

"I understand, but would you remember to tell him I called, concerned about his injuries?"

"I will be sure to give him that message."

"And Chan, if you could, would you also tell him we just heard the message he'd left on our phone, inviting my fiancé and me for cocktails this evening. We were due, he'd invited us for six-thirty. We're getting married the end of the summer here on the island. Mr. Woodbridge was putting a proposal together for us. The rehearsal dinner, the reception, rooms, everything. He left word he'd finished it. I'd like you to ask him when you have a chance, if he thinks he'd be feeling well enough sometime tomorrow or Monday morning to meet with us. We're heading home about noon on Monday. Am I making myself clear? Could you—"

"Most certainly, Miss Travis, and congratulations. If you could please hold I will see if he is awake. Perhaps I can ask him your question now."

Kelly was placed on hold for several minutes. I should have remembered to say we could come down to see him virtually any time, at his convenience, she thought to herself.

"Hello, Miss Travis? I am sorry to have kept you waiting so long. Mr. Woodbridge says that he'll be available after your round of golf on the Jewel tomorrow morning. He realizes how much the two of you were looking forward to that. If he is not in his office at the hotel then, he will arrange to have a copy of his proposal left in your name at the front desk. He invites you to call him with questions and to discuss it.

"He also asked me to tell you he encourages you to pick the August date, even though the September date would be better business-wise for the hotel. He wants you to have a beautiful, sunny day for the wedding."

Kelly laughed. "Chan, please tell him I have so much confidence in him, I think he can probably arrange for—even guarantee—nice weather, too."

"I will, Miss Travis. I will."

As Kelly hung up, she was thinking that Mike and she should probably finalize the August date with Terry Noonan and Irene Taylor tomorrow morning. They could possibly change if there was a major difference in prices for the later date. Funny, she thought. I told Mr. Woodbridge in my note about our plans to attend church tomorrow morning and meet with the pastor immediately following the service. Maybe he didn't remember with all his concerns, everything else on his mind. I hope he doesn't have a serious head injury. Everything else Chan related to her made sense. The comment about playing golf on the Jewel was the only one that seemed a little odd. Oh, well.

Mike stepped out of the bathroom, dressed in his boxer shorts. Seeing Kelly still perched on the bed next to the phone, he asked, "Were you able to get through to him? How's he feeling?"

Kelly answered she hadn't been able to talk to him directly. She told him who Chan was and the gist of the conversation. "Mr. Woodbridge must not feel too badly. He hopes to be in his office here at the hotel around noon tomorrow and see us. If he's not up to that, he'll arrange for a copy of his proposal to be left at the desk for us, inviting us to call with any questions."

"Sounds as if it went well. I was fearful I might get washed down the drain, being in the shower so long." His smirk conveyed the message, 'waiting for you.'

"I'm sorry," Kelly said, smiling. "Chan did leave me on hold for nearly five minutes. Honest."

"I believe you. We still have some wine left. Would you like a glass now?"

"In a minute or two. I think I'll shower first." She grinned. "This hasn't been the romantic weekend we both envisioned yet, has it? Maybe a nice candlelight dinner followed by some dancing can change that." Whistling 'I'm In The Mood For Love,' Kelly removed some underwear from one of the dresser drawers and pranced by Mike, giving him a light kiss on the lips as she headed into the bathroom.

Mike smiled to himself as he began to get his clothes out. He'd been primed for the weekend. *I remind myself of some young teenage stud who's been anticipating his date with the prom queen. Polishes up the family car, scouts out a place they can park after the dance, buys some Binaca mouth spray. Then his high hopes and romantic dreams for the evening are deflated by two flat tires. That's Kelly and me this weekend. Not minor glitches, big-time interruptions.* He smiled to himself again. *The weekend's not even half over. Things could change for the better.*

•

And they appeared to be doing so. Their dinner had been a delight. An attentive and friendly waiter, four courses which would have pleased the palates of anyone, and a delicious bottle of Merlot. Kelly looked stunning with her dangling gold earrings reflecting in the candlelight. Her light blue dress matched the color of her eyes. Mike was reminded of Roy Miller's comment about Kelly resembling Princess Di. He especially noticed it now. *I'll be the envy of every man in the ballroom, spinning around the dance floor with her tonight,* he thought.

Kelly was having similar thoughts. *Mike looked dashing tonight in a black blazer, checked pants and the geranium-patterned Mackinac tie she'd surprised him with tonight. She'd spotted it earlier in the window of one of the stores downstairs and had called down and had it sent up. She'd done it when Mr. Woodbridge's line was busy the first time she'd dialed his number.*

"Let's review our plans for tomorrow," Mike suggested. "I know about the ten-thirty services at church and our meeting afterwards with the minister. But what else do we have planned? What time are we supposed to meet with Mr. Woodbridge? That is, if he's feeling up to it."

"Right after church and our meeting, I guess. Chan said that Mr. Woodbridge hoped he'd be able to come up to his office here at the hotel late tomorrow morning, by the time we finished our round of golf."

"Tomorrow morning? I thought you'd told him in your note about our plans for church and meeting with Terry and Irene following the service."

"I thought I had, too. But with everything that's happening, the stress he must be under with these meetings, he could have easily forgotten what I'd written. Chan did relay the message that Mr. Woodbridge was aware of how much we were looking forward to playing the Jewel, the Grand's new course."

Mike scrunched his face, staring at Kelly with a questioning look. "That's strange. I can understand how he might not have picked up on our going to church from your note, but remember, I also spoke with him this morning. It was the first time I'd met him. He asked what our plans were, what we'd be doing while we were here. He specifically asked whether we'd have time to work in a round of golf at the new course. He said he could arrange everything—clubs, balls, green fees—at no cost to us, as his guests. I remember smiling and asking if we could have a rain check, telling him we wouldn't have time this visit. I explained that we'd brought along our tennis racquets and that we also had plans to go horseback riding, and the golf would have to wait for another time. I thanked him, of course, and I think I said something about maybe getting a look at the course while we were out riding. But there's no way—no way at all—I would have left him with the impression we'd be playing golf. To the contrary—I was very emphatic we wouldn't have time."

Kelly nodded her head, her expression one of concern. "I'm sorry I didn't say something earlier, Mike. This bothers me. I had . . . I don't know how to put it. When Chan related Woodbridge's comment, the fact he'd said he knew we were looking forward to playing golf, I had strange vibes. A thought that something wasn't ringing true, even without knowing about your earlier conversation."

"Maybe we're reading too much into this—our police mentality in overdrive," Mike joked, but with no trace of a smile. "Let's think this out," he said as he motioned to their waiter.

They'd originally turned down his offer for coffee, thinking they'd be heading to the ballroom to dance.

"We've changed our minds," Mike said, smiling at the waiter. "We'd like some coffee after all. De-caf, Kelly?"

She nodded, deep in thought. "Make it two."

They sat for a few minutes, mulling over their respective thoughts, sipping their coffee.

"Let me run a scenario past you," Kelly finally said. "This may be off the wall, but what if it wasn't an accident this afternoon? What if the entire incident was staged? An elaborate plan to take Mr. Woodbridge hostage in his own home? To force him to take steps to cancel the meetings?"

"I don't think that's farfetched at all," Mike said. "But remember, Chamberlain mentioned something about the possibility of Mr. Woodbridge experiencing a mild concussion. It might be more serious than that—an injury that's impacted his thinking."

"I realize that's the more logical explanation. But the other statements Chan related, supposedly after speaking to Mr. Woodbridge, didn't sound the least bit odd. I have the gut feeling Woodbridge was trying to send me some kind of message, to alert me to the fact that everything wasn't as it appeared. Doing it with a remark which would appear innocent enough to anyone but me—anyone but us. Now, how do we go about checking on whether my supposition has any validity?"

"I don't think we do," Mike said. "I think we should contact Stuart, tell him of our concerns and let the FBI get into it."

"That sounds logical," Kelly responded. "It probably wouldn't be too wise for us to be prowling around Mr. Woodbridge's home at this hour of the night."

Mike nodded with a slight smile as she continued on.

"They should be able to quickly discover if something is amiss or if maybe I've just overreacted. We could stop by the offices now on our way to the ballroom and see if Stuart's there. If not, maybe we can reach him at that number he gave us. Ready?" Kelly concluded, standing and pushing back her chair.

•

As Kelly and Mike came out of the dining room and down the hall into the lobby, they noticed over a dozen people in line in front of the entrance to the ballroom.

"Saturday night, I should have realized they would probably have a full house, even this early in the season," Kelly said. "Why don't I get in line while you try to locate Stuart and brief him?"

65

Mike nodded. "But a better suggestion might be to reverse that. I'll get in line while you try to find him. He may have questions regarding your conversation with Chan that I couldn't answer. Hopefully, you'll find me inside at a table."

Chapter 19

"I'm not sure just who's back there," the young woman sitting behind the desk said. She recognized Kelly from her earlier visits. "I could check for you, but why don't you go back on your own? Maybe you'll see a familiar face."

Kelly nodded as she navigated around the desk and through the doorway which led to the office area, which was now familiar to her. Steve Richards' office was empty, with the light turned off. Although the lights were on in many of the other offices, they too were vacant. The entire area appeared to be deserted. As she stuck her head into the last office on the left, she heard a familiar voice behind her. "Can I help you?"

She turned to see Fritz, the younger agent she'd met this afternoon—the one who Stuart had sent to find Mike. There was no sign of recognition as he stared at Kelly.

"Hi, Fritz. I'm Kelly Travis, we met this afternoon. I'm looking for Stuart."

With more of a smirk than a smile, he replied, "As you can see, he's not here."

Kelly hesitated a second or two before saying, "It's in regards to Mr. Woodbridge."

"Stu's aware. We've all been told about the accident."

"I was sure you had been. I just wanted to check and see if you knew how he's doing."

"If you want my candid opinion, I think he's losing it," Fritz replied, pointing a finger to his head and making circles. "A little touched. Have you ever been in his office? Everything's fastened or glued down—the chairs, tables, lamps, paintings—even the ashtrays."

Kelly was well aware of Mr. Woodbridge's desire to have everything in its place. As Fritz was talking, she recalled a meeting in Woodbridge's office when she'd worked for the Grand. He'd spread some sketches of plans for the hotel on his desk and Kelly had attempted to inch her chair forward to have a closer look. He'd laughed, explaining how everything in his office was anchored in place. He'd found himself getting angry and all worked up every time his office was cleaned. His solution eliminated the problem. Fritz was no longer speaking, just smiling at Kelly, sensing her irritation over his reply.

He's waiting for me to ask again, explain myself. He knew the purpose of my question—an inquiry about Mr. Woodbridge's injuries and how he was faring. It was a brief battle of wills, staring one another down before Fritz said, "He's lucky a doctor was there when the accident occurred. We've been told he wasn't seriously injured. His own doctor, I guess he's the only one on the island, was going to be stopping by and looking in on him tonight. I don't think we've heard from him."

As he talked, Fritz inched closer to Kelly and placed the palm of his left hand on the wall next to her face. I can't believe it, she said to herself. He's coming on to me. He just met Mike this afternoon.

"By the way," Fritz continued, "you might know the other doctor—he's from Ann Arbor. George Overbeck. His address as I recall was on Airington."

"Probably Arlington," Kelly said. "Not far from where my parents live."

Fritz had moved even closer, cornering her in the narrow hallway, the palm of his outstretched arm continuing to press against the wall next to her face. Kelly quickly bent her knees and ducked under his arm. She took a couple of steps forward and then turned, glaring at him. He'd also swung around to face her, an expression of surprise on his face.

He can't believe I could possibly be turning him down, Kelly surmised. What a creep!

"I'd still like to speak with Stuart," Kelly blurted, her face flushed in anger. "Are you aware that I'm a former FBI agent myself?" she asked, her voice rising in volume.

Fritz smiled and nodded, obviously pleased he'd succeeded in rousing Kelly's dander.

"Stu's upstairs, on guard duty with some of the others. I actually don't expect to see any of them back down here for an hour or so." He edged closer towards Kelly again as he added, "Richards filled in for Woodbridge at dinner, formally welcoming the group here for the meeting. They began their opening session right after dinner, about an hour ago."

Kelly stepped back a few paces, keeping her distance. Fritz was having trouble taking no for an answer. He's not being very subtle, that's for sure, Kelly reasoned. His message was clear. If you're so inclined, we could probably use one of these offices without being disturbed. Her adrenaline rising, Kelly had to caution herself against kicking him in the groin.

"Could you get word to him? Tell Stuart I need to speak to him. Have him call our room."

Kelly's persistence confused Fritz and raised his curiosity. "I'll try, but I could also relay a message."

She shook her head. "Just have him contact me as soon as possible, please."

He smiled again, slowly nodding his head. Kelly could read his mind— Lady, you just blew the opportunity of a lifetime. She quickly turned and hurried down the hallway. Glancing over her shoulder, she saw he hadn't moved—still standing, staring at her with that sickening grin on his face.

Chapter 20

Mike was near the head of the line when he noticed Roy Miller standing at a table, waving at him, holding up two fingers and pointing to the two empty chairs at the table. What should I do? Mike thought. The ballroom appeared packed and maybe there wasn't even an option. Hoping Kelly wouldn't be too disappointed, Mike waved back and made his way along the edge of the dance floor towards the Millers' table.

"Where's Kelly?" Mr. Miller asked.

"She'll be along in a minute or two," Mike answered.

"Sometimes you ask the dumbest questions, Roy," Martha said, implying it should be obvious that Kelly must have stopped off at the ladies' room.

Ignoring her, Roy pointed to the camera on the table in front of his chair. "They found it, out behind the hotel under a fire escape. They assume it was either dropped or tossed there. Doesn't appear to be damaged, though. I won't know for sure until I have the next roll processed. Damned if they didn't remove the film, though. Guess I should be happy I'd only taken a couple of shots."

Mike nodded as he seated himself next to Martha Miller as her husband continued talking. The orchestra had started to play "Lollipop." Martha's face lit up as she pulled on the sleeve of her husband's sport coat. Roy smiled at his wife and jumped up.

"You'll have to excuse us, Mike. This is one of our favorites, right Martha?"

She smiled as he pulled back her chair. "We're anxious to hear about your horseback riding," she said to Mike. "We won't be long."

•

The orchestra had swung into a rumba and Mike watched in admiration as the Millers, with looks of glee, began to swivel their hips. It was amazing how graceful and light-footed they were, especially considering their hefty builds. I hope I don't embarrass Kelly too much tonight, Mike thought. Though loving music, he'd never considered himself a good dancer. He was trying to recall the last time he'd danced, when he spotted Kelly. He stood and waved and moved forward to greet her.

"Guess what?" he said, grinning. "You'll never guess who invited us to join them at their table."

Kelly's concerned expression changed to a smile. "Really?" Glancing around the room as Mike escorted her towards their table, she commented, "I guess we should consider ourselves lucky to even get a seat."

"Were you able to locate Stuart?"

Kelly shook her head. "The only person there was the agent he sent to locate you this afternoon, Fritz. I don't even remember hearing his last name."

Mike nodded as he pulled out a chair for her at the table. "Frederick U. Stanton III."

Kelly looked up over her shoulder in surprise as she was seating herself, amazed Mike knew his full name. "You probably know what the U stands for, too."

"Actually, I do. Underwood. His mother's maiden name."

"You must have become pretty close friends in just a few minutes today. That certainly hasn't been my experience. I think he's a jerk."

Mike's eyebrows raised, startled by the harshness in Kelly's voice. "My observation too, and I was only with him for a couple of minutes. But what happened just now to turn you off?"

Kelly quickly told Mike of the confrontation with Fritz. "I didn't mention anything about our concerns for Mr. Woodbridge, just that we needed to talk to Stuart."

"Did you tell him to let Stuart know we'd be here in the ballroom?"

Kelly shook her head. "No. I asked him to tell him to call us in our room. I thought—"

"You two should be out there dancing." Martha said as she and her husband came up to the table. "The orchestra's wonderful! You can practice up for the wedding. You are planning for dancing at the reception, aren't you?"

Kelly smiled and nodded her head as she stood up to greet the Millers. "We are. Hopefully, this same group—or at least some of them—will be available."

"It's pretty old-fashioned stuff right now," Roy said. "But we've heard things liven up at midnight. After the oldsters head for bed."

"Maybe we should get out on the floor now, then," Mike said to Kelly. "I have enough trouble with the Fox Trot, let alone some of that stuff you probably thrive on, Kelly."

What he was saying was probably true, Kelly thought, but she also sensed Mike was making an excuse for them to get away from the Millers for a few minutes so she and Mike could continue their conversation.

•

As Roy had indicated, the orchestra was into the oldies. Kelly and Mike were delighted at how quickly their steps came into sync during the first dance of their courtship.

"Are you having as much fun as I am?"

Mike nodded, squeezing her a little tighter and brushing his lips across her cheek. Laughing, he said, "I could dance the night away—and I never thought I'd ever be able to make that statement."

The two decided to head back to the hotel office area in another thirty minutes or so. Hopefully Stuart would be there, or someone other than Fritz, to tell of their concerns in regard to Mr. Woodbridge. The opportunity presented itself a few dances later, when to the delight of many of the younger couples in the room, the orchestra switched over to the type of music which had more appeal to them. Kelly and Mike navigated past the many couples coming out onto the dance floor, faces shining, hands clapping, to return to their table to say goodnight to the Millers.

"You make a very attractive couple out there on the dance floor," Martha said.

On hearing Kelly and Mike were planning on calling it a night, the

Millers exchanged knowing glances. Roy started to make a comment, but Martha grabbed his arm before he was able to say anything.

"We'll be heading up soon ourselves," Martha said. "If we don't see you at breakfast, good luck with your meeting with the minister. I'm sure we'll see you again before we check out tomorrow. Roy's already arranged for a late check-out, haven't you, dear?"

He nodded. "Remember, if you're in the market for—"

"Now stop that, Roy," Martha said, laughing. "Remember, we're on vacation."

Chapter 21

It was past eleven and no one was manning the desk in front of the hotel offices. The door leading into them was unlocked and Kelly and Mike stepped into the hallway. There were just a few lights on and there was no sign of anyone. Just as they were about to leave, Mike held up his hand.

"I think I hear someone talking at the end of the hallway," Mike said. "It's a woman's voice."

Kelly nodded, indicating she was hearing the voice, too. "Sounds as if she's talking on the phone. I only hear one voice."

Walking down the hall in the direction from which the voice was originating, they heard the sound of a phone being hung up. As they approached the office from which they'd heard the voice, they nearly collided with a woman coming out the doorway. She jumped, startled to see them. It was the young woman, Mary, the agent they'd met earlier that afternoon.

"You scared me," she said with a broad smile, raising a hand to her chest. "Stuart was trying to reach you a couple of minutes ago. He and Jim just headed down to Mr. Woodbridge's house. You just missed them."

"Do you think we could catch up to them?" Kelly asked. "We had something we wanted to discuss with him."

"Fritz did brief him about you wanting to speak with him. That's why he called your room. I doubt if you'll catch them. I said they'd just left, but it was at least ten minutes ago, and I think they took a taxi." Mary smiled. "A carriage."

"Do you expect to see him when he gets back?" Kelly asked.

"If it's in the next hour, yes," she answered, smiling again.

Glancing at Mike, Kelly began to relate to Mary their concerns and suspicions in regards to Mr. Woodbridge and his accident.

"I've had the gut feeling he may have been trying to send us a message."

Mary nodded in understanding. "You may be onto something. Mr. Woodbridge's doctor—the island doctor, not the one who treated him after the accident—phoned Mr. Richards less than an hour ago. I think his name is Solomon. He'd tried to reach Mr. Woodbridge all evening and had received only a busy signal. He finally went over to his house shortly before ten. A man who works for Mr. Woodbridge—I think his name is Chan—told him Woodbridge was sleeping and had left explicit instructions he didn't want to be disturbed. The doctor said he has a very close relationship with Mr. Woodbridge, and Chan too, for that matter. He thought it was rather strange he couldn't get inside the door to have a look at his patient and called Richards to tell him. Richards told Stuart. After they tried to reach Mr. Woodbridge on the phone, getting a busy signal, Stuart and Jim headed down to take a look around.

"I could try to page Stuart and have him call, so you or I could relate your concerns. He may already be there. I certainly hope he and Jim aren't blindly walking into trouble. I should warn them. But Stuart might elect to use Mr. Woodbridge's phone to call me to answer his page, and then it might be too late for a warning. He left his cell phone here with me." Shaking her head, Mary picked up the phone and dialed Stuart's pager.

•

While they'd been awaiting the call back from Stuart, Mary briefed them on the events of the evening. The initial meeting had been far more fruitful than anyone had expected. Discussions had continued until nearly ten-thirty, and a breakfast session was scheduled for eight a.m.

"The spouses who are here will be going over to the Governor's Summer Home at about eight-thirty for breakfast. I think there will be around ten or eleven involved. I'll be one of the escorts."

Glancing at her watch, it was now nearly a quarter to twelve, Mary said, "I would have thought we'd have heard from Stuart by now. I think I'll page him again. I'm certain he's wearing it."

Five minutes later, they heard footsteps coming down the hallway and a second or two later, Stuart and Jim entered the office. Acknowledging Kelly and Mike with a nod and smile, Stuart started the conversation by apologizing to Mary.

"I received the page, but I wasn't able to get to a phone, Mary. I'm sorry. My apologies to you, too," he said, turning to Kelly and Mike. "I heard you wanted to talk to me. Who wants to start? Is that why you paged me, Mary?"

She nodded. "Why don't you begin by briefing us? Actually, I paged you to warn you something might be awry at Mr. Woodbridge's. Is he all right? Did you see him?"

Both men nodded. "Yes, we did see him," Stuart said, "and we also spoke with him for a few minutes. Is he all right? Is there anything—using your term—awry? I don't know. Jim and I were asking ourselves those questions on our way back here. The house was completely dark when we arrived. No sounds or sign of anyone."

Catching the look from Kelly as she started to say something, Stuart said, "Steve Richards briefed us on the fact Mr. Woodbridge's bedroom is soundproofed, with electric panels which can be lowered over the windows. So the darkness and silence, especially due to the hour, didn't alarm us."

Kelly nodded. Stuart had anticipated what she'd been about to say. The totally black, soundproofed room was, like Woodbridge's office with everything fastened in place, one of the quirks islanders talked about in discussing this living legend.

"We rang the doorbell three or four times," Stuart continued. "We could hear it ring, but we must have waited for nearly five minutes before someone finally came to the door." Jim nodded in agreement as Stuart went on. "It was Charles Woodbridge himself. He looked a little pale, very agitated—angry. He asked what in the hell we were doing waking him at that time of night and whether something had happened, gone wrong at the Grand or with the meetings, to prompt our visit. I explained that to the contrary, everything was going smoothly and that Steve Richards had done a good job pinch-hitting for him. I told him we'd just come to check to see if he was okay, because we hadn't been able to reach him by phone because his line had been busy. He gave us an incredulous look, explaining he'd taken the phone off the hook so that he wouldn't be disturbed. If he could get a good night's sleep, he said he planned to be up at the hotel by seven-thirty or eight o'clock tomorrow morning. I guess I should say this morning. He told us if he felt up to it, he wanted to help the Governor and his wife host the wives of those attending the meetings."

"He never once invited us in," Jim said. "He chastised us like two schoolboys for interrupting his sleep when we should have known better. Stuart even asked if he could use his phone."

Stuart smiled. "He just glared and told us to get back where we were supposed to be, where we might be needed."

"That's so out of character for him," Kelly commented. "He truly is the nicest, sweetest man you could imagine. I don't recall him ever speaking harshly to anyone."

"Our taxi driver said about the same thing," Stuart said. "We'd asked him to wait for us. He could see we were a little rattled, I think, when we climbed back in the carriage. He said Woodbridge was almost paranoid about getting a full eight hours' sleep. He knew all about the 'black' room. But when I quoted what Mr. Woodbridge had said to us, wondering what the hell we were doing waking him up in the middle of the night, the driver appeared shocked. He told us we must have really upset the man, because he'd never heard of him ever swearing before."

"That's true," Kelly said. "He has the reputation of never, ever using profanity."

"We won't spoil it," Stuart replied. "It was understandable, with the accident, the late hour, the tension with the threats about the meetings and all. Our lips are sealed.

"And that's about it, isn't it, Jim? Anything I failed to mention?"

"No, I think you pretty well covered things. We both did try to peer over his shoulders while he was at the door to see if we could see anyone else inside. We didn't. And one other thing Stuart and I both commented on later. Mr. Woodbridge appeared to grimace in pain as he was shutting the door as we were leaving. We think he may have injured his shoulder or hand in the accident."

"You didn't see his houseman, Chan?" Kelly asked.

The two men shook their heads. "We didn't think to ask about him, either," Stuart said. "It was really a brief confrontation, a somewhat tense situation. We did take time to walk around the house and grounds before we left, however. We didn't see anyone else, or anything out of the ordinary. You were anxious to talk to me, Kelly. What was that about?"

Kelly glanced at Mike, who motioned for her to take the lead in telling the two men of their concerns. Kelly quickly told them of her conversation with Chan and Mike's talk that morning with Mr. Woodbridge.

"Granted, we could be reading too much into it, but we both sensed that Mr. Woodbridge might have been attempting to send us a message of some sort."

Stuart sat for a minute or two, contemplating, stroking his chin with one of his hands, glancing over at Jim. Finally, he said, "You may be right. The entire incident could have been planned—really no accident. The fact Doc Solomon couldn't get inside Woodbridge's house to examine him also raises concern, a red flag so to speak. Even so, I don't think there's much more we can do at this juncture. But if Woodbridge doesn't make an appearance by eight a.m. and we haven't heard from him, I promise you we'll get back down there and force our way in. Does that make sense?"

Kelly was still concerned. Yes, it did make sense, but she wished there was another option. Mary and Jim, along with Mike, were nodding their heads, agreeing with Stuart's assessment and suggestion.

•

As Kelly and Mike crossed the lobby, heading towards the stairway, they saw the Millers coming out of the ballroom.

"Oh, no," Mike said. "They've seen us."

The Millers came down the stairs, hand in hand, their faces beaming. "Did you two decide to take a stroll in the moonlight?" Martha asked.

Kelly and Mike grabbed one another's hand and nodded their heads with a smile. "And I think we're in store for another lovely day tomorrow. There are plenty of stars out," Mike said.

"That would make it nice for our last day," Roy replied. "I think you're just in time for a last dance."

Kelly shook her head. "No, I think we're really ready to call it a day now, but it was fun. Thank you for letting us join you."

"Our pleasure," Roy said. "There's only a dozen or so people left in there." Holding up his and his wife's clasped hands, he grinned and started to sing, "Two o'clock in the morning, time to be—"

"Oh, sheesh, Roy," Martha said, laughing. Winking at Kelly and Mike, she said, "Don't let him fool you. He's going to be snoring in five minutes."

•

A few minutes later, as Mike was standing in front of the sink in their bathroom, clad in his boxer shorts, brushing his teeth, Kelly tapped him on the shoulder.

"I just had an idea, Mike. I think I'll call information and see if there's a listing for that doctor from Ann Arbor. The one who—"

"I hear you," Mike mumbled with the toothbrush in his mouth, indicating he understood what she was saying. "Good idea!"

Chapter 22

Kelly was sitting on the side of the bed in her nightgown when Mike came out of the bathroom. She looked up and said, "There's no listing for a Doctor George Overbeck. On Arlington or anywhere else in Ann Arbor. No office phone, either."

"What about an unlisted number?"

"I asked," she said. "There isn't. There's a George Overbeck, but no doctor. It's a Chelsea address."

Mike nodded. Chelsea was a small town a few miles west of Ann Arbor. "Did you ask her to check under the University of Michigan Medical Center? I think some of those doctors don't have a separate listing."

"I did and she couldn't find his name there, either."

"Maybe Fritz had the name wrong. You mentioned he was mixed up on the street. We should probably pass the information on to Stuart. Let him use their resources to check it out. He can also verify the name. He might have it, or he can easily check with Fritz or someone else."

Kelly nodded and picked up the phone, dialing the number Stuart had given them. She didn't recognize the man's voice who answered, and left word for Stuart to call their room.

They climbed into bed and embraced, sharing a long, romantic kiss. Kelly started to laugh as they were still kissing.

"What's the matter?" Mike asked as they broke the kiss and he leaned back, a smile on his face.

"I think you know," Kelly answered, smiling back. "The great romantic weekend we both envisioned has had to take a back seat with all that's happened. I know I'm exhausted, and here we are waiting for Stuart's call."

Mike laughed. "Maybe we'll be in the mood for a 'morner'."

With a questioning look, Kelly asked, "What's that? I'm not with you."

"A 'sooner nooner'," Mike replied, grinning.

Kelly laughed and playfully punched him in the ribs. "Sounds great to me!" she said, bending over and giving him a kiss on the lips.

•

Ten minutes later, Stuart called. Mike had dozed off and Kelly jumped up and walked around the end of the bed to answer the phone. The conversation was brief. As Kelly hung up, Mike mumbled, "What did he say?"

"He thanked us. Said they were remiss if someone hadn't already checked out Overbeck's credentials. He thinks that's the correct name. He said he'd handle it, and for us to get a good night's sleep."

Mike had already fallen back to sleep as Kelly talked. Smiling as she climbed back into bed, she leaned over and kissed him.

Chapter 23

As Mike opened his eyes, he was surprised and disappointed to see Kelly was already up and dressed. He glanced at the clock. Ten after eight.

"Good morning," he said. Kelly had been standing in front of the mirror over the dresser, checking out her appearance. She glanced over her shoulder in response to his greeting, smiling.

"I thought I'd go down and see if Mr. Woodbridge has arrived yet. Hopefully have an opportunity to speak to him before he leaves for the Governor's Summer Home."

"I can be ready in five minutes," Mike replied, throwing off the blanket and swinging his legs off the side of the bed as he sat up. He grimaced and then smiled. Leaning sideways, he patted his fanny as he said, "I can feel the results of our ride yesterday. How about you?"

"A little. I know what you mean." She walked over and gave him a kiss. "Are you going to be in shape for another kind of a ride tonight?"

He blushed and grinned, grabbing her hands, nodding his head. "For sure!"

Kelly laughed. "Is that an answer or a question?"

"I hope it's an answer," he said, laughing, standing up and taking her in his arms. "Do you want to wait or have me catch up to you?"

"Why don't I go down ahead. I'll see you in the office area or in the lobby. I won't go into the dining room without you."

"Fair enough. In the lobby or the offices by eight-thirty. Good luck!"

•

Kelly didn't recognize the young man behind the desk fronting the office area. She asked him if Mr. Woodbridge had arrived.

"Not yet," he answered with a smile. "He called in though, saying he'd be here around ten. Is there something I can help you with?"

"Is there anyone in back?" Kelly asked, motioning behind him.

"I'm not sure. Mr. Richards and some of the others had a matter to attend to and just left a few minutes ago. Some others left to accompany a group of hotel guests who are just leaving for breakfast at the Governor's Summer Home. I'll check and see if anyone else is still here. Your name?"

"Oh, I'm sorry. I'm Kelly Travis," she said, holding out her hand. "I've been working with Mr. Richards and Mr. Kreicheff. Mr. Kreicheff's associates will also know who I am."

The young man nodded as he said, "I'll just be a minute."

A moment or two later, he came back through the door with Fritz Stanton following him.

"Yes?" Stanton addressed Kelly.

She felt her body stiffen. No 'good morning,' no recognition by name, no question of whether he could help her or answer her questions.

"Are you the only one here?" Kelly asked.

Rather than answering her directly, he said, "Stu's busy on another matter. You're probably wondering about Woodbridge. He called to say he wouldn't be coming up until about ten."

"Did he offer any explanation of why he wasn't coming sooner?"

Fritz shrugged his shoulders. "I wasn't the one who spoke with him. Not that I know of. Hold on a minute, though. I'll see if I can find out." He turned and went back into the office area, closing the door behind him.

At least he's starting to treat me half-way civilly, Kelly thought as she stood waiting as the young man and she small-talked about the nice weather.

"Yes, this has been amazingly good weather for June," he was saying as Fritz came out the door again.

"Really no explanation, just the change in time for when he'd be here. He did pass on a message to be relayed to you, however. I'm sorry no one contacted you, we got sidetracked. He said to tell you he wouldn't be able to make church this morning with you and, is it Mike?"

Kelly nodded, alarm bells sounding. This had to be another message of distress, or warning. There was never any talk of Mr. Woodbridge's joining them for church. She strained her memory. Didn't she remember him attending St. Mary's, Mackinac's Catholic Church?

"Is Stuart available? I need to speak to him."

Fritz shook his head. "I thought I'd explained he's not here. He's involved in an important matter that just came up. I'd even hesitate to disturb him at this juncture. Are you sure I can't help you?"

For a brief second, the thought flashed through her mind that she and Mike could investigate on their own. She quickly discounted it, however. Neither had a gun, for one thing.

"Yes. I mean I need to confide in you. Maybe back in the office area," she suggested, tilting her head towards the young man at the desk, implying she'd rather not talk in his presence.

Rather than answering her, Fritz simply opened the door behind him and nodded, indicating she could come into the office area. He held the door for her as she preceded him. Closing the door, he said, "Okay. What's this all about?"

"I'll get right to the point. Mike and I believe Mr. Woodbridge might be being held hostage. His houseman, Chan, relayed a message to me yesterday which didn't make sense. Just now, you said Mr. Woodbridge told someone to tell me he wouldn't be joining Mike and me at church this morning. That was never discussed—never in our plans. We think the accident may have been staged. There's no doctor in Ann Arbor by the name of Overbeck. We think Mr. Woodbridge and Chan are being held captive, possibly being threatened or tortured by those people who want the meetings cancelled."

"Slow down, let me get this straight." Fritz had a smile on his face rather than a look of concern. "Does Stu know anything about this? Have you discussed your . . . theory with him?"

"Everything but the message that Mr. Woodbridge wouldn't be meeting Mike and me for church."

Fritz frowned. "Have Mike and you had breakfast yet?"

"No, but—"

"Maybe you could stop by in an hour or so and we could provide you with an update. I'll contact Stu right away. This might sound cruel, but at this moment Woodbridge isn't—how should I put it—our top priority. Our resources are . . ."

This isn't going well, Kelly thought. More than ever, she was certain Woodbridge needed their help. Timing could be critical.

"Mike and I could go down to Mr. Woodbridge's house right now and see if something's wrong. Could you loan us a gun? Maybe one for both of us?"

Fritz appeared to be shocked by her suggestion and request. "No, definitely no! I mean, as far as the two of you doing anything on your own. I realize you're a former agent, but . . ." He paused. "I'm going to share something with you, in strict confidence. I wasn't planning to, and I probably shouldn't be. You have to promise not to discuss it with anyone else." He hesitated again. "I'm certain you will with Mike, but no one else. I'm relying on you to caution him as well." He appeared to still be debating whether he should confide in her.

"I understand, we'll—" Kelly started to say as Fritz interrupted her, saying, "A bomb's been discovered in one of the guest rooms. We just got word a few minutes ago. One of the meeting attendee's rooms. His wife was getting ready to go to the breakfast they're having for spouses at the Governor's Summer Home and dropped one of her earrings on the floor. She couldn't seem to find it and had her husband get down on his hands and knees to search for it. He spotted the bomb, an explosive device of some kind, under a coffee table. We assume it was probably planted there yesterday, possibly last night, while the welcoming dinner was underway. The particularly sorry part is it still hasn't been disarmed. There's no timer. It–"

A man poked his head out of one of the offices a few yards down the corridor. Seeing Fritz, he gestured for him to come join him. Fritz told Kelly he'd just be a minute, and hurried toward the office.

Kelly took a deep breath. Fritz's news helped to explain his earlier comments, the fact Woodbridge wasn't their major concern. Fritz came out of the nearby office a moment later, smiling.

"We're in luck. It's been disarmed. All the other attendees' rooms are being searched now—the entire west end of the hotel, for that matter. This one alone would probably have caused massive damage; demolished several rooms. It was very tense there for a few minutes with us not having any idea as to the timing, when a signal would be transmitted to set the device off. Thank God it's been disarmed. The concern, of course, is whether or not another—or others—have been planted."

Kelly was shaking her head, aware of the risks the men who'd been defusing the bomb had been taking; the elation they must have over having been successful.

"That other agent I just spoke with is contacting Stu now. He should call me in a minute or two. I'll bring him up to date. Please, this is all confidential. We still don't know for certain where we stand. The ramifications are enormous, considerations such as whether we should vacate the hotel."

Kelly nodded. "Thanks for confiding in me—us."

Fritz placed his hand on her shoulder and Kelly tensed. He noticed her reaction and immediately removed it, a smile crossing his face again. "I'm certain Stu will be trying to keep you informed. I'll be telling him what you've told me. And thanks for volunteering your help, but . . ." He hesitated a moment, shaking his head.

Kelly sensed he wanted to tell her to stay out of the way, to get lost. There was still a tenseness in the air.

"Remember, sealed lips—and don't get any . . . don't do anything on your own. It could complicate things for us. Understand?"

Kelly nodded her head again. Does he have any idea how obnoxious he is—how demeaning? she thought. He'd turned and was heading back down the hallway.

Chapter 24

Kelly saw Mike standing next to the desk, talking to the young man she'd met earlier, as she came through the doorway from the office area. The Millers were standing a few yards behind him.

"There you are," Mike said. "I met the Millers on my way down and they'd like to join us for breakfast." Suppressing a grin, he winked as he asked, "Okay?"

"Sure," Kelly replied, forcing a smile. "But I just learned the minister wants to meet with us before the service now, a change of plans. We'll have to make it a quick breakfast. We're due to see him at nine-thirty."

The Millers were overhearing Kelly's comments and smiled at her as she came around the desk.

"I'm sorry you won't have time to fully enjoy breakfast," Martha said. "We've been told they really out-do themselves on Sundays, but we know how important that meeting is. We'd still love to join you, though, if we aren't intruding."

"Oh, heavens no, you aren't," Kelly replied, smiling. "I'm just sorry we won't have more time."

"No problem," Martha said. "Roy will probably more than make up for what you won't have time to sample."

He laughed, patting his stomach. "Now don't you start spreading stories about me, Martha. I just like to show the kitchen staff all their hard work is appreciated."

As they made their way toward the dining room, Mike leaned over and whispered in Kelly's ear. "Was Mr. Woodbridge there? Did you have a chance to speak to him?"

She shook her head. "No. He called to say he wouldn't be up to the hotel until close to ten." Still whispering, she explained, "We really don't have an earlier meeting with Terry Noonan, I just made that up. We need to talk in private. Let's try to be out of here within half an hour, okay?"

Mike nodded, glancing at his watch. "That would be about ten after nine. Anything further I should be mulling over during breakfast?"

They'd reached the maitre d' stand and he was greeting the four of them warmly, explaining he had a lovely table next to the front windows for them.

"Guess that'll have to wait," Kelly said as they followed the Millers into the dining room.

•

They'd been able to excuse themselves according to plan, shortly before nine-fifteen. With the number of people waiting in line for breakfast, milling around the lobby and on the stairway, Kelly delayed saying anything to Mike until they were in the corridor which led to their room. She'd suggested going back upstairs so they could talk in private.

"First off, Mr. Woodbridge left a message for us that he'd be unable to join us this morning at church."

Mike's eyebrows raised in surprise. "He what?"

Kelly continued. "I'm certain it's another plea for help."

"Who told you? Have you informed Stuart?"

"Fritz. Stuart wasn't there. He promised to inform Stuart right away. I also told Fritz about our prior concerns, finding no listing for a Doctor Overbeck in Ann Arbor, everything."

Two housekeepers were standing in the hallway next to a service cart as Kelly and Mike neared their room. Kelly raised a finger to her lips.

Mike smiled at the two women and said, "You're early today. You didn't get to these rooms until mid-afternoon yesterday. Do you rotate?"

The ladies smiled and shook their heads as one replied, "You're right, we are early. We usually always start with the suites at the west end of the hotel. For some reason, they reversed it today. We don't know why. Marge and I were just saying we can't remember that ever happening before."

Kelly surmised the reason for the change. That was the next piece of information she was going to share with Mike.

"We're down here at the end room," Mike said to the women. "We'll just be a few minutes, and then we'll be out of your way."

•

As Mike closed the door behind them, Kelly immediately started to tell him all she'd learned from Fritz—the discovery of the bomb, the fact it had been successfully dismantled, the search of other attendees' rooms, actually the entire western end of the hotel to see if any other explosive devices could be found.

"Stuart's involved in the search. Fritz said he'd try to track him down and update him on the message from Mr. Woodbridge. He also said that they'll try to keep us informed. I volunteered our help, saying we could go down to Woodbridge's house. I even asked for a gun."

"And?" Mike asked, already quite sure what Kelly would say.

"He suggests we don't get involved. That's a nice way of phrasing it. A better description would be a warning or a demand that we don't. In fairness to him, however, he did take time to listen to what I had to say, and confide in us about finding the bomb. He probably thinks he went out of his way to be polite."

Mike nodded, collecting his thoughts. "We aren't due at church for another hour, right? I don't think we'd cause any harm if we paid a social call on Mr. Woodbridge beforehand."

Kelly smiled. "You're getting pretty good at reading my mind, aren't you?"

Mike laughed. "It didn't take a genius in this case. We should probably try to reach him on the phone first, though."

"Makes sense," Kelly said, reaching into her purse. "I have his number right here."

Removing a small slip of paper on which the number had been written, Kelly walked over to the bedside phone. She hung up after dialing the number and tried again.

"Not even a busy signal," she explained to Mike. "The line's dead."

Chapter 25

Fifteen minutes later, Kelly and Mike were heading up the sidewalk to Mr. Woodbridge's front porch. There was no sign of anyone. Mike rang the doorbell. They could hear the chimes inside. After waiting for perhaps a minute, Mike pushed the button again. Still no response. Mike opened the screen door, pleased to find it unlocked, and tried the main door.

"Locked," he said to Kelly. He then knocked on the door loudly and they waited a few more moments.

"There's a possibility he may have gone up to the hotel," Kelly suggested. "We may have just missed him. Chan could have accompanied him. Gone along in a carriage to assist him."

"I hope you're right," Mike replied. "While we're here, we may as well stroll around the yard and check the rear entrance."

Kelly nodded and followed Mike down the steps and around the side of the house. There were two large garbage cans sitting next to the back door. Mike attempted to pull the lid off one, finally prying it off with his thumbs. Holding the lid in his hand, he peered into the container. His eyes widened and handing the lid to Kelly, he reached inside the container. He pulled a beige-colored towel out, holding it up by the corner.

Kelly gasped, seeing it was heavily stained by what appeared to be blood.

"There appears to be a bloodstained sheet in there, too," Mike said. "I wouldn't think his injuries from the accident resulted in this much bleeding."

Kelly nodded, having come to the same conclusion, contemplating their next step.

Mike walked over and tried the door. He was surprised to find it unlocked. Motioning for Kelly to step back, he pushed the door open and shouted, "Is anyone here?" There was only silence.

"I'd like you to go over there by the lilac bushes, Kelly. I'm going inside. You be ready to take off to seek help. Whatever you see or hear, don't come in. Just take off and find a phone."

Kelly moved back toward the cluster of bushes, nodding her head in understanding. She watched as Mike disappeared inside, hoping her growing anxiety was unwarranted.

•

Mike moved cautiously up the short stairway which led from the back hall into a small kitchen. Light from two large windows over the sink illuminated the room. There was a swinging door to his left. Pushing it open, Mike saw the dining room. There was a large table and chairs for at least a dozen people. Light from windows on the south wall eliminated the need to switch on the pewter chandelier which hung over the table. He felt for a light switch as he entered a dark hallway leading toward the front of the house.

As the light came on, Mike saw a chair propped against the door knob of a door on his left, about fifteen feet ahead of him. Approaching closer, he noticed the door was padded. This must be the 'black' room, he concluded. The soundproofed room he'd heard described. Removing the chair, he twisted the knob and pulled the door open. The room was in total darkness, with only the light from the hallway giving him an indication of the vast size of the room. It took him several seconds to locate the dimmer light switch. Two desk lamps and a floor lamp came on as he turned the dial.

He was standing in a combination bedroom and study. Bookcases lined the wall to his right, fronted by a large, ornate desk. To his left was a bed with a man lying on it, all but his face covered by a blanket, either asleep or dead. It was Woodbridge. In addition to the brief meeting with him yesterday morning, he'd seen dozens of photos of him on the walls in the lower level of the Grand.

Mike quickly approached the bed, grimacing as he observed a massive bruise on Woodbridge's swollen cheek. He placed his hand under Woodbridge's chin, feeling for a pulse. He was relieved to find one, though rather feeble. His skin felt cold and his face was ashen. Pulling the blanket down, he saw Woodbridge's hands were tied in front of him. Removing the blanket, Mike observed his ankles were also bound. He attempted to raise one of Woodbridge's eyelids. There was a faint groan and a slight movement as the man's head twitched.

He must be drugged, Mike thought. As he attempted to untie the rope binding Woodbridge's hands, Mike noticed one hand was swollen to nearly twice the size of the other. He compared the hands as he worked with the knot. He grimaced again, shaking his head, trying to be as gentle as possible. Every finger on Woodbridge's right hand appeared to have been broken. In the accident? No, Mike thought, he'd been tortured. He was surprised he hadn't seen any sign of blood.

Mike removed the rope and pulled Woodbridge's robe open, still seeing no trace of blood. As he began to untie the rope around his ankles, Mike noticed the phone on the bedside table. The cord had been cut. It was clear the man needed immediate medical attention, Mike thought as he turned and raced out of the room.

•

Kelly kept checking her watch, straining her ears. Mike had been inside for over five minutes. She jumped as he came bounding out the door, motioning to her. He quickly told her what he'd found, including the severed phone cord.

"There's no sign of Chan. He might be in one of the other rooms. I didn't explore any further than Woodbridge's bedroom. The blood doesn't appear to be his. He's in bad shape, though. I think he's been drugged. He probably needs to be taken to the mainland, flown there. Maybe a helicopter could land in the park next to the tennis courts. You'll need to find a phone, Kelly. Try to alert Stuart, call Doc Solomon, too."

Kelly nodded. "No sign of whoever's responsible?"

Mike shook his head. Kelly turned and quickly moved around the corner of the house, breaking into a run.

•

Mike removed the rope from around Woodbridge's ankles and attempted to stretch his legs into a more comfortable position. There was a bathroom, complete with a shower, adjoining the room. Mike went there and dampened a washcloth. He came back and gently wiped Woodbridge's face. The man stirred, turning his head slightly when Mike touched his bruised cheek.

I'd better look for Chan, Mike thought. He might be in more desperate need of attention than Woodbridge. Remembering the blood on the towel and sheet, Mike wondered whether he was still alive. He went into the hallway and headed towards the front of the house.

Chapter 26

Kelly had found a woman at home two doors away. She'd excitedly explained to the woman who she was and the fact she was a police officer.

"Charles Woodbridge has been badly injured. I need to use your phone."

The woman immediately led her to a phone in a small study and asked if there was anything else she could do.

"Should I go stay with him while you're calling?" she asked.

Kelly shook her head as she dialed Stuart's number and said, "No, there's another officer with him. Thank you."

The woman backed out of the study as Kelly listened to the phone ringing. She was just ready to hang up and dial again when someone answered hello.

"Hello. This is Kelly Travis and this is an emergency. Is Stuart Kreicheff there?"

"No, he's not. As a matter of fact, I'm the only one here."

"Are you an agent?"

"Am I a what?"

"Who is this?" Kelly asked, trying to remain calm as a feeling of panic began to surface. Her options were limited; where else could she turn?

"My name's Ralph. Ralph Blackburn. I'm just here servicing the copier. The phone rang so long I thought I'd better answer it."

"Is Mr. Richards anywhere close by?"

"That's the manager? No, I haven't seen him. Just a Mr. Stanton, I think he said his name was. I think he's using the restroom. Said he'd be back in a minute or two, but that was at least ten minutes ago."

"I'm glad you answered the phone. But listen carefully, this is truly a life and death matter. Someone needs immediate medical attention. Go see if there's anyone, maybe a young man or woman at the desk just outside the door leading into the offices. If no one's there, look for the bell captain. I need to talk with someone right away. I'll hold on."

As she waited, Kelly wondered if she should be having the woman whose phone she was using locate another phone and notify Doc Solomon. Should she hang up and do it herself? And then call back? Dialing 911 would only take a minute or two.

"Hello, Kelly. What's this all about?" She recognized Fritz's voice.

"Mike's at Mr. Woodbridge's house. Woodbridge needs immediate medical attention. He's been beaten and tortured, tied up and possibly drugged. We found a towel and a sheet soaked in blood in his garbage can. It doesn't appear to be his and we still haven't found Chan. Woodbridge's phone lines have been severed. Mike thinks he'll need to be taken to the mainland and suggests you could arrange for a helicopter with a medical team to land in the park."

"Guess I was wrong to tell you to stay out of it," Fritz answered. "You think he's really in serious condition? You're not over-reacting?"

"I haven't been inside to see him myself. But yes, it's serious. Mike thinks they may have broken all the fingers on his one hand."

"Okay," Fritz said. "We'll have someone down there with you in a matter of minutes. I'll start making calls now. Any sign of the culprits?"

"No. Mike hasn't taken time to check out the entire house, though. He may be doing it now, seeing if he can find Chan."

"I'll have someone there soon and the two of you need to be careful. We don't—"

Kelly hung up the receiver. I just hope he'll be true to his word and move quickly, she thought as she picked up the receiver again and dialed 911.

Chapter 27

Kelly called out for a second time as she cautiously started down the hallway.

"Mike! It's me! Help's on the way."

She heard his voice from upstairs. "I'll be down in a minute or two. I still haven't seen any sign of Chan."

Kelly walked past the open padded door on her left and looked into the room. Woodbridge was lying on the bed with his eyes closed. Kelly immediately noticed the bruise on his swollen cheek. Mike had draped a blanket over him. As Mike had previously done, Kelly felt for a pulse. Weak, but he was still alive.

She pulled the blanket back and cringed as she noticed his right hand, swollen with its fingers pointing crookedly in all directions. She recalled being told how Mr. Woodbridge had appeared to wince last night as he shut the door in Jim's and Stu's faces. No wonder. She placed her hand on his forehead as she asked in a quiet voice, "Can you hear me? It's Kelly. You're going to be fine." Was it her imagination or had there been a trace of a smile? She heard footsteps coming down the hallway and turned as Mike entered the room.

"People have been using the beds upstairs. No sign of Chan, though. Look," Mike said, pointing behind her with a surprised look.

Kelly turned to see Woodbridge's eyelids fluttering, his eyes opening, squinting. She grabbed his left hand and gently squeezed it.

"You're safe now. You're going to be fine." Once again she thought she observed the trace of a smile. His lips were moving, slowly opening and closing, similar to the movement of the mouth of a fish. "Don't try to talk, just relax. Help's on—"

Woodbridge was straining to say something. Kelly leaned down towards him as Mike placed his hand on her shoulder. "I . . . I . . . ." He was having difficulty as he struggled to speak.

Mike went into the bathroom and came back with a handful of facial tissues. Kelly took them and reached into Woodbridge's mouth, attempting to clean out the phlegm with the tissue.

"I . . . knew . . ." he began again. There appeared to be a spark in his half-closed eyes. ". . . you'd . . . come."

Kelly felt her eyes tearing up. "I'm only sorry we didn't come sooner." She gently squeezed his hand again as she glanced over at Mike, who was now standing on the opposite side of the bed. Tears had also welled up in his eyes. Woodbridge was trying to say something else. Kelly leaned down again.

"Did . . . they . . . the bomb?"

Kelly glanced up at Mike. "One bomb, an explosive device of some kind, was discovered at the hotel," she explained to Woodbridge. "They've defused it. There wasn't a timer. The plan must have been to trigger it with some remote signal of some kind. There's been no damage to the hotel."

Once again, Kelly thought she saw signs of a faint smile on Woodbridge's face.

"Do you know where Chan is?" Mike asked. "Do you know if they took him along with them when they left?"

Woodbridge's eyes darted in Mike's direction. There was a look of pain, of fear, Kelly thought. He was mumbling, trying to answer Mike.

"I think he used the word bed," Kelly said. Mike nodded.

There had been three bedrooms upstairs—two with queen-size beds and one with two twin-size beds. All had been recently slept in. Mike had checked under them and found no sign of Chan or any trace of blood.

Woodbridge was trying to say something again.

"Under . . . under . . ."

No, I checked under the beds, Mike thought. And then it dawned on him. He dropped to his knees and bent down to look under the bed Woodbridge was on, pulling up the skirt. Kelly had dropped to her knees on the opposite side of the bed.

Chan was there. At least, a middle-aged Asian man was, trussed up as Woodbridge had been. However, in this instance, Chan's hands were bound behind his back and there was a strip of adhesive tape covering his mouth. Kelly gasped as she pointed to Chan's bare feet. Mike nodded. Slash marks and dried blood covered the soles of his feet. Mike was feeling for a pulse. Kelly could see his head nod.

"It's a strong one," Mike explained. "He's probably in better shape than Woodbridge, in that respect anyway." Mike was attempting to wedge his hands under Chan's shoulders. Slowly and gently, he began to slide Chan's body out from beneath the bed. Kelly jumped up and came around to Mike's side of the bed to see if she could assist him.

"I wouldn't be surprised if they gave Chan a higher dosage of whatever drug they used to sedate them," Mike said. "The age difference, for one thing. They may have been worried about a possible overdose in Woodbridge's case."

Chan's body was now stretched out on the floor next to the bed. Mike gently rolled him onto his shoulder as Kelly untied his wrists. Mike removed the strip of adhesive tape as Kelly worked on the cord binding his ankles. She grimaced as she observed the soles of his feet.

"Why don't you get a washcloth, Kelly," Mike suggested as he massaged Chan's wrists. Kelly jumped up and headed to the bathroom as Mike said, "I think at least four people were involved. There are four beds upstairs and they've all been slept in. There might have been more people, sleeping in shifts. The torturing might have gone on non-stop. I'm thinking they began with Mr. Woodbridge, trying to get him to take steps to cancel the meetings. When that didn't work, they probably started on Chan, in hopes that would motivate Woodbridge. I would guess—"

"Mike, he's trying to say something!" Kelly exclaimed as she came out of the bathroom. Mr. Woodbridge was holding up his left hand with three fingers raised. Mike immediately noticed his hand with the fingers extended.

"There were three men involved?" Mike asked him. Woodbridge was trying to nod his head. As he did he also lowered two of the extended fingers, trying to signal with one. Kelly thought she knew what he was trying to communicate.

"Three men and one woman?" she asked.

He was trying to nod his head again.

"How long ago did they leave?" Mike asked. "Any idea?" Glancing at his watch, he said, "It's about ten-thirty now, Sunday morning."

Woodbridge's eyes indicated he'd understood the question. He tried to say something, but the words were unintelligible. Kelly noticed him move the hand he'd used to communicate with earlier. She pointed it out to Mike. In addition to the one extended index finger, the one next to it was bent at the knuckle. The other two fingers were clenched in a loose fist.

Mike was smiling and nodding his head. "An hour-and-a-half ago?" he asked, watching Woodbridge's hand. The bent finger was moved back into his fist with the other two, and Mike asked, "An hour ago?" The bent finger was raised again. Mike laughed. "We're getting this down to a science. Between an hour and an hour-and-a-half ago? That's it, isn't it?"

The two saw relief in Woodbridge's eyes and his head appeared to nod again, though the nod was barely perceptible.

Kelly was smiling. Under the circumstances, it was amazing what they'd learned over the course of the past few minutes. From finding Chan, to learning four people were involved—one a woman—and for good or for bad, Kelly and Mike must have arrived about a half-hour after they'd cleared out.

Kelly heard the sound of a siren and saw that Mike had also heard it. "I left the front door ajar," he said. "Why don't you go out and meet them, though, and direct them back here?"

Kelly reached down and squeezed Woodbridge's good hand once again before she headed out the bedroom door.

Chapter 28

Stuart, Jim and another man were racing up the walk as Kelly arrived at the front door. She stepped out onto the porch and held the door open for them.

"We found Chan. He's also injured, still unconscious. He and Woodbridge are down the hall there, in the room to the right, with Mike.

Considering the fact Mr. Woodbridge can barely speak, we've learned a great deal in the past few minutes. Mike will fill you in."

Stuart nodded. "A medical team is being flown in by helicopter. Either from Petoskey or Traverse City, I'm not sure which. They should be landing near the tennis courts in about twenty minutes or so. You've heard the siren, of course. It's the island's EMS unit. Fritz notified them."

Kelly nodded, wondering if Fritz had also taken credit for the plan to land a helicopter in the park. She felt a twinge of guilt. Who's getting the credit shouldn't even be a concern. The important thing was to get Mr. Woodbridge and Chan medical attention.

"You're going to wait for them here at the door?" Stuart asked.

Kelly nodded again.

"Kelly, thank you for your persistence. I'm sorry our attention became focused elsewhere."

"Did you find any other bombs?" Kelly asked.

"No. And there's been a pretty thorough search. Ian McKenzie and his people have done a tremendous job. Steve Richards also called in about a dozen off-duty people to help. With most of us involved as well, everyone seems fairly confident we'd have discovered another bomb if there had been one to be found. At least in the west wing of the hotel."

"That has to be a relief," Kelly replied. "How many agents do you have here?"

"Ten now, four more arrived last night. Just the one woman who you've met, Mary. She's currently up at the Governor's Summer Home at the breakfast, keeping an eye on things."

The agent Kelly knew as Jim and the other agent had already headed down the hall.

"I better catch up," Stuart said. "I'll be anxious to hear what Mike has to say."

•

The EMS vehicle, its lights flashing, pulled up in front a minute or two later. Kelly had gone out to the street to meet them and to advise them that there were now two injured men.

Three people quickly exited the vehicle. Two, a woman and man in their late twenties or early thirties, were dressed in white uniforms. They immediately went to the rear of the vehicle and began to remove a stretcher. The third person was also a man, maybe in his late thirties, dressed in a golf shirt and Dockers. He had a black leather satchel in one hand. He extended his other hand toward Kelly, introducing himself.

"Hi, I'm Richard Solomon."

Kelly was surprised to see 'Doc' Solomon was such a young man. "Kelly Travis. I'm one of the people who found Mr. Woodbridge. And Chan, now, too. They've both been injured."

"You're the one who called 911? We actually had two calls. So Chan's also been injured. Seriously? Will we need a second stretcher?"

Kelly nodded. "Are you aware a helicopter will be arriving in a few minutes with a medical team?"

"We are. We planned to attend to any immediate needs, maybe get them both on IVs. We'll hopefully have them on board in this vehicle and over at the park before the copter arrives." Looking over his shoulder, Dr. Solomon said to the other two, "Hear that? We'll need two of everything. The two of us," he gestured toward Kelly, "can help you carry things in."

Turning to Kelly again, he asked, "Are they both in Mr. Woodbridge's bedroom?"

Kelly nodded as the woman handed her two bottles of IV solution.

"Why don't you lead?" Dr. Solomon suggested. "We can get the rest of the gear or make a couple of trips."

•

Kelly was impressed with how quickly Richard Solomon and the EMS personnel took charge, evaluating the condition of the two men. They were already administering oxygen to Mr. Woodbridge. Kelly could sense he was their bigger worry. Solomon had been very gentle, whispering in Woodbridge's ear as he checked him over and started an IV. Stuart had wanted to have Woodbridge take a look at the enlarged photos of the two men who'd been in the crowd on the dock. He also had a computer sketch of the bogus FBI agent who'd come to Kelly's room yesterday morning. But Solomon had waved him off, saying that would have to wait. Woodbridge appeared to be resting comfortably now with his eyes closed.

Kelly was seeing the computer drawing for the first time. It had been done in Washington on the basis of her description and faxed to Stuart. She didn't know when he'd received it. It was fairly accurate, actually very good. There were some things she would have changed, though—especially the nose.

Mike was with Stuart, discussing the information he and Kelly had obtained from Mr. Woodbridge, as the medical team made preparations to move the two men out into the EMS van.

"You're certain he used the singular, then?" Stuart asked, referring to Woodbridge's question about whether a 'bomb' had been set off.

Kelly nodded along with Mike.

"I'm wondering if I should be sending some of our agents down to the waterfront," Stuart said, thinking out loud. "See if they recognize anyone from these photos and the sketch, boarding a boat for the mainland. We'd have to cover both docks, probably the Yacht Club dock as well. We're spread so damn thin already, though. I'm not sure we should chance it. I'd love to believe they're hightailing it off the island, though—abandoning their attempt to sabotage the meetings. Probably wishful thinking on my part."

Stuart considered his options for another moment or two before taking a portable phone from the inside pocket of his blazer as he explained to Kelly and Mike, "I think I should get at least three agents down there at the docks now. I'll use one of the other rooms. I can probably get a clearer connection."

"Could Kelly or I be of any help?" Mike volunteered. "We could—"

Stuart waved his hand. "Aren't you supposed to be at the Little Stone Church, making wedding plans?"

"We could skip church, just meet with the minister," Kelly replied. "And maybe we could re-schedule."

Stuart shook his head. "We appreciate all you've done, especially in this instance." He was gesturing toward Mr. Woodbridge and Chan. "But really, this shouldn't be your concern." He shook his head. "That's really not an apt term. Of course you're concerned. You've been directly and indirectly involved from the beginning. Thank heavens we only have about twenty-four more hours before . . . I need to call now. Thanks, but please go ahead with your previous plans."

Kelly and Mike exchanged looks of disappointment as Stuart left the room. "At least we offered," Kelly said. "We tried."

Mike nodded. "Did you know the bomb was discovered in our room? I mean the suite we were initially in?"

Kelly gasped in surprise. "Really?"

Mike nodded. "Stuart just told me. I would have thought that Fritz would have said something to you."

"He may not have been aware it was the room we'd been in," Kelly said.

Mike just shrugged his shoulders, glancing over to where the EMS personnel were lifting the stretcher holding Chan.

Kelly's mind was visioning the suite they'd been in, picturing the coffee table positioned in front of the easy chairs they'd sat in. The man who'd posed as an FBI agent possibly came up with the idea of where to conceal the bomb when he'd been talking to her. She remembered hearing the explosive device had been discovered under a coffee table during the search for an earring.

•

Kelly and Mike followed the attendants carrying Woodbridge out of the house and down the front walk. Richard Solomon, who was walking just ahead of them, looked over his shoulder.

"I think you probably saved his life. An hour or two delay could have been fatal for him. I think Chan's going to be fine. There doesn't appear to be any life-threatening injuries. You can't imagine how painful the healing process for those feet is going to be, though. I feel for him. How much longer are you here for?"

Kelly explained they planned on leaving by noon tomorrow.

"It's a shame you won't have more time to enjoy the island this visit," Solomon said. "I hear you'll be back at the end of the summer for a wedding, though. That's wonderful, congratulations!"

Kelly and Mike smiled, thanking him in unison. Both shared the thought of how fortunate the island was to have Solomon as its doctor. Personable, caring, capable—everything one could want, a very appealing man.

Mike pointed up at the helicopter in the distance, flying over the Straits toward the island.

Doc Solomon glanced up as he was about to climb into the front seat of the EMS vehicle and smiled. "Our timing appears to be perfect."

Jim Waters and the other agent who Kelly and Mike had just met, Marc Marowitz, had positioned themselves, fireman-style, on the back step of the van. The park was just north of Woodbridge's house, not more than an eighth of a mile's drive.

"As soon as Stuart's here, we're on our way," Jim said, looking up towards the front porch of Mr. Woodbridge's home. Kreicheff was charging down the steps. He stopped next to Kelly and Mike.

"Three of our people are already on their way downtown. The search is continuing. There's still no sign of another explosive device. Keep your fingers crossed.

"In regard to this," he continued as he gestured toward the EMS vehicle, "the story we're circulating is that Mr. Woodbridge's injuries from the accident were more serious than originally thought. That's the reason we're giving for having him flown to Petoskey."

Kelly and Mike nodded, indicating they understood and would remain mum on the events of this morning.

Stuart concluded with a grin. "And thanks again for ignoring Fritz's advice."

Chapter 29

"I think we'll just be in time for the tail-end of the service," Mike said, looking at his watch. "Have you decided on what we're going to be telling Terry Noonan? Still want to lock in the August date?"

Kelly nodded. "There's still a number of questions to be answered, though, as to timing. We need Mr. Woodbridge's input on that. An early afternoon wedding with the reception in the gardens below the hotel, or a later wedding with an evening reception in the hotel."

"What's your preference, Kelly? Let's plan it that way, then if we have to make a change, we'll see if we can."

•

Ten minutes later, Kelly and Mike were proceeding up the walk in front of the Little Stone Church. Standing outside the door, they could hear the congregation reciting the Lord's Prayer. They waited until the organ music began before opening the screen door and stepping inside. The church was about two-thirds filled, maybe fifty or sixty people. As they slid into an empty pew and reached for a hymnal, they saw Irene Taylor sitting next to the aisle in about the third row. As the congregation stood, she glanced over her shoulder and spotted Kelly and Mike. Her face lit up and she lifted her arm to view her watch. Kelly and Mike nodded and smiled. The poor woman had probably been worried we weren't going to show up, Kelly thought.

As the minister was giving the benediction, the sound of a siren could be heard, growing louder as he spoke. As he concluded, a car raced past the church, apparently heading in the direction of the Grand.

Kelly and Mike exchanged looks, both wondering if this was related to the other events of the morning. The discovery of further explosives, or the possibility a bomb had been detonated and people had been injured or killed.

As people began to file out of the church, Irene made her way back to where they were standing.

"Good morning," she said. "I was concerned something may have come up. I'm glad you were here before we heard that siren—I really would have been concerned. We don't hear sirens very frequently on the island, at least usually not until July or August. Someone may have had a heart attack or fallen from a horse. With all our visitors, it's probably surprising we don't have more instances."

Kelly and Mike nodded as she talked. They apologized for their late arrival and to have caused her concern.

"We were actually at Mr. Woodbridge's house," Kelly said. "We'd hoped to be able to meet with him before our meeting today with you and Pastor Noonan."

"I knew you wanted to do that," Irene said. "Did it work out? Were you able to get everything squared away? I'm aware he was injured in an accident. How's he doing?"

"Hopefully, he'll be fine," Mike said, wondering how much should be said. "He's now being flown to a hospital in Petoskey."

"Really? I had no idea his injuries had been that serious. I'll have to tell Terry. Here he comes now."

The minister was approaching them, a broad smile on his face. "You must be Kelly Travis and Mike Cummings. I'm Terry Noonan. I've been looking forward to meeting you." He shook hands with both of them as he said, "Congratulations, I hear a wedding is in the offing. Any final decision yet on the date?"

"Yes, we've decided on the August date," Kelly replied.

"They still haven't been able to finalize the reception plans, though," Irene explained to Noonan. "They've had to take Mr. Woodbridge to the hospital in Petoskey."

"Oh, I'm sorry to hear that. He's such a nice, kind man. A true gentleman, a great booster for the island. Do they think he'll be okay?" he asked, addressing Kelly and Mike.

"Given time," Kelly answered, like Mike, hesitating to say too much.

The four of them sat down in one of the pews for the next several minutes, discussing some of the options open to Kelly and Mike in regards to the actual wedding service.

"We don't have to decide everything today," Terry explained. "I just want you to be thinking about these details."

They established an immediate rapport with Noonan. Both were thinking how wonderful it was that he would be available to perform the service. After everything that had occurred this weekend, it was nice to finally have something so easily falling in place. Kelly thought how pleased her parents would be as she made a list of things she'd give them the opportunity to have input on. It was nearly twelve-fifteen before they wrapped up their discussions.

"You have my address and phone number," Irene said to Kelly as the four of them were exiting the church. "Now, don't hesitate to contact me if you have any additional questions, if something comes to mind we haven't covered. No matter how trivial you think it may be, just pick up the phone."

"I will," Kelly replied with a smile. "You've helped so much already with all your suggestions. Thank you! Mike and I really appreciate it. We're looking forward to working with you."

Terry grinned. "You'll be even more amazed the day of the wedding. She's helped many a couple, making it possible for them to truly enjoy the moment without having to fret over the details."

Irene blushed as she removed her bicycle from the rack.

"The only thing she can't control is the weather. I think Kelly's aware because of spending summers here, Mike, but you might not realize just how lucky you've been with the weather this weekend. It's probably ten degrees warmer than normal for this time of the year. This is more like a July day on Mackinac. I hope you're going to be able to enjoy it. What are your plans for this afternoon?"

"We brought our tennis racquets," Kelly replied. "We still haven't had a chance to get out on the courts. I think that'll be on today's agenda. We really haven't discussed what we'd be doing—meeting with you was the most important thing on our calendar. Thanks for meeting with us."

Terry nodded. "Our pleasure. I'm going to be playing some tennis myself later today, around four. We have a group, usually eight to ten of us, who get together every Sunday for mixed doubles. I know everyone would love to have the two of you join us. We have a fun time, maybe more laughs than great shots, but everyone's fairly competitive. Stephanie Solomon's probably the best; she played varsity tennis in college. She's the wife of the island's only doctor, a lovely lady. Ed Merryweather and his daughter, Susan, will probably be there. They publish the island's newspaper, the Town Crier. They're no doubt involved now in seeing if there's a story behind our island's police car heading up towards the Grand with its siren on. That doesn't happen too often."

"Irene said the same thing," Mike said. "As far as the tennis, we'd enjoy joining you, if you're sure we wouldn't be intruding." Kelly was nodding in agreement.

"You won't be. Everyone loves to see new faces, the 'added competition'."

"I think we'll need to get down to the courts a little early then," Kelly said, turning towards Mike, a grin on her face. "Practice up a bit so we don't embarrass ourselves."

Terry laughed. "You don't have to worry on that score, I'm sure."

Chapter 30

Hands joined, Kelly and Mike headed up the sidewalk toward the Grand. Both were elated over how smoothly the meeting with Terry and Irene had gone.

"I'm sure it's about the tenth time I've said it, but wouldn't it be great if we had a day like today for the wedding?" Mike said.

She smiled back at him. "It's worth repeating, it's so lovely today. And aren't we lucky to have Irene and Terry?"

"That's for sure. They're wonderful."

"Must have been right about here where the accident occurred," Kelly said as they began to ascend the hill which led up to the Grand. "I sure hope Mr. Woodbridge and Chan are going to be okay."

"Me, too. But I think you were right in assuming it was no accident. It'll be interesting to hear what Mr. Woodbridge and Chan have to say about their ordeal."

"Maybe we should stop by the offices on the way to our room. Stuart might be able to give us an update and also tell us what that police siren we heard was all about," Kelly said. "Nothing appears out of the ordinary up ahead of us. I don't see the police car or any flashing lights."

"Sure doesn't seem like anything's amiss, from the expressions on people's faces," Mike replied. "Everyone seems to be wearing a smile."

The nice weather had brought swarms of visitors to the island. There was a steady procession of people passing them on the sidewalk, returning from the Grand, and an equal number walking in their direction. The street was jammed with carriages, bikes, and people on horseback. The sound of happy conversations was coming from all directions.

As they reached the crest of the hill, they saw a couple dozen people waiting in line to enter the east entrance of the hotel. Non-guests had to pay an admission fee to tour the Grand, but the charge could be credited against the hotel's elaborate buffet lunch. Kelly remembered stories of how controversial it had been when the policy was initiated several years ago. Now, no one seemed to question it.

An attractive young woman in a red blazer with the hotel's crest asked if they were hotel guests. Kelly and Mike nodded and she gestured for them to come around those in line, explaining they should be prepared to show their guest passes just inside the entrance.

Mike asked her about the police car and was told it had stopped near this entrance and a couple of men had joined the officers inside. They'd driven off toward Harrisonville. She was quite certain its arrival had nothing to do with any incident at the hotel.

•

The young man they'd seen that morning was manning the desk in the lobby. He spotted Kelly and Mike as they headed toward him. His face lit up as he waved to them. They were still a couple of yards away when he began speaking.

"I'm glad I saw you. I'd been told to keep an eye out for you. Mr. Kreicheff's anxious to see you. I'm afraid he just left, though. I'll check and see if anyone here knows what it was about."

He went into the office area and was back in a matter of seconds, followed by Marc Marowitz, the agent they'd met earlier at Mr. Woodbridge's house.

"I'm glad we were able to locate you," he said as he shook hands with both of them. He appeared tense, a troubled look on his face. "Could you please follow me? We'd like to take you up on your offer to help us, if it's still open."

Closing the door behind him, he led them down the hallway. Kelly and Mike saw Fritz on the phone through the open door of one office as they passed. He also saw them and nodded. Marc directed them into the next office and motioned to the two chairs in front of the desk.

"I need to update you. There's been a major new development." He continued speaking as he sat down on the corner of the desk facing them. "Six women are missing—wives of those here for the meetings. We believe their carriage was highjacked—that they were kidnapped on their way back to the hotel from the Governor's Summer Home. They'd had breakfast there this morning."

Kelly and Mike glanced at one another, startled by this news. They'd been aware of the morning plans for the wives, but this came as a surprise. They'd expected news of a discovery of another bomb, or a sighting of one of the men in the photo. But this was shocking.

"There were two carriages involved. Mary Zuckerman was riding in the second one, the last to head back here to the hotel. The drivers planned on coming back together, but Mary's was delayed by one of the wives having to go back inside to retrieve her purse. Mary told the other driver to go on ahead and they'd catch up. We don't know if that had a bearing on what happened or not. Maybe we'd have over a dozen women missing if it hadn't. When Mary returned with her group and found the first carriage hadn't arrived yet, there was still no major concern. Everyone assumed that the driver had taken a detour to show the women some additional sights. But it's been nearly two hours now, and there's still no sign of them. We haven't been contacted, or received any threats or ransom demands. We haven't interrupted the meetings—the husbands still aren't aware of what's happened. Or, at least they weren't up until a few minutes ago. Stuart and Steve Richards should be briefing them about now. All of our people have been involved in trying to find out what's happened, trying to locate them."

"Did you check out the house in the Annex area?" Kelly asked. "Where I—"

"Yes—one of the first things we thought of, too. Two of our agents say it doesn't appear anyone's been back there since they disappeared yesterday. They're in the island's only police car."

"We heard it as it passed the Little Stone Church with its siren on, headed up towards the hotel," Mike explained. "We wondered what the trouble was."

"Well, now you know," Marc replied. "Turning on the siren was a mistake. We're still attempting to keep a tight lid of secrecy on everything. The meetings, Anderson's murder, the discovery of the bomb, what happened to Mr. Woodbridge and his houseman, and now this. As a matter of fact, Sam Pacquette, the island's police chief, still hadn't been brought into the loop until this latest fiasco. I'm glad we did—he appears to know every nook and cranny on this island.

"Stuart immediately called back the three people he'd sent to watch the docks to help locate the missing women. That's why we're so in need of your help. To keep an eye on the two main docks, at least. We still haven't figured out how to cover the Yacht Club dock. You'd recognize the faces of the three we know are involved. Chances are, you won't spot them, though. They're probably with the missing women, wherever they are. But as you know, we still aren't certain how many people we're talking about."

"We'd be glad to fill in. It'll take a few minutes for us to change out of these church clothes. Probably bikes are the quickest way to get downtown. Maybe you can line a couple up while we're changing," Kelly said.

"Will do. One other thing—Stuart says to tell you we can supply you both with handguns, if you desire. It's your call. You know the faces of those three men. The danger is, they know yours, too. We don't think you'll be placing yourselves in danger, with the crowds and all, but you decide. Regardless, we don't want either of you to attempt to arrest or detain any of those men—just notify us immediately if you see anyone. I'm going to be giving each of you a cellular phone. I wish you could be working as a team, but you'll need to split up to cover both docks."

They all looked up as Fritz came into the room. "The carriage has been found," he said to Marc. "At the north end of the island, near a place they call British Landing. The driver, too. They're still questioning him."

"Did they have a boat there?" Kelly asked.

Turning toward Kelly, Fritz answered. "I think that's what they want us to believe. There's a bunch of footprints on the beach leading into the water. We notified the Coast Guard earlier. Hopefully, we'll have some more answers soon. Maybe the driver knows something."

Turning to Marc again, Fritz asked, "Are they going to help?"

Marc nodded and explained that Kelly and Mike were going to change their clothes while he arranged for some bikes.

"A carriage might be faster. Have they had lunch?"

Marc looked over to Kelly and Mike for the answer. While shaking their heads, Mike said, "That's no concern, though. We can both find a snack near where we'll be positioned."

"See if you can get a couple of box lunches for them, Marc," Fritz said. "They need to get down there right away. You've given them phones? What about the handguns?"

Kelly and Mike glanced at each other, annoyed that Fritz was addressing them through Marc. Marc handed them two miniature phones as he asked, "Did you decide on the guns?"

"Yes," Mike replied. "One for each of us."

Fritz was shaking his head. "Remember—you're just supposed to notify us. Stuart says the guns are your call. I don't . . . they're just to be used to protect yourselves, remember that. Shit happens, but we've got enough problems on our hands without having any further complications."

If she wasn't aware of the possible importance of what they'd been asked to do, Kelly would be reconsidering. She knew Mike must be furious over the shabby treatment Fritz was dishing out. Marc appeared to be sensitive to it also, embarrassed by Fritz's attitude.

"I'd suggest you get started," Fritz said as Marc handed Kelly and Mike the two revolvers, explaining they were already loaded. "We'll have a carriage and box lunches ready out front in five minutes." Turning to Marc again, Fritz said, "I'm going up and tell Stu they've agreed to help. Watch the phones, and dial me up if you learn anything." With no further comment to Kelly or Mike, he hurried out of the office.

"You can see everyone's pretty tense right now," Marc said, attempting to somehow explain away Fritz's rudeness. "I want to assure you of how appreciative everyone is. We're lucky you're available and willing. Do you have any additional questions?"

Kelly and Mike both shook their heads as they rose from their chairs. "Do we use the same contact number?" Mike asked.

"Yes, good question—but I forgot to mention it's already programmed into your phones for speed dialing. Number eleven—one, one. They're special phones, it's the only number you can dial. I'm sorry we don't have ones where you could keep in touch with each other. You can do that through us, though."

Chapter 31

Kelly was enjoying the sunshine. Now dressed in Bermuda shorts and a sleeveless top, she blended in nicely with the swarms of tourists on the dock. The great weather and the fact that it was a Sunday had resulted in a near-record number of island visitors for this time of year. Kelly's sunglasses didn't look at all out of place in the bright sun, and they gave her the opportunity to closely observe people without them being conscious of it.

Mike was stationed at the other main dock, a hundred yards or so to the west of her. Kelly glanced at her watch—just past two-thirty. There had been no sign of any of the three men. She felt fairly certain Mike hadn't spotted any of them either, or she would have been alerted. The time was quickly passing. People-watching was fun. The families with young children were particularly fascinating to Kelly, observing the contrasts in how differently parents reacted to their children. There were already good-sized lines for the two three-o'clock departures; one to Mackinaw City, the other to St. Ignace. Most of those in line would soon be in their cars heading down-state, with memories of their vacation to savor during the long ride home.

•

At Mike's suggestion, Kelly had taken time to phone Terry to advise him it was doubtful they'd be able to join him and his group for tennis. He hadn't been home, and Kelly had left word with his wife. After promising to pass the message on to her husband and saying how disappointed he'd be, she told Kelly how impressed Terry had been with them, and how enthused he was to be a part of their wedding. Kelly was sorry she'd had to hurry the call and hadn't been able to chat longer.

•

Kelly frowned as she saw a little boy drop his ice cream cone. She'd been watching him, waiting in line for the boat with his parents, relishing every lick. Now he was standing with tears streaming down his face, sadly looking down at the scoop of ice cream melting on the dock. The parents had a quick discussion before the father grabbed his son's hand and leaned down, whispering in his ear. The small boy's face lit up and they marched back toward the main street.

Kelly smiled, seeing where they were headed. A giant red and white umbrella hovered over a push-cart with a sign on its side reading, "Famous Mackinac Island Fudge Ice Cream Cones." A young man, in summer whites and wearing a red baseball cap, was standing next to it, serving cones to the dozen or so people waiting in line.

Kelly smiled again to herself as she fell in behind the small boy and his father. An ice cream cone would taste good about now. It wouldn't distract from her being able to scrutinize the crowd. In fact, it would probably help her blend in with the scene even better.

I hope he doesn't run out before I reach the head of the line, Kelly thought as she positioned herself in line behind the father. She noticed people were also getting flavors other than the Fudge. Strawberry, Lemon, Butter Pecan, and plain old Vanilla. But she decided to go for broke.

"Mackinac Island Fudge, a double dip," she said to the young man as she reached the front of the line.

"A smart choice! Satisfaction guaranteed!" he replied, a big grin on his face.

She handed him a five-dollar bill as he gave her the cone. She couldn't stop herself from having a lick as she waited for her change.

"Is that you, Kelly? It's been ages!"

Kelly turned to see Virginia Campbell, a neighbor of her parents' from Ann Arbor. She use to baby-sit for her daughter. Kelly felt like a child who'd just been caught with a hand in the cookie jar as she stood facing her, holding the cone.

"Hello, Mrs. Campbell. Care for a bite?"

"It looks good, but no thanks. You look great!" Mrs. Campbell's face was beaming. "Kate's here with Chuck and me and a friend of hers. We're staying just down the street, at the Chippewa Hotel. I know she'd love to see you! Are you here just for the day? And Kelly, please, it's Ginny."

Kelly quickly explained to Ginny what had brought her to the island, about Mike, and their wedding plans.

"Is he nearby? I'd love to meet him. We all would. Any chance the two of you could drop by the Pink Pony later today and join us for a drink? You used to work here on the island, didn't you, Kelly? I'm sure you remember the Pink Pony Cocktail Lounge."

Kelly nodded, smiling again. The Chippewa Hotel's cocktail lounge was one of the long-time favorite watering holes on the island. She'd spent many an evening there, partying with other college kids. During the yacht race weekends, the Pink Pony was the place to be, and to be seen.

Mrs. Campbell had asked several questions, and Kelly debated for a moment over how she should answer her.

"We'd love to do that. I don't think I've seen Kate for at least six years. Is she in school?"

"Yes, she is. She's just completed her junior year at Michigan State. She's trying to follow in your footsteps, Kelly. You were her absolute favorite baby-sitter. Mine, too, for that matter. She always dreamed of growing up to be just like you. And I couldn't imagine a better role model. I cut out all the articles about that major case you were so deeply involved with this past fall and mailed them to Kate."

She smiled as she added, "I'd send them with a care package of snacks. Some of the same kinds of candy that evil man taunted you and those people he was blackmailing with, Hershey's Hugs and Kisses, for example. We were so proud of you."

Kelly blushed, flattered by Ginny Campbell's comments. "I'm anxious to see Kate. And I also want all of you to meet Mike. We'll do our best to get over to the Chippewa, possibly around five-thirty."

Marc had informed them earlier of the FBI's plans to bring in more people, possibly the State Police. He'd said in all likelihood, others would be relieving them by three-thirty or four this afternoon, definitely by five o'clock.

"If something comes up so that doesn't work out, we'll call and leave a message."

"That sounds perfect! You'll want to see our room, too. They've poured an immense amount of money into remodeling and redecorating. We have a lovely view of the harbor. We're on the top floor. Kate and her girlfriend have been horseback riding this afternoon. They should be back way before then. Chuck's waiting for me now, I better keep moving. Hope we'll see you later."

The ice cream cone had melted faster than Kelly could eat it as the two had talked. As she watched Mrs. Campbell head in the direction of the Chippewa Hotel, a few doors up the street, Kelly attempted to salvage what remained. She leaned over, licking the cone, holding it away from her body so it wouldn't drip on her clothes. From that awkward position, she noticed something familiar about the man passing a few feet in front of her, heading in the same direction Mrs. Campbell had taken. He was dressed in yachting clothes—white cotton pants, dock-siders and a boat captain's cap. Though he now had a mustache, Kelly recognized the face of the man who'd come to their room yesterday, posing as an FBI agent. The one who'd identified himself to her as Brett Anderson. I'm sure of it, she said to herself as she tossed the ice cream cone into the trash container next to her and followed the man. Though nearly positive, she hesitated to call in without being absolutely sure. It might be possible to get another look without him recognizing me, she thought.

The man glanced at his watch and he turned to his right and entered the Chippewa Hotel. Kelly was only a few steps behind him as he turned. She was able to get a good look at his profile. Yes, it was definitely him, she concluded, envisioning the face absent the mustache. She hesitated a moment and then headed through the door after him. He was just ahead, turning down a corridor to his left. A sign on the wall to the right of the hallway he'd entered read 'Restrooms - Telephones.'

The man looked over his shoulder before settling in a chair in front of one of the phones. Kelly saw it was one of the two pay phones. There were also two house phones to his left. I need to call, she thought as she glanced at her watch. It was exactly three o'clock. I better go back outside to do it, she thought.

"Kelly, I didn't think we'd see you again so soon."

She spun around, recognizing Mrs. Campbell's voice, and saw her standing next to her husband.

"Hello, Mr. Campbell," she said, holding out her hand. "Did your wife explain she's invited me and my fiancé to join you for a cocktail in a couple of hours?"

He nodded. "She sure did. We thought we'd just step outside for a few minutes for a little shopping. Maybe buy some fudge to take back to our neighbors in Ann Arbor who are picking up our newspapers and mail. Is Mike with you?" he asked, gesturing towards the men's room.

"No," Kelly answered, smiling. "I just stopped by to use the restroom myself. I was just leaving. We'll be back around five."

They continued talking as they went out the door. Kelly could see they were headed west, toward the center of town, and explained she was headed the other way, up to the fort, to meet Mike.

"We'll see you in a couple of hours then," Mrs. Campbell said as they turned in opposite directions.

●

Kelly had continued walking a few yards, to the end of the block, before removing the small phone from her carry-all bag and dialing the one-one number. As she waited for someone to answer, she moved onto the grassy area along the waterfront, distancing herself from the people passing on the sidewalk.

"Hello." It was Fritz.

"Hi, Fritz, it's me, Kelly."

"Yes, I recognized your voice."

"I've seen one of them, the man who visited me in my room yesterday morning."

"Boarding a boat?"

"No. He passed by the dock, just walking down the street. I followed him to the Chippewa Hotel. He's inside now, using a pay phone."

Kelly was taken aback with Fritz's reaction. He was laughing.

"He's talking to Stu on the other phone," he explained. "He called about half an hour ago, telling us to round Stu up and he'd be calling back at three sharp, which he has. Stu's trying to keep him on the line. We've already traced the call. We know which pay phone it is. Two of our people should be there any minute. They'll try to follow him. He hasn't spotted you, has he? Where are you?"

"No, at least I don't think so. I'm outside now, in the park to the east of the hotel."

"Not near the docks?"

"No, I told you, I followed him. I wasn't sure at first if it was actually him." Why do I feel like I have to explain myself? Kelly thought. He's probably going to chastise me now for leaving my post.

"I don't want him to see you," Fritz said. "Understand? It could screw everything up. Be careful working your way back to the dock area, maybe use the other side of the street across from the Chippewa. Our men should be at the hotel in a couple of minutes. Damn! Stu just hung up. You should be relieved within the hour. And thanks."

Kelly jerked her head back as Fritz slammed his handset down, hanging up on her. She'd wanted to question him as to whether there had been any new developments. Had they learned anything from the carriage driver? From the Coast Guard? Her hand was shaking as she slipped the small phone into her bag. Don't let him get to you, she reminded herself. This is their case, not yours. As she crossed over to the far side of the street, heading back toward the dock, she wondered what the man had said to Stuart. Had he made ransom demands? She glanced over at the Chippewa Hotel's entrance, directly across from her. She hoped Fritz was right, that the two agents had already arrived, and that they could successfully tail the man without exposing themselves.

Kelly's eyes widened as she observed the man she'd followed coming out the front door of the Chippewa. He adjusted the yacht cap on his head and quickly moved off in the direction she'd just come from. Kelly moved back next to one of the storefront windows, maneuvering between the many tourists passing by in both directions. She watched as the man continued down the street, keeping an eye out for the two men whom she assumed would be following him.

A number of other men had also come out of the hotel, but all had either headed in the opposite direction or crossed over to her side of the street. She couldn't identify anyone, on either side of the street, who seemed to be tailing the man. He crossed the street, starting up the sidewalk which bordered the park beneath the fort, after first having waited for a carriage to pass. They're either good or they didn't arrive in time, Kelly thought, still seeing no sign the man was being followed. He passed beyond her line of vision as she contemplated what she should do.

Fritz hadn't given her the opportunity to describe how the man was dressed, or to explain he now had a mustache. The two agents who are supposed to be tracking him should be informed of those facts, she thought as she reached into her bag for the phone again.

She headed back towards Marquette Park while still trying to keep an eye on the Chippewa Hotel's entrance, for signs of the two agents. Passing the grocery store on the corner, she cautiously peered around the side of the building.

The man was now halfway up the block, apparently heading to the walkway which ramped its way up the hillside to the fort. Kelly stepped back and nearly collided with a woman coming out of the grocery store, holding two bags of purchases.

"Oh, I'm sorry," Kelly said to her, reaching out to steady one of the bags.

The woman smiled. "No, it's my fault. I should have made two trips. My bike's just around the corner."

"Let me help you," Kelly said, taking one of the bags.

Kelly followed her around the corner of the building. The bicycle leaning against the wall had a large wire basket on each side of its rear tire. The woman placed the bag she was carrying in one and grabbed the handlebars of the bike, righting it and moving it away from the wall.

"That one can go right in there," the woman said, nodding her head toward the other wire basket. "Thank you very much. Now if I can keep my balance, I should be just fine. As you've probably surmised, I've had a little experience with this routine."

As they'd placed the two bags of groceries in the bike's baskets, Kelly had tried to keep an eye on the man. He had removed a bike from the rack at the base of the hill, just left of the walkway leading up to the fort, and was now pedaling down the street towards them.

"I'm glad I could help you," Kelly told the woman, before quickly moving around the edge of the building, back in front of the grocery store, so the man wouldn't see her. Out of the corner of her eye, she caught sight of him bringing the bike to a halt at the stop sign. She turned her head to the right to conceal her face. He removed his right foot from the pedal, extending his leg to steady himself as he waited for a gap in the traffic. Dozens of tourists were passing in front of him on their bikes, about to wrap up their day on the island. He also had to wait for a couple of carriages to pass before he could cross the street. Standing up to gain momentum, he headed up the road to the east, rather than turning towards town.

As he turned his back to her, Kelly stepped out to the edge of the sidewalk, glancing in all directions to see if she could tell if someone was following him. Bringing the phone out of her bag, she called Fritz.

Kelly was relieved to hear a woman's voice answer. "Is that you, Mary? This is Kelly. Kelly Travis."

"Hi, Kelly. Have you sighted any of the others?"

"No. Just the same one who I guess was talking on the phone to Stuart. He's on a bike now, on the main road—Huron—heading east, across from Marquette Park. The reason I called is I don't see any of your people following him."

"Are you positive? One is dark-haired, very tall, six-foot-three or -four, wearing a light blue shirt and tan slacks. The other one's also a man, average build, sandy-haired, in Bermuda shorts, dark blue or black, a printed golf shirt, possibly shades of dark green."

"I haven't seen them, I'm sure of that."

"Hold on a minute, Kelly. Let me check with Fritz."

Kelly could still see the man, now nearly a hundred yards in the distance. She glanced around, wondering if she could quickly locate—beg, borrow or steal—a bicycle. As a carriage passed in front of her, she thought of commandeering one. She wondered if it would be fast enough to catch up to him.

"Hello, Kelly. You're right. Fritz is furious. He just spoke with them. They'd hopped in a carriage to go through town and there was an accident. A woman stepped off the curb in front of their horse. They lost some valuable minutes. The driver didn't want them to leave until they'd explained to someone he hadn't been at fault. Fritz chewed them out for not having one of them go on ahead. They were supposed to call in after they'd arrived at the Chippewa. They're probably racing there now by foot. We still haven't heard from them."

Kelly could hear a man's loud voice in the background as Mary talked. Possibly Fritz's, but she couldn't be sure.

"Hang on," Mary said. Kelly glanced back towards the Chippewa as she waited, in hopes of seeing the two men Mary had described.

"Kelly, Fritz wants you to go over to the Chippewa. See if you can find our men—Mitch Allen and Mark Krondelmeyer. Mark's the tall one. Point them in the direction the man is headed, with a description. If you don't find them, see what you can do on your own. We'll brief Mitch and Mark. We'll tell them to look for you heading east on the main road. If he should turn off it, either wait for them to catch up or find someone you can rely on to watch for them so they can tell Mitch and Mark the direction you headed. Fritz wants you to check in every few minutes, and to be careful. No heroics. Under no circumstances are you to approach him on your own."

Kelly wanted to ask what the man had said to Stuart. Had he made a ransom demand? Instead, she said, "Understood. He's nearly out of sight and I should hang up."

"Good luck, Kelly. And thank you."

Chapter 32

Kelly dashed across the street dodging fellow pedestrians. Inside the hotel, she glanced down the hallway where the phones were located and then scanned the lobby. She saw no one who even remotely matched the descriptions she'd been given. Turning and heading out the main door, she hoped she wouldn't run into the Campbells again.

An empty carriage taxi was just passing the hotel. She raised her hand to flag the driver down. He noticed her, but shook his head, indicating he wasn't available. She ran alongside of him, yelling that it was an emergency.

"I need to catch up to someone. He's about a quarter of a mile ahead of us on a bike."

The driver finally reined the horse. "Damn it, lady. I'm on call and I'm already late. I'm headed to the Island House—I can't take you any farther."

Kelly nodded as she jumped aboard the carriage. "Please hurry as fast as you can. It's very important!"

The driver gave her an incredulous look. "I'm not about to lose my license. We have strict speed limits, especially anywhere near town. I'll do my best, but don't expect miracles. You'll have to take full responsibility in case we're stopped."

Flicking his switch, striking the horse on its hindquarters, he urged the horse on as he said, "I don't know why I'm even doing this. You better have a good reason, not just a lover's quarrel." Seeing Kelly reach into her bag, he added, "You better have some money in there in case you need to bail me out of jail."

Kelly flipped open her billfold and showed him her police badge. The driver's eyes bugged in surprise. "Sorry, I hadn't realized," he said, urging the horse into an even faster trot.

Luckily, most of the traffic—other carriages and bicyclists—was headed toward them. They were making good time, but a carriage a short distance in front hid Kelly's view of the road and she couldn't see if the man on the bike was still in sight. Her driver maneuvered their carriage around the one in front of them.

The other driver screamed and shook his fist at them. "You damn idiot! Slow down! Are you crazy?"

"I'm afraid there's going to be some heavy-duty explaining to do,"

Kelly's driver said, chuckling with a broad grin on his face. "I hope you're going to be available in case I need you."

Kelly smiled and nodded.

The Island House Hotel entrance drive was coming up on their left. As the driver turned to her again, Kelly felt certain he'd be saying this was as far as he could go. But instead, he said, "We've made such good time, I can probably take you on ahead a little farther if you'd like."

Kelly smiled and placed her hand on the middle-aged man's shoulder. His bark was worse than his bite.

"You're nice to offer. I still don't see the man I was trying to catch up with, though. I have no idea where he was headed. He may have already turned off somewhere and we passed him. But it would be great if you could take me a few blocks more, maybe another mile."

He gave her a look which read, 'Don't press your luck, lady,' and glanced again at his watch before replying, "The State Park begins sooner than that. There's really nothing much beyond the Mission Pointe Resort. I'll drop you off there. It's the best I can do."

As they sped along, Kelly assured him how much she appreciated his help. She reached into her bag for the phone, thinking she should be calling to explain where she was. She waited, not wanting Fritz to know she may have lost the man. A few seconds later, she gasped in delight.

"I think we've caught up to him. That man on the bike, wearing a yachting cap." They were less than a hundred yards behind him. As they closed the gap, Kelly was more certain than ever it was the same man.

"Slow down, I don't want him to see me."

As the driver tugged on the reins, slowing the horse down to first a slow trot and then a walk, he glanced back at Kelly with a confused look.

"Let me get this straight, it was almost a life or death matter for you to catch up to him. Now, you're telling me you don't want him to see you. Are you sure this is police stuff? You're not spying on your boyfriend or husband, are you?"

Kelly grinned. "No, nothing like that. All I can say is, I'm on a police matter."

"Well, what do you want me to do? He's almost at the Mission Pointe Resort. You should be able to rent a bike there. That is, if he doesn't stop at the Resort. I'm sorry, but I really need to get turned around. Is this a drug bust of some kind?"

"Wish that's all that it was," Kelly replied, shaking her head. She opened her billfold and removed two twenties and a ten, handing them to the man.

"Thank you," she said. I'd nearly given up hope of catching up to him."

The driver studied the bills for a second or two, his face lighting up. "Thank you, Miss! And good luck with whatever you're up to."

As the driver turned the carriage in a wide semi-circle to head back in the opposite direction, Kelly provided him with a description of the two agents who were hopefully following her.

"I don't know if they'll be in a carriage or on bikes. But if you do happen to see them, please tell them where you dropped me off. Tell them I'm in close pursuit. They'll understand."

Kelly jumped down from the carriage as the driver nodded. Another carriage approached as Kelly walked along the left side of the road, toward the Mission Pointe Resort. She smiled to the driver and the passengers. The carriage was filled with a dozen or so people and their luggage. Kelly assumed they were probably departing guests from the Resort, on their way to catch a boat to the mainland. Her assumption was verified as the carriage drew abreast of her and she overheard one woman say, "I sure hope we don't miss this boat. It's probably going to be midnight before we're home as it is."

Kelly glanced at her watch. Twenty to four. Hopefully, their boat departure was for four-thirty or four-fifteen, rather than four o'clock. The two horses pulling the carriage were just ambling along. A thought came to her and she looked up at the couple sitting in the last row of seats.

"Did you happen to notice a man riding a bike, wearing a yachting cap, as you were leaving?"

The couple glanced at each other before the man replied, "Not that we recall."

A family of four, a couple with two children, probably six and nine years of age, were sitting in the row in front of the couple. The older of the two children tugged her mother's sleeve and Kelly overheard her say, "We did, Mom, remember? He nearly hit Will. It was Will's fault. He stepped out in front of him just before we boarded the carriage."

"I did not," the young boy shouted at his sister. "You're just trying to get me in trouble."

Kelly had turned and was jogging slowly alongside the carriage. "Did you see if he went inside?" she asked the young girl. As if to check before talking to a stranger, the girl glanced at both her parents before answering. She nodded as she explained, "He was parking his bike near the front door. He was putting down the kick-stand. I think he was going inside."

The girl's mother smiled at Kelly. "I think I recall him now, too. Maybe about thirty years old, in white pants and a blue shirt, maybe a mustache?"

"That's him," Kelly answered, continuing to jog at a slow pace next to the carriage.

"I saw him go inside, yes. He was holding the door open for an elderly woman. I think he followed her in."

Kelly was elated. She halted in the road and shouted, "Thank you!" The passengers turned their heads to look back at her as she waved to them. Kelly was laughing, relieved and excited. She hadn't lost him.

As she turned and headed back towards the Mission Pointe Resort, she reached into her bag for the phone. Mary answered again. She quickly explained her luck in catching up to the man.

"Have you heard from Mark and Mitch?" Kelly asked.

"Yes, I just spoke with them. They're on bikes, approaching St. Anne's Church. I'll call them back. They should catch up to you in a few minutes."

"Have you spoken to Mike?"

"I have, and he knows about you. His replacement should be there any minute. He's chomping at the bit to catch up with you. I'll also call him as soon as we hang up, and tell him where you are."

"Any sign of the missing wives?"

"No, but the other line's ringing, Kelly. I'll talk to you later. Good luck."

Slipping the phone back into her bag, she turned into the drive leading to the Resort.

Chapter 33

Mike had just been updated by Mary. He hoped the woman being sent to spell him would arrive soon. Standing next to the bike he'd just rented, he was primed to head to the Mission Pointe Resort the second she did.

"Mike!"

At the sound of his name, Mike turned and saw Terry Noonan on a bike on the opposite side of the street. A carrying case containing a tennis racquet was draped over his shoulder. Terry waited for two other cyclists to pass and then maneuvered the bike over to Mike's side of the street.

"My wife gave me your message. Sorry you and Kelly won't be able to join us." Terry pulled alongside the curb and Mike shook his outstretched hand.

"We are, too. I hope you'll give us a rain check."

"Definitely. But the next time I'll probably be seeing you will be the wedding. Unless you visit again before then, to finalize the arrangements. Which might not be a bad idea."

"I'd love to, but that's Kelly's department. I'm sure we'll be on the phone with you and Irene in the next few weeks, though."

"I forgot to mention how delighted I am you picked the August date," Terry said. "I didn't want to say anything earlier to influence your decision, but that will save me an extra trip up here. We head back to Canton and my regular church commitments on Labor Day weekend."

"Oh, you should have told us. I'm glad August is better for you. So your church is in Canton? That's not far from Ann Arbor. Kelly and I will definitely drive over some Sunday for your service. Which church is it?"

Terry smiled. "Canton, Ohio, sorry. Not Canton, Michigan. I'd still love to have you visit, but there's a few hundred miles difference. It's the First Presbyterian Church."

Mike laughed. He'd been too hasty in his assumption. If Terry's church had been in Canton, Michigan, he felt sure it would have come up in the discussion that morning. He should have realized that.

"We met a couple coming over on the boat Friday from your Canton. They're also staying at the Grand. Roy and Martha Miller. He's the Chevy dealer there. I think the dealership operates under the Miller name."

Terry shook his head. "Their names aren't familiar. And I know he's not the Chevrolet dealer. His name is Bob Evans, same as the restaurant chain. He's a member of my congregation."

"That's strange, I thought for sure they told us Canton."

"Maybe there's a third Canton somewhere."

"No, it's definitely somewhere in Ohio. We talked about the Michigan-Ohio State game."

"That is a biggie. I've been to the game in Columbus several times over the years," Terry replied. "Never Ann Arbor, though."

"We'll have to see that you do," Mike suggested, still wondering how he'd gotten confused in regard to the Millers.

"I better get going, I'm going to be a little late as it is," Terry said, checking the time. "Tell Kelly you both have a rain check."

"I will," Mike replied, waving as Terry headed across the street and turned up the side street toward the courts.

"You must be Mike Cummings. I'm here to relieve you. I didn't want to interrupt."

Mike had been thinking about the Millers and hadn't noticed the woman who was now extending her hand towards him. "I'm Sally Sumberlund."

Mike returned her smile as he shook hands with her. An attractive woman, nearly the same height as Mike, he guessed she was in her late twenties.

"I'm sorry, I'd been on the lookout for you, too. I'm glad you're here."

"I know you're anxious to catch up with . . . is it your fiancée?"

Mike nodded. "You're right, I am. I'm sure you've been briefed, but do you have any questions before I leave you?"

Chapter 34

Kelly noticed the lone bike standing next to the walk which led to the front porch and main entrance. Several others were parked in a rack off to its left. Probably his, Kelly thought, wondering if she should wander down to the end of the building to wait for Mark and Mitch. She could keep an eye on the bike from there, yet still be in a position to conceal herself behind the corner of the building in case the man appeared.

She glanced through the glass doors. The lobby appeared empty. A woman was by herself at what Kelly presumed was the registration desk. An idea came to her. She looked towards the road to see if the two men were in sight yet as she reached into her shoulder bag and quickly removed a twenty-dollar bill. She crumpled it in her fist, then straightened it out as she walked up the steps and reached for the handle of the door. There were five or six people in the lobby, but no sign of the man she'd followed.

Kelly walked up to the registration desk and smiled at the young woman who had lifted her head, saying, "Good afternoon, can I help you?"

"Yes," Kelly answered, showing her the twenty-dollar bill. "I just found this wadded up on the ground next to a bicycle parked outside near your front door. I was down by the road, but I think I saw the man who dropped it. He was wearing a yachting cap, maybe a mustache, probably—"

"I know who you're referring to. He's over there, using the house phone. He'll be delighted, that's very nice . . ."

Kelly had glanced over her shoulder in the direction the young woman had indicated.

"He's gone now. He was there a few seconds ago."

The young woman frowned, thinking how best to handle the situation. "He's not a guest. I don't know his name. He asked for a room number and I told him I wasn't permitted to give out room numbers. I suggested he call the party on the house phone, and get the room number from her."

Kelly nodded, thinking he must have done so and now be on his way to the room.

The young woman laughed. "I think I'm reading your mind. Let me check with our operator."

Kelly watched as she picked up the phone, giving a brief explanation of the problem and asking for the name of the person and the room number the man had been connected to. Kelly tried not to be obvious as she strained to see what the woman was writing on her note pad. The 337 was easy to see. The name appeared to be Sandra with a long last name, beginning with what looked like the letter R.

"Thanks, Virginia. No, I can dial her direct. I'm going to wait a minute or two, to give him time to get to the room."

As she talked, the young woman had glanced at Kelly and sensed her interest in what she'd written on the note pad. She flipped the pad over as she said, "You heard. I'll call in just a second or two."

Kelly smiled, answering, "I'm sure it belongs to him. Why don't I just leave the money with you? I have to meet friends."

"I'll call now," she replied, picking up the phone. "What if it's not his?"

Kelly grinned. "Then let it be your reward for having tried to find the owner. Besides, the rightful owner might contact you about it."

Kelly backed away from the counter and turned, quickly heading out the door.

Two men who matched the descriptions Kelly had been given were parking their bikes in the rack. Kelly quickly headed toward them.

"Mitch? Mark? I'm Kelly Travis."

The taller of the two, who matched the description she'd been given for the one named Mark, immediately began to apologize. "We're sorry, Kelly. It's been a comedy of errors. Mary probably told you. Where do we stand?"

Beaming, Kelly explained she thought the man was upstairs now in one of the rooms.

"Room 337. It's registered in a woman's name, and I think she's there with him."

Mitch's expression was one of surprise as he asked, "How on earth were you able to find that out?"

Before she could answer, he grinned and said, "I know, good training." Laughing, he added, "They told us you used to be with Bureau."

Kelly quickly told them of the ruse she'd used to gather the information. The two men appeared duly impressed.

Looking over Kelly's shoulder, Mark casually placed a finger to his lips. Kelly turned and saw a woman heading towards them, probably just having come out of the hotel. She's probably coming after her bike, Kelly thought as the three of them sauntered into the drive and walked toward the main road. Sure enough, the woman was working the combination on her bike lock.

"Have you spoken to Stuart?" Mark asked. "Does he know what you've just told us?"

Kelly shook her head.

"Why don't we have her call while we're inside checking this out?" Mitch suggested to Mark. Turning to Kelly, he said, "By the way, Mary told us that Mike, your fiancé, is on a bike headed here as fast as he can. That was over five minutes ago, probably ten minutes ago. You could call Stuart while you're waiting for him. Make sense?"

Kelly nodded. It was clear that's what the two of them thought best. With some reluctance over being left out of the center of action, Kelly asked, "Should we be waiting for Mike? To have the two of us perhaps backing you up? Maybe nothing more than watching the exits?"

Mark smiled as he looked over at Mitch. "Timing might be important, Kelly, and I don't think we should waste any time. I think we'll be able to handle things on our own. Hopefully, we can get you and Mike back to enjoying the weekend. Can't tell you how much we appreciate what both of you've done already. Learning the room number," he said with a laugh, shaking his head.

The two men turned and started toward the steps as Kelly reached for her phone.

•

Mary answered her call, but quickly put Stuart on the line. After her update, he was lavish in his praise. He asked her to call back immediately with the hoped-for news that they'd apprehended the man who'd used the name of Brett Anderson, and whoever else was with him.

"There's been a major development, Kelly. In a nutshell, the man you're after contacted me. He and his cronies want to turn the clock back. Try to get everyone to agree this weekend and all that's happened never took place. It's complex. Hopefully, sometime I'll have an opportunity to fill you and Mike in on all the details. I'm going to send the island's police car or one of the EMS vehicles out there as soon as we hang up. Let Mark and Mitch know. Good work, Kelly."

While Kelly had been on the phone, she'd noticed the woman who'd interrupted her conversation with Mitch and Mark earlier was still standing next to the bike rack. She appeared to be mumbling to herself and had given one of the bikes a kick. As Kelly slipped the phone back into her bag, the woman looked over at her and smiled.

"Do you have any idea how these damn combination locks are supposed to work?" she called out. The woman appeared to be about Kelly's age. She was slightly taller and slimmer than Kelly, with her dark hair tied in a ponytail. Kelly smiled back as she walked toward her.

"I'll see if I can be of help, but don't get your hopes up. Things like that aren't my forte."

A few moments later, Kelly was kneeling next to a bike as the woman standing behind her told her the combination. Kelly was twisting the cylinders when she felt an object being pressed into her back. The woman behind her had leaned down and was now whispering in her ear.

"If you ever want to walk again, you'll do exactly as I say. This bullet would shatter your spine."

The woman's voice was almost a hiss, full of venom and hatred. Kelly froze in surprise and fear.

"You're going to get up and walk in front of me. We're going to go down there to the corner of the building, then out behind the resort. Just act as normal as possible. I promise you, I won't hesitate to use this." With this last remark, she jabbed what Kelly now knew must be the barrel of a gun into the small of her back.

"Careful now. But we need to move quickly. Don't even think about trying to outwit me or you'll be spending the rest of your life in bed on your back, thinking about your mistake."

Kelly slowly stood up. Glancing over her shoulder, she saw the woman's tense expression and a look of hatred in her piercing, dark eyes. Her tone of voice gave Kelly the impression the least little thing might trigger her to carry through on her threat.

The woman jammed the gun into Kelly's back again and whispered, "Okay, Miss Travis, let's get moving."

Chapter 35

Mike rose up from the bike seat and used his leverage to pump the pedals even faster. I should be there in another five minutes, he concluded as he accelerated past the houses and trees lining both sides of the road. He was perspiring heavily and gasping for air. His anxieties had been building over the past few minutes. He hoped Kelly was all right, that she hadn't been injured. These were vicious people they were confronting. The injuries to Chan and Woodbridge were still very vivid in his mind.

Several times during the course of the afternoon he'd thought about going over to the Arnold Dock and joining Kelly, fearful she might be in danger if she encountered any of those men on her own. He couldn't be second-guessing himself now; he just prayed Kelly was safe.

He hoped the two agents he'd been told about had caught up and were with her now. The entrance drive to the Mission Pointe Resort was just ahead. He could see the sign on his left.

Chapter 36

The line had been busy the first two times the young woman had dialed room 337. When on her third try she'd gotten through, it had initially been awkward. She'd asked the woman who answered if a man had just come up to her room. With her question being met with dead silence, she quickly realized her mistake and began to explain why she'd called. The woman interrupted her and put a man on the line. He was very friendly and cordial. He asked if the woman who'd found the twenty-dollar bill was still there. She explained that no, the lady had gone out front to meet someone.

He thanked her and said he'd be down in a few minutes to pick up the twenty-dollar bill. Then he laughed and told her better yet, why didn't she just hold ten dollars for him, keep five for herself, and see if she could get the other five to the woman who'd actually found it.

•

The two men who'd asked to speak to the manager were still at the desk. One was now on the phone, talking to him. It had taken the woman several minutes to track her manager down.

"He'd like to talk to you," the man who'd been speaking to the manager said as he handed her the phone.

"Yes, Mr. Rosen, this is Shelly again." She listened a moment and started to say something to him. He must have cut her off. "Yes, I'll give them one right away," she said.

Hanging up the phone, she immediately went into the office behind her and returned, holding up a key. She started to explain about the woman who had found a twenty-dollar bill, but the man who'd been on the phone held up his hand as he reached for the key with his other.

"What's the quickest way there?"

"The stairway over there. Third floor. It'll be to your left."

The men were already on their way toward the stair door as they thanked her.

Chapter 37

Kelly and the woman behind her rounded the corner at the rear of the building. They both saw the man Kelly had been following coming down the fire escape, only a few rungs from the bottom. He'd changed clothes and the mustache was gone. He was now wearing a blue baseball cap and carrying what appeared to be a heavy duffel bag.

He grinned as he saw them. "Perfect timing, I'd say," he said as he approached them. "I really didn't expect to be seeing you again, Kelly. You should have taken my suggestion and distanced yourself from this mess."

He placed the duffel bag down in front of him as he continued talking, smiling as he said, "We're almost twins," referring to the fact his yellow shirt and light tan pants matched the colors of Kelly's blouse and shorts.

"I'll take the gun now," he said, reaching out his hand toward the woman. Rather than handing it to him, she pulled her hand back, keeping the gun pointed at Kelly.

Kelly sensed the tenseness of the moment as she stared at the woman, whose dark eyes were flashing with emotion, her intense glare focused on Kelly.

The man patiently waited for the woman to hand him the gun. "You don't need to worry," he said to the woman. "I won't be any more hesitant than you to use it." Turning towards Kelly, he continued. "You need to be fully aware of that, too. If you give us the slightest provocation, bang! Got it?"

Kelly nodded, the thought going through her mind that she'd be better off with the gun in the man's hand, hoping he'd win the current battle of wills.

The woman's lip quivered for a second and she seemed ready to say something, before she angrily handed him the gun.

"Let me have her bag, too."

The woman had taken Kelly's carry-all bag earlier and it was slung over her shoulder. She slipped it off and handed it to him.

"Now grab the duffel bag, we're going to be taking that path."

There was a stretch of approximately twenty yards of grass behind the resort, fronting the wooded hillside. Kelly could see the opening for the path he'd referred to, heading into the woods, probably weaving up the hill.

"She should be the one carrying it," the woman snarled.

"Good idea," the man answered, smiling again. "My thought is to have us take turns, though. You first, until we're out of sight of the hotel. I think we'll make better time that way initially."

Shaking her head, the woman grabbed the straps of the duffel bag and hoisted it to her shoulder.

Chapter 38

The room was vacant. Whoever had been there had cleared out in a hurry. A toothbrush was still in the bathroom. Two half-filled glasses of pop were on the table next to the morning's Detroit Free Press. Mitch was checking out the waste baskets as Mark went through the dresser drawers.

Mark went to the window and glanced out, noticing the fire escape stairs a few feet to the right.

"Mitch, come here. What do you see up there?"

"It looks like a couple people, maybe three, hiking up the hill. Nearly to the top. I think it's a woman in front, wearing a yellow top." Mitch turned and stared at Mark.

"Could be Kelly, couldn't it?" Mark asked, knowing Mitch was having the same thought. "No way of being certain from this distance. The other two could be the ones we're after, though."

The two men were already racing out of the room as Mitch said, "Let's hope we find Kelly's still out front."

•

Mike was describing Kelly's appearance to the young lady at the registration desk. She was smiling and nodding her head when she gasped in surprise, as the two men she'd directed to room 337 came charging out the stairway door and quickly raced out the front door.

Mike turned his head and saw them. Quickly concluding who they were and realizing something must be amiss, he ran after them.

They were rounding the corner at the end of the building with Mike in close pursuit, when one of the men, sensing Mike's presence, glanced over his shoulder. Still running, he tugged the sleeve of the man next to him and gestured that someone was behind them. He looked over his shoulder too, and slowed his pace, enabling Mike to catch up.

"Are you Mike Cummings?"

Mike nodded as one of the men said, "We think they have your fiancée with them. We spotted three people at the crest of the hill. Just a couple minutes ago from an upstairs window. We'll lead the way." The man pointed at his chest, saying "Mark," and pointed to the other man, saying, "Mitch." No time for last names.

As the three men raced along the narrow pathway, Mike noticed the two ahead of him taking guns from their pockets. Mike reached for his as a branch slapped into his face. The man named Mitch looked back toward Mike with a look of apology. He acknowledged it with a wave, indicating he was fine.

Mike's worst fears had come to pass. At least Kelly was still alive and wasn't injured, at least he prayed that was still true. The long bike ride, combined with the dash up the hill, was taking its toll. Mike stumbled, caught himself, and then, panting, continued after the two men.

At the crest of the hill, the path forked off into two directions. Mike saw Mark direct Mitch to take the trail to the right. Looking back at Mike, he said, "You stick with me."

Chapter 39

"Keep taking the one to the left until I tell you differently," the man said to Kelly as she approached another spot where the path forked. This time there were three options.

"A little faster, too," he said as Kelly led the way along the trail he'd directed her to take.

"It's about her turn, isn't it?" Kelly heard the woman say.

"Here, I'll take it," she heard him reply.

"Why in the hell are you babying her?" the woman said. "The bitch asked for this. I can't believe you're actually catering to her, treating her–"

"Cool it, Sandy," he snapped.

Kelly remembered the name the young girl at the desk had jotted down on her note pad, Sandra something. Had she used her real name? Maybe she needed to pay with a credit card. More likely, it's an alias, a name chosen for this caper.

"The one to the right this time, Kelly. Hell, you're probably more familiar with these trails than I am. I should be asking you."

Kelly was surprised by his comment. How much did he know about her? He must be aware she was acquainted with the island. Maybe she'd mentioned she'd worked here when he'd conversed with her posing as an FBI agent.

They still hadn't seen another person, or heard anyone. They'd been skirting some of the roads the carriage tour used. But it wasn't surprising that at this time of day, especially on a Sunday afternoon, no one was about. People were on their way to the mainland or cleaning up for dinner.

"We're going to be crossing a road up here in a minute or two," the man said. "Remember what I said about no tricks. You'd regret it for the rest of your life." He laughed. "But it could be a short one. The trail begins again on the opposite side of the road. We should be about halfway there."

•

125

Mark had stopped at another point where the trail branched off in opposite directions. Mike caught up as Mark said, "We'll need to split up. How good are you at whistling? Show me."

It was the first time Mike had smiled since he learned Kelly had been taken hostage. He placed two fingers in his mouth and launched a loud, high-pitched whistle.

Mark returned his smile as he said, "You must have been in scouting. I want you to be careful. The second you spot them I want you to whistle. Maybe every thirty seconds or so. But just wait for me to find you. Don't expose yourself to them."

Mike nodded in understanding. As to following all those instructions, though, the circumstances would dictate that. Rescuing Kelly was his main goal.

Mark headed off to the left and Mike to the right, both breaking into a run once again.

•

The three of them had crossed another of the roads which wound through the island and were now on a trail which meandered through a heavily wooded area. Kelly surmised they were a ways north of Fort Mackinac. She believed the road they'd recently crossed led to the Fort Holmes and Skull Cave area.

"I suggest we stop for a short break," the man said as he slipped the duffel bag off his shoulder and onto the ground. "This bag does get heavy. Why don't you sit on it, Sandy?"

The man bent down and plopped onto his hindquarters in the middle of the trail. Kelly was still standing as the woman sat down on the duffel bag.

"Better rest yourself up, Kelly. The next leg with the duffel is yours."

Kelly kneeled down on her knees, resting on her haunches.

The man had taken Kelly's carry-all bag and was peering into it. He reached in and removed her revolver. Smiling, he hesitated a moment or two before he said, "Here, Sandy—catch."

Kelly couldn't help but cringe. Even with his threats, she'd felt safer with the gun in the man's hands. The woman sensed Kelly's thoughts and a trace of a smile appeared on her face. It was clearly intended to intimidate her.

"Does this phone connect directly to Kreicheff?" the man asked.

Kelly nodded. "You simply dial one-one."

The man nodded and smiled again. He glanced at his watch. "I think it's time to give the old bugger a call. Shake him up a little, give him an update. Let him know you're still alive, for one thing. He should also have some answers for me.

"I don't know how much you've been privy to, Kelly," the man said. "Maybe everything—maybe nothing."

"The latter is closer to the mark," Kelly replied.

The young woman was staring at Kelly, shaking her head. Glancing at the man, she said, "I don't think she realizes the predicament she's gotten herself into. Sitting there on her haunches and carrying on a conversation as if we were having a picnic. She should be terrified."

Hearing her, Kelly wondered if this was a compliment or another threat.

The man answered her question by saying, "Lay off, Sandy. The fun and games are over." Turning to Kelly, he said, "I'm going to tell you just enough so you'll be able to understand my conversation with Kreicheff, or do you call him Stuart?"

Kelly ignored the question and realized her mistake when a look of anger appeared on his face and he shouted, "Which is it? Didn't you hear me?"

"Stuart," Kelly answered in a whisper, hoping her quiet tone might help to simmer him down.

He nodded. "We've made a proposal to Stuart. I should probably say we've made three demands. This weekend has been botched. This isn't our cause, anyway. We were roped into it. Now we're trying to get out of it. We've asked for three things. First, that everyone who's come for the meetings be off the island by seven o'clock tonight. No more meetings. Second, that the heads of state of all four nations pardon us—grant us total immunity—in regard to the events of the past couple of days. Yes, that refers to Anderson's demise, for one. By the way, that wasn't intended. It just happened. There's a side you probably haven't heard. It wasn't cold-blooded murder. We also need to get the state and local authorities to back off. We need all these guarantees in writing. Can we trust them? Probably not. But we think they'd be hard-pressed to pursue and aggressively prosecute us, knowing we can and would put these written assurances in the hands of the news media.

"Third, we're asking for two hundred and fifty thousand dollars in cash. Not blackmail money. It just better enables us to bow out. We didn't deliver. You don't need to know the details, but it will help put everything back the way it was. Before all this shit happened, before we were foolish enough to become involved.

"What does Kreicheff get in return? What do they get? The wives back, safe and unharmed. You, too, now. We disappear and promise to keep this entire incident a secret. They took great pains to keep these meetings under wraps. They're convinced, and they should be, that if knowledge of them becomes public, any progress could go down the tubes.

"So, what do you think, Kelly? Do you think it will fly? How, pray-tell, would you vote if you were one of those making the decision?" He smiled again. "You don't have to answer. But now you're up to speed."

Kelly's mind was racing. Even though meeting those demands might be in her best interests, would it be the right decision? He'd just alluded to the entire affair as an 'incident'. Was the death of an agent, was the torture of Woodbridge and Chan, just an 'incident'?

"I appreciate you telling me what's happening," Kelly said. "As to how I'd vote, I'd have to give it some serious thought before answering."

The man smiled. As he dialed the one-one number, he looked over at Kelly and said, "I'll probably be asking you to say something to Stuart to prove to him you're alive and well. I'm sure no reminder is needed, but please—don't try to be clever. Just tell him that, period."

Chapter 40

Mike jogged out of the woods and onto the graveled road. He stood catching his breath, glancing in both directions. Still no sign of Kelly or any other person. Reaching in his pocket and removing the small, portable phone, he dialed the one-one number.

A woman answered. He recognized Mary Zuckerman's voice.

"Hi, Mary. It's me, Mike."

"Oh, Mike, I'm sorry. Stuart just finished talking to Mark Krondelmeyer. He told us about Kelly. Stuart's back on the phone now, talking to the man Kelly was following. He overheard me and just flashed me a thumbs-up sign. I'm sure that means he knows Kelly is . . . alive. Maybe he's spoken to her. He's nodding yes, Mike."

Though relieved to hear this, Mike still had many questions. Had Kelly been injured? Was she still being held hostage? Was she in danger? Thoughts of Woodbridge and Chan crossed his mind.

"You can't imagine how relieved I am, Mary. Can I hold on the line? Maybe get a more detailed update from Stuart when he's finished?"

"I'm not sure how long he'll be. And we need these lines free. Where are you now, Mike?"

Mike explained he was on one of the island's roads which ran east and west. He told her where he believed he was, relative to the fort.

"Fort Mackinac?" Mary questioned.

"Yes. I didn't realize there was more than one."

"There is, though it's not nearly as large or impressive. Fort Holmes is more to the middle of the island. I should have known you meant Fort Mackinac. Mark can't be too far from you. He's also somewhat lost, complaining about the maze of trails. He said the foot paths branched so often he'd lost count. He told us you'd split up and that Mitch headed in another direction even earlier. My guess, from what Mark said, is that he's on the same road you are, probably a few hundred yards to the west of you. Why don't you head that way. I'll call Mark and have him come your way. Stuart told Mark that he'd try to locate Mitch and you and get all three of you back here to the hotel as quickly as we can.

"Stuart's already sent a carriage to meet you. He's still on the phone. I'll have him call you as soon as he's through, okay?"

"Fine, Mary. If I run into a sign that gives me a better idea of where I am, I'll call you back."

"That makes sense," Mary replied. "And try not to worry, Mike. I'm sure Kelly is going to be just fine."

•

Kelly was just hearing one side of the conversation. But from what she'd heard, it appeared as if Kreicheff and the others were attempting to meet the demands.

The man had given the phone to Kelly at the beginning of his conversation with Stuart, to assure him she hadn't been harmed. He'd then immediately grabbed it back, asking Stuart a series of questions.

They argued briefly over whether the husbands of the six women who were being held hostage should leave the island with the rest of the attendees. The man seemed to accept the fact the six men would be waiting together somewhere for news of their wives, and agreed it might as well be on the island. He made the comment it might mean a few hours delay in being reunited with their wives, indicating the reunion wouldn't be on the island. He'd noticed Kelly's stare as he said that, and had turned his back on her as he continued the conversation.

Kelly had the feeling he wasn't truly leveling with Stuart. From what little she knew, she was aware the question of whether or not the women were still on the island hadn't been answered.

"Oh, that's ridiculous, Stuart, and you know it. I realize it's a Sunday, but I bet you can find that much cash in the tills of the fudge shops alone. That should be the least of your worries." For perhaps the third time in the conversation, the man said, "Time's a-fleeting; I spelled out the time-table."

From what had been said earlier, Kelly believed that only one of the people whose signature was required on the statement of pardon, or agreement not to prosecute, was holding out. The rest—everyone from Sam Pacquette, the island's police chief, on up to the President—had seemingly acquiesced.

Amazing, Kelly had thought as the man had gone through the names with Stuart. From the Governor to the county sheriff, from the Director of the FBI to the Canadian Mounted Police. And many names, probably political leaders in Canada, Britain, and France, which were only vaguely familiar to Kelly.

The one person seemed to be the only stumbling block in all the demands being met. The man finished his conversation with Stuart by saying, "The others better start applying leverage, and I mean now. I know there's a time difference, but they'd better haul his ass out of bed if that's what it takes. I'll call you back in thirty minutes, Stuart. I'm counting on you to have every single one of those signatures and all the money in your possession by then. I also want to hear that all the attendees except for those six husbands are back on the mainland, or soon will be."

The man smiled as he clicked the button to disconnect the call, a smug look on his face.

"I can't believe it's been so easy," Sandy said. "You didn't think it would be, either," she said to the man, who was now grinning. "That they'd be willing to move this quickly."

He held up his hand. "Let's not count our . . . Remember what, who was it said—Casey Stengel or Yogi Berra—it's not over 'til it's over."

Glancing at Kelly, he said, "They could still be laying a trap for us, too. Right?"

He sat for a moment, pondering as he stared at Kelly, who'd merely shrugged her shoulders with a blank facial expression. She realized he was trying to decipher her reaction. She'd also been taken by surprise over how quickly Stuart and the others involved had appeared to capitulate.

Chapter 41

Mike was on the phone, explaining to Stuart that he had just observed Mark come into view, walking towards him on the road. Stuart had called Mike. For the past few minutes he'd been explaining what was happening.

"How are you going to get the letters of assurance and money to them?" Mike asked.

"We're still in the dark on that," Stuart replied. "The man who I've been in communication with says he'll give us instructions in due course. They seem to have that figured out, a plan of some sort in mind. I asked the same question and he told me not to worry about it, just to make sure we got everyone's signatures and the money. He says they're going to trust our word that the meetings have ended, that everyone, all the attendees, have left the island, or soon will."

"Except for the six husbands?" Mike asked, hoping they'd agreed to that exception.

"That's right," Stuart responded. "He finally made that concession."

Mark was now within twenty or thirty yards of Mike. They'd been walking towards one another as Mike spoke to Stuart.

"Just a minute, Stuart, I'll ask Mark if he needs to speak to you."

Mark shook his head. "You can probably brief me, Mike. But has he heard from Mitch? Any idea where he is?"

"Did you hear Mark?" Mike asked.

"Yes. He can't be far from you. You should be seeing a carriage in another minute or two, which will bring all three of you here. We'll see you soon. And Mike, please be assured Kelly's welfare is one of our highest priorities. We aren't contemplating anything to put her in further jeopardy, I promise you that."

"Thanks, Stuart. I needed that assurance."

•

The man and woman had moved off a few yards down the trail, and had been engaged in a hushed conversation for the past few minutes. They'd both made some additional threats before they'd left her, cautioning her not to try anything stupid. They were returning now. The man in particular appeared to have a satisfied smile on his face.

"Rested up? Time to move on. Be careful with that duffel bag. Sandy's reminded me it's your turn to tote it."

Kelly was surprised at the weight of the bag and was curious about what it contained. No wonder Sandy had complained about carrying it, Kelly thought, calculating that it must weigh over twenty-five pounds.

She was in the lead, with the man just behind her, still holding the gun in his hand. Sandy was bringing up the rear, and Kelly was relieved to see there was no longer a gun in her hand.

They were headed west, in the general direction of the Grand Hotel. If they stayed on this course, they'd be approaching the hotel from the back. A large tree limb had fallen across the path and Kelly placed her foot on it and stepped up, preparing to jump onto the trail on the other side of the limb. There was a loud crack as the limb broke.

Kelly found herself tumbling to the ground, sprawled in the middle of the trail. She groaned and grimaced in pain. She'd twisted, or maybe even broken, her ankle.

Rather than springing to her aid, the man had appeared to lunge behind a cluster of trees they'd just passed. He was struggling to his feet with a shaken expression on his face.

"Damn it!" he snarled in anger. "I told you to be careful with that duffel!"

Kelly had maneuvered into a sitting position and was reaching down toward her ankle, her face scrunched in pain.

"I think she may be seriously injured, Webb," Sandy said as she walked towards Kelly and kneeled down.

The man glared at Sandy and she sensed her mistake. She looked at Kelly, who was rocking in pain with her eyes partially closed, to see if Kelly had heard her slip—the mention of the man's name. He had also knelt down next to Kelly, reaching toward her ankle.

"No, no," Kelly said, inching her leg away from him. "Please give me a minute or two first."

The man and woman looked at one another, a questioning look on her face; a look of concern on his.

"That was stupid of me," Kelly said as the pain began to subside.

"We're all in agreement on that," the man replied, with little of the anger he'd first shown. Looking at Sandy, he said, "We'll just have to alter our plans somewhat. We can still pull it off."

Seeing Kelly's stare, he smiled. "Guess the good news is, we don't have to worry about you running off. Do you think you've broken a bone, or is it just a nasty sprain?"

Kelly shook her head and answered, "I'm not sure."

"Let's get you up and see if you can put any weight on it," the man suggested, as he motioned to Sandy to get on Kelly's other side.

The two placed their hands under Kelly's armpits and began to lift her. Kelly struggled to her feet and tried to place some weight on her injured, right ankle. She grimaced in pain and collapsed in their arms.

"I don't think she's that good an actress," Sandy said. "It seems she's really hurt it."

As they lowered Kelly back to a sitting position, Webb turned to Sandy and said, "You'll need to hightail it to Fort Mackinac. It's not too far. See if you can locate some crutches—better yet a wheelchair." Checking the time, he said, "The fort may be closed for the day. But I'm sure you'll be able to find someone who can help you. Boy Scout troops come up to the island all summer, taking turns for a week and camping out." He smiled. "It may just be scouts to the rescue. Who knows, Kelly? Maybe we can find one to put a splint on to hold you until we can get you to a doctor."

Turning back towards Sandy again, he said, "If she can handle it, we'll come along behind you as quickly as we can. I'm hoping that will be possible, she can lean on me. If not, we'll see you right back here. Time's growing short, so you should hurry."

Sandy nodded and asked, "I go back across the road and take that right fork where we veered left?"

"You got it. See you in a few."

Chapter 42

"I'll have you there in five minutes," the driver said as he flicked his buggy whip, urging the horse on. As Stuart had indicated, the carriage driver had located Mark and Mike a few minutes after they'd finished their conversation. It had taken another ten minutes to locate Mitch. He'd actually become lost in the maze of trails.

"I can't fathom Stuart giving in to those demands," Mark said. "Someone has to be applying immense pressure."

"Probably the husbands of those missing women," Mitch suggested. "As to cancelling the meetings, they may think they accomplished everything they can now, already. On the other hand, maybe they became stymied over some issue and reached a loggerhead. What I'm trying to say is, maybe that's no big concession. But letting them get away with the murder of an agent—I'm amazed, too."

The carriage pulled up near the east entrance of the hotel and the three men quickly disembarked, thanking the driver.

"We should head upstairs to the offices right away," Mark said. "But first, I need to stop at the men's room."

Mitch decided to join Mark, as Mike waited outside for them.

"Mike?"

It was the second time today he'd heard his name called out. He turned and saw the Millers coming out of the nearby gift shop. Martha was holding a large bag with the Grand Hotel logo.

"We're just winding up our visit. We're leaving on the seven o'clock boat," she said, smiling and holding up the bag for Mike to see.

"How about the two of you?" Roy asked. "Did you have a good day? Is Kelly powdering her nose?"

Mike shook his head. "I was hoping to see you. I have a question for you. Where are you from? Where's your auto dealership located, Roy?"

Both looked at him with nervous expressions. Was it his imagination, or was there a trace of fear on Martha's face? They were avoiding looking Mike in the eye.

"Seems we've been found out, Martha."

She glanced at her husband and nodded.

"We really are from Canton, Ohio," Martha said. "But Roy's just a postman. We made up all that stuff about him being a successful Chevy dealer." Her face was flushed in embarrassment. Roy sheepishly looked up at Mike.

"We had more success making friends with fellow travelers using that story. I knew we'd get caught someday. How did you find out?"

Mark and Mitch had come out of the men's room and were standing, waiting for Mike. He introduced them to the Millers. Mixed thoughts were going through his mind. Was this as innocent as the Millers would have him believe? The entire island visit had been one of confusion. After talking to Terry, Mike's imagination had gone wild. One scenario had the Millers involved in the conspiracy to sabotage the meetings. Now, he wasn't sure.

Martha Miller interrupted his thoughts as she told Mike what an enjoyable time they'd had being with Kelly and him. "Please apologize to Kelly, too. We didn't intend any harm."

"We really should be going, Mike," Mark said.

Mike nodded. He really didn't know what to say to the Millers. Finally, he said, "I'll tell Kelly. We enjoyed being with you, too," and turned to follow Mitch and Mark.

"That seemed awkward, Mike. What was that all about?" Mark asked.

"I'm still not sure," Mike replied. "It's somewhat involved. Maybe I'll get a chance to explain it to you later."

Chapter 43

As Sandy disappeared from view, the man asked Kelly if her ankle was feeling any better.

"Maybe a little," she replied, reaching down and tenderly massaging it again.

"Good. We can make good use of our time while she's gone. You can start by taking off your blouse and shorts."

Kelly stared up at him with a shocked expression. This can't be happening.

Webb laughed. "Not what you think. I should have provided you with some prior knowledge of my intentions. Sandy was going to be the courier to pick up the money and letters of pardon. When you became available, we changed plans and made the decision to use you. We still plan to."

He pulled the duffel bag over in front of him and unzipped it as he continued talking. "We have some gear in here that Sandy was going to wear, only now it will be you. Don't be frightened. If all goes according to plan, you have nothing to fear."

Webb was carefully removing what resembled a life vest from the duffel bag and held it up so Kelly could see it. "I'm going to be helping you put this contraption on. You'll find it's somewhat cumbersome and heavy. I'm sorry about that, what with your ankle. I don't want to scare you, but this will turn you into a human bomb."

A few seconds ago Kelly feared he had intentions of ravishing her. Now he was talking about putting her into a sort of wet-suit, minus the sleeves and legs, stuffed with what he was indicating were explosives. She couldn't help but shudder at the thought of donning that device.

As if reading her thoughts, Webb was smiling again. "You're probably not relishing what you're hearing, but at least you know now why I asked you to take off your blouse and those Bermudas. You can put them back on after we have you in this. Hopefully, they'll fit over it and conceal what's underneath."

He'd been holding the vest aloft in his left hand and was now pointing to the two straps resembling seat belts, which dangled from the bottom. "These will be fastened between your legs. Pay close attention. We don't want any accidents. When I snap them in place, this light will come on, indicating . . ." He paused for a moment. "Indicating you've been activated. There's no timing device or anything of that nature."

He reached in the duffel again and removed what resembled a TV remote control unit. "However, if this button is pushed while that light is on, you'd be blown to smithereens. Not only you, but probably everything and everyone within a hundred or so feet of you. What you need to be aware of, and remember, is that any attempt to unclasp these belts while the light is on will result in the same consequences. I don't want you or anyone else to think they can wriggle you out of this without dire results. Believe me, there's no way it can be done without triggering the explosives. You're only going to have to be wearing this for a short time. If everything goes according to plan, probably less than three hours. You're going to be leaving the island on the seven o'clock boat to Mackinaw City."

As he talked, he put the control unit back into the duffel bag and removed a roll of toilet paper. A grin appeared on his face. "Just like I hope those scouts are, we're prepared, too. You might want to relieve yourself," he said, tossing her the roll of paper. "Even though as I said, you won't be trussed up all that long, it could be a little messy if nature calls after we have you into this contraption. I should be calling Stuart about now, anyway. I'll just turn my back on you to give you some privacy. But don't get any ideas. You'd just be asking for more trouble."

He gestured with the gun. The message was clear—he wouldn't hesitate to use it.

"Sandy was prepared to wear this and she still could. I have to say, she was elated when I told her of the change in plans and my decision to involve you. Don't move off too far. You'll be able to hear my instructions to Stuart. It'll save time not having to tell you, too. You'll be fully apprised of our plans and the role we're orchestrating for you. The number is one-one, right?"

Kelly nodded as the man swung around and dialed the number.

•

Kelly had removed her blouse and shorts. Squatting to urinate had been awkward as well as painful, as her ankle continued to throb. Webb had raised his voice to enable her to better hear what he was saying.

"That's right, I want you to put everything into Kelly's suitcase, the one with the piece of red yarn tied to the handle."

Kelly was surprised. She was trying to recall if her luggage had been visible to him when he'd come to her room. He must have noticed it when I was on the phone, discussing switching rooms. She wondered if he'd made the decision then to use her suitcase. No, this was a change in plans. They were probably confident then that their other actions would succeed in getting the meetings cancelled.

"Just send it down in time to be loaded on the seven o'clock boat to Mackinaw City, the one leaving from the Shepler Dock. Understood? Kelly will be on that boat. She'll be seeing that her suitcase gets into her car at the dock in Mackinaw City. She and Mike used valet parking. Make sure the car's there when she arrives. I'm sure he has the claim check. I don't want any of you on the boat with her. You know a few of our faces—and we know yours, too. This can all work smoothly, or it could result in a disaster. It's up to you."

Webb went on to describe the device Kelly would be wearing; the fact it—she—could be detonated by remote control if any attempt was made to entrap them.

"I'm going to be putting her on the line now to verify what I've just said. Just so there are no surprises, I want you to know she's had an accident, a badly sprained or broken ankle. She might be boarding the boat in a wheelchair. You might want to alert the Northern Michigan Hospital in Petoskey to be on the lookout for her, around nine tonight. Here she is."

Webb turned around and walked over to Kelly, who was sitting in the middle of the trail, clad only in her bra and panties, and handed her the phone.

"Hi, Stuart. I'm okay. My injury was an accident."

Webb leaned down to listen to Stuart's response.

"I'm relieved to hear that. I'm sure Mike will be, too. I'm expecting to see him in another minute or two. Is what I've been told pretty much true? They have you wired up?"

"I'm afraid so," Kelly replied. Before she could say anything more, Webb had yanked the phone from her hand.

"Her fate and the fate of those other women is in your hands, Stuart. No tricks, no games. Have her suitcase on the seven o'clock boat." He terminated the connection before Stuart could reply.

Smiling, he said, "Now let's get you outfitted. We're under a tight timetable."

Chapter 44

Fritz was talking to Stuart when Mike entered the office, followed by Mitch and Mark. There were two people seated in chairs facing Kreicheff's desk, both dressed in warm-ups. One was a man who appeared in his late sixties or early seventies. The woman next to him was probably half his age, possibly his daughter. There was a definite family resemblance, Mike thought.

"Good timing," Stuart said to the three men. "I just spoke to Kelly, Mike. She assured me she's all right, considering. She's injured her ankle, badly sprained or broken. She's still with them."

Mike had a mixed reaction, definitely relieved to hear Kelly was still alive, concerned hearing about her injury, and realizing the predicament she was in.

"First, let me introduce you to Ed Merryweather and his daughter, Susan," Stuart was saying. "They're the publishers of the Mackinac Island Town Crier, the island's local paper."

The man stood and reached out to shake Mike's hand. "We were supposed to be playing tennis with you this afternoon, with you and your fiancée."

Mike nodded as he replied. "I wish we had. Things might be a little less complicated."

His daughter, Susan, had also risen from her chair and took Mike's hand. "We're sorry, we hear you're here to plan a wedding for later this summer."

Mike nodded again as Ed and Susan also shook hands with Mitch and Mark.

"The Merryweathers became privy to much of what's been happening these past couple days," Stuart explained. "In exchange for being brought into the loop, somewhat of a promise for an exclusive, they've agreed to keep this story under wraps for now. They've also promised not to reveal any details to any other news media for the time being. In turn, we were just in the process of bringing them up to speed."

Looking back toward the Merryweathers, who were seated once again, Stuart said, "I'll be repeating myself, but I want to brief these men on my latest conversation before I start to address your questions. You're welcome to stay, or if you'd rather use the time to contact anyone, make a call, you could use one of the other offices and we'll come get you when I've finished up with them."

Ed and his daughter exchanged looks. "Maybe you could phone Mom, Susan. Tell her I'm not sure when I'll be home for dinner. Don't say anything to worry her."

Susan nodded her head, a brief smile surfacing as she rose from her chair, excusing herself. Fritz also excused himself, explaining he'd be back momentarily.

Stuart spent the next few minutes relating the details of the earlier call. Mike sensed that the others were attempting to steal a glance to see his reaction as Stuart described the bombing mechanism Kelly was being forced to wear, and the threats that had been made.

"The Grand Hotel's dray will be leaving to take luggage down to the dock for that seven o'clock departure in less than half an hour," Stuart said. "Could you go up to your room now, Mike, and bring Kelly's suitcase down? You'll need to—I'm sure you'll want to—empty things out of it."

Mike nodded. He was quite sure Kelly had completely emptied her bag when they'd unpacked, though. However, it would still take a few minutes to get the suitcase. He'd better hold his questions until after he'd gotten it.

•

On the way upstairs, Mike had been able to mull over much of what he'd just learned. *Maybe I can persuade Stuart to call back and try to convince them that I should bring Kelly's suitcase to the boat. I could use the* argument that Kelly would have difficulty driving the car with her injured ankle. He wondered if it was her left or right one, it would strengthen his case. It was the only thing he could think of that might work to enable him to join Kelly. He was worried that even without anyone wanting it to happen, the explosives strapped to Kelly might be ignited. Accidents happen. He wanted to be with her.

He opened the door to the room and went directly to the closet. Kelly's bag was sitting next to his on the closet floor. He picked it up and placed it on the bed. As he had thought it would be, it was completely empty. As he closed it, he noticed the red yarn tied to the handle. Kelly had been so proud to have devised that simple way of identifying her luggage. It was a popular make and model. He remembered her telling him that on nearly every flight she'd been on, at least one person, usually more than one, had the identical bag. The yarn also made it easily identifiable by someone else, probably the major reason for instructing them to use it as a container for the money and letters.

As Mike headed back downstairs, additional worries filled his mind. Stuart had indicated that the Bureau wouldn't be doing anything to jeopardize Kelly. Did that mean that they were acquiescing to all the demands? That they were truly going to sit back and allow these villains to escape and avoid any punishment? Stuart might be sincere, but could he guarantee everyone was of the same mind?

•

As he came down the hallway toward Stuart's office, Mike could overhear a conversation in progress. It was Fritz's voice.

"I think they've planned to use her for some time. This isn't spur of the moment stuff. Maybe he decided to involve her after talking to her that morning in the room. He knew about the red yarn tied to the handle of her suitcase. He knew they'd used valet parking in Mackinaw City. I don't think he's just learned those things from her now. Maybe it was a secondary plan. Regardless, I think he did a pied-piper bit on Kelly, banking on her naiveté. He got her to follow him to the Mission Pointe Resort. I bet he had a big chuckle when she pulled that amateur stunt with the twenty-dollar bill. All I'm saying, Stuart, is that you have to remember she isn't some innocent bystander. God sakes, she's a former agent, still in law enforcement. She's a big girl now, we shouldn't be basing all our decisions on her safety. She's chosen to get involved. She—"

Mike's face flushed in anger as he strode into the office, carrying Kelly's suitcase. Barely glancing in Stuart's direction, he turned and glared at Fritz as he said, "Damn! You think you have all the answers, don't you? You've treated Kelly and me with contempt from the first moment we met you. You . . . you . . . you must have ice water in your veins."

Mike was steamed, breathing heavily as Stuart raised his hand to simmer him down.

"Hold it, Mike. Cool down. We need to focus on the real bad guys."

"Sorry, Mike, but I was just expressing my opinion," Fritz said. "I didn't realize you could hear me, but damn it, it wouldn't have made any difference. I was only expressing my opinion. Kelly might be saying the same thing if she were here. It would be a crime to let those people go unpunished."

"The problem is, Kelly isn't here," Mike replied, his face still flushed. "I wish you were there in her place, Fritz, so she and I could debate your welfare."

"I'm sure you'd prefer it if that was the case," Fritz said. "But it isn't. And we need to make some decisions. Be fair, don't you agree it would be a shame to let those people off scot-free?"

Mike nodded as he appeared to calm down. He turned toward Stuart.

"You promised me that Kelly's safety would be a high priority. I want to know if that's still true."

"It definitely is, Mike," Stuart answered. "For what it's worth, I wasn't buying into Fritz's argument, either. That's probably why he was coming on so strong when you arrived. I think they've pulled this together on the fly. That seizing Kelly—"

The phone rang and Stuart paused to answer it.

"Yes, Mike just arrived with it. That's right, it will just go down with the Grand's other luggage."

Stuart was still talking when Rick Sobelinski entered the office. He nodded to Mike and Fritz and flashed an OK sign to Stuart with his thumb and index finger as he picked up Kelly's suitcase.

"Rick's just taking it with him now. You should have everything there."

Mike started to speak up as Rick left with the suitcase, but then decided to wait until Stuart had completed his conversation. As he hung up, Mike said, "I had a thought when I was on my way upstairs to get Kelly's bag. I'd like to run it past you. You said they want Kelly to drive my car down to Petoskey after she gets to Mackinaw City. I know we aren't sure how badly her ankle's injured, but that might present a problem with driving, especially if it's her right ankle.

"In light of that, I'm thinking we could contact the man you've been talking to, and volunteer my services. I know he was emphatic about you not involving any of your people—on the boat, in surveillance, whatever. But maybe they look at me in a little different light. I could chauffeur Kelly. I could also carry the suitcase onto the boat, rather than sending it on the baggage wagon."

"And you'd feel a lot more comfortable if you were with Kelly. I see where you're coming from, Mike. I'm not sure I'd be able to get them to buy into it, though. I suppose we could give it a try. You're shaking your head, Fritz. Not a good idea, or are you thinking they won't agree?"

Mike glanced over at Fritz and saw he was holding up two fingers. He was replying to Stuart's questions.

"Probably both, but there're two reasons I'd hesitate about even making the proposition to them. Hear me out, Mike. Remember, I'm just expressing my opinion. It's one of the ways I earn my salary. Right, Stu?"

Stuart nodded. "Just give us your reasons, okay?"

A touch of a smile crossed Fritz's face as he spelled out his concerns. "My first thought is that Mike's too emotionally involved. Witness what just took place. If he were to—"

"That's nonsense!" Mike said, his face flushing in anger. "And you know it!"

Stuart held up his hand to quiet Mike and nodded for Fritz to proceed.

"All I'm saying is that in the best interests of everyone, probably Kelly in particular, Mike should step back. It's a potential risk that's not necessary. They know what she's capable of doing, or can't do, with her injury. If they were the ones to suggest Mike's involvement, that would be a different story. I guess I'd support it, providing we had certain assurances from Mike."

Mike was taking a series of deep breaths, biting his tongue, as Fritz continued.

"My second concern is the same one I expressed to you earlier, Stu. I think there's a hidden agenda we aren't privy to in directing you to send Kelly's suitcase down to the boat with the Grand's other luggage. I'm sure they want us to believe the reason for that is to minimize our participation. Avoid having another person involved, if someone were to hand-carry it. But as I told you earlier, I'm suspicious it's being done so they can get their hands on the bag—really, its contents—before it even reaches the dock. That Kelly's involvement, talk of her driving to Petoskey, is just a ruse.

"I think they've planned to take possession of the suitcase, maybe just remove the contents, during the time it's on the dray. Maybe a plan to switch bags, substitute another with a similar strand of red yarn tied to the handle. If I'm right, the suggestion to have Mike bring it to the boat would be turned down. That alone is no problem. The risk is in alerting them we're suspicious of their intentions. It could make our surveillance that much more difficult. We'd run the risk—"

"Hold on," Mike said, interrupting Fritz. "What surveillance? What are your intentions? To apprehend someone if they try to take the suitcase? Wouldn't that increase the risks to Kelly and those other women?"

"Surveillance, period, is all I've suggested to Stu," Fritz answered. "I think we can do it without them being aware of it. We could move in after Kelly and the women are out of danger."

Fritz was just validating Mike's fears. They'd been quick to agree to the demands because they really didn't actually intend to honor their promises.

"That's just a suggestion Fritz made, Mike. We haven't agreed to it, there's been no decision yet."

The mere fact it was being considered was alarming enough, Mike thought.

"I'll just say I think Fritz has his risk calculations screwed up," Mike said, shaking his head. "Viewing my involvement more of a risk than what he's proposing, and you're agreeing?"

"You should know more than most, Mike, that all options have to be explored and evaluated. Contrary to what you may be thinking, I'm leaning towards contacting them and having you involved. Fritz delights in playing the devil's advocate. I suggest that each of you take no more than two minutes to state your case again, and then I'll make the decision."

Chapter 45

Kelly was attempting to button her blouse. It wasn't going to work. The vest she was now strapped into was far too bulky.

"Don't worry about that, Kelly. I was intending for you to wear a windbreaker, anyway. I'll help you into it."

The man removed a light-colored jacket from the duffel bag. He smiled as he said, "An official Mackinac Island windbreaker."

Kelly couldn't help but smile as she observed the logo—a box of Famous Mackinac Island Fudge. She extended her arms as he helped her put it on. The temperature had dropped over the past hour. Even though she realized the windbreaker's main purpose was to conceal the contraption she'd been put in, she appreciated the added warmth.

The man hoisted the duffel bag and leaned down so Kelly could comfortably place her arm around his shoulders.

"Let me know if you're in pain. I really don't want you to aggravate your ankle. If need be, we can just wait here for Sandy. But if you can handle it, so much the better. We'll be cutting it close as it is."

Kelly was surprised as she placed weight on her foot that the pain was now minimal. The body has an amazing capacity to heal itself, she thought, as she stepped forward on her foot again.

•

They crossed the same road they had earlier and continued along the trail, making surprisingly good time.

"If you want to rest for a few minutes, just tell me."

Kelly shook her head. "As you can see, I'm handling this far better than I anticipated."

"Do you hear voices?" the man asked, stopping.

She had. They sounded like young boys.

Sure enough, a minute or two later, a half-dozen boys in scouting gear appeared, carrying a stretcher. Sandy was following them with a middle-aged man, also dressed in scouting gear. She introduced the two of them to the scout master, Richard Smith, and members of Troop 461 from Kalamazoo. She'd been clever in how she handled it, without identifying either Kelly or Webb by name.

"I'm sorry we don't have crutches or a wheelchair available," Smith explained to Kelly. "The island doctor's office is near the base of the hill from the fort. Hopefully, the office will still be open or someone will be there. I'm sure they'd probably have both. My boys are excited about using the stretcher to get you there," Smith said with a grin. "You'll be able to take credit for getting them a special merit badge. We did bring a bag of ice."

Kelly smiled as she thanked him and the scouts. They lowered the stretcher on the ground next to her. She started to kneel down, with plans to lie down so that they could lift her or she could work her body onto the stretcher. As she did, her leg buckled. She groaned in pain as she tumbled to the ground.

Everyone grimaced. Richard Smith and three of the scouts immediately came to her aid, gently lifting her and placing her on the stretcher. Kelly was still in pain, with her eyes clenched shut. She whispered a thank-you as she opened them. The scouts looked to their scoutmaster for direction before spreading out, three to a side, and lifting the stretcher.

Webb explained to the scoutmaster that they were anxious to get her to the mainland as quickly as possible, to get her to the hospital in Petoskey, as he adjusted the bag of ice on Kelly's ankle.

"I think there's a boat to Mackinaw City at seven o'clock. Do you think we could make it?"

"Hear that, men?" Smith asked. "We're going to have to hurry, but yes, we should be able to."

He quickly turned and took the lead, followed by the scouts carrying Kelly on the stretcher. Sandy and Webb brought up the rear. A ringing sound, which seemed to be originating from the duffel bag the man was carrying, startled the group as they approached the fort. Two of the young boys were pointing to the duffel bag as he slipped it off his shoulder and onto the ground.

He quickly unzipped it and took the cellular phone out. He motioned to the scoutmaster for him and the others to continue on, as he turned and stepped back a few steps, lifting the phone to his ear.

The caller was Stuart Kreicheff, and he quickly presented Mike's proposal. "In addition to driving the car, Mike could also bring Kelly's suitcase to the boat," Stuart suggested.

The man smiled, about to summarily turn down the proposal. He hesitated, perhaps recalling Kelly's difficulty in positioning herself to get on the stretcher, before replying.

"We probably should have thought of that ourselves. Fine. Tell Mike to meet Kelly on board the boat. Remind him not to engage in any heroics, though. He'll be as vulnerable as she is. We don't want her killed any more than you do. I hope you're following my instructions to the letter. Still, send Kelly's bag down on the dray, rather than with Mike. For your sake, I hope we'll find the money and the letters of pardon are there."

"You will," Stuart replied.

•

What had begun as a fun endeavor for the young boys had turned into work. As they proceeded down the walkway from the fort towards town, the scoutmaster asked his boys if they wanted to take a short break. They assured him they were doing fine and that it wasn't necessary. Nonetheless, Richard Smith and Webb took positions across from one another alongside the stretcher, to help the boys. Smith asked Kelly and Webb if they wanted to go by the medical center to see if anyone was there. Webb replied for Kelly as well, explaining there wasn't time, they should go directly to Shepler's Dock.

Webb smiled down at Kelly. "Do you have your return ticket, or does Mike have it?"

"Mike has them both," Kelly answered.

"I've got a surprise for you," he said with a grin. "Mike's going to meet you on the boat. He can drive the car. But do you have money for a ticket in case he doesn't get there in time?"

Kelly nodded. She had some money in the pocket of her shorts.

"When we get to Main Street, Sandy and I are going to bid you farewell. Hopefully, this will all be over for you in a couple of hours. But remember, it isn't yet. I'm sure we won't be getting invitations to the wedding," he said, smiling again, "but I hope your ankle will be ready for dancing. You may see Mr. Woodbridge in Petoskey. Tell him he has my admiration. Tell him that his injuries, and those of his houseman, too, weren't my doing."

The scouts were glancing at one another, wondering if any of them understood what was being discussed. Kelly's thoughts were confused. The man had created such havoc. Still, he'd been kind to her, considering. She wondered how he'd gotten mixed up in all this.

They'd reached the corner next to Doud's Grocery on Main Street. Webb removed three twenty-dollar bills from his billfold and handed them to the scoutmaster.

"We have to leave you now. Thanks for your help in getting her to the boat. This money is for Troop 461."

Richard Smith pulled back his hand. "That's not expected, nor necessary. We were glad to be available to help."

Webb tucked the money next to Kelly on the stretcher. "Make sure they take it. Maybe you can treat them all to an ice cream cone at the dock."

Chapter 46

Mike had managed to find space for most of Kelly's clothes in his suitcase. He'd been able to obtain a large shopping bag with handles from the hotel gift shop and had used it for her robe, slippers, and cosmetic and toiletries case. He checked the dresser drawers one last time to make sure he hadn't missed anything. He had to hurry—it was already twenty past six.

He'd been so elated as he'd sat across from Stuart, hearing the proposal to allow him to accompany Kelly on the boat and chauffeur her had been accepted. Fritz had made a major issue of the fact they hadn't wanted Mike to bring Kelly's suitcase with him. Maybe Fritz was right in thinking they intended to obtain it or its contents while the suitcase was being transported on the Grand Hotel's horse-drawn dray. But in case that didn't occur, Mike pondered the possibilities of how Kelly and he would be notified or intercepted on the mainland in order for them to take possession of Kelly's suitcase.

Stuart had asked him to stop by the office before leaving for the boat, saying they wanted to get him set up so there could be two-way communication with him. Tossing the room key onto the dresser top, Mike picked up his suitcase and the shopping bag and dashed out of the room.

•

"I think that just about does it, Mike," Stuart said. "Remember, just cough to notify us that we should cease communication. For example, if you think someone may be overhearing us or if we're interfering with a conversation. A second cough will alert us we can pass a message on to you again. They've perfected this equipment so much in the past year or so. I'm pretty sure you'll be the only one able to hear us."

Mike nodded. Stuart had provided him with a miniature receiver, which was now in his ear. The size and natural coloring made it almost invisible. Someone would definitely have to know what they were looking for in order to spot it. Even then, they might have difficulty. Though familiar with similar devices, Stuart was right. Great strides had been made in the technology. This unit was half the size and offered twice the clarity of anything Mike had previously seen. The same was true for the hidden microphone, pinned on the inside of Mike's shirt.

"As I said," Stuart repeated, "the range is amazing. We shouldn't have any difficulty in communicating to you or in hearing you and those around you, even in Mackinaw City. That could change, though, when you're in the car and headed towards Petoskey. And as I said, they might instruct you to head in another direction—across the bridge and into the UP, for example. That could complicate things as well. Any questions?"

Mike shook his head. "No, I think you've addressed them all. You took care of the hotel bill?"

"Already done. And good luck, Mike," Stuart said, grasping his hand. Fritz also came over to shake Mike's hand, a nod suggesting he wished him well, too. Mike appreciated the fact neither was reminding him to be careful. Fritz had more than covered that issue as they were debating whether to attempt to get him on the boat with Kelly.

"The carriage is out front," Fritz said, glancing at his watch. "The driver should have you at Shepler's Dock in about five minutes."

Mike nodded again and headed out the door.

Fritz waited a minute or two before asking, "Any change in your thinking?"

Stuart shook his head. "No, I thought we'd decided that. I've also assured Mike we'd refrain from any surveillance."

Fritz smiled as he replied, "Just thought I'd ask."

Stuart's phone rang as he was shaking his head. He answered it and Fritz watched as a delighted smile began to surface on Stuart's face.

"Fantastic! Could you hold for a minute?" Stuart asked, covering the receiver with his hand as he excitedly conveyed the news to Fritz.

"They've found the women, alive, in a heavily-wooded area just north of British Landing. Can you round up Mary and Rick and whoever else is around? Steve Richards, if he's here? Have them all come in here."

•

A few minutes later, six people in addition to Fritz were present in the office. All were ecstatic. Mitch and Mark exchanged high-fives. Ian McKenzie's and Steve Richards' faces were beaming with smiles of relief.

Stuart hung up the phone and turned to them with a huge grin on his face. "Our prayers have been answered," he began. "The two dogs the State Police brought with them were the key. I mean in addition to Sam Pacquette.

It was his suggestion to concentrate in the area in which the women were found. Asking each of the husbands to provide us with an article of their wives' clothing paid off.

"The women have been drugged and they're still unconscious. An EMS team and Doc Solomon are on their way there now. Everything indicates they're going to be fine, probably coming out from under the effects of whatever drug was used over the next couple hours. No one appears to have been injured.

"The Michigan State policeman who first discovered them thought he'd come across a mass suicide by some religious cult. The women had been placed side-by-side, on a couple of blankets. A sheet of canvas covered them, propped up by a series of sticks to allow a few inches of space above the bodies. Leaves had been scattered over the canvas to serve as camouflage. Marc is the one who I spoke to. He thinks we were very lucky. He says we could have walked right past the area without noticing anything. As I said, the dogs were the key.

"There was no sign of anyone other than the women. It doesn't appear that they were being watched. No lookout in case one or more regained consciousness earlier than anticipated, or in case they were discovered. They weren't tied or gagged. I think whoever's responsible was confident they'd be able to accomplish their aims, obtain the money and letters of assurance, before either occurred."

"Are we still going to let them, as you put it, accomplish their aims?" Fritz asked. Heads first turned to look at Fritz and then turned toward Stuart.

"The picture has changed," Stuart said, addressing Fritz's question. "I'll be the first to admit that. But we have to remember, Kelly Travis is still in a very precarious position. My thinking from the start was to immediately launch every resource at our disposal to track down, apprehend and prosecute these terrorists, as soon as those women were out of harm's way. They are, that's true. But now we have to factor in Kelly."

"But Stu, she can't be looked at the same way as we viewed the wives," Fritz interrupted. "We were probably right in classing them as innocent victims. But Kelly's different. She's in law enforcement. She chose to get involved, nobody coerced her. How would you act if it was one of our agents in her position?"

"I would hope it would be in the same way I am now."

There were a number of snickers and Fritz's face flushed as Stuart added, "Maybe if you were the agent, Fritz, I might have different thoughts.

But as it stands, I'm concerned right now that our discovery, our rescue of the women, once it's known by those responsible, might precipitate some stupid reaction. They might know already. Seeing the EMS vehicle headed towards British Landing might send up a red flag, rouse their suspicions.

"My belief is, even if they become aware, they'll still wait to see if they're able to get the letters and money. They realize, of course, they're still holding the Kelly card. And they might think that alone is sufficient motivation for us to meet their demands. They might also assume that it's too late for us to alter things and pull back. Fritz believes they might already have the letters, having obtained them as the luggage was being transported to the dock. I think he's probably right. I'd vetoed the idea of trying to prevent that or putting a tail on the person or persons who seized the suitcase."

"So we're just going to sit by and let them get away with everything?" Fritz asked. "Anderson's death? The kidnapping? The torture of—"

"Hold on, Fritz. That's not what I'm saying. The second we hear Kelly's out of danger, I'm ready to move. I realize the window of opportunity for apprehending them is going to be much smaller when that occurs. We'd have to retrieve those letters. Get them back before any copies are made.

"The money is relatively unimportant. And their third condition— having all the attendees to these meetings off the island—is now for the most part meaningless. They have to realize the meetings have already accomplished, or failed to accomplish, their purpose.

"What I am willing to do is prepare for when we learn Kelly's safe. Or, perish the thought, learn she's no longer alive. Fritz, if you and some of the others want to hop into a speedboat now and try to get to Mackinaw City ahead of Kelly and Mike, that's fine. Better yet, we could probably get you there faster by plane," Stuart suggested, after looking at his watch. "But I want you to remain invisible until we've been assured of Kelly's safety."

Fritz jumped up. "Who's going to come with me?" he asked, looking around the room. "Damn it, Stu, we should have been planning this all along."

Chapter 47

Only a handful of people had been present to see the scouts carrying Kelly through the fort complex, down the ramp and along the sidewalk towards town. This changed as they neared Main Street. Kelly was the focus of attention, as dozens of people turned to stare. It resembled a scene from the children's book, 'Make Way For Ducklings,' as carriages and bicyclists halted to allow the procession of scouts carrying Kelly to cross the street in front of the Chippewa Hotel. Pedestrians continued to stare and the scouts and their scoutmaster found themselves fielding questions.

As they passed the entrance to the Chippewa Hotel, two men were coming out the door. They were engaged in a heated discussion. The taller of the two had turned to face the other, wildly gesturing with his hands as he stepped backwards.

He was unaware of the activity behind him and collided with two of the scouts. The two small boys stumbled as they tried to maintain their balance, losing their grip on the stretcher. It tilted to the side and Kelly, fearful she was about to slide off, frantically attempted to grab hold of the stretcher's sides.

The man turned in surprise, horrified to see what he'd inadvertently caused to happen. He quickly reached for the stretcher, attempting to right it. In doing so, he placed his hand on Kelly's shoulder to hold her in place in the center of the stretcher.

The scoutmaster, who'd been a few paces ahead leading the group, had wheeled around to help.

"That was a near disaster," he said as he explained to the man. "Her ankle's broken. We're taking her to catch a boat so she can get some medical attention on the mainland."

The man nodded. "A back injury, too. I felt her brace."

Smith was surprised by that statement, and looked toward Kelly for verification. But she'd draped her hand over her eyes.

"Are you okay?" he asked.

"I'm fine, just catching my breath," she replied. Thinking she'd been about to tumble off the stretcher onto the sidewalk, she'd been fearful the explosives might be set off. Though unaware at the time, she now understood the reaction of Webb when she'd dropped the duffel bag. He'd thought that might trigger an explosion. That's why he'd leaped behind a clump of trees, to take cover, Kelly thought.

The man who'd bumped into the scouts was still apologizing, asking how he could be of help. Smith assured him that he and his boys had everything under control.

Kelly removed her hand from across her eyes and smiled. She was relieved. "I'm in good hands. Don't worry, there wasn't any harm done. You boys are fine now, aren't you?"

The two scouts the man had bumped into both grinned, assuring her they were okay.

Starting forward again, they passed the Arnold Dock. The Shepler Dock was just ahead.

"Oh, no," Kelly said, slapping her fist into the palm of her hand.

The scouts jumped, thinking she was experiencing some pain.

Kelly smiled. She'd just thought of Ginny Campbell. *I never called to tell her that Mike and I wouldn't be able to meet her and her family for a drink. Or did I? Did I ask Stuart or Mary to have someone call?* She couldn't remember. *Hopefully, none of the Campbells witnessed the scene just now in front of the Chippewa. She wouldn't have wanted to face their questions. She'd dodged the man's question about her having a back brace. I'll have to call Mrs. Campbell and apologize.* But there were more major concerns now.

●

Passengers were boarding the boat as they approached. She asked Smith if he and the boys could carry her up to the top deck. She still hadn't seen Mike. Had Webb lied to her?

"Why heavens, Kelly! Is that you?" Martha Miller was staring down at her. "What happened? Where's Mike?"

Kelly smiled up at her. "I had an accident. I think I may have broken my ankle. Mike wasn't with me, he's supposed to meet me here."

"Roy," Martha called out. "Come here. Kelly's been injured."

Roy joined his wife, both peering down at Kelly.

"She thinks she's broken her ankle," Martha explained.

He nodded. "Have you had a chance to have a doctor look at it yet?" he asked.

Kelly shook her head. "Mike's going to be driving me down to the Petoskey Hospital."

"That's good," Martha replied. "Roy and I will keep an eye out for Mike while they're getting you on board."

Kelly thanked them and introduced Smith and the scouts to the Millers. "They've been wonderful! They're going to carry me up to the top deck, the same spot where Mike and I met you on Friday."

"I can't believe the time flew by so quickly," Martha said.

Kelly's thoughts were the opposite. It was amazing how much had occurred in the past forty-eight hours. It seemed ages ago since they'd met the Millers.

"I'll see if I can find a chair," Roy suggested. "I don't recall seeing any up there on our way over. Probably one reason there weren't many of us on the top deck."

"Remember, it was pretty chilly, too, Roy," Martha said as he nodded, turning to go look for a chair.

"That's nice of him," Kelly said to Martha as she and the scouts crossed the gangplank. Following Smith's directions, the scouts managed to tilt the stretcher so that she'd be going up the stairs head-first.

Chapter 48

Mike was beginning to panic as he glanced at his watch again. Several carriages had pulled over to the side of the street a couple minutes ago to allow an EMS vehicle with its lights flashing to pass. Mike recognized Richard Solomon in the front seat as the vehicle passed. He's having a busy day, Mike thought.

Two of the carriages in front of his had collided as they maneuvered back into the street. It was taking time to sort out the damage, assessing who was at fault.

"I guess I'm going to have to walk," Mike said to his driver. "I was cutting it close as it was. If I run, I think I can still make it."

"Sorry about this, mister," the driver replied as Mike climbed out of the carriage and grabbed his suitcase and the large shopping bag.

Dodging pedestrians, he hurried toward the dock. He was fortunate he had only a short distance to cover. He veered to avoid striking a young child with the suitcase.

The communication was working well. They were apparently having no difficulty hearing him, and the agent who was monitoring him was coming in loud and clear.

"I'm just about there," Mike said as he saw the sign for the Shepler Dock a few yards ahead.

"According to my watch, you still have four minutes," the agent replied.

•

Mike saw a boat was still at the dock as he dashed toward it. Looking up, he spotted Kelly standing next to the rail on the upper deck, waving and smiling.

A feeling of relief swept through him. Tears were welling up in his eyes as he put the shopping bag down and waved back at her, blowing her a kiss. The boat's horn sounded, indicating departure was imminent.

Mike picked up the bag and ran towards the gangplank. Two crew members were just about to pull it aboard the boat. Seeing Mike, they smiled and waited.

•

Kelly was elated. Seeing Mike's smiling face seemed to minimize her concerns and fears. People on the dock were smiling up at her, having witnessed the scene. Kelly smiled again. They must think they've just seen a scene from a movie, she thought. Two lovers being reunited as the movie ends.

Martha was standing next to her and sighed, saying, "That was so romantic. Mike throwing that kiss to you. I think you have yourself a keeper. But he's pretty lucky, too."

"That's for sure," Roy said. He'd been standing on Kelly's other side.

•

One of the crew members took the suitcase and shopping bag from Mike as he came on board. "I'll just put them over there on that dolly."

Mike looked to see where he'd gestured and saw several pieces of luggage on two baggage carts. Kelly's suitcase with the strip of red yarn caught his eye. It was on the top row of one of the carts.

"Thank you," Mike said, reaching for his billfold.

The young man smiled and shook his head, anticipating Mike's intentions. "That's not necessary. Free luggage handling with the price of your ticket. Did you use valet parking?"

Mike nodded.

"I'll take your claim check and call ahead. We'll have your car waiting for you."

As Mike removed his billfold, he explained, "I don't have the claim check. The hotel said they'd notify you."

"Fine, they probably have. You might be asked to show some ID, though, to verify against the registration."

Mike nodded as he handed him a two-dollar bill. The young man grinned as he thanked Mike.

"We called ahead, Mike. Your car will be waiting for you." It was Stuart's voice on the miniature receiver in his ear.

"I hear you, thanks," Mike said.

The boy looked back toward Mike with a confused expression. "Did you say something?"

Mike smiled and shook his head. He'd have to be a little more careful.

"I heard that," Stuart said, chuckling.

•

Kelly had limped over to the stairway and grinned as Mike's face appeared as he came dashing up the steps. He embraced her as he told her how delighted he was to see her.

"The feeling's mutual," she replied. "But be careful, don't hug me too hard."

Feeling the padding underneath her windbreaker, Mike nodded and grabbed onto her hands as they kissed.

Martha and Roy glanced at each other and winked. As Kelly and Mike stepped apart, still holding hands, Martha asked, "Did you injure your back, too? How did it happen?"

Roy interrupted, saying, "Let's get Kelly onto this chair first, Martha, and then she can answer your questions."

As Mike and Roy assisted her, Kelly told Mike how helpful the Millers had been. "Roy carried the chair up from down below."

As Kelly was talking, Stuart's voice came over the ear mike.

"A word of caution, Mike. We're picking up indications there's another listening device near you. They probably have Kelly wired. She might not even be aware of it. They probably worked it into that gear they have her in. You might want to check with her to see if they're communicating with her like I am with you. That could be possible."

It made sense, thought Mike. They'd be able to direct them when they reached the mainland. Give them instructions about Kelly's suitcase.

Sensing that the Millers were staring at him, Mike wondered if they could be overhearing Stuart. He coughed.

"Read you," Stuart replied in a hushed tone.

The boat had been backing out into the harbor as they'd assisted Kelly over to the chair. Now turned toward Mackinaw City, the engine had been shifted into the forward gear and turned on full throttle. Mike held onto Kelly's hand as the wind blew through their hair.

"Kelly and Mike might want to have some time alone, Roy. Why don't we go downstairs for a few minutes," Martha suggested.

Roy nodded in agreement. "We'll be back shortly, though. I want to take another photo of the two of you," he said with a wink.

As the Millers started down the stairs, Mike removed his billfold and took out a business card. Taking his pen, he wrote, 'You may be wearing a mike,' and showed the card to Kelly. She nodded her head in understanding. He then wrote, 'Are they communicating to you?'

Kelly gave him a confused look and Mike bent down and pointed to his ear. It took her a few seconds to spot the hearing device. When she did, she nodded and then shook her head, indicating no.

"Our car's going to be waiting for us on the dock," Mike said. "How long a drive is it to Petoskey?"

"Not far, about fifty miles, probably an hour's drive," Kelly replied.

"How's your ankle? Are you in pain?"

Kelly reached for Mike's pen and the business card. As she answered him, she wrote, 'Fine!'

"I think I've probably broken a bone or two. And yes, it hurts."

Mike grinned and squeezed her hand as she continued talking, saying she thought she'd need surgery, that the pain was so intense she could hardly place any weight on her foot. As she made this latter statement, she rose from the chair and walked around in a small circle, hardly showing any sign of a limp.

"The crew seems nice," Mike said. "I'm sure I can recruit some help in carrying you downstairs and getting you into the car. Maybe you can stretch out on the back seat. I think I have a pillow in the car. We could use your robe, too. It's in a Grand Hotel shopping bag; the rest of your clothes are in my suitcase."

Kelly seated herself again and the two continued to make small-talk. They discussed some of the island's landmarks that were now beginning to fade from view, the balmy weather, and their wedding plans.

At one point during the conversation, Kelly had placed a finger to his lips and unzipped her shorts. She had Mike bend down to see the clasped belts between her legs and the lit, red bulb. Mike shuddered as the seriousness of their predicament was brought home. During the past few minutes, he'd tried to divorce it from his mind. Kelly's attitude was amazing. He squeezed her hand again and kissed her as she zipped up her shorts.

As Mike was suggesting they should be docking in another ten minutes or so, the Millers appeared, coming up the stairway. Roy had his camera and took a couple of shots, one with Kelly and Mike at the rail, another with Mike kneeling down next to Kelly as she sat in the chair.

"You can caption this one as 'The Proposal'," Roy joked.

Roy and Martha explained they'd had so much fun they were thinking of staying in the area another full day, heading back to Canton early Tuesday morning.

"We know you're an expert on Mackinac Island, Kelly," Roy said with a grin. "How about the rest of this area? Any suggestions? A little sightseeing, maybe some gift shops for Martha to browse in. Notice I said browse, Martha, not shop," he added with a laugh.

"I've read about the Petoskey and Harbor Springs area," Martha said with a twinkle in her eye. "What do you think, Kelly?"

"A perfect choice! It would actually be my first recommendation."

"Where would you suggest we stay?" Roy asked.

Kelly thought for a moment before replying. "Probably the Perry Hotel in Petoskey. I think you'd enjoy it, it's an old historic hotel that's been refurbished. It has a wonderful dining room, and you can walk to the Gaslight shopping area."

"Sounds perfect!" Martha said. "Why don't we call from here and see if there's a room available?" she suggested, turning to her husband.

The horn sounded, indicating they were just about to dock.

"Can I help you get Kelly down the stairs, Mike?" Roy offered. "Better yet, I'll make arrangements for some of the crew to come up and carry her down. How's that?"

Kelly smiled and thanked him as Mike replied, "Would you? That would be great."

"Who knows?" Roy said. "Maybe Martha and I can come visit you at the hospital tomorrow."

Kelly glanced over at Mike and winked. The Millers were something else.

"There's our car, Roy. Trunk open and all set to go. They really do an efficient job, don't they?"

Kelly and Mike nodded. Martha had pointed out a Lincoln Town Car. Mike wondered if Kelly had noticed, and questioned why a Chevy dealer would be driving a Ford product. She'd begun thanking the Millers, saying she hoped their paths would cross again soon.

As Roy shook Mike's hand, he leaned over and whispered in his ear. "Does Kelly know about our little deception? Have you told her yet?"

Mike smiled and shook his head. He'd intended to, but with Kelly possibly wearing a listening device, he hadn't discussed it with her yet.

"I'm not sure I'm going to be," Mike whispered.

Roy blushed as he replied, "You're a good man, Mike."

As the Millers left, it dawned on Mike he hadn't given Stuart the signal to communicate again. He coughed and Stuart immediately said, "I wondered if you'd forgotten about us. Has anyone attempted to contact you, advise you on what you should do now?"

"No, nothing," Mike replied. "And Kelly hasn't heard anything, either."

He was taking a risk in saying so much, but Mike was hopeful Stuart would understand he was saying Kelly wasn't set up to hear any instructions.

"I read you," Stuart said. "You're still coming through clearly. One other thing. Kelly might not be wired after all. There was quite a stretch without any reading to suggest another listening monitor nearby. We picked up something again when your friends, the Millers, joined you, however. Did you happen to notice if he's wearing a hearing aid? Either of them, for that matter? I've never heard of one giving us the reading we've been getting, they're not supposed to. Technology changes so fast, though. That could be the problem."

Mike had wandered down the deck a few yards, with his back to Kelly, so his comments couldn't be picked up if there was a monitor on her.

"I didn't notice any hearing aids. Of course, I wasn't particularly looking."

"I'd still be cautious, Mike," Stuart replied. "I think if we were calling the shots, we'd have Kelly wired. This should all be over in a very short time." He seemed to realize that the statement hadn't been said as he'd intended. "I meant that in a positive way, that Kelly and you would be out of the woods. We're praying that will be the case."

"Thanks, Stuart. We are, too."

•

Kelly watched as Mike talked. The fact she might be wearing a mike had really confused things. So much was going unsaid. She wondered what Mike was being told, what he was saying. He looked concerned. She couldn't say, 'Penny for your thoughts,' because he probably couldn't tell her.

"Kelly."

She turned at the sound of her name and saw Roy's smiling face protruding from the stairwell.

"Just thought I'd tell you you're all set. They'll be up to get you as soon as the other passengers and luggage are off the boat. And Kelly, tell Mike they've already been tipped, handsomely."

"Thank you. That wasn't necessary. I hope you and Martha will enjoy Petoskey."

"I'm sure we will."

•

Mike was deep in thought, having some negative vibes about what Stuart had said. He recalled his thoughts when Terry Noonan had told him he didn't know the Millers, but he knew for sure he wasn't the Chevy dealer. He'd wondered then if they were possibly involved with the group trying to sabotage the meetings. He was having similar thoughts now. Was one of the Millers wearing a monitor? Was he being deceived again? He hadn't mentioned anything to Stuart about the Millers. Stuart could have easily verified whether or not they were really from Canton. He still could. As he pondered these questions, he strolled back toward Kelly.

As he approached, Kelly told him that Roy had made arrangements for some of the crew to help her get off the boat and into the car.

"It'll be a few minutes. They wanted to get the luggage unloaded first."

Mike nodded and smiled. Maybe his concerns were unwarranted. The Millers were probably as innocent as they appeared. Standing next to Kelly, he watched the activity on the dock. The dollies had been unloaded and he could see Kelly's suitcase on the dock, a few feet apart from where his sat with the shopping bag next to it. Most of the other luggage had been claimed, some bags being carried by people to their cars parked in the lot at the foot of the dock. Dock porters were assisting those who'd used the valet service, loading luggage into their trunks. One of the young men was helping the Millers.

Mike's eyes widened as he saw that one of the bags being loaded into the Millers' trunk was an exact duplicate of Kelly's suitcase, minus the red yarn identification.

"I'm going to check on something," Mike said to Kelly as he hurried toward the stairs. "I'll be right back."

One of the crew spotted Mike as he came hustling down the stairs. "We'll just be another minute or two, Mr. Cummings. We haven't forgotten you."

"I wasn't worried about that, but I'd like to ask you a question."

"Sure," the young man replied, nodding his head. "I hope I can answer it."

"On our way over, did you happen to notice if anyone . . ." Mike hesitated, considering how he could best phrase the question. "Did you notice anyone opening their luggage or shifting their bags around?"

"Do you think you're missing a bag?" the young man asked, rather than answering Mike.

Mike shook his head. The frustrated look on his face reminded the young man he hadn't answered Mike's question.

"No, I don't recall seeing—wait a minute. That friend of yours, the one who made arrangements to have us help you with your, is it wife?"

"Soon-to-be," Mike answered, anxious to hear the rest of the answer.

"He was getting some pain killers out of one of the suitcases for her."

"Can you describe the bag he opened?"

"I really can't, I was talking to his wife." He smiled. "She bombarded me with a whole bunch of questions."

To purposely distract him? Mike wondered as he looked to see the Millers' car just beginning to drive off. He darted over the gangplank and squinted at the license plate. An Ohio plate, he could just make out the numbers.

Could the Millers have possibly switched bags with Kelly's? Switched the yarn? Was it just a coincidence they had a bag identical to Kelly's? He'd learned not to believe in coincidences. He should notify Stuart.

"We can help you now," one of the other crew members was saying to Mike.

Do I ask them to wait a minute until I go up on deck and talk to Stuart? Mike wondered. No, it will have to wait.

"Fine," Mike answered him as he came back onto the boat and followed the two young men up the stairs.

One of them turned and said, "We can handle her, if you want to go out to your car and point out your luggage. One of our people will help you with it."

That would allow him to pass on the info to Stuart now. "I think I'll take you up on that," Mike said. "We're in the black Explorer."

•

Mike pointed out the three pieces to be loaded to one of the young men on the dock. Slipping him a two-dollar bill, he explained that two of his coworkers would be carrying Mike's fiancée off the boat in a minute or two.

Jumping into the front seat, Mike said, "Stuart, can you hear me?"

"Loud and clear, what's up?"

"Take this down, a Lincoln Town Car with an Ohio plate. The license number is PVN 913. It's the Millers' car, the people you heard us talking to."

Mike quickly spelled out his concerns to Stuart.

"Have you opened Kelly's suitcase, Mike?"

"I haven't had a chance to yet. I just wanted to fill you in rather than waiting. I was planning on pulling up at the other end of the dock and checking it. They're just coming with Kelly now."

"I understand," Stuart replied. "You also need to verify if the gear Kelly's wearing is still armed."

Mike hadn't been reprimanded, but two points had been made. Verify your suspicions before alarming us. Our hands are still tied as long as Kelly's in danger.

Mike jumped out of the Explorer and went around to open the passenger door for Kelly as the two young men approached with her. They'd locked their arms to form a chair on which she was sitting, her arms draped around their necks.

•

Mike adjusted the passenger seat as far back as it would go, to give Kelly plenty of leg room.

"I'm going to swing by the restrooms," he explained to Kelly. "How about you, do you need to stop?"

She shook her head. "That's not easy, I can wait."

Mike looked at her as he pretended to unzip his pants and bend down to look between his legs. She nodded, immediately picking up on his message. She unbuttoned her shorts and pulled the zipper down. Mike had stopped the vehicle and craned his neck to look as she glanced down.

Damn, the red light was still on. Putting his finger to his lips, he announced he'd only be a second or two. He clicked the rear window open and jumped out, moving to the rear of the vehicle. Reaching in, he laid Kelly's suitcase flat and unzipped it. As he raised the lid and saw the contents, he had mixed emotions. The suitcase was filled with magazines and a few newspapers. Kelly was looking over her shoulder at him and he twisted the bag around and tilted it so she could see. With a surprised look, she nodded her head.

•

"What's he doing?" Mark asked.

Fritz lowered the binoculars and replied, "I think he just opened Kelly's suitcase. I really can't see."

Fritz and Mark were parked in a corner of the lot over a hundred yards from where Mike had pulled over in the Explorer. Mary and Mitch were in a car closer to the entrance to the lot. The four had been flown over by helicopter and had just positioned themselves less than ten minutes ago.

Looking through the binoculars again, Fritz reported, "He's wandered over behind the restrooms. He's probably talking to Stu."

Mark nodded. They'd just been on the phone to Stuart a few minutes ago. Up to then, he'd told them that Kelly and Mike still hadn't received any added instructions. They were just planning to head to Petoskey. Stuart had warned Fritz to get no closer than a mile of them as they followed. That would hold true until he informed them Kelly was out of danger.

•

"I realize the switch could have been made earlier," Mike was saying to Stuart. "But don't you agree the duplicate suitcase has to be more than a coincidence? And I know, it could be they're playing games with us. Wanting us to assume the Millers made the switch."

Mike listened as Stuart explained they'd be checking to see whether a Roy and Martha Miller lived in Canton, Ohio, and whether they had a Lincoln registered in their names.

"They still hold the ace card though, with Kelly. Let me know the minute that light goes off."

If it does, Mike thought as he replied, "We'll be checking every few minutes."

"Just head to Petoskey," Stuart instructed. "I'll keep briefing you on any developments. You pull over if need be, if you have something to tell me."

Chapter 49

Mike winked at Kelly as he climbed into the front seat. "Sorry I took so long, there was a line. That should take care of me until Petoskey."

Kelly smiled, understanding his remarks were for the audience that was possibly listening. She pointed to her crotch, shaking her head, indicating to Mike the light was still on.

Mike wished they could talk without the fear of someone hearing every word. As he drove toward the exit, he spread the palm of his left hand and pretended to write on it with his other hand.

Kelly quickly picked up on his message and opened the glove compartment. She removed a note pad and then moved maps and other papers aside, searching for a pen or pencil.

Seeing what she was doing, he tapped her on the shoulder, holding up his hand. He reached into his pants pocket and removed the pen he'd used earlier. Taking the pad from Kelly, he put it on the center of the steering wheel and began writing.

"You'll have to direct me, Kelly," he said, turning left out of the lot, talking as he wrote.

"There will be a sign for Petoskey up there at the next light," Kelly said, picking up on his charade. A sign had been staring Mike in the face when he'd asked his question. "We'll turn right onto Highway 31 in about two or three miles. It leads us right into Petoskey."

Mike had finished writing and handed the note pad to Kelly. He'd written, 'Millers? I think they have your suitcase.'

She read what he'd written and then reread it a second time. She was already aware someone had switched bags with hers, or replaced its contents with magazines and newspapers. But the Millers? Why on earth would Mike think they were the ones involved?

She looked up at Mike with a questioning look. Could that be possible? Roy Miller was the one who'd supplied the photograph that had made it possible to identify two of the men who were involved. Why would he have done that if he and his wife were also involved? It didn't make sense.

Mike was merely nodding his head, indicating he believed what he'd written was true.

"Here's the turn up ahead, Mike." As she spoke, another thought flashed through her mind. Maybe Mike's suggesting an involvement with Stuart, the Bureau. Maybe the FBI recruited the Millers to make a switch with the suitcase. She peered down and looked between her legs. The light was still on.

She found it hard to believe that Stuart would put her at greater risk, gambling that the reaction of this group wouldn't be fatal to her when they discovered the switch had been made. She reached for the notepad and pen and wrote, 'Millers with FBI?,' and handed it to Mike.

He read it and looked up with a questioning look, which gradually changed to one of surprise, then concern.

Stuart began talking to Mike over the earphone as Mike grasped the meaning of Kelly's message.

"We were in luck," Stuart was saying. "The Millers' daughter had just stopped by the house to pick up the mail and the newspapers and answered the phone. She says her parents are on vacation, and she thinks they're on Mackinac Island."

"Has she spoken to them in the last day or so?" Mike asked, grimacing as he caught himself. *This has to be a one-way conversation unless I pull over.*

"The same question we asked, Mike. She hasn't, but says that's not unusual. She expects she might hear from them tomorrow, though. It's her father's sixtieth birthday. The Lincoln is registered in Roy Miller's name. Good credit reference. They've lived in the same house for over twenty-five years. He recently retired from a position in government service.

"They don't seem to fit the profile of the type of people we suspect are involved, Mike. I probably should have asked the daughter a few more questions, but I was having difficulty enough making up an excuse for my call. I should have had her give me a physical description of her parents. Roy Miller looks a little young for a sixty-year-old. There's a possibility these Millers switched identities with the real ones. But you have to admit, Mike, that would be stretching things a bit. I think your suspicions are probably unfounded, that the similar suitcase was just a coincidence."

Mike would have liked to respond, but he restrained himself as Stuart continued.

"You'll be interested to know that four of the wives have regained consciousness. Susan Merryweather has already interviewed two of them. Nothing much there. There were three people involved, all wearing ski masks. One may have been a woman. There was no talking, just the use of signs similar to flash cards to threaten the women and instruct them. They simply verified what we'd already learned from the carriage driver.

"I'm disappointed, though not surprised, that Kelly hasn't been disarmed. They're probably wanting ample time to clear the area. I suspect those responsible may be headed to the mainland on a later boat, with the letters and money. Fritz was probably right in assuming they'd make their move while Kelly's bag was being transported to the dock. I'd thought they'd wait until you arrived on the mainland. That's why I cautioned you to be on guard for them staging an accident of some sort and retrieving it from you then."

Stuart's voice was starting to fade and Mike was hearing the first sounds of static. He strained to listen as Stuart continued.

"Kelly and you are still my first priority. As a matter of fact, I still haven't told everyone the letters and money are missing."

The thought crossed Mike's mind that Stuart was probably referring to Fritz. Mike sensed that if Fritz was calling the shots, the danger to Kelly would be magnified.

Stuart's voice was even fainter as he discussed the possibility Kelly's apparatus might not be disarmed prior to their arrival in Petoskey.

"We really can't risk you entering the hospital. Maybe you could have a bite to eat while you're waiting for the light to go off. Probably best to go to some fast-food outlet and park in a remote corner of the lot. I . . . ."

His voice had completely faded out. Mike wondered if he should pull off to the side of the highway and get out and talk to Stuart. He really didn't have much to say, except to let him know he'd been able to hear most of what he'd said. He was in a line of cars; if he pulled off now, he might be delayed getting back into the flow of traffic. He decided to just keep moving. They were just approaching Pellston.

"You've heard of Pellston, haven't you, Mike?"

He'd nearly forgotten about her. He imagined the thoughts that must be racing through her mind, and how isolated she must feel, having no one to talk to.

"It usually has the coldest temperature in the state, or maybe it's just the lower peninsula. They have the area's major airport here, too."

Mike smiled. Kelly was doing her best to keep her spirits up. As he swerved to avoid a car which was making an abrupt turn in front of them, he tried to make small talk as well.

"You have to be getting a little hungry."

Kelly nodded. The Mackinac Island Fudge ice cream cone was a distant memory.

Chapter 50

"Damn that Stu, why didn't he tell us?" Fritz said, slamming his cellular phone down on the car seat next to him. He'd just been told about Kelly's suitcase by one of the other agents who'd answered his call to check on any new developments. The agent had inadvertently said something about the missing letters and money, believing Fritz and the others had previously been informed. Fritz quickly briefed Mark.

"I don't understand why, if that's the case, Stuart's still having us keep so far behind Mike's car," Mark said. "For that matter, why are we even following them? Shouldn't we be back watching for a familiar face on a later boat?"

"Probably to pick up the pieces," Fritz replied, grinning at Mark.

Mark shook his head, glaring at Fritz. "Sometimes . . ."

"Sometimes what?" Fritz asked.

"I find it hard to understand you," Mark replied.

"Don't you mean hard to tolerate me? Damn it, say what you really think."

Mark shook his head again and stared out the side window as Fritz accelerated and started to pass the car in front of them.

•

"I'm sorry," Rick was explaining to Stuart. "I thought you'd already told them."

"I can see why you would," Stuart replied. "I hadn't mentioned anything about the Millers, or Mike's suspicions either. I can probably use that as the reason I delayed informing them." I'll say I wanted to check the Millers out before saying anything, Stuart thought. He picked up the phone and dialed Fritz's number.

•

Ed Merryweather had overheard the conversation between Stuart and Rick. He sensed there had to be friction between Stuart and Fritz. Stuart had explained earlier how he'd vetoed Fritz's idea to maintain surveillance on the Grand Hotel dray. And Stuart now agreed that was probably when the group switched bags, or the contents of Kelly Travis's suitcase. This was going to make one hell of a story for the Town Crier, Merryweather thought. At the same time, he wondered how much of this story they'd be willing to let him and Susan tell. Maybe we'll collaborate on a book, he thought.

•

Stuart had just finished relating all the details about the Millers and Mike's suspicions to an irate Fritz. Surprisingly, Fritz had cooled off as he listened.

"I hear what you're saying, Stu," Fritz said as Stuart concluded. "And I know I've given Mike a pretty rough going over. But the man's no dummy. Besides that, he has law enforcement experience. I wouldn't totally discount his vibes or his hunches just yet, Stu. He may be onto something."

"That was my reaction too, until I spoke with the Millers' daughter. Everything she said pointed to their innocence. Maybe she just lulled me into discounting Mike's conjecture."

"Did you put an alert out for the Lincoln?" Fritz asked. "Has it been seen? If the Millers aren't heading to Petoskey, where you said Kelly suggested they go, that might tell us something, too."

"I didn't put anything out on the car. But I could call the Perry Hotel. Kelly not only suggested they visit Petoskey, I overheard her suggest where they stay and why. The Millers were going to call ahead for a room. I'll call now and see if they did."

•

Though Fritz had been exceeding the speed limit for the past ten miles or so, they still hadn't caught up to Kelly and Mike. Mark was scanning both sides of the highway, seeing if the Explorer might have pulled into a gas station or convenience store. He was also on the lookout for the Millers' Lincoln. Fritz had alerted Mary and Mitch, in the car behind them, to keep an eye out for the two vehicles as well.

Chapter 51

As Mike eased the Explorer to a stop at the traffic light, Kelly pointed, saying, "That's the turn for Harbor Springs. It's a very picturesque, upscale resort area. We'll have to go there someday. There's a beautiful drive along the shoreline in front of some huge, old Victorian homes. Most of them have old-fashioned front porches highlighted with colorful flower boxes."

Mike grinned as he replied, "Let's hope that visit is a little less exciting than the one to Mackinac. Maybe it's a possibility for a mini-honeymoon after the wedding. Not to replace Hawaii this winter, though. I still want to take you there."

"If that's the case, Harbor Springs might be a good choice," Kelly said, placing her hand on his and returning his smile.

The two had been very cautious in their conversation, knowing they were being overheard by Stuart and possibly others. As the light turned green and they started forward, Kelly said, "We're only about ten minutes or so from the hospital."

Send them a message, Mike thought as he said, "I'm really surprised we haven't been flagged down, that someone hasn't approached us yet to get your suitcase." He didn't want them to know that they were aware of the switch. "Stuart said we shouldn't risk going into the hospital while that device you're in is still armed. You need to get that ankle looked at as quickly as possible. Let's hope something happens soon. It's not fair for them to leave you traumatized like this for so long."

"What do we do if the bulb's still lit when we reach the hospital?" Kelly asked.

"Probably try to have a bite to eat in the parking lot of some fast-food outlet and just keep waiting, I guess."

•

"This looks like them, about four cars in front of us," Mark said.

Fritz nodded, having also seen the Explorer up ahead of them.

"Are you planning on catching up and pulling alongside of them?" Mark asked. "To let them know we're here?"

"I think we should," Fritz replied. "Stu was going to let them know about us, but I don't know if he was able to. When he called just now to tell us the Millers had made a reservation at the Perry, he also said he hadn't picked up any communication from Kelly and Mike for the past ten minutes or so. He assumes that's also probably true in the case of Mike, that he hasn't been hearing Stu. There's a remote possibility that Kelly's been disarmed. If that were the case though, I'm sure Mike would have stopped and called Stu on a pay phone. Unless Mike thinks Stu is still hearing him."

Mark was shaking his head. Seeing his reaction, Fritz continued. "I agree, everything suggests that the gear's still armed. Otherwise they would have stopped and gotten her out of that apparatus. If they'd stopped, we'd have caught up to them sooner than we have."

"And I'm sure Stu would have notified us right away if he'd heard from them," Mark replied. "Maybe it's best if we just hang back a little longer."

Fritz seemed to be weighing what would be accomplished by advising Kelly and Mike they were nearby. "I guess all we could offer is moral support at this stage," Fritz said. "I really empathize with the hell those two are going through."

Mark looked over at Fritz in surprise. Noticing him, Fritz laughed. "Hey, I'm not really the insensitive son-of-a-bitch I'm often made out to be. I think you're right, it's just a few more miles to the hospital. We'll hang back and see what happens."

•

"Maybe we should stay up here a few more days while you recuperate," Mike said. "We could sample Harbor Springs now."

"I really should get back though, Mike, and you should, too. I think David's leaving on Wednesday for a conference and we both have things we need to review with him before he leaves."

"That's true, it's the annual meeting of police chiefs, I think he said it's in Phoenix this year. But we could probably cover those items by phone tomorrow or Tuesday," Mike suggested. "Neither of us is indispensable, the troops can cover for us."

The implication of what he'd just said about not being indispensable suddenly dawned on Mike. If the explosives were ignited, they both would be history. It could happen anytime, either intentionally or by accident. As he opened his mouth and started to say something, Kelly gasped and shouted, "The light's off!" A huge smile appeared on his face as he reached out to squeeze her hand.

"We need to get you out of that device right away." Mike silently mouthed his next statement. "And notify Stuart, too."

Kelly nodded in understanding as they both looked for a spot they could turn off which would allow them some privacy. They'd just entered Bay View. Old, well-kept homes lined both sides of the road, many decorated with U.S. flags.

"It's Sunday night, Mike. This is an historic, Methodist cottage community. Most of the residents in this area will be attending a program of some sort up there on the hill at this time of the evening. You can probably take any of these streets to the right, down towards the lake."

As Mike turned at the next street, he smiled at Kelly. "You continue to amaze me with your knowledge about this area."

As Kelly had indicated, no one seemed to be home in the houses they passed. There were only a few. The road dead-ended at the waterfront, less than a hundred yards from the highway. Mike immediately jumped out of the vehicle, rushing around to the passenger side to assist Kelly. She already had the door open and was sliding out of the seat. He grasped her under the armpits and eased her to her feet.

Testing the injured ankle, she grimaced a little, but said, "It really feels pretty good, Mike."

"Maybe by comparison. I can see you're still in pain."

"Not much, really," she replied, standing and letting her shorts fall around her ankles. Mike was on his knees in front of her. With a little prayer, he reached up and slowly disconnected the clamp holding the belts between her legs. Even though the lamp wasn't lit, his hands were shaking, fearful the bulb had merely burned out and the device was still activated.

They both sighed in relief as the detached belts dangled between her legs. Kelly slipped out of the windbreaker and quickly unbuttoned her blouse. Mike helped her remove it and watched as she unzipped the vest.

Moving behind her, he carefully assisted her as she eased the contraption off her shoulders. Though he'd expected the gear to be heavy, he was still amazed to find it weighed so much. And she never mentioned it, never complained.

They heard the sound of soft clapping directly behind them and quickly turned. Fritz and Mark were both applauding with broad smiles on their faces. Mike was holding the harness device in his hands. Kelly, clad in only her bra and panties, her shorts around her ankles, raised her right arm to cover her chest.

"We can relieve you of that, Mike," Fritz said, reaching for the gear.

"Then give you some privacy, Kelly," Mark said.

"We'll wait over there while Kelly's getting dressed," Fritz said, taking it from Mike. "Then we can talk, update one another."

Kelly started to pull up her shorts. "These are pretty dirty, Mike, my blouse too. It's also starting to cool off. I think I'll change."

"I have all your clothes in my bag," Mike said. "Just tell me what you want."

"Maybe those tan slacks with the matching dark-blue and tan golf shirt. Get the dark blue cardigan sweater, too, please."

Mike hadn't moved. "First, can I just give you a hug?" He glanced over his shoulder and saw the two men had moved off about thirty yards, with their backs turned. Stepping forward, he embraced Kelly and she placed her hands around his waist, giving him a big hug. Tilting back, he leaned down and kissed her, a long, lingering kiss.

As they broke apart, Kelly sighed. "With all that love, I'm not even chilly."

He laughed, remembering she was clad only in her underwear. "I'll have your clothes in a minute. How about shoes?"

"Why not? These might be better for my ankle, but why don't I try on those dark blue flats."

Mike nodded as he opened the rear door of the vehicle. "You must have illusions of meeting one of those handsome, young doctors we see on TV."

"Not so, Mike, not so," Kelly replied, grinning. "It's just for my best beau, you."

•

It had only taken Kelly a matter of minutes to dress. As Mike helped her into the sweater, he called out to the two men. They immediately turned and came toward them. Observing Kelly and her different attire, Fritz whistled.

If you'd done that earlier, you'd have had a fat lip, Mike felt like saying. But it was evident the whistle had been meant as a compliment.

Mark was also impressed by Kelly's appearance and grinned as he said, "The people in Emergency are going to find it hard to believe you need their services, Kelly."

"It's really remarkable after the ordeal you've gone through," Fritz added. "You look fabulous! Mike's a lucky guy."

Mike nodded in agreement as he glanced at a blushing Kelly.

"We'll need to update Stu," Fritz said. "I'm sure he'll be relieved. Mike's aware, and you might be too, Kelly, that he put a freeze on us. Now we can try to undo what's happened. Try to apprehend everyone involved. We all realize the odds are heavily weighed against us. First, we need to recover the letters prior to any copies being made. Otherwise, they'd have them to use against us, to use with the news media or in court."

"We want to at least try to identify who's involved," Mark said. "So we could at least keep them under surveillance, make sure they really are closing up shop. This gear they had you in, Kelly, could be of help. Maybe we'll be able to piece together the origin of the parts. We also need your suitcase—or the one they left in its place. Have you been able to tell if this one's yours?"

Kelly shook her head as Mike replied, "She hasn't had a chance to. We can check while you're contacting Stuart. I should give you these, too," Mike said as he removed the miniature receiver from his ear, untucking his shirt to reach for the hidden microphone.

"Fine," Fritz said as he took them from Mike. "I'm sure Stuart will want to talk to both of you," he suggested. "I was hoping your hunch that the Millers were involved would prove out, Mike. I'm sorry it doesn't seem to be."

Kelly was confused. Hadn't Mike implied that Stuart and his people might have recruited the Millers to switch bags? That thought ran counter to what Fritz and Mark were indicating now. Are they still attempting to hide the fact they had, increasing the risk to her? No, she reasoned, those people wouldn't have disarmed the apparatus she'd been wearing if they didn't have the letters and money. As these thoughts and questions swirled through Kelly's mind, Mike was continuing to talk about the Millers.

"I'd love to get the opportunity to open their suitcase to make sure," Mike was saying.

"Maybe you can," Fritz replied. "According to Stu, they took Kelly's suggestion and made a reservation at the Perry Hotel."

Mike shook his head. "That certainly doesn't lend credence to my suspicions. If they were involved, you'd think they'd want to just disappear now."

"Not necessarily, Mike," Fritz replied. "By not disappearing, by following through on Kelly's suggestion to stay at the Perry Hotel, they divert suspicion. We could be dealing with some very clever pros. We really don't have much else to work with, unless we learn something from Stu. I don't think we should give up on the Millers yet."

"We could stop at the Perry Hotel on our way to the hospital," Kelly suggested. "It's right on the way."

"Good idea, let's get Stu on my car phone first and then we'll be on our way."

As Fritz was calling Stuart, Mark explained that Mary and Mitch had been following them in another car.

"We told them to continue on to the Perry Hotel and we'd catch up to them there."

Kelly glanced at Mike, surprised to hear a stop at the Perry had already been planned. Either they shared Mike's suspicions regarding the Millers, or Mary and Mitch were going on ahead to retrieve the letters and money from them. Kelly was anxious to talk to Mike in private. She was still having difficulty fathoming the possibility the Millers were part of the group who'd caused all this havoc—a murder, kidnappings and torture.

•

The phone call to Stuart had been a short one. He was overjoyed to hear Kelly was safe and unharmed. He informed them that all the wives had regained consciousness and were alert, without any apparent signs of side effects following their traumatic experience. Though not optimistic, and mainly at Mike's urging, he gave his blessing to tracking down the Millers and hopefully, learning for certain whether or not they were involved.

"Remember the legal boundaries though, Fritz. We don't need the Millers making a public issue of being harassed by the Bureau. And don't get the idea you can conceal the Bureau's involvement by putting Mike or

Kelly up to something. And they certainly don't need added problems after what they've been through. Understood?"

"Yes, boss," Fritz answered, chuckling. "Anything else?"

•

Mike was shaking his head. "No, to tell you the truth the thought the Millers had been enlisted by Stuart had never crossed my mind until your note. I don't think he'd have done anything to put you in added jeopardy. If I'd thought he or maybe Fritz, without Stuart's knowledge, had arranged for the Millers to switch suitcases, I'd have been even more terrified than I was. But I can easily see why you were having those thoughts."

Kelly and Mike were finally alone without the fear of being over-heard as Mike continued. "If what you thought was true, I don't see the motivation for them to keep up the charade. You're safe now. I'd think they'd level with us. There's the possibility that Fritz might have worked some-thing out with the Millers on his own and doesn't want Stuart to know just yet. I still don't trust him the way I do Stuart."

"Anything's possible, I guess," Kelly said. "I'm relieved my assump-tion was probably wrong. And I tend to agree that Stuart wouldn't have been a party to it. He seemed genuinely concerned about me. It's the next turn to the left, Mike. That's the Perry over there."

•

Mike and Kelly had led the way because of her familiarity with the area. Fritz and Mark were just behind them as they drove into the parking lot and each of them found a space to pull into.

As Kelly and Mike climbed out of the Explorer, they noticed Mary and Mitch walking across the parking lot toward them. Fritz and Mark had parked a couple of spaces away and were also exiting their car. Mike no-ticed Kelly was still limping slightly as they approached Mary and Mitch.

"Do you think we should just head to the hospital and leave this to them?" he asked her.

Shaking her head, Kelly replied, "No way. I'm really in pretty good shape. Just a touch of pain, I'm sure it's just a sprain."

"Their Lincoln's parked over there," Mitch said, pointing to the other side of the lot. "We looked inside, but we didn't see anything."

"How about the trunk?" Mike asked.

Mary glanced at Mitch and then answered, "We didn't want to risk causing any damage by prying it open without input from the rest of you." She was directing the statement to Fritz and Mark, who had now joined them.

Fritz thought for a moment, stroking his chin. "It's probably best if we go in and confront them, get their permission to open the trunk. They may have taken the suitcase up to their room with them, anyway. I'd certainly think they would."

Heads were nodding as Mike glanced at Kelly. He smiled as he said, "I might have a solution. The Millers' daughter told Stuart that her father's birthday was tomorrow, his sixtieth. Lincolns have a combination door lock. We could try his birth date, people often use it."

Fritz also smiled as he replied, "It's worth a try."

As they moved across the lot toward the Millers' car, all of them glanced around to see if they were being observed. The lot appeared to be deserted except for the six of them.

Fritz entered the date into the digital panel on the outside of the driver's side door. They all could hear the sound of the lock being triggered. Mitch slapped Mike on the back as Fritz opened the car door and looked for the button to open the trunk.

"I think the ignition has to be on," Mark said as Fritz pushed the button. They all could hear the trunk snap open.

"Guess not," Fritz said as his face broke into a smile.

Mark quickly moved to the rear of the Lincoln. "It's here!" he exclaimed as he reached inside the trunk, hoisting the bag out by its handle.

"Lay it down on the trunk of this car," Fritz suggested, pointing to the Buick Park Avenue next to the Lincoln. Mark did so and immediately proceeded to unzip the suitcase.

They all stared in amazement. The bag was filled with packets of cash. They all exchanged looks. Kelly reached out to grab Mike's hand, realizing how elated he must be to have had his hunch pan out.

"I'll be damned!" Mitch said.

"Should I get Kelly's bag and make a switch?" Mark asked Fritz.

He nodded. "Remember, you'll have to remove the yarn from hers."

As Mark dashed back to his and Fritz's car, where they'd placed Kelly's suitcase, Fritz was moving his hands through the stacks of money. "The letters aren't here. They must have removed them. Hopefully, they still have them."

The others were nodding, realizing the possibility the Millers might have already passed them on to someone.

Mark approached with Kelly's suitcase and placed it in the trunk of the Lincoln, carefully maneuvering it into the same spot the other bag had been, and then closed the trunk.

"It's a whole new ball game," Fritz announced, smiling again. "I suppose we should advise Stu, think out where we go from here."

Fritz turned and started back towards his car. Mark zipped the suitcase containing the money back up, motioning to Mitch that he could have the privilege of carrying it.

•

Stuart was awed by their news. Fritz used the speaker phone to enable everyone to hear the conversation. Initially, Stuart reacted in anger, thinking Fritz and the others were in cahoots, teasing him. As Fritz sung Mike's praises, describing how they'd opened the trunk, Stuart realized that wasn't the case.

"Just a minute," Stuart said, "I'll get Rick involved. I'll have him try to reach the Millers' daughter again. We'll see if she can fax a recent photo of her parents to us, or at least provide a description."

Fritz shook his head as they waited for Stuart to come back on the line. "We should be deciding our next move here. I think Stu's going off on a tangent."

"I heard you, Fritz. Think about it. What do we have? An illegal search. A possible accusation of having planted evidence. Though I'd love to see the looks on their faces when they open that suitcase and see it was switched on them this time, I'm thinking you should switch them back.

"If it works out as I think it could, we can get a warrant for their arrest to you in the next couple of hours—for car theft and suspicion of kidnapping. You can keep an eye on the car and hopefully, arrest them as they're getting in it. Search them and the car and discover the suitcase with the money then."

"That could be sometime tomorrow, Stuart," Mitch remarked. "Shouldn't we be trying to get our hands on those letters sooner than that?"

"I'm with you," Stuart replied. "I'm not suggesting the warrant for their arrest is our only option. I think we can safely assume they still have the letters with them. If they'd passed them on to someone, chances are they would have passed on the money, too.

"We need to put a plan in place which could also lead us to the others involved." Stuart was speaking slowly. They could tell he was mapping one out as he spoke. "You'll need to determine if they've made any calls from their room. If so, to whom and where. My hunch is they probably made contact on a public phone. Perhaps at the same time they called the Perry to make a reservation. The Perry staff should be questioned to see if anyone recalls the Millers using a phone in the lobby.

"The ideal thing would be to intercept the physical delivery of those letters. Tie in at least one person other than the Millers. We have to realize they could have had an envelope prepared in advance and already mailed the letters. If they still have them, chances are they're in their hotel room. They'd be pretty bulky to carry around, but I suppose Mrs. Miller could do that in a large purse. They haven't been there long. Let's hope they've taken Kelly's suggestion and are having dinner in the hotel. On the basis of us soon having warrants, for the Millers' arrest and a search warrant, you may be able to obtain a key to the Millers' room and conduct a search while they're at dinner. Once they're back in the room, it'll be more difficult. You'd have to use some sort of ruse to get both of them out of the room. You'd have to be careful, we don't want to alert them. And we've seen they're pretty clever, smart enough to see through anything I can think of now.

"Give it some thought. You're pretty creative, Fritz. But don't get too cute. If you set up a false alarm, a fire drill, chances are the first thing they'd grab to take with them would be the letters. Let's hope a ruse isn't necessary, that you can get in the room before we're able to get the warrant."

"We'll think of something," Fritz said. "I'm sure we can either sweet-talk or scare the Perry staff into cooperating."

"You'll need to keep close tabs on the Millers in case anyone contacts them," Stuart continued. "I know they'll recognize you and Mary, Fritz. You were with me when I gave those photographs to him. How about the two of you—Mitch and Mark?"

The two agents exchanged looks. Mitch appeared ready to say the Millers shouldn't recognize them when Mark said, "They saw us outside the men's room in the lower lobby of the Grand when Mike was talking to them. It was very brief, they might not remember our faces."

"Better not chance it, the risk's too great. I'll see how soon I can get some of the local police, possibly State Police, over to help you. Most of us will fly down as soon as possible—"

"Mike and I could help," Kelly volunteered. "We could see if we could join them for dinner, stay glued to them the same way they tried to do with us. We can say the visit to the emergency room was a quick one and the doctor said I only had a sprain. I can say they took x-rays and I'm supposed to stop back in the morning."

"But you should have that ankle attended to, Kelly," Mike said. "Maybe Mary could take you and I can tell the Millers they're keeping you overnight."

Mary was nodding her head, agreeing to Mike's suggestion.

Kelly smiled. "My ankle's really feeling quite good, it probably is just a sprain. I could go there later tonight after dinner, after the Millers have turned in."

"That's probably the best bet, Kelly, if you're sure you're up to it," Stuart said. "I feel guilty about what we've put you through already, though. Mike's suggestion is a good alternative. It's your decision. The rest of you should be on the lookout for any of the local police or state troopers I enlist. Do you have a suggestion as to where they could meet you? Also for the people who will hopefully be bringing you the warrants?"

"We need to have someone watching the Millers' car," Fritz said. "Why don't we say the entrance drive to the parking lot at the rear of the Perry."

"Fine. I'll keep in touch. We'll probably see you in about two hours."

Chapter 52

Fritz was on the phone talking to the Perry Hotel's manager. The decision had been made to obtain a room for Kelly and Mike near the Millers' room, hopefully next door or across the hall. He was also going to try to secure a room with ready access to the parking lot and from which the Millers' car could be easily observed. His main objective in making the call, however, was to lay the groundwork for gaining access to the Millers' room. They were all in agreement that Fritz should try to accomplish as much as he could on the phone, rather than risk the possibility of being seen by the Millers at the registration desk while arranging to speak to the manager.

Mitch and Mark had switched the suitcases again while Fritz had been on the phone. He'd been talking for nearly ten minutes. He smiled as he hung up and stepped out of his car to brief them on his conversation.

"Good news and bad news," he began. "First the good news. The

Millers just went into the dining room a couple of minutes before I called. Mr. Miller stopped by the offices about twenty minutes ago and asked to use the copy machine. He made his own copies and tipped the registration clerk twenty dollars. The assistant manager, who I've been talking to, questioned her while I was holding on the line. She says Miller made about twenty copies, one copy each of a stack of papers he had with him. She believes he took everything back up to his room before they came down to dinner."

Everyone's faces were beaming as Mary clenched her fist and raised it in the air to indicate 'right on.' This meant the Millers still had the letters, that they hadn't passed them on yet.

Fritz was grinning at their reactions as he continued. "We've also had another lucky break. Miller asked to use their fax machine. Fortunately for us, it's down. A repairman is supposedly on his way. Miller was told it should be working by the time he and his wife were finished having dinner."

"We are in luck," Mark said. "Did you happen to ask if anyone saw whether Mrs. Miller was carrying a handbag, and the size of it?"

"I did, and no one recalls one way or the other. The letters and copies might be in their room. But here's where the bad news sets in. The Perry Hotel is under the same management—ownership—as the Bay View Inn. We passed it just before Mike turned off the highway. A couple of years ago there was an incident at the Bay View with some striking similarities to what we're involved with here. A man and woman had checked in who closely resembled the description of a couple who had just pulled off a major bank robbery. They were having dinner at the Inn while the police searched their room. The Inn provided a key and the room number. It was a case of mistaken identity."

Glancing over at Kelly with a smirk on his face, Fritz continued. "When the police searched the couple's luggage, they found an assortment of kinky sex toys. One of the officers involved must have told someone and I'm sure the story was embellished as it spread. The couple was celebrating an anniversary. The man was the superintendent of schools in a town just south of here, Charlevoix. The end result was the man lost his job and the couple ended up leaving the area. But not before instituting a major lawsuit against the Bay View Inn. There was a costly settlement."

Heads were nodding, they were seeing where Fritz was headed.

"I think I mentioned, it was the assistant manager I spoke to and he's trying to reach his boss. But as it stands now, he's not about to tell us the Millers' room number, let alone provide us with a key. I have rooms for us, but I've no idea where yours is in relation to the Millers," Fritz said to Kelly and Mike. "He indicates the other room is ideal for us, with ready access to and a complete view of the parking lot."

"So, what do we do?" Mitch asked.

"I've been thinking of two possibilities. First, call Stu and see how he's doing, how he's coming along with obtaining the search warrant and the warrant for the Millers' arrest. It's a big if, but if he's been successful, we could perhaps have the judge who signed them, or will be signing them, call the Perry. That might work. In a town this size, they might well be personally acquainted." He laughed. "The ideal would be to have them faxed to the Perry, but what's been a blessing in the one instance presents a problem now. Besides, I doubt if the warrants have been prepared and signed yet. As we all know, that can often be a time-consuming process.

"I think we should get Kelly and Mike into that dining room, to hopefully team up with the Millers, just as quickly as possible. Don't even take time to go to your room, we'll take your luggage up. You might want to put on a sweater or blazer, Mike. Kelly's fine with what she's wearing. You could use the downstairs restrooms to freshen up.

"The two of you could ask the Millers about their room, the view," Fritz suggested. "Volunteer your room number and see if they do the same. You'll have to be subtle, but it could work. Mike could excuse himself to go to the men's room and pass the information on to us. That's probably our best hope, unless any of you have a better idea."

"Sounds good to me," Kelly said. "I think we might be able to pull it off, don't you, Mike?"

He nodded. Any qualms about being a party to an illegal search had vanished after the ordeal Kelly had been put through.

•

Fritz phoned Stuart while Mike made a quick change with Kelly's help. He donned a fresh shirt, switched over to his loafers and slipped on a blue blazer.

Mark came forward to meet Mike and Kelly as they came back to Fritz's car. Mike was carrying his suitcase and the Grand Hotel shopping bag.

"We'll get those up to your room for you," Mark said, reaching for the two items. "We'll check the two of you in while you're using the rest rooms, get you a key and let you know your room number."

Fritz had just finished his call as they approached his car. "We'll have to rely on your ingenuity," he said to Kelly and Mike. "They were able to reach the daughter again and she's described her parents as tall and slender. She's going to fax a photo. Stu and the local police have had a problem rounding up a judge, though. We might not get the warrants until tomorrow morning. I thought he might have a problem.

"You stay here, Mitch, and watch the car," Fritz instructed. "The locals should be here soon, you can be on the lookout for them. We'll let you know as soon as we have a room." Looking at the others, he said, "Let's get a move on."

Chapter 53

The hostess greeted Kelly and Mike with a smile as they entered the dining room. "Good evening. Will it just be the two of you tonight?"

As Kelly and Mike nodded, the Millers noticed them from across the room. They broke into smiles as Roy jumped up from his chair and started towards them. The hostess had just started to lead them to a table.

"We'll just say hello to our friends first," Mike explained to her. The young woman smiled and told them there was no hurry, to take their time.

"We didn't expect to see you so soon," Roy said as he approached. "You look fantastic, Kelly! Have you been to the hospital yet? Any report?"

"They think it's just a nasty sprain," Kelly replied. "They took some x-rays and want me to check back with them in the morning. They're real efficient, they had us in and out in a matter of minutes."

"I would say so," Roy responded. "Your suggestion of this place was perfect, Kelly. Martha's delighted. Would the two of you care to join us? We're just starting our salads."

Kelly glanced at Mike, thinking how perfectly this had worked out. "We'd love to, wouldn't we, Mike?"

He smiled at Roy as he nodded in agreement.

The hostess had overheard their conversation and led them over to the Millers' table. Kelly gripped Mike's arm, limping ever so slightly as they crossed the room. Martha rose to warmly greet them.

"This is wonderful!" she exclaimed. "I hope you're feeling as good as you look, Kelly." Glancing at Mike, she added, "And you look pretty dapper yourself. I didn't mean to ignore you."

As they seated themselves, Martha gushed over how pleased she and Roy were with Kelly's suggestion of Petoskey and the Perry Hotel.

"And driving through Bay View on the way here, what a charming area. We plan some sightseeing tomorrow. When we were checking in, another couple was raving about Harbor Springs."

"Are you pleased with your room?" Kelly asked.

"Nothing special, but yes, it's nice," Martha replied. "We have a view of the water. But we probably won't be spending all that much time in our room anyway."

"What's our room number, Mike?" Kelly wasn't wasting any time, Mike thought as he answered, "Two-Eighteen."

"Why, that's close to ours," Roy said. "We're in—"

The hostess had been standing with menus in her hand and picked that precise moment to interrupt, asking, "Would either of you care for a cocktail? Sherry is your waitress tonight, but I can help with a drink order. Would you like to see our wine list?"

"Oh, you'll like Sherry," Martha said. "You'd think she was still in college, but she has three kids, two boys and a girl. The oldest is nine."

"I'll just have a glass of iced tea," Kelly said to the hostess, who was patiently waiting with a friendly smile on her face.

"Make that two," Mike said.

"That's right, they probably have you on medication of some kind for the pain, don't they, Kelly? Best not to mix booze with pain killers," Martha said, laughing. "You're nice to keep her company, Mike. I hope our wine doesn't bother you."

"Not at all," Kelly said. "We were just talking about our rooms."

"Yes, you must have the same view we do," Martha said. As she talked, Kelly noticed the large handbag which was hung over the back of Martha's chair. "We're just . . ." She noticed Kelly staring at her handbag.

"Do you like my bag? Roy bought it for me as a birthday gift a couple of years ago, in Boston. It's great, I can carry just about anything in it." She lowered her voice to a whisper as she continued. "When we're traveling, I always keep my jewelry and other valuables in it. Roy's camera's in it now."

Kelly and Mike were having the same thoughts. Twice they'd come close to learning the Millers' room number. They should keep trying even though the letters and the copies were probably in that handbag.

"I'll get your orders in right away so you can catch up with Mr. and

Mrs. Miller, if you've decided?"

Kelly and Mike looked up into the smiling face of the attractive young lady who was ready to take their order.

"Sherry, you haven't even told them about your specials yet," Martha reprimanded her. "Just hearing you describe them whet our appetites."

"Oh, I'm sorry. I thought you may have told them."

"Even if we did, we couldn't do them justice like you do. We had a difficult time choosing, didn't we, Roy? They all sounded so good. Roy's having the duck and I'm having the whitefish."

Sherry was charming. She told Kelly and Mike about the specials and also described some of the popular items on the regular menu.

•

During dinner, Martha and Roy had asked Kelly numerous questions about the area, what to see, shops they shouldn't miss, and a suggestion for lunch tomorrow. Mike was pondering how best to again broach the subject of what room the Millers were in. During a pause in the conversation, he asked, "So you think your room's pretty identical to ours?"

"We're not sure about that," Martha said, glancing at her husband. "But it's easy enough to find out. Our rooms are close to one another. When we go up, we can show you our room."

"It would save Kelly a few steps if we just had a look at theirs, we go right past it," Roy suggested.

"That's fine with us," Kelly said, smiling at Mike. "You might have to run up ahead of us though, Mike, and make sure we're presentable. We hurried so fast to get down here before the dining room closed."

Mike had gotten the message. Fritz and some of the others might be in their room, using it as a staging area. They'd have to be warned.

"Oh, that won't bother us," Martha was saying. "But we don't have to do it tonight, we could wait until tomorrow."

•

Mary walked over to the house phone to call Fritz. She and Mark had taken turns in the lobby, in hopes Mike would come out and tell them the Millers' room number. She'd just strolled by the dining room and could see the waitress clearing Kelly's plate.

"I don't think they've been successful, Fritz. The waitress is just starting to take their plates."

"Damn! I was getting worried that might be the case. Listen carefully. When we checked in, I noticed they have the old-fashioned room slots for keys and messages. I'm going to call and leave a message for the Millers. I'll say I'm calling to confirm their dinner reservation for tomorrow night. There's a brochure on our table, the Pier in Harbor Springs seems to be a popular spot. Go to the front desk and ask them some questions. Hopefully, you'll be able to see the room number of the slot the note is placed in."

•

Mike wished he was still wearing the hidden mike. Fritz, or whoever was listening, would have been able to have heard how close he and Kelly had come to learning the Millers' room number. They could also have probably heard Martha's comments on the handbag and drawn the same conclusion he had.

Sherry was asking if they'd saved room for dessert. Smiling and cracking a few jokes, Martha and Roy assured her they had. It was fun to watch the Millers' expressions as Sherry described the desserts with the same flair as she had the main menu. Martha and Roy were able to convince Kelly and Mike to join them. She chose a scoop of Mackinac Island Fudge ice cream, and he opted for cherry pie a la mode.

Kelly was still finding it difficult to comprehend the Millers' involvement. They seemed so genuine, seemingly without a care in the world, taking time to enjoy their lives and one another. But I saw the suitcase of money in their trunk, heard Fritz tell us about the letters being copied, and Stuart's description of the real Millers from Canton, Ohio. Still, something didn't feel right.

"Oh, this is so good!" Martha said. "Would you like a taste?"

Kelly smiled and shook her head, but Mike sampled a small bite.

"You made a good choice," he said, gesturing to Kelly that she might want to reconsider.

•

Mary was running out of questions. She'd been conversing with the young man at the registration desk for nearly five minutes. As she searched

184

her mind for another possible question to ask, a young woman came through the door behind the young man. She caught Mary's stare and smiled. She was carrying several slips of paper in her hand. Mary watched over the young man's shoulder as the woman proceeded to put them in room slots.

She was elated to see the first slip being put in the slot for Room 217. Even though they'd refused to cooperate in regards to revealing the Millers' room number, it appeared they'd given Mike and Kelly the room across the hall. A second slip was being placed in the slot for Room 228. The woman checked the room number again on the last message, before placing it in slot 214.

Three options, Mary thought, committing the three room numbers to memory as she thanked the young man, apologizing for having taken so much of his time. She immediately headed toward the house phones and relayed the information to Fritz.

•

"Kelly, I think I'll go and phone the hospital and see if anyone's had a chance to review those x-rays yet. There's no sense in going up to the room if by chance they want to see you again tonight."

"Fine, want me to come, too?" Kelly replied, sensing Mike was trying to save her a few steps in that they'd probably be heading to the emergency room right away.

"No, that shouldn't be necessary," Mike answered with a grin. "I'll just be a minute or two, back before you're finished with your coffee."

•

Mike spotted Mary near the house phones as he came out of the dining room. She also noticed him and started to wander down the opposite corridor, where he caught up with her.

"We came close, but we weren't able to find out their room number. Mrs. Miller has a rather large handbag with her. I think the two sets of letters may be in it."

Mary nodded and explained how they'd been able to obtain three room possibilities. "One's right across the hall from yours, the other two are close by, in the same corridor."

"This may help," Mike immediately replied. "The Millers told us we'd be passing our room on the way to theirs. That's why I came out ahead of them. We're going to be stopping by our room with the Millers, and we didn't want to walk in on any of you."

Mary nodded. "That does help, it points to Room 228. How much time do you think before you'll be coming upstairs? Maybe you can stall them. Fritz and Mark are probably upstairs now. I'll go up and let them know what you've told me. You're probably right about the letters being in her handbag, but we can still hope it's otherwise and search their room."

•

Mark knocked on the door of 217 and there'd been no response. As Fritz watched, he used a small tool to unlock the door. Opening it, they were surprised to see the safety chain was connected.

"What the hell! Can't you read? We hung the do not disturb sign on the door." The man glaring at them had a sheet draped around his waist. "Who are you?"

Fritz responded by saying, "Please excuse us, they must have given us the wrong room number. We thought our wives were here."

The man laughed. "I hope it's not your wife." As he closed the door in their faces, he mumbled, "Okay, no harm done."

"I felt sure that was the room," Fritz said. "That they'd given Kelly and Mike the room across the hall. Let's try 214."

They moved down the corridor and knocked on the door, once again getting no answer. Mark had them inside the room in a matter of seconds.

"I'll check the closet while you're going through the dresser drawers," Mark suggested.

Fritz nodded, hurriedly moving over to the bureau and pulling open a drawer.

Mark was inside the closet when he heard Fritz laughing. He came out to see him holding up a tiny pair of ladies' bikini underpants.

"These sure can't be Mrs. Miller's. It must be 228."

•

Mike had come back to the table and explained that the doctor who'd examined Kelly wanted to see her again.

"He suggests now, this evening, while he's still there."

"Oh, that's too bad," Martha said. "I certainly hope that doesn't mean there's a break after all. If it's not too late, past midnight, when you get back, give us a call. We're in Room 228. We'll be anxious to hear what they have to say."

Kelly thanked her for her concern and suggested they could slip a message under their door. She couldn't help but smile, finally having discovered the Millers' room number.

As they passed the registration desk, the young man at the desk called out to Mr. Miller.

"I'm glad I saw you, I was just getting ready to call your room. I'm sorry, but our fax machine still isn't working. We can receive, but we can't send. They're saying they'll have us a new machine by noon tomorrow."

Was that true, Kelly wondered, or had Fritz arranged to have that message communicated?

"No problem," Roy replied to the young man. "I'm in no hurry."

"Look Roy, I think there's something in our box," Martha said.

"Seems to be," he replied, telling the young man their room number.

Roy looked baffled as he read the message on the slip of paper he'd been handed.

"It's a message with our name, confirming a dinner reservation for tomorrow night," he explained to Martha. Addressing the young man, he said, "You must have some other Millers registered, we're heading back to Ohio tomorrow afternoon."

"I don't think so, but I'll check," the young man said as Roy handed the slip back to him.

Mike remembered his conversation with Mary and thinking quickly, said, "That note may be my doing, Roy. I was going to surprise Kelly, but I made a dinner reservation for tomorrow night and was hoping the two of you might join us, our treat. I gave them both our names. They were booked solid, but said they'd get back to us if something did clear. I wasn't going to say anything until I was sure we had a reservation."

"Oh, how nice, Mike," Martha said. "Do you think we could stay an extra day, Roy?"

He grinned. "Why not? Especially since Mike says it's his treat."

Mike noticed there was something in the slot under his and Kelly's room number and asked the young man to check for him. "I'm Mr. Cummings."

The young man handed him two faxes. Glancing at the top copy, Mike saw it was a photograph of a man and woman. He quickly folded the sheets and tucked them into the pocket of his blazer.

"Hope it's not bad news," Roy said.

Mike smiled. "No, just an update from the office that I'd asked them to send me."

"Ready to head up, Roy?" Martha asked. "These two are probably anxious to get over to the hospital."

"Do you think I should go up and get your cosmetics kit, in case they want to keep you overnight?" Mike asked Kelly.

"Might be wise," she replied. "It would save you a trip. I sure hope that's not the case, though."

"We'll go up with you, Mike," Martha said. "You can give us a peek at your room, we'll see if it's the same as ours."

"Maybe we should stay and keep Kelly company," Roy suggested.

"That would be nice," Mike said. "It should only take me a minute or two to get her stuff. We'll show you the room tomorrow."

•

Mark had quickly obtained entry to Room 228. The three hurriedly began searching for the letters and the copies. Fritz lifted the mattress and peered underneath as Mary began to go through the dresser drawers.

Mark had searched the closet and then moved into the bathroom. Fritz was beginning to think Kelly and Mike were probably correct in assuming the Millers had the letters with them, when Mark called out from the bathroom.

"Hey, we're in luck! I found the copies taped under the sink."

Mary and Fritz quickly approached the open door to the bathroom.

"Just the copies, not the originals?" Fritz asked.

Mark nodded and pointed out where he'd found them underneath the bathroom sink.

Fritz was considering their options as he checked his watch. Should they continue searching for the originals? There was a knock on the door, possibly the housekeeper.

"We're all set, thank you," Fritz called out.

"It's me, Mike."

Mark immediately opened the door.

"I thought I'd find you here," Mike said. "Sorry we weren't able to come up with this room number sooner. Mary may have told you we came close a couple of times."

"Close only counts in—" Fritz was starting to say as Mark cut him off.

"Forget it, Fritz. You know, you can be a real bastard."

Mike's fists clenched. He was glad Kelly wasn't there to have heard Fritz. She'd tried so hard to learn the Millers' room number. Attempting to control his emotions, Mike said, "The desk clerk told Mr. Miller that they won't be able to fax anything out until noon tomorrow. I'm glad you were able to get his cooperation."

"You can credit Mark with that," Fritz responded. "Some people are more creative than—"

"Let it be," Mark said, glaring at Fritz. He was clearly embarrassed by Fritz's comments. If Mary hadn't been present, Mike believed he would have been tempted to slug Fritz and wipe that smirk off his face.

"I'm thinking we should leave the copies where they are," Fritz said to Mark. "Without the originals, there's a problem. We now know where the money is and where the copies of the letters are. Hopefully, the Millers will lead us to some of their accomplices."

"We found the copies under the bathroom sink," Mary informed Mike.

He nodded as he explained, "I'm taking Kelly over to the hospital now to check out her ankle. The Millers are staying with her until I get back with her toiletries kit."

"I hope she's okay," Mary said.

"Me, too," Mike answered as he turned to leave.

Chapter 54

"I think it's just a nasty sprain," the doctor on duty said. "We'll get you down for x-rays just in case."

"Can you give us a report on Mr. Woodbridge and Chan?" Kelly asked.

The young doctor smiled. "You can probably stop by and see Mr. Woodbridge on your way downstairs. He was wide awake when I last saw him. He's been making sketches of the people who injured him. For a man his age, he's made quite a remarkable recovery. Mr. Hatcher has, too, but he's sound asleep."

He noticed their questioning looks and offered an explanation. "Chandler P. Hatcher III, nickname Chan."

Kelly smiled at Mike. Funny how one can jump to false conclusions, she thought, having assumed Chan had an unpronounceable Chinese name.

The doctor had just left them when the two heard a voice behind them. "I finally found you."

Kelly and Mike turned to see Stuart approaching them.

"You look good, Kelly. Have they been able to determine if it's just a sprain?"

"We're just heading down for x-rays," she replied. "Anything new back at the Perry?"

Stuart nodded. "Yes, they found the copies of the letters in the Millers' room. They left them where they found them, taped under the bathroom sink. We have nearly a dozen people available now. We're hoping we can keep tabs on the Millers in hopes they'll lead us to some of the others involved."

Mike had already told her where the copies of the letters had been found, and the fact Fritz had suggested leaving them there. Stuart must not have the warrants, she surmised, otherwise she felt sure they would have apprehended the Millers and searched her bag for the originals. Caught red-handed, they could perhaps be convinced to identify their accomplices.

"Fritz said you didn't show him the copy of the photo I faxed to you, Mike. You did receive it, didn't you?"

Mike had shown Kelly the photo during the drive to the hospital, a vastly different-looking couple than the Millers—older, thinner and taller. Stuart's accompanying note had suggested they might be able to use it with the Perry Hotel manager to obtain added cooperation.

Mike nodded, a sheepish grin on his face. "It wasn't intentional, it slipped my mind. Fritz—"

Stuart held up his hand. "No explanation required. I gave him another copy, so we're all set. Mary mentioned Fritz was giving you a tough time. I apologize, he . . ." Stuart seemed to decide what he'd been about to say was probably best left unsaid.

"We expect the warrants will be ready for us by mid-morning tomorrow. If the Millers haven't phoned or made personal contact with anyone by noon, we're planning on proceeding with their arrest. I suppose your plans will probably hinge around the results of the x-rays. I guess you had originally planned to head back to Ann Arbor tomorrow afternoon. We'll have hopefully wrapped this up one way or another by then. I don't think we'll need you as witnesses. If so, we know how to contact you.

"Do the two of you want to stop by and see Mr. Woodbridge and Mr. Hatcher after the x-rays? I was planning on seeing them now, if they're awake. If I find they've been dozing off and on, I'll probably just stay in hopes they'll wake up again soon."

"Why don't we accompany you now?" Kelly suggested. "The doctor told us Mr. Woodbridge made some sketches of the people who held him hostage. I'm anxious to see them before I head down for the x-rays."

Chapter 55

His light was on and Mr. Woodbridge was sitting up in bed as the three of them entered the room. A delighted smile appeared on his face.

"I was hoping you'd come, I haven't been able to sleep. I've been so anxious to show you these."

He reached over to grab several sheets of paper with his good hand as he spoke. His other hand was heavily bandaged. The bruise on his face was more pronounced than ever, but his face had much more color now compared to when they'd last seen him.

His eyes twinkled as he said, "I haven't had an opportunity to truly thank the two of you yet. They say you probably saved my life. I was hoping you'd be able to understand my pleas for help."

As he talked, he handed the sheets of paper to Stuart. They were pencil drawings of faces.

"And I definitely owe you an apology, Stuart. I think I overdid it in my rudeness when you came to check on me."

"No, to the contrary," Stuart replied, smiling. "When I described your behavior and language to Kelly, it just provided an added reason for her to believe something was terribly wrong."

Nodding, Kelly said, "Mike and I are just sorry we took so long to get there."

"You came, that's the important thing. And the wedding festivities," his eyes were twinkling again and he chuckled, "at least a good portion of them, are going to be my gift to you, my thank-you."

"Oh, you don't need to do that," Mike said.

"No, definitely not," Kelly echoed.

"I know I don't need to, but the fact is I want to. But I'm worried my offer may prompt you to skimp. I want it to be your shindig, not mine. I'll take care of expenses up to a hundred dollars a person. That'll go a long way toward covering the costs—flowers, the orchestra, food, champagne . . . you'll be responsible if it goes over that amount, and I hope it does. Deal?"

Both were grinning, astounded by his generosity. "We'll see," Kelly said.

"None of this we'll-see stuff," Woodbridge replied, grinning back at them. "Let an old codger have his fun, okay? Tell me what you think of my artwork, Stuart."

Stuart was studying the sketches he'd been handed as the others were talking.

"I knew you were a man of many talents, but these are marvelous," he said, handing them to Kelly as Mike looked over her shoulder. "I clearly recognize three of the people we know are involved."

Kelly shuddered as she saw the first drawing. It was the face of the girl, Sandy, who'd taken her hostage. Mr. Woodbridge had captured the same menacing glare in her eyes Kelly had seen. The word 'Evil' had been written and underlined beneath the drawing.

"Is that the same woman who took you hostage, Kelly?" Stuart asked.

"Not even a question," she replied. "It's her. This sketch is so good it's almost making me relive the experience. I'd use the word evil to describe her, too," she said, looking up at Mr. Woodbridge.

"She was one crazy lady," he replied, shaking his head. "When those other two men started breaking my fingers—without success I should add." A slight smirk was on his face. "Oh, they broke them easily enough, but I still refused to give in to their demands."

Kelly cringed as she pictured the scene in her mind.

"She went ballistic when she realized they weren't going to be able to force me to cooperate that way. 'Break 'em all', she screamed."

Kelly was now looking at the second page of sketches. The two men she'd first seen from the boat, and later in the photograph, were portrayed. At the bottom of this page, Woodbridge had written the word 'Flunkies.'

Kelly and Mike both had an ominous feeling as they looked at the next drawing. It appeared to be a man, but he was wearing a dark-colored hood, with cutouts for the eyes. Woodbridge had captured an intense, piercing look in the man's eyes.

"I don't think this is Webb, the man who held me hostage with that girl," Kelly said. "But there's not much to go on except for the eyes."

"Looks like a . . . new one to the mix," Stuart said. He smiled. "I was going to say face, but in this instance we don't have one."

Woodbridge had written the words, 'Silent Sam' under this sketch.

"He was present most of the time," Mr. Woodbridge said. "Never said so much as one word, though. He wore dark gloves, too. Gave me the creeps. Even though he didn't say anything, he still appeared to be the one calling the shots. He'd gesture with a hand to give them direction to proceed ahead with what must have been a preconceived plan."

Kelly couldn't help but gasp as she looked at the final drawing. It was Roy Miller. At least the man they knew as Roy Miller. Any remaining doubts she harbored over his involvement vanished as she studied the amazing likeness.

"You truly have a talent," she said to Mr. Woodbridge. "Mike and I just finished having dinner with this man and his wife an hour or so ago."

Mr. Woodbridge's eyebrows arched in surprise. Underneath this drawing, he'd drawn a question mark. Kelly held the drawing so everyone could see it.

"That one has me a little confused, you see my question mark," Woodbridge said. "He might be the ringleader. He really lashed into the others when he arrived. I only saw him for about five minutes. He took in the scene and his face flushed in anger. Not like the woman—his was controlled, but just as emotional. He called them idiots and a whole bunch of other names before he had the four follow him out of the room and into the hallway. Five minutes later, the four came back and gave Chan and me an injection of some kind. That's the last I remember."

"How is Chandler, by the way?" Stuart asked. "Have you been able to see him, talk with him?"

A look of sadness appeared on Mr. Woodbridge's face as he answered. "I have. I think he's sleeping now. They have him on a great deal of pain medication. He's been through hell. My injuries don't hold a candle in comparison to his. And speaking of injuries, how about yours, Kelly? You look great to me. I wouldn't have guessed anything was wrong if I hadn't been told."

"I'm really fine. I think I just sprained my ankle. We're on our way now for an x-ray just to make certain."

"If it's only a sprain, it's a nasty one," Mike added. "She's experienced considerable pain. She—"

"I'm fine, Mike," Kelly said, holding up her hand to silence him. "The pain's almost gone."

"Mr. Kreicheff?" One of the nurses had stuck her head into the room. "You have a phone call, a Mr. Stanton. You can take it in here or out at the desk, whichever you prefer."

"Be my guest," Woodbridge said, gesturing to his phone.

"Fine," Stuart said. "The three of you will probably be interested in hearing what he has to say, too."

"I'll transfer it in, then," the nurse said. "It'll just be a second or two, and the phone will ring."

•

While Stuart was on the phone, Mr. Woodbridge reviewed some of the decisions Kelly and Mike would have to make.

"I'll put together a complete packet along with a letter, hopefully by the end of the week. They're talking of keeping me here for another couple days. Chan might even have to stay longer."

"We were really impressed with the Grand," Kelly said. "You've made so many improvements since I've been here. Of course, it was Mike's initial visit."

"And I was awed, too," Mike said. "Even after the glowing description Kelly had given me to build up my expectations, the hotel far exceeded them."

Mr. Woodbridge smiled in pride. "We'll do our best to have it even more spiffed up for your wedding. That visit should be far more enjoyable than this one's been. I—"

Stuart had just hung up the phone and Mr. Woodbridge stopped talking so they could hear what he had learned.

"Two things you'll be interested in. First, Miller just went out to his car and put the letters inside the suitcase with the money. Not the copies, the originals. Mitch and Mark opened the trunk and checked. It means we know where everything is now. We'll have a minimum of two people maintaining surveillance on the car throughout the night, and the Millers' room as well.

"The second bit of news is that the Millers slipped a message under your door. They've invited you to go shopping with them at ten o'clock tomorrow morning in Petoskey. If you want to join them, you're to leave a message in their box. They'll meet you in the lobby."

"They're playing games with us, aren't they?" Kelly said. "They have to be aware at this stage that we're wise to them."

"I would think so," Stuart said. "But they still appear to be acting with a great deal of confidence. I don't know if you should really be trying to handle a couple hours of shopping with that ankle, Kelly, but it would be good for us if you could. Fritz believes, and I tend to agree, that the Millers might attempt to ship the letter copies with one of their purchases tomorrow morning. It's as if they relish the added challenge of accomplishing it under your noses.

"If you were to catch them in the act, you would be empowered to apprehend them and seize the copies of the letters."

"I certainly hope that's the scenario that unfolds," Mr. Woodbridge said. "I was so disappointed when I learned there was a chance these people might go scott-free, not be penalized for their dastardly deeds."

"We better get you downstairs for that x-ray," Mike said to Kelly.

"Will you be sure to call and let me know the results?" Stuart asked. "Better yet, I'll come down with you now. I don't want to be asking you to do anything which would further aggravate your injury, Kelly."

"I think we're going to find it's just a sprain," she replied. "I'm actually surprised over how well I'm doing."

•

Kelly's arrival had been anticipated and the x-rays were immediately taken. The technician explained they'd have them developed in about twenty minutes. The doctor who'd seen her earlier would be coming down to review them and then meet with her.

"If you want to have a coffee or something in the cafeteria while you're waiting, I'll tell him you're there."

"Why don't we," Stuart suggested. "I have a few more things to discuss with you and I hesitated to do it in front of Mr. Woodbridge. You'll understand why."

•

Gathered around the table in the nearly empty cafeteria a few minutes later, Stuart spoke in a hushed, confidential tone.

"Fritz has been contacted by Washington. There have been a flurry of calls the past few hours. There's considerable pressure being applied on the Bureau to just let matters rest. To honor the assurances made in those letters in hopes those involved will honor theirs. They don't want any details of the events of the past few days leaked to the news media. There's even been direct contact with Ed Merryweather and his daughter, making sure they can be relied on to keep a lid on the story.

"Fritz was told the meetings were far more productive than anyone anticipated. But he was also told that the negotiations are at a delicate stage. There's a worry that they could be back to square one if the public is made aware of the secret meetings and the fact other countries were involved."

Stuart gave the two of them a moment or two to digest what he'd said as he took another sip of his coffee. "We certainly don't want to do anything to undercut these negotiations. And we're sensitive to the fact that in the overall scheme of things, the hoped-for results of the negotiations dwarf other concerns. The Canadians believe that in less than three months, a solution will have either been hammered out or the whole process will unravel.

"Fritz and I believe there's still a small window of opportunity to apprehend those involved. That it could be done without public knowledge. It would give the Canadians time to cement an agreement without the fear that this group was still trying to derail the negotiations. There would have to be enormous concessions. Plea bargaining would probably result in only minimal, if any, prison time for those apprehended. Still, we'd at least know who they are. We could probably have them on probation during the critical phase of the negotiations.

"Washington points out the risks. Even with the originals and the only copies of the letters in our possession, it would take just one of those involved, with a smart attorney, to spoil everything. Imagine the President, for example, being subpoenaed to testify whether or not he signed a letter, agreeing not to pursue or prosecute someone we have in custody. Just the assertion being made to the media in conjunction with details about the meetings is something we all want to avoid."

"So where does this leave us?" Kelly asked. "Do you think you'll have to back off? That the risks are too great?"

"Possibly," Stuart answered. "That's why I'm going into such detail with the two of you. For Brett Anderson, for Woodbridge and Hatcher, for you, Kelly, and those wives and possibly the real Roy and Martha Miller— I still want to try and pull this off. But I don't have the final say. We can just lobby our case.

"For the time being, I'd like you to plan on joining the Millers tomorrow morning. But that could change. We might be instructed to make an arrest before then. Or be told to just let the Millers waltz on their merry way, to completely back off. At the least, I think we'd be allowed to take possession of the letters and money, so it wouldn't be a total victory for them and their accomplices. Maybe they won't even go along with that.. Some might think we shouldn't do anything that could trigger a reaction which—"

"There you are." It was the doctor who'd examined Kelly earlier. "The good news is, you won't be needing any surgery. But I'm sorry to report there is a slight fracture. My suggestion is to make you a boot to furnish some protection, help ensure the bone correctly mends. You won't have to wear it all the time, mainly when you're up and about. The Velcro straps make it easy to get on and off."

Kelly nodded as he spoke. She was somewhat familiar with what he was describing. One of her co-workers had fractured a bone in her foot a few months ago and had worn a similar device.

"How long do you expect she'll need to wear it?" Mike asked.

"Probably about three to five weeks. I'd suggest you have another x-ray in about ten days, Kelly. I don't foresee any problems. It should heal completely. In a couple of months, you'll probably have trouble remembering you had a problem. But in the meantime, you will be experiencing some pain. You might want to keep some extra-strength Tylenol handy. I don't think you'll need anything stronger. If you're planning any traveling, you should seriously consider using a wheelchair. Anytime, really, when a great deal of walking is called for."

"Kelly was planning on doing some window shopping tomorrow morning," Stuart said. "Do—"

"Yes," the doctor interrupted. "She should use a wheelchair. We'll fix her up with one tonight. Give me about ten minutes and then come upstairs, just to the north of the Emergency area. I'll be in the third room on your right."

•

"Maybe I should accompany the Millers on my own," Mike suggested. "There's no sense in you aggravating your ankle any more than necessary."

The two smiled as Stuart commented, "I don't think that's going to work, Mike. I'm not suggesting you have bad taste, but Martha Miller is

197

going to be interested in Kelly's input, not yours. True, it's a dual invite, but I think you're just along for the ride, Mike."

"I think he's right," Kelly said. "Besides, I'm up to handling it. You didn't hear him suggest we postpone the shopping."

•

The next few minutes were spent discussing tomorrow morning's probable schedule.

"I'll give you a call between nine and nine-thirty to finalize things," Stuart concluded. Glancing at his watch, he explained he was going to check in on Chandler Hatcher before heading back to the Perry Hotel.

"Get a good night's sleep. I'll be talking to you in the morning. Even sooner, if anything comes up."

Chapter 56

It was after midnight when Kelly and Mike arrived back at the Perry. As Mike wheeled her up the ramp toward the rear entrance, Mitch came out the door.

"What can I do to help?" he asked. "It really was broken?"

"Just a small fracture," Kelly replied with a smile. "This is really just precautionary," she explained, gesturing to the wheelchair and foot brace. "I think with Mike's help, everything's under control. But thanks for asking. Anything new here?"

Mitch shook his head. "I assume you know about Mr. Miller putting the letters in the suitcase?" They both nodded. "Nothing's happened since then. The Millers haven't placed any calls that we know of, and they haven't received any, either. Are the two of you planning on joining them in the morning?"

"As of now, we are," Mike replied. "Remember, we should leave a message for them," he reminded Kelly.

"Sure there's nothing I can do? How about filling your ice bucket?"

"We're all set, I think," Mike replied with a grin as he pushed Kelly through the open door as Mitch held it.

"Well, pleasant dreams, then. You've both had a busy day."

•

"Do you realize we forgot to ask if you're supposed to keep that on when you're in bed?"

"I think not," Kelly replied. "I'm just to wear it when I'm up and about, remember?"

Mike nodded. "You tell me what I can do to help you. I'll get your nightgown."

Kelly grinned. "Remember, I'm far from being an invalid. There are probably a few restrictions, and I'm truly sorry about some of them, Mike. It looks like it'll be hugs and kisses again tonight, for one thing."

Mike grinned back at her as he walked over and embraced her. "And to think your mother was worried about us."

•

Mike had fallen asleep within a few minutes, but it was over an hour before Kelly finally drifted off to sleep. Her ankle wasn't the problem. Her mind had been racing.

In addition to recapping the events of the previous day, the past three days actually, she found herself thinking about what was in store for them. How could she have been so deceived by the Millers? Until tonight, the thought of them being part of the conspiracy to sabotage the meetings had never even entered her mind. She smiled to herself as she thought about her early impressions of the Millers—country bumpkins who were becoming pests. Later, they'd won her over—she'd actually been enjoying their company. Of course, they'd flattered her ego with all their questions about Mackinac. She didn't characterize herself as being gullible, the reverse, if anything. A vivid imagination made her far more suspicious than most, certainly compared to Mike. Yet in this instance, he'd been the one who was first to see through the Millers' charade.

She wondered what had happened to the real Millers. Were they being held captive? Were they even alive? Had Brett Anderson been the only one to be murdered? Mr. Woodbridge had also come close to losing his life. She wasn't sure why, but she remembered feeling relieved when Mr. Woodbridge said the man posing as Roy Miller hadn't been a participant in his and Chan's torture. To the contrary, it seemed he was the one who brought it to a halt, angered that it had occurred.

She'd surprised herself at dinner. Knowing the Millers' involvement, she'd questioned whether she'd be able to maintain her composure, act as if she had no idea they were parties to the ordeal she'd just experienced. It had been easier then than it would be tomorrow, really later this morning. Until she'd seen Mr. Woodbridge's sketch, she'd still had a speck of doubt about their involvement. That cinched it.

Hopefully, she thought, she and Mike could play a role in apprehending the Millers and finding out where the real Martha and Roy Miller were. It would be icing on the cake to apprehend the others, too. Their faces flashed through her mind—the two who'd taken her hostage, Sandy and Webb; the two men she'd first seen on the dock; the man wearing the hood to conceal all but his piercing eyes; and of course, Martha and Roy Miller. Those same faces appeared in her dreams after she fell asleep.

Chapter 57

Mike was already in the shower when Kelly's eyes fluttered open. She glanced at the digital reading on the bedside clock radio. It was nearly eight-fifteen. Tossing the covers aside, she sat up and swung her legs over the side of the bed. She put her weight on her left foot as she started to stand, and then carefully tested her injured ankle. She winced as a burst of pain shot through her foot. It only lasted for a second or two. She cautiously took a couple more steps and smiled with pleasure. There was hardly any pain.

The sound of the shower had stopped and the bathroom door opened a moment or two later. Mike had a towel wrapped around his waist. Seeing Kelly, a broad smile appeared on his face.

"How does that ankle feel this morning?"

"It's much better, thank you. There was just some minor pain, initially. But now there's next to none."

"How about breakfast in the room?" Mike asked. Pointing to the menu on the bedside table, he said, "They have just about anything."

"Sounds good to me. If you want to order while I'm in the shower, make it an English muffin and a bowl of strawberries for me. Mixed berries, if they're available—blueberries, raspberries, whatever. And, of course, coffee."

"Are you sure that's all? How about a poached egg?"

She smiled. "Why not? We're on vacation, right?"

•

"This is probably a good time to call David," Mike suggested as he and Kelly were finishing up with their breakfast, sipping coffee. "We should be hearing from Stuart in the next half-hour or so."

"I should talk with David, too," Kelly said. "Get his input on the MacNamara case. I still don't think we have enough yet to go to Rasmusen."

Rasmusen was the Washtenaw County Prosecutor. He'd bounced several cases back to the police department over the past two years, chastising them for lack of evidence and witnesses to support the suggested charges. Kelly was critical of Rasmusen for only wanting to pursue 'open and shut' cases. That wasn't the real world. The legal process was often necessary to get to the truth of a matter. Rasmusen took delight in his near one-hundred percent conviction record. Kelly believed that many potentially guilty individuals were allowed to escape punishment because of his stance.

Mike had asked them to bring the morning Petoskey paper with their breakfast. Kelly found a brief article about Mr. Woodbridge. The owner and general manager of the Grand Hotel had been involved in an accident on the island, and was recovering from his injuries at the Northern Michigan Hospital. The article provided only sketchy details of the accident.

"I'll call David now," Mike said.

Kelly listened as he informed David of her injuries. A few minutes later, Mike signaled Kelly with a thumbs-up sign and asked him to hold for a minute.

"McConnell's going to stand trial. Blackburn is going to rule today that he's mentally competent. David heard the news early this morning."

Kelly was elated. Mike and she had played an important role in the arrest of Joseph McConnell. As Mike continued his conversation with David, Kelly reminisced about that case. McConnell had been carrying out a vendetta against the University with an elaborate blackmail scheme targeted at several high-profile campus personalities. He'd manufactured the evidence and used candy to taunt his victims and the police. He'd been seriously wounded during his capture and had been hospitalized for several months. His defense attorneys had been successful up to now in alleging he was crazy, mentally incompetent and physically unable to face trial. Kelly, Mike, and others felt McConnell was manipulating the legal system. They'd convinced the prosecutor to hang tough and expose McConnell's con game. It now appeared that all their hard work was going to bear fruit. After seven months of uncertainty, McConnell was going to be tried. Kelly could envision the mood at headquarters this morning. Everyone had to be elated.

•

"David says he could be arraigned as early as this afternoon," Mike said. "Of course, this doesn't mean that he can't use a claim of insanity as a defense. None the less, it's a giant step forward. I hope he spends the rest of his life in prison."

"Maybe it's an omen it's going to be our lucky day," Kelly commented. "That we'll be successful in the first step of putting the Millers and their cronies behind bars, too."

"That would be nice," Mike replied. "But after listening to Stuart yesterday, I wouldn't be at all surprised if he was ordered to back off, let things lie and hope for the best. Allow a few people to escape punishment so that millions can benefit. It's a tough call. I'm glad you and I aren't the ones who have to make that decision."

There was a knock at the door. It was nine-fifteen, they were expecting Stuart's call any time now.

"Maybe that's him," Kelly said, as Mike stood and headed towards the door. She was right.

"Good morning," Stuart said. "Your line's been busy, besides, I needed to get these to you." As he spoke he held up a small paper sack. "We need to equip you for this morning. The Millers are downstairs having breakfast. We've checked their room and they've removed the copies of the letters that were hidden under the bathroom sink. By the way, Kelly, how's that ankle? Must be feeling pretty good, you two look happy."

"Much better, thank you," Kelly answered. "And we are happy. We just heard news about a case Mike and I worked on last fall. The judge just ruled the man's competent to be tried, and he might be arraigned as early as this afternoon."

Stuart smiled as Kelly was talking. "I heard the news, too. It's been on TV this morning. As a matter of fact, I just hung up from talking to Susan Merryweather, and we were talking about the two of you and that case. Susan says you two played the key roles in finally catching him."

Kelly and Mike glanced at one another, surprised to hear Susan knew so much about the case. True, there had been a great deal of publicity at the time. The candy connection and the twists and turns in the case as McConnell was being pursued, had captured the public's imagination. But still, it was surprising she'd remembered their role.

Stuart, seemingly reading their minds, went on to explain. "In preparation for doing a story, possibly even a book, about what's been happening these past couple days, she began doing some research on some of the people involved. She found out all about your involvement in the McConnell case. Of course, she's saddened that she and her father probably won't be able to do a story on the Mackinac doings. I joked that they might want to collaborate on a book about the Ann Arbor case. I told her about McConnell possibly being arraigned today, and thus, the story was still unfolding.

"She's really a delightful lady. She laughed and picked up on the idea. She said her father had an expression, 'When life gives you lemons, make lemonade.' I think I'd already said something about when one door closes, sometimes another opens, in reference to being frozen out of this story. Anyway, I think she's going to be talking to the two of you. Our conversation had started out on a dismal note, but at the end she was enthused and excited. She's even come up with a possible title for the book, 'The Campus Candy Caper'."

Kelly frowned. "I'll have to give that some thought. In my mind it sort of trivializes what McConnell did. What's your reaction, Mike?"

"I guess I'm a little skeptical. Not just the title, the entire project."

Stuart nodded. "My thought is that probably someone is eventually going to write a book about the case. It's better to be someone the two of you could relate to, who'd be open to your suggestions. I think Susan would be. Who knows," Stuart joked. "Maybe the book will turn you into celebrities."

Kelly and Mike exchanged smiles. "And in the meantime, you've been successful in channeling her creative smarts in a different direction, away from the events of the past couple days," Kelly said.

Stuart returned their smiles. "Exactly. What I really want to discuss now, though, are the plans for this morning."

Reaching into the small sack, he removed two miniature microphones, the same type Mike had worn yesterday. "I have one of these for each of you in case you get separated. Chances are, we'll be getting the same feedback through both. That won't be a problem, we can always tune one out. We thought about equipping both of you with an ear piece, like the one you wore yesterday, Mike. But there's really no reason to risk the possibility the Millers might hear or see it. Instead, I'm going to give each of you one of these small, vibrating pagers to carry, preferably in a pants pocket. We'll use them in case we have something to tell you. You can make some excuse and distance yourselves from the Millers. We'll make contact and hand you a note or deliver a verbal communication. Possibly to alert you we're about to arrest them."

The phone rang as Stuart was handing the equipment to them. Mike crossed the room to answer it. It was Martha, calling to let them know she and Roy had gotten their message and were delighted they'd be joining them this morning. She asked about Kelly, and Mike explained that the x-ray had shown only a small fracture. He also described the brace they'd provided to give her ankle some protection.

"Don't be surprised when you see her in a wheelchair. She's able to stand and walk with very little discomfort, but the doctor advised her she should use it when she might be planning to be on her feet for a period of time."

"Maybe going shopping with us isn't the best idea," Martha replied. "We certainly don't want her to aggravate her ankle on our behalf."

"Oh, no," Mike said. "We're both looking forward to it. Did you want to meet around ten?"

"If that's good for you. It's another lovely day. Why don't we just plan to see you on the front porch, in about half an hour?" she inquired.

"Sounds fine. We'll see you then."

Stuart and Kelly had been able to understand the gist of the call, and Mike quickly briefed them on the full conversation.

•

Stuart was reviewing what he expected might occur in the next few hours.

"Fritz and Mitch will be staying here, keeping an eye on the Millers' Lincoln. There's a possibility they're using this shopping spree to draw us away from the Perry so someone can remove the suitcase from their car. I can't believe they'd assume we're dumb enough to allow that to happen. But anyway, there'll be over half a dozen people watching the parking lot.

"We'll have nearly a dozen people keeping an eye on the two of you, positioned virtually everywhere. Don't be surprised if you see a few familiar faces. We'll hear if anything unusual occurs, and we'll be able to move in immediately if they try to pass the letters on to someone. I think you should carry the gun we gave you, Mike. I don't envision you having to use it, but at least you'll have it for security. How about you, Kelly? Do you think you should have one too?"

She shrugged her shoulders as she looked to Mike for input.

"If one's easily available, I think you should," Mike suggested. "I don't intend on leaving your side, but it's probably a good precaution."

"I agree," Stuart said. He smiled as he took a small revolver out of the sack. "I thought you might want to have one."

As he wadded the small sack in his hands, Stuart said, "Please bear with me a couple more minutes while I point out some things you should probably be on the alert for. Then I'll get out of your way so you can get ready."

"By the way," Stuart said with a wink, "the Millers were told again this morning that the fax machine is still down."

Chapter 58

The Millers were on the porch waiting for them as Mike pushed the wheelchair out the front door of the hotel.

"You always dress so attractively," Martha said to Kelly with a broad smile as Roy nodded. "That color looks so nice on you."

Kelly had chosen a periwinkle-blue blouse to wear with the same slacks she'd worn the previous evening. She smiled at the Millers as she replied, "Compliments are great medicine when you're not feeling up to par, thank you." She would have liked to return the compliment, but was tongue-tied as she observed the matching Hawaiian shirts the Millers were wearing. While colorful, Kelly also thought they were garish. Not quite the Polo-look you were accustomed to seeing people in Petoskey wearing.

Mike and she both immediately noticed Martha was carrying the large handbag.

"Why don't you and I lead the men, Kelly?" Martha suggested. "They can protect our rear flanks."

Roy laughed. "That's quite an awesome task in your case, Martha."

Pretending to be shocked and insulted, she replied, "I guess I set myself up for that, didn't I?"

Once again Kelly was awed by the composure of the Millers. They appeared to be completely relaxed, showing no outward signs of tension. They crossed the street with Martha walking next to Kelly as she was being pushed by Mike. They passed a series of shops as they headed towards the main shopping area. One was a children's clothing store.

"They seem to have lots of cute things," Martha said. "Want to come in with me and have a look, Kelly?"

"Maureen's not pregnant, is she?" Roy asked.

Martha laughed. "Not yet, but you never can tell. You know they're working on it."

Roy elbowed Mike in the ribs as he whispered, "That's the fun part."

"But we need to get a baby gift for Sally and Ralph," Martha said. "I've been putting it off."

"Sure, I'd like to join you," Kelly said, answering Martha and getting out of the wheelchair with Mike's assistance. Her mind was racing. Wasn't Maureen the name of the real Millers' daughter? The woman who'd provided the photo?

Mike was folding up the wheelchair as Roy suggested he could probably leave it outside, next to the door. "I don't think anyone's going to be stealing it."

•

The four of them browsed around the store for several minutes, Martha asking for Kelly's opinion on several items. Martha inquired about Kelly's plans for children.

Kelly's handling this better than I am, Mike thought. The conversation he was attempting with Roy was more strained.

Martha finally decided on a purchase and as she took it to the counter, Roy told her he'd be waiting out front and asked Mike if he'd like to join him.

"I can grab a puff on this," he said, pulling a pipe from his pocket.

Mike was surprised. They'd spent several hours with the Millers over the past few days, and this was the first time he'd seen the pipe. Maybe he'd be using it to send a signal to an accomplice. The copies of the letters were probably in Martha's handbag. That and the fact he'd asked Mike to join him probably meant he wasn't going outside to pass them off to someone.

•

Kelly tried to appear casual as she kept a close eye on Martha and the handbag as she made the purchase. Martha was taking the item with her rather than having it sent. One thing Stuart had warned them to watch for was the possibility the Millers might try to send the copies with one of their purchases.

Mike and Roy were outside talking, mainly about the weather. Mike glanced around in hopes of possibly seeing a familiar face, perhaps one of those from Woodbridge's sketches. He thought he recognized the woman with a small child on the opposite side of the street as the one who'd re-lieved him at the dock yesterday. But, he couldn't be sure.

•

They stopped in two additional stores, but there had been no further purchases. Window-shopping was the main focus of activity. Kelly and Martha were currently surveying the windows of a corner store named Gattle's.

"This store does a huge business in monogrammed linens, towels and bedspreads," Kelly explained.

"They seem to have nice stuff," Martha remarked.

"And it probably runs a pretty penny or two," Roy said, smiling. "Shouldn't we be thinking about lunch?"

Mike glanced at his watch, a quarter past eleven.

Ignoring her husband, Martha asked, "Would you and Mike like a set of towels or perhaps a monogrammed bedspread as a wedding present?"

Kelly blushed in surprise as Martha continued. "I know we won't be invited, we didn't expect to be. But you two have been so nice to us. What do you say, Roy? You'd like to give them a nice present, wouldn't you?"

He shrugged his shoulders and replied, "If you say so, Martha. Yes, I think that's a great idea."

Kelly was shaking her head, grinning at Mike. "No, definitely no. We hardly know you, although we've also enjoyed being with you."

Careful, Kelly, Mike was thinking. They might be attempting to throw us off guard.

"Why don't we just treat them to lunch as a wedding present?" Roy suggested.

"Let's go in and at least have a look," Martha said. "I want it to be a gift to be remembered."

"We'll treasure the memory of lunch, too," Mike said. "Roy's idea is a good one, don't you agree, Kelly?"

She nodded and replied, "Yes, but they really shouldn't be doing anything. We should go Dutch treat."

Martha winked and gestured for Kelly to follow her inside the store.

•

Kelly couldn't help but smile inwardly as one of the clerks, an older woman, noticed them with a somewhat aghast expression on her face and immediately rushed over to wait on them. She's probably one of the owners, Kelly assumed. The reception was similar to what they'd experienced in some of the other stores they'd visited. Not only did the loud, colorful shirts of the Millers attract attention, they also prompted the same reaction. Clerks seemed intent on getting the Millers out of their stores as quickly as possible. They seemed concerned that the garish shirts might turn off other prospective customers.

Martha asked the woman about their selection of monogrammed towels. In seconds, she was showing her the full array of colors and monogram styles available.

"You really shouldn't be considering doing this for us," Kelly said.

"Nonsense," Martha replied. "Think how happy you'll make Roy and me by us being the first ones to give you a monogrammed gift of any kind. Do you like this shade of blue? Maybe the monogram in white?"

Martha was not about to be dissuaded. The blue shade she pointed out was very appealing to Kelly.

"What do you think, Mike?" Kelly asked.

He smiled. "That they shouldn't be doing it."

"But what about the shade of blue?" Martha asked him.

Roy was keeping quiet, a huge grin on his face.

"I like it," Mike answered. "How expensive are they?"

The woman started to explain the pricing and Martha held up her hand. "They don't need to know. Roy, why don't you escort Kelly and Mike outside for a few minutes? Get their address, though. You can bring it back in."

The pager in Kelly's pocket started to vibrate. She glanced at Mike, who gave her a barely-perceptible nod as he said, "Come on, Kelly. It doesn't appear we're going to convince them."

Kelly nodded, unsure of her next move. She wanted to keep an eye on

Martha. Maybe she should suggest Mike leave while she stayed to provide the address and offer input on the style of monogram. Mike had grabbed her hand. She should probably go outside with him. They might want us out of the way so they can step in and arrest the Millers. They might have already apprehended others, maybe someone attempting to remove the suitcase from the Lincoln. With these thoughts racing through her mind, Kelly walked toward the door with Mike, following Roy.

•

Outside, they briefly discussed what address the towels should be sent to, finally deciding on Kelly's parents' home in Ann Arbor. Roy started back inside to relay the message to his wife.

"We'll only be about five minutes, I would think," Roy said. "Why don't you head up that way with your window shopping and we'll catch up to you."

Kelly and Mike nodded as she said, "Now tell her not to go overboard, two sets of towels are plenty."

He smiled as he turned, heading back inside.

•

Kelly and Mike spotted Marc Marowitz across the street, staring into a window. Waiting a moment or two for the traffic light to change, they crossed the street.

Marc had seen their reflection in the store window and turned to meet them.

"You were able to break away quickly, how's it going?" he asked.

"You won't believe it," Mike replied. "They're in there buying us a wedding gift, some monogrammed towels."

Marc smiled. "They're carrying this charade out to the fullest, aren't they? We're going to be bringing it to a head now, though. We discovered they'd replaced the copies of the letters under the sink. We can thank Mary for suggesting we look again. She just had a feeling and it paid off."

Kelly and Mike were surprised by Marc's revelation. What were the Millers up to? They'd been certain Martha had been carrying the copies in her handbag.

"No one's approached the car or their room. The decision's been made to arrest them. I'll be going into Gattle's with that couple you see standing in front of the store next door. Stuart's out in back with a number of others, ready to come in the rear entrance. A UPS truck pulled up out back just a few minutes ago to make a delivery, maybe a pick-up, too. It should be leaving shortly and then we'll go in. Stuart should be contacting me any minute, he knows you're clear. He was able to hear what's been happening."

During the conversation over the Millers' desire to buy them a wedding gift, Kelly and Mike had nearly forgotten they were both wearing microphones. As Marc cupped his hand to his ear, they could tell from his expression that he was receiving an update.

"The truck's still there," Marc informed them. "Those drivers usually move fast, though."

A moment or two later, Marc checked his watch as he advised them the UPS truck had just pulled away.

"We'll be entering Gattle's in three minutes. I suggest you wait here."

•

Kelly and Mike watched Marc and the other two agents enter the store. Mike kept looking at his watch. He and Kelly were both expecting to see the Millers ushered out the door any second.

As the minutes passed, Kelly suggested, "Maybe they took them out the back way."

Mike nodded. "It would make sense, trying to keep a low profile for the store's benefit and ours. If we don't see someone in the next couple of minutes, why don't we go over and try to find out what's happened."

•

Mike had been inside for nearly five minutes. Kelly returned the smiles of people strolling past her as she sat in the wheelchair, wondering what was detaining him. She was about to enter the store on her own as Mike came out the door.

He was shaking his head. "You won't believe it, the Millers have disappeared. They found their shirts stuffed in the bottom of a waste basket in the restroom. Initially, they thought they were hiding somewhere in the building, possibly the basement. But now they think they left in that UPS truck. Stuart's put out an alert."

Kelly was having difficulty comprehending what he was saying. Peering through the window over Mike's shoulder, she could see Stuart talking to the woman who had waited on Martha.

"Stuart was calling Fritz when I left to come notify you," Mike said. "He wants to know if the suitcase is still in the trunk of the Lincoln, if the letters and money are still there."

Mike continued to provide details to Kelly as they entered the store and made their way to the back. It was apparent to Kelly that Stuart was devastated. He appeared shell-shocked, his face void of color. Kelly glanced at Mike, wondering how best they could help.

Stuart motioned for Marc to hand Kelly and Mike an envelope. Their names were written on the front of it. Someone had already torn it open.

Mike removed a sheet of folded note paper with a few sentences written on it, holding it so both of them could read it.

'Dear Kelly and Mike. Sorry to leave you without saying goodbye. You make a marvelous couple and we know you'll have a wonderful life together. The wedding will be special and we're sorry we won't be there to help you celebrate. Martha and Roy Miller are alive and well, at the Park Sheraton in New York City. We're sorry mistakes were made. We didn't intend for anyone to be hurt or killed. Tell your friends to back off and we'll still keep our end of the bargain. Our lips are sealed.'

There wasn't a signature, just a drawing of two smiley faces, but with their mouths drawn in a straight line rather than as a smile or a frown.

Stuart approached them just as they finished reading the note. "You can see this had to be planned," he said. "There's no telling when that note was written. Fritz says the suitcase is still there, along with the letters. Maybe as much as half of the money is missing, they're still counting it. I suppose Miller could have taken some out last night when he put the letters in, or maybe long before that. We never actually determined if it was all there. I've informed Washington, and they're actually somewhat relieved. They're tracking down the Millers—the real ones."

Kelly and Mike could sense Stuart was personally taking the full blame for the massive screw-up. They empathized with his deep despair as he continued talking.

"Fritz says we shouldn't take much satisfaction in the fact we have the original letters and the copies the Millers made. He suggests they probably taped our verbal assurances, mainly mine, regarding the letters. Even though they haven't the letters to back them up, the tapes alone would leave us stymied.

"We should leave, we've inconvenienced these people too much already. The two of you can ride back to The Perry with me. Give us a couple of minutes, we'll pull up out front and pick you up."

•

The couple of minutes turned into closer to ten, as Kelly and Mike waited in front of Gattle's. Mark Krondelmeyer was driving when the car eventually pulled up to the curb. Mark helped Mike put the wheelchair in the trunk as Kelly climbed into the back seat.

Stuart was sitting in the front passenger seat, looking even more crestfallen than previously. As Mark and Mike entered the car he explained, "The UPS truck was found a few blocks from here. The driver was bound and gagged in the back of the truck. It doesn't appear he's been injured."

Nothing further was said during the short drive back to The Perry until Stuart asked Mark to drop him off at the front entrance. He suggested to Kelly and Mike that they would probably have an easier time coming in the rear entrance, where there was a ramp. Stuart told them he'd get word to them if there was any further news.

As Mark drove the car around to the rear of the Perry, he told Kelly and Mike the reason he and Stuart been delayed earlier was due to Fritz.

"He arrived just as we were about to leave to pick you up. He's up to his old tricks. He really chastised Stuart and me and the others who'd been watching Gattle's rear entrance. I think I was the one who said we should have been suspicious when we saw an overweight UPS driver. Fritz really zeroed in on that, ranting and raving over our stupidity. Roy Miller probably had a UPS shirt on under his Hawaiian one, and she probably had a cap for him in her handbag.

"I'm sure Mike already explained to you, Kelly, that the Millers asked to use the restroom while the woman waiting on them wrote up the order. Gattle's doesn't have public restrooms, just a unisex one right next to the back door. The UPS truck was backed up to the freight door. We assume the Millers must have confronted the driver as he was about to leave, taken him hostage and put him in the rear of the truck with Mrs. Miller. Fritz can't understand how everyone failed to see it was a different man who climbed in the truck and drove off. He can be a real bastard. Stuart tried to make excuses for the rest of us, but Fritz wouldn't let up."

Chapter 59

The registration clerk recognized Mike as he and Kelly passed through the lobby on the way to their room.

"Mr. Cummings, there's a message for you. A David Benton called a few minutes ago."

Mike steered Kelly over to the counter and thanked the young woman as he took the slip of paper from her outstretched hand. Kelly saw the look of surprise appear on his face as he quickly read it.

"And we thought it was going to be our lucky day." Shaking his head in disgust, he handed the note to Kelly.

The note read, 'McConnell's vanished. You may have already heard the news. Few details, I'm on my way to the Forensic Center now. If you want to call, they'll be able to page me. David.'

Kelly had thought she'd be reading something about a legal delay or a change in the decision regarding McConnell's competence to stand trial. Not this.

"Oh, Mike, this is unbelievable. Just having learned he was finally going to face trial . . ." Kelly didn't finish her statement. "Let's go up to the room and call David. They might have something about it on a newscast. We can check while you're trying to get through to him."

•

Kelly and Mike were surprised to find McConnell's escape and disappearance was one of the lead stories on the local channel. There were hardly any details though, the coverage was mainly historical, a rehash of McConnell's alleged crimes and the fact he had been scheduled for arraignment tomorrow morning. There was an aerial shot of the Ypsilanti Forensic Center where McConnell had been housed, and scenes of the University of Michigan campus.

Mike chatted briefly with David's secretary. She promised to immediately notify him that they'd called. She was sure he'd be back to them momentarily, he'd been expecting their call. Mike told her they'd be waiting in their room.

Mike propped several pillows on the bed so that Kelly could sit with her legs extended and rest her ankle while they were awaiting the call.

"Are you hungry?" he asked. "I can call room service."

Kelly shook her head. "Between the Millers and McConnell, I think I've lost my appetite. How about you?"

"I feel the same way. Maybe we can grab a bite downstairs later, after we've spoken to David."

"Stuart may be calling us, too," Kelly reminded him. "He promised to, if he learned anything new, remember?"

Mike nodded. "Sure do. I have several questions I'd like to ask him. I'm sure you do, too."

"Shouldn't our first question be whether he still needs us?" Kelly asked. "I think we belong in Ann Arbor. The first thing David's apt to ask us is, how quickly can we be there."

"Not necessarily, Kelly. I would bet that David's already taken precautions with respect to Judy and Steve, protection or getting them out of town for the time being. He may be relieved we're not there. It would be less complicated if we just stay put."

She nodded, understanding where he was coming from. Judy Wilson and Steve Rentz had both played a major role in McConnell's arrest. Judy had been the one to provoke him into exposing himself. Steve had been the one who fired the multiple shots that nearly led to McConnell's demise. Would he just flee now, or would he seek to retaliate against those responsible for thwarting his plans for revenge against the University? In addition to Judy and Steve, she and Mike topped that list.

"I hope we'll be able to convince David that we belong back in Ann Arbor," she said. "Having us involved in attempting to recapture him." Reading into Mike's expression, she added, "This ankle isn't going to slow me down."

He smiled. "It hasn't thus far, that's for sure. My initial thought also was how soon we could get to Ann Arbor. I was thinking of trying to convince Stuart to fly us down to save time, versus the driving. But your ankle needs time to heal. Maybe we—"

"So what are you suggesting?" she interrupted angrily. "That you fly down and I stay here to recuperate? That I drive back alone after you're sure I'm no longer in danger?"

"Damn it Kelly, I wasn't suggesting that. That didn't even cross my mind. Why are you so uptight?" Mike immediately regretted what he'd said. He wished he could take those words back. Good Lord, she'd been through a harrowing experience. She had to be in pain. She'd been through hell, and here he was jumping on her.

"So you think I'm uptight? Maybe I am. Perhaps I'm overreacting, but just because I'm going to be your wife doesn't give you the right—" Seeing the surprised and shocked expression on Mike's face, Kelly shook her head and started to laugh. "I'm sorry, Mike. This shouldn't be happening. I'm—" The phone rang, interrupting her.

"That's probably David," Mike said. "Let's hope he has good news, that McConnell's back in custody." And then we can forget all about these past few minutes of conversation, he thought.

It was Stuart, checking to see if they were in their room and available for him to come up and update them.

"For one thing, the real Roy and Martha Miller have been located, safe and happy. I'll be right up."

•

Kelly and Mike were amazed over the change in Stuart's demeanor, a sharp contrast from the dejected man they'd viewed less than an hour ago. Excited and smiling, he seated himself next to Kelly on the bed.

"As I said on the phone, the Millers have been located, unharmed at the Park Sheraton in New York City. A truly happy ending, considering what we imagined we might discover. They were in their room waiting for a phone call. Not ours, one from the producers of Candid Camera."

Kelly and Mike glanced at one another in surprise as Stuart continued.

"The Millers arrived in Mackinaw City on Friday, around three-thirty. With ample time to catch the four o'clock boat to Mackinac Island, they decided to forego the valet parking service and find a place to park on their own. Mr. Miller is very protective of his Lincoln and he chose a fairly deserted section of the lot in which to park. Lo' and behold, just as they were about to exit from the car, a small sports car drove up and parked right alongside of them. Mr. Miller decided to switch to another space, again far removed from other cars. The sports car, with a young couple inside, followed them and pulled up alongside Mr. Miller's car door. As he started to open his door, the young woman in the sports car did, too. He pulled his shut to allow her to get out first. She did the same. He opened his door again, just as she did. This continued for several minutes, with Mr. Miller becoming totally frustrated, wondering if he should change places again. Finally, the young woman climbed out of the sports car and opened Mr. Miller's door. As he climbed out in confusion, she announced, 'You're on Candid Camera'.

"The young couple complimented Mr. Miller on what a good sport he'd been and then went through a lengthy explanation of what this all meant. They were to be flown to New York City for the weekend as guests of Candid Camera, all expenses provided. They were told they'd be appearing on Monday night's show, live. They'd have a chance to see the actual film footage before being asked to sign a waiver giving Candid Camera permission to use the film on the show.

"They gave the Millers one thousand dollars in cash, two airline tickets, and a hotel voucher for the Park Sheraton. They were also given the keys to the sports car and instructed to drive to Traverse City to catch their flight, which would be departing in four hours. They were told that their car would be driven back to their home in Canton, waiting for them on their return from New York. They were given choice theater tickets, for both Saturday and Sunday. They were to enjoy the weekend and then be contacted on Monday, this afternoon, in their room by a Candid Camera representative. By the way, when they arrived in their room they found a large bouquet of flowers and a bottle of wine on ice. The Millers say the weekend was one of the highlights of their lives."

Mike was sitting next to Kelly on the opposite side of the bed from Stuart, and felt Kelly grip his hand. She winked as he looked up. Stuart noticed and grinned as he continued.

"Mr. Miller described it as a third honeymoon, saying they'd celebrated their twenty-fifth anniversary in Hawaii as a second honeymoon. It's quite a story, isn't it?"

Kelly and Mike were both smiling, shaking their heads. They'd envisioned the worst as they'd contemplated over the Millers' possible fate.

"I hadn't even realized 'Candid Camera' was still being broadcast," Kelly said. "My parents always used to watch it. I remember Alan Funt and then I think it was his son who hosted it. I don't think my parents realize it's still on the air."

"It isn't," Stuart said, laughing. "The Millers were embarrassed to admit they hadn't watched the show in years. Sounds far-fetched, but they really reeled the Millers in. Just as well, probably, there's no telling what may have happened if the Millers hadn't bought into the Candid Camera bit. Believe it or not, we're coming out heroes in all this. The Director spoke to me herself, congratulating us for the recovery of the originals and copies of the letters. The Canadians are delighted. They believe we acquiesced to their request to let the instigators of all this grief go free. Maintaining a lid on any publicity about the Mackinac meetings is their primary concern."

"Does this mean you'll no longer need us?" Mike asked.

"I hope that's the case," Stuart replied. "Except for possibly helping the Merryweathers with their book. I didn't commit you, but I did tell Susan you might be willing to."

"I guess you haven't heard the news about McConnell," Kelly said.

"In addition to the fact he's going to face trial soon?" Stuart asked.

"Yes," Mike replied. "He's missing. He escaped this morning. We're awaiting a call from our boss, David Benton, with an update."

Stuart was taken by surprise. "I had no idea. I've been on the phone since I left you earlier. I'm sorry, I know what you went through to catch him. Maybe there's a way to get the Bureau involved. I'd like to help, possibly pay back a little of the debt we all owe the two of you. It's been a triple whammy for you these last twenty-four hours, hasn't it, Kelly? The ankle, the Millers' disappearing act, and now McConnell's. I hope you both realize how much we've appreciated your help. I can't begin to thank you for all you've done. Could I treat you to lunch? After your phone call?"

"It depends on what we learn from David, we may be jumping in the car and heading to Ann Arbor," Mike replied. "Thanks for the offer, but it may not work out."

"I understand. But if you don't leave, the invitation is open. I'd say dinner, but it's Fritz's birthday. I shouldn't assume, but I'm thinking you'd just as soon avoid those festivities. I'll be anxious to hear what you learn from Benton. If you have time, give me a call."

"We will," Kelly replied. "You've been very considerate in keeping us so well informed. We've appreciated that, also the opportunity to get to know you. Mark told us what happened this noon, Fritz's blow-up. We're both sad that it happened. Leading the troops can often be a lonely and frustrating position. Mike took a great deal of heat when we were pursuing McConnell. I know I speak for both of us in saying we think you've done a tremendous job. And even though we aren't thrilled by the fact that those responsible might be escaping punishment, we're happy for you things have panned out as well as they have."

"Thank you," Stuart replied. "Thanks to both of you. I hope I haven't misled you, though. I didn't mean to imply that this incident is over. We've already checked the Millers' room for prints. Our people indicate we might not come up with much there. Though some of the water glasses were used, they were void of prints. We think the Millers probably used latex gloves. We'll also be going over the car for prints, as well as the suitcase and the letters.

"I really don't have to detail all that for you, though, do I?" Stuart said. "It's all familiar stuff to you. We also have the contraption they strapped you in, Kelly. That and the explosives might produce a lead for us. We're not going to slow down our efforts in trying to identify these people. We've already forwarded Mr. Woodbridge's sketches to Washington."

"Were you able to come up with anything at Mr. Woodbridge's house, prints or other evidence?"

Stuart shook his head.

"Didn't Roy push your wheelchair a couple times this morning, Kelly?" Mike asked. "Maybe there's a possibility for prints there."

"And on the paperwork and the money at Gattle's," Kelly said. "Roy gave his billfold to Martha, I think so she could pay cash. You confiscated it, I hope."

Stuart chuckled as he nodded his head. "Maybe I was too quick to say we wouldn't need you any longer. I can see why McConnell didn't stand a chance with the two of you on his trail. I can imagine you're anxious to get back to Ann Arbor and match wits with him again. As for Fritz, the problem is he was probably right in much of what he had to say. Isn't it amazing how simple things can have a major impact? The Hawaiian shirts, for example. Everyone was primed to look for them. All of us probably see several UPS trucks and drivers every single day. As a result, we weren't as alert as we should have been at Gattle's."

Kelly and Mike nodded. "It's like many a witness," Kelly said. "Able to relate every detail as to what a person was wearing, from a description of the shoes and whether they had laces, to a precise description of a logo on a shirt. Yet when asked if the person had facial hair or was wearing glasses, the witness draws a blank."

"Precisely," Stuart replied, smiling. "And it happens to the best of witnesses."

The phone rang and Mike reached for it. He mouthed, "It's David."

Chapter 60

Stuart offered to leave, but Kelly assured him he should just wait. "David's not long-winded, Mike should just be a few minutes. It'll save us having to call you."

Kelly and Stuart weren't able to decipher much of the conversation, Mike was mainly listening. While he did so, Kelly and Stuart talked in hushed tones. He told her what they'd been able to learn from the UPS driver. He also told her that Chandler Hatcher had made great strides and would probably be discharged at the same time as Mr. Woodbridge, on Wednesday or Thursday.

Kelly's ears perked up as Mike was ending the call. She'd heard Mike say that they'd be back on Wednesday. She frowned at Mike, mouthing, 'Why the delay?' He nodded and flashed her the okay sign.

"We'd really prefer coming back this afternoon or evening," Mike said a few moments later. After listening to David's reply, he said, "I understand. I'm sure Kelly will, too."

The remainder of the conversation consisted of Mike's answers to questions about Kelly. "Why don't I let her tell you herself? She's right here."

She assumed David must have said that would have to wait, as Mike replied, "She'll understand," rather than handing her the phone.

•

"There's been no sign of McConnell," Mike said. "I'll try not to jump around, but first let me tell you about the Ann Arbor News story. There were only minutes to spare to make today's edition. They held it up and featured the article on the front page, with a photo of McConnell. David's delighted with that part, a photo of McConnell out on the street within a couple hours of his escape. They used the headline, 'Sweet Ending Turns Sour.' The article described the elation in our department and the prosecutor's office over the court decision to allow McConnell's trial to go forward. It implies, probably rightly so, that the decision prompted McConnell's escape. The rest of the story was a brief synopsis of the case. No details on the escape were available when they went to press. There still aren't many."

Mike coughed and asked Kelly and Stuart if they'd care for a glass of water. They both shook their heads, absorbed in Mike's recounting of his conversation with David.

"I'll get one for you, Mike," Stuart offered.

"Thank you. Let's see, where was I?"

"Just starting to tell us about his escape, I think," Kelly replied.

Mike nodded. "At about nine o'clock this morning, one of McConnell's attorneys came to visit him. The security guards verified his ID and his name was on the master list of authorized visitors. Everything was done to the letter. They examined his briefcase, patted him down and had him empty his pockets. It was raining this morning in Ann Arbor and they had him leave his umbrella with them. He was wearing a raincoat. One of the security guards ushered him back to see McConnell. David says there are at least three locked doors you need to go through. The attorney stayed for about thirty minutes. The same security guard escorted him out to the parking lot.

"At close to ten o'clock, two more attorneys appeared. One gave the same name as the attorney who'd just been there. But it wasn't the same man. One difference was the fact the first one had a beard. The two attorneys were detained while the two staffing the security desk contacted their superiors. One of them recognized one of the two men as a previous visitor. Calls to their law offices and the courthouse eventually established the fact these two men were who they said they were. One of the guards escorted them back to see McConnell. His room was empty. They sounded an alarm and the staff conducted a thorough search of the building. They found no sign of him.

"David first heard the news from Greg Collier. He's a reporter for the Ann Arbor News," Mike explained to Stuart. "He's the one who wrote the stories, when we were pursuing McConnell, to infuriate him so he wouldn't flee the area. He received a mysterious call informing him of the escape. The head of the Forensic Center called David a few minutes after Greg's call.

"In less than thirty minutes, the story was being broadcast, both on radio and TV. Neither Greg nor David had orchestrated it. David had been busy dispatching officers to the Forensic Center, and he's still attempting to piece together the puzzle of how the story circulated so fast. Our people were on the scene in a matter of minutes, questioning all the staff. They also conducted a search of their own, finding nothing. David says the security guard who accompanied the man who visited McConnell earlier this morning is probably the key. He's been traumatized by this, at least he's pretending to be."

"What about the possibility that McConnell masqueraded as the security guard, accompanying the lawyer out?" Stuart asked. "You mentioned he escorted the man into the parking lot."

"That's true, but he also came back inside. There are four or five witnesses testifying they know the security guard and that he was definitely the one who escorted the lawyer out to the parking lot."

"My mind was moving in the same direction as yours," Kelly said to Stuart. "I kept waiting for Mike to say they'd found the guard, bound and gagged somewhere, or worse. This is really a puzzler, it has to have been an inside job."

"That's a valid assumption, but I haven't told you that over half of the staff have already voluntarily submitted to a lie detector test," Mike said. "All have passed, thus far, and more are being tested right now."

"You said that David thinks the traumatized security guard is the key to unraveling this mystery. Did he say why?" Kelly asked.

"Yes. The other personnel say he was behaving strangely, that it wasn't customary for someone to accompany a visitor out into the parking lot. He was actually one of those who volunteered to take a lie detector test. Midway through the test he went into convulsions. Up until then, there'd been no indication he was lying. David believes McConnell could have swapped places with the attorney, wearing a beard and the raincoat. But even if that's true, where did the other man disappear to? Someone pulled a vanishing act. Your hunches, thinking McConnell masqueraded as the security guard, made more sense. The guard could have blended in with the scene with a new uniform after McConnell and the man posing as his attorney departed. But several witnesses dispute that scenario. They're certain it was the same guard, and not McConnell who accompanied the lawyer outside."

"So any way you look at it, the fact is one person seems to have vanished," Kelly said. "Either McConnell or the attorney."

"That's the crux of it," Mike replied. 'Hopefully the other lie detector tests will point to an answer. David's suspicious of an inside job, with the strong possibility more than one person was involved."

"And here I thought I was the only one—" Stuart was interrupted as the phone rang again. Mike answered it and turned to Stuart.

"It's for you. I think it might be Fritz."

•

While Stuart was on the phone, Kelly questioned Mike as to why they'd be waiting until tomorrow to drive back to Ann Arbor.

"You heard me," Mike replied. "I told him we'd prefer to come down today. But as I suspected, one of the first things he did was take precautions in the case of Steve and Judy. She's already out of town. Steve's in a little more difficult situation, no longer being employed. David's arranged for round-the-clock protection for him and his family."

"And David's the one saying we should delay going back?" Kelly asked.

"That's right, he brought it up before I did. His point is that they'll have one less thing to be concerned about if we're up here. Everyone can be committed to tracking down McConnell."

"I heard you tell him I'd understand, and I do," Kelly said. "It doesn't mean I agree. I still think our value in being there would far outweigh the risks. Our being there might also entice McConnell to stay in the area, possibly expose himself. That strategy worked before, with Judy."

Mike nodded. It was true they had been successful in setting up Judy Wilson in a way to infuriate McConnell and lead him to retaliate. Using her as a decoy had worked, but it was dangerous to go to the well too often. That strategy had come close to resulting in disaster.

Kelly smiled. It was clear to her that Mike didn't want to become embroiled in another argument with her. "Did David say when he might be contacting us again?"

"Not really. He suggested we call him around five o'clock. I'm sure he'll get word to us if anything major happens."

Stuart was just telling Fritz that he'd be coming down to the room in about five minutes. He turned to Kelly and Mike as he hung up.

"It was Fritz, he's anxious to be on his way. He wants to drive the Lincoln down to Detroit, possibly Chicago, where they have the facilities and equipment to check everything out." Stuart winked. "He's the only one he trusts not to screw up in getting all that evidence into the proper hands. He suggested that Mark join him. I want to verify that the tests can be done in Detroit, and also make sure they'll be taking everything they should.

"As far as the McConnell situation, I wish I could help. I thought the security guard might have been acting in a strange manner because the attorney had a gun pointed at him. But you said the lawyer was searched when he arrived. I'm at a loss. As Benton suggested, the key probably lies with that guard.

"The luncheon invitation is still open, by the way. I expect to be finished with my business in fifteen or twenty minutes. I could meet you in the dining room. But don't wait for me, go ahead and order."

•

They had the same waitress they'd met the previous night when they were with the Millers. Mike explained to her that Mr. Kreicheff would probably be joining them for lunch, but that Kelly and he would just go ahead and order.

"Good idea," Sherry said with a cheerful smile, glancing at her watch. "We'll be ending luncheon service in about fifteen minutes, so it's best to get your orders in as soon as possible."

They both ordered a glass of wine, which was not a normal routine for either, particularly not with lunch. They'd decided they might as well relax and enjoy the remainder of their mini-vacation.

"Would you feel up to a tour of Harbor Springs this afternoon?" Mike asked.

Kelly smiled and raised her wine glass. "Certainly, I'd love to. It's such a gorgeous day, we should really make the most of it."

As Sherry brought their entrees, she commented, "That's really strange about the Millers, they seemed like such nice people. I heard they just vanished, leaving everything behind in their room. I thought that the four of you were longtime friends, but I guess you're with the FBI, too. Were the Millers in trouble? I heard you were taking fingerprints in their room."

Rumors circulate quickly in any organization, Kelly thought. The fact they'd done so among the Perry Hotel staff came as no surprise.

"We aren't privy to all the details," Kelly replied. "We're not with the FBI."

"Oh, I'm sorry, some of us were assuming you were."

Mike shook his head to verify they weren't as he explained, "We have as many questions as you do. We've been told to keep everything hush-hush, though."

The young woman was flustered and blushed. "We were told that, too. I'm sorry. I shouldn't have said anything."

A thought came to Kelly, and after assuring Sherry she hadn't been out of line, she asked, "Remember last night at dinner, the Millers were sharing a dessert menu and she spilled some coffee on it?" Sherry nodded.

"Would there be any possibility that it's available?"

Sherry shook her head. "It was stained, I threw it out myself. Those are the rules—always an immaculate menu. You're thinking of fingerprints, aren't you?"

She was a sharp young lady, Mike thought, as Kelly nodded her head.

"I'm sorry, I think it's long gone," Sherry said, and then her face suddenly lit up. "They asked to see a photo of my children. Both of them handled it as I pointed out who was who. Do you think that would help?"

"Maybe," Mike replied, smiling at Kelly.

"It's in my purse. I'll get it."

•

Sherry was soon back, carrying a small handbag. Kelly and Mike were elated to see it was a framed photograph, rather than just a snapshot, as she removed it from her purse.

"What's going on here?"

Stuart had approached their table while they were occupied with the photo. Mike was now holding it in his napkin.

"Perfect timing!" Kelly said, smiling at Stuart. She introduced him to their waitress and quickly explained the meaning of the photo.

"What do you think?" Kelly asked. "You should be able to get some prints off the frame, shouldn't you?"

Stuart was smiling. "The two of you continue to amaze me. This might be the best opportunity we'll get as far as the Millers are concerned. Fritz and Mark are just about to leave, I should get this to them. Could we borrow this for a few days?" he asked Sherry.

"The dining room's just about to close," Kelly said. "Mike can probably run that out to them while you order."

Stuart and Mike both nodded. "They're in the Lincoln. If you don't catch them, I can call and have them double-back." There was a happy grin on Stuart's face.

Chapter 61

Mike dashed out the rear of The Perry, the photo clutched in his hands. He was in luck, the Lincoln was just backing out of its parking space. Mike called out as he raced toward the vehicle. Mark was in the passenger seat and turned to see him approaching. Fritz remained in the driver's seat, with the motor idling, as Mark opened the car door and climbed out to greet Mike.

"I'm glad I caught you," Mike said. The passenger window was down and Mike leaned down so Fritz could hear him as he explained to Mark. "This photograph belongs to the lady who waited on the Millers and us last night. She says both the Millers held it. We're hoping you'll be able to get their prints off the frame."

Fritz and Mark appeared to be impressed. "It's worth a try," Fritz said as he unlatched the trunk. "Be sure to wrap that napkin around it carefully, Mark," Fritz instructed. "Maybe it should go in the suitcase."

As Mark walked to the rear of the car, Fritz smiled at Mike. "I don't know how you ended up with that, but congratulations to whoever's responsible. Does Stu know about this?"

Mike nodded. "Yes, Kelly and I are having lunch with him now. I volunteered to run it out to you."

"Well, good show! You two are even making Stu look good, and that's—"

"What in the hell?" Mark explained. "They've armed this damn thing again, the light's on!"

Mike started back toward the open trunk. Fritz was just reaching for the door handle as the car phone rang. He answered it and a moment later shouted, "Who is this?"

Mike and Mark watched as Fritz's expression changed as he listened to the caller, his anger subsiding, the color draining from his face. A moment or two later he mumbled, "I understand."

Fritz appeared frightened rather than angry as he repeated the statement in a louder voice. "Yes, I said I understand."

He seemed confused as he lowered the phone to his lap. Mike and Mark stood next to the driver's side door, staring through the lowered window at him. He turned to look at them, shaking his head.

"Someone is observing us," he explained. "They've used a remote device to arm those explosives in the trunk."

As Mike and Mark began to swivel their heads to look, Fritz cautioned them. "Don't look now, that's only the half of it. I've been told the car doors are on a circuit. If it's broken it will trigger the explosives."

"Let's not panic," Mark said, quickly comprehending what Fritz had said. "Mike and I can help you maneuver out this window."

Fritz immediately shook his head. "I was told if I make any attempt to do that, they'll blow up the car. I'm supposed to head north on 31, they'll be calling back with additional instructions."

The three men exchanged looks, all with similar thoughts. Was this a bluff? No, Mike and Mark had seen the bulb lit on the gear in the trunk. Even if the car doors weren't wired, it didn't matter. Even if they weren't being watched, there weren't any options. Fritz couldn't risk not following the instructions he'd been given.

"You two stand clear. Alert Stu as to what's happened. I was told to stay off the phone, leave the line clear so they can contact me. They've warned against anyone following me. Tell Stu I'll try to call him."

The two men backed away from the car as Fritz shifted into reverse. Mike wished there was something he could say or do. Fritz had to be terrified.

"Good luck," he called out, with a slight wave of his hand.

Fritz nodded his head, his forlorn expression acknowledging he'd need it.

"Let's find Stuart," Mark said, turning and quickly walking towards the rear entrance to the Perry.

•

Kelly was worried, wondering what was delaying Mike. He should have been back five minutes ago. Maybe he was immersed in an argument with Fritz, bawling him out for lashing out at Stuart this morning. She was finished with her lunch and Stuart was halfway through his.

"Maybe I should go check," Stuart said, reading her thoughts. "I've had about enough, anyway. My stomach's still churning over today's events." He pushed his chair back and was just about to stand when they noticed Mike and Mark hurrying across the dining room towards their table. They could readily tell from the two men's expressions that something was wrong. Mike deferred to Mark to explain what had taken place.

•

Stuart was shaking his head, clearly awed by Mark's revelations. "They were probably going to contact you and Fritz by phone after you were on the road. The fact you discovered the device was armed the way you did was just an accident. You're lucky you're not in the car."

"I think it's also fortunate that both of you were able to see the device was armed," Kelly said. "Just hearing the caller describe what had been done might have tempted one of you to call their bluff. Seeing the bulb was lit gave credence to the other things Fritz was told."

All three men nodded. It could still be a bluff. But if it wasn't, the thought of the consequences of miscalculating was a sobering one.

"I hope Fritz doesn't panic and do something foolish," Stuart said. "I'm wondering if we should risk following him in spite of their warning. I think not. We need to get back to the room, I left my phone there. Fritz may have already tried to call. I think Mitch is there in the room, I'm sure he'd answer it."

Stuart quickly led them out of the dining room. "You're welcome to come with us," he said to Kelly and Mike.

•

Minutes later, they were in the room overlooking the parking lot. After asking if he'd had any calls and learning there hadn't been any, Stuart quickly briefed Mary and Mitch.

"I've concluded we shouldn't follow him," Stuart said. "We certainly don't want to do anything to place him in further jeopardy. I'm thinking they'll direct him to some out-of-the-way place where it would be difficult to follow him anyway. Have him open the trunk so they can obtain the letters and the remainder of the money."

Stuart paused for a moment and then continued. "What worries me is what could occur after that. They might elect to trigger the device and destroy the car and the remaining contents in the trunk. I just hope they'd allow Fritz the opportunity to get out of the car and far enough away so he wouldn't be injured."

That might be the scenario, Kelly thought. What would they hope to accomplish by his death? If they were seriously hoping the Bureau would act as if the events of the past weekend never occurred, they certainly wouldn't kill him. They'd have to realize that Fritz's murder would only prompt a massive effort to search them out.

Stuart was continuing to verbalize his thoughts as Kelly and the others listened. "There's also the possibility they've reached the conclusion we're not to be trusted, that we're already committed to seeing them brought to justice and that the letters assuring them to the contrary were probably written in invisible ink. In that frame of mind, they might be wanting to make a spectacular statement to ensure the Mackinac meetings become front-page news. They could be planning to blow up the car with Fritz aboard in a crowded area, for example. An incident we'd have little chance of concealing. Maybe they plan to detonate the explosives as he's driving across the Straits of Mackinac Bridge. Though fewer people might be killed or injured, with the bridge probably having to be closed due to damage, there'd be no chance of killing the story."

Stuart's phone rang and he answered it after the first ring. He immediately whispered it was Fritz as he listened. After a few seconds, Stuart said, "You need to know we didn't follow you, we didn't want to do anything to place you in greater danger."

Stuart listened to Fritz's response and started to reply. He stopped, his expression indicating Fritz had already severed the connection.

"They've been in contact with him twice, having him continue north on Highway 31. He just passed through Conway. They're toying with him, calling him Mr. Underwoody."

Kelly exchanged looks with Mike. He was the one who had told her the U in Frederick U. Stanton III's name stood for Underwood, a family name.

"He's getting more nervous by the minute, wondering why they haven't—"

The phone rang again and Stuart immediately answered again. It was Fritz.

"I want to apologize for my behavior this morning, Stuart. I was way out of line. In case I don't survive this, I'd like you to promise to do everything you can to bring these people to justice. I know you will. Thanks."

He disconnected the line before Stuart could respond. Kelly could see from his expression, that whatever he'd been told had had a sobering effect on him. He explained the gist of the call to everyone, suggesting all keep their fingers crossed. Kelly noticed that except for Mike, the others seemed to be avoiding eye contact with Stuart. Was it just her imagination, or had she seen a smirk on Mary's face? It was strange how differently people reacted in a time of crisis.

Mike reached out and grabbed her hand. Fritz's predicament just re-emphasized for him the trauma Kelly had experienced yesterday. Her strength and courage in dealing with her fears and anxieties had been amazing. Though he and Fritz had had their share of confrontations over the past couple of days, he empathized with him now. He glanced over at Mark to see his reaction—he could have easily been with Fritz now. Mark was looking at his watch. Mike checked his, three twenty-five. He noticed Mitch was also glancing at his watch.

"We just have to hope for the best," Stuart was saying. "I know we've all had our moments with Fritz, but we all have to be praying for him now." He shook his head. "And it's his birthday."

There was a knock at the door. Mitch had been standing next to it and quickly opened it. Marc and Rick entered the room, followed by four others. Kelly and Mike weren't sure of their names, but recognized them as other agents who they'd previously seen. Word of Fritz's plight had quickly circulated, they assumed, impressed to see his fellow agents assembling to show their concern.

Stuart's phone rang again as the other agents were introducing themselves to Kelly and Mike. It was Fritz again.

Stuart cringed. "He's been told to drive to the bridge and stop when he's half-way across."

Stuart's worst fears were being played out. He hardly noticed as Mark grabbed the phone from him and held it aloft as he stepped into the middle of the room and the other agents surrounded him.

"Happy birthday to you, happy birthday to you."

As the others joined in chorus, Kelly looked up in shock at Mike and saw he shared her reaction. The agents were grinning as they sang.

Stuart looked befuddled and surprised. His face flushed in anger as the song ended and the group began a chorus of 'stand up, stand up.' The words had been altered.

"Wise up, wise up, this has all been a hoax, wise up, wise up."

"I can't believe you would do this," Stuart shouted. His glare swept the room. "Were you in on this, too?" he asked Kelly and Mike. Both shook their heads, their looks of dismay also telling him they hadn't been.

"He's only been delayed an hour or so by this," Mark said to Stuart. "We did this as much for you as for us."

"You heard his reaction when we offered to host a birthday party for him," Mary said.

Stuart nodded. "I hear you, but this went far beyond a practical joke. It was a cruel thing to do. I'm amazed you all seemed to be a party to it."

Glancing at Kelly and Mike again he said, "I think we'd all feel more comfortable if you were to excuse yourselves while we discuss this. I apologize for what's happened. I'm probably responsible in a way, ignoring Fritz's actions the way I did."

There was a deathly silence as Kelly and Mike turned to go.

"Get Fritz on the line, Mark. I want him involved in this discussion."

Chapter 62

"It appears we aren't the only ones that Fritz has clashed with," Mike said as he wheeled Kelly down the corridor towards the lobby.

"But there are limits, Mike. They exceeded them."

Mike nodded. Probably more than anyone because of the same situation she'd experienced, Kelly had to have been identifying with Fritz. Knowing first-hand the thoughts that had probably been going through his mind.

"But I have to admit, I would have loved to have seen his face when he realized he'd been conned," Kelly said. "He has to be livid."

"From what Mary said, I think they pulled this all together pretty quickly," Mike suggested. "Fritz's reaction to their offer to help him celebrate his birthday must have triggered the idea."

Kelly nodded. "The idea was born and probably developed a life of its own. They were swept into it so fast they didn't take time to really think it through."

"You'll have to admit, they couldn't have orchestrated it any better," Mike said. "I had a feeling something was up, though, when I saw everyone checking their watches."

"I noticed that too," Kelly said. "I remember Mary's reaction, the glint in her eyes, was strange."

They saw a message in their box as they passed the registration desk. It was from David. Mike quickly skimmed it and handed it to Kelly.

'Still no sign of McConnell. We've more or less pieced together how he escaped. Call me at your convenience.'

The time of receipt was noted at three twenty-five p.m.

"We might as well call him now," Mike suggested. "Looks as if Harbor Springs is going to have to wait until our next visit."

"Not necessarily," Kelly replied. "We could go there for dinner. Let's see what David has to say. I hope he doesn't suggest we stay here a while longer. He'll have a tough sell as far as I'm concerned."

"Why don't you talk to him this time?" Mike suggested. He grinned as he added, "Not that I think you'll get any different answers than I would, I just think he'd enjoy hearing from you."

"Fine with me," she replied with a twinkle in her eye.

•

David asked about her ankle. She joked that Mike was being very attentive and that she was enjoying the royal treatment.

"I think he may be starting to tire from it, but I haven't yet. It's been a delight being spoiled."

"I never did get all the details as to how it happened," David said, chuckling over Kelly's comments.

"There's lots to tell," she replied. "It's a rather long story. We'll fill you in after we're back."

She and Mike hadn't shared the events of the weekend with David yet. Not that they weren't intending to, it was more a question of timing. It would take far more than a couple of minutes to convey the story.

"Let me bring you up to date," David said. "As my note said, there still hasn't been any sign of McConnell. Not for lack of effort, we've had wonderful cooperation from our neighboring jurisdictions. But other than his photo, we've been limited in what we could provide them. No idea of how he's dressed or possibly disguised, or his mode of transportation. We're quite certain he's been able to distance himself from the Forensic Center. Even so, we're still searching the grounds and the nearby wooded areas. We've been interviewing residents within a half-mile radius."

"Did you discover anything in his room that could help?" Kelly asked.

"No, nothing. Of course, all his personal effects and clothing were left behind. But no notes, and no candy."

When they'd been pursuing McConnell, he'd taken great delight in taunting the police with messages and candy, from Nerds to Dum Dum suckers, Zero bars to Nestle 100 Grand bars.

"We've pretty much figured out how the escape was arranged. When I spoke with Mike earlier, I said we believed one of the security guards could provide the answers. He has, his name's Tony Mondini. He's in his early thirties, recently married and described as a jovial type, one of the best-liked men on the staff. Some of the other guards had described his behavior as strange or out of character this morning, when he escorted the attorney out to the parking lot. The guard at the final security checkpoint wisecracked, 'What's your problem, Tony, you're acting like . . .'" David hesitated a moment, "'like you have a pole in your rectum.'"

Kelly smiled, thinking to herself, that's not a direct quote. He's cleaned it up for my benefit.

"The guard said that Tony usually gave as good as he got and he'd expected a laugh and some flippant remark in return. But instead, he didn't answer, didn't even crack a smile. When Tony came back inside, he headed right to the men's room. He didn't come out for about twenty minutes. The guard asked him if he was feeling okay, and Tony answered much better than he had been and flashed a smile. The guard remembers thinking that Tony must have had a touch of diarrhea. The other two lawyers arrived about then and there wasn't any further conversation. Tony was one of the first to volunteer to take a lie detector test. Halfway through it, he more or less collapsed. It was nearly two hours before we were able to question him any further. I don't think he's held anything back.

"He was the one who escorted the attorney, or the man who posed as an attorney, to McConnell's room. The two had joked and chatted on their way. Tony unlocked the door to the room and the lawyer and McConnell warmly greeted one another. He's uncertain how it actually happened, but Tony was overpowered in some way and recalls blacking out. The next thing he remembers was coming to, sitting on the floor in a corner of the room with the attorney seated on a chair in front of him. He didn't see McConnell, but another man he didn't recognize was standing next to the attorney, smiling down at him. He was dressed in work clothes and his shirt had a logo for Hutzel Plumbing. He also had on a cap with a similar logo. Tony knew they'd had a plumbing problem at the Center that morning and that two men from Hutzel had arrived to repair it. He hadn't seen them, but he remembered seeing their names on the master sign-in sheet.

"You certainly know I'm not a chauvinist Kelly, but I think I'd find it easier talking to Mike at this stage."

Mike had just gone into the bathroom. But rather than explain that, she merely replied, "I'm a big girl, David. I think I can handle anything you have to say."

"You're right, I shouldn't have said anything. I told you Tony was sitting with his back propped against the wall. His fly was unzipped and his penis was protruding from the opening in his boxer shorts. The attorney was holding a thin wire in his hand which was attached or wrapped around the base of Tony's penis. The other man warned him that he'd be castrated if he didn't do everything they instructed him to do. The lawyer gave the wire a gentle tug to emphasize the point. As you might well imagine, Tony was terrified. With his heart pounding, he listened as the man explained what they wanted him to do. And that was to lead the two men out of the complex. The man made it clear that if there was any screw-up, a quick yank on the wire would sever his manhood and leave Tony singing soprano.

"The attorney walked closely behind Tony as he led them out through the series of locked doors. Tony stood right next to him at the security desk as he signed out. The other man had hung back after they'd gone through the previous door and it was just Tony and the attorney who headed into the parking lot. The guard at the desk didn't notice the wire coming out of the back of Tony's pants. As I mentioned, he made a wisecrack to Tony and the attorney as they stood bunched together at the desk. The attorney's raincoat hid the fact he was gripping the wire in his hand."

Kelly pictured the scene and couldn't help but identify with the young newlywed's plight. He had to have been panicked, Kelly thought. It's no wonder he didn't react to the other guard's comment.

"When Tony returned from the parking lot, he headed directly into the men's room. It took him a while to remove the wire. It had been looped around his penis several times, slightly embedded in the skin. It had caused some bleeding.

"While he was occupied doing that, the man wearing the Hutzel shirt and cap appeared at the security desk, explaining he needed to go out to his truck to get a part. Thinking he'd only be a minute or two, the guard didn't take the time to sign him out. The other two lawyers appeared shortly after that. In the confusion, calling the court and their law offices to establish their identities and discovering McConnell was missing, the man in the parking lot was forgotten. The same guard wasn't manning the desk when the two actual Hutzel plumbers left.

"I'm sure you've figured it out by now, Kelly. We're fairly certain that McConnell and the man posing as his attorney swapped clothes while Tony was blacked out. Not only the clothes, but the thick-lens glasses and beard as well. The man probably was wearing the Hutzel uniform under his suit, the cap perhaps in the sleeve of his raincoat. Dressed as the attorney, McConnell was careful not to say anything to Tony, the other man did all the talking. Tony was probably so nervous that it wouldn't have made any difference, but they were careful.

"I said McConnell didn't say anything, that was true until he and Tony were in the parking lot. He grinned at Tony and said, 'You owe me big-time.' He had Tony promise him a ten-minute window before telling anyone what had happened, and handed Tony the wire. I truly believe Tony was so relieved, that it still hadn't dawned on him that the man was McConnell."

"Do you have any idea who the other man was?" Kelly asked.

"No, none whatsoever. We think McConnell had this planned for some time. But how and who he recruited to assist him is still a mystery. We don't have any idea as to the car or other vehicle McConnell and his accomplice used, either. Tony left McConnell standing in the parking lot and didn't see him enter a vehicle or head towards one."

"What's going to happen to Tony?" Kelly asked. As David replied, there was a knock on the door. Mike went to answer it.

"I'm just happy we aren't the ones who'll be determining that," David was saying. "I feel sorry for him."

Kelly saw Fritz Stanton standing in the doorway with a large, gift-wrapped package in his hands. It must be a large serving tray, maybe a picture, Kelly thought as Fritz smiled at Mike and nodded, acknowledging her over Mike's shoulder.

"He was probably negligent in allowing himself to be overpowered by McConnell and the other man," David continued. "But his real problem is the fact he kept mum after he re-entered the Center."

Mike and Fritz were conversing as Kelly talked. Fritz was apologizing about the interruption and just wanted to leave the package. Mike was telling him Kelly would just be another couple of minutes, asking him to wait.

"We have a visitor," Kelly explained to David, "but I want you to know that Mike and I will be driving down early tomorrow morning and should be there shortly after noon."

"Fine, why don't you come directly to headquarters. Hopefully, we'll have some good news for you. Otherwise, we can just discuss what precautions we might need to take. I think I've covered everything, unless you have any other questions. I hope you've been able to enjoy the extra time up there."

"We'll tell you all about it tomorrow," Kelly replied.

•

Fritz was smiling as he explained he'd taken a detour through Harbor Springs on his drive back to Petoskey.

"I had a little thinking to do, but I must have been guided. I found this," he said, referring to the package now leaning against one of the chairs. "I had to get it for you. I guess it'll be your initial wedding gift now. Stuart told me about the Millers'. I had to chuckle over that."

Talk about a personality transformation, Kelly thought. Fritz was exhibiting none of the arrogance they'd grown accustomed to seeing.

"Mark and I will be leaving for Detroit in just a few minutes, but I just had to deliver this personally first. Would you like to open it?"

Kelly and Mike exchanged smiles as he carried the package over to her. She carefully unwrapped it and gasped in surprise and delight, as she turned the framed picture so Mike could see it. It was a painting of the Little Stone Church. Fritz was beaming over their reaction.

"This is lovely, Fritz," Kelly exclaimed. "All the flowers make it so colorful. I'd love it even if it wasn't the church we're going to be married in."

"It's very special, Fritz," Mike said, patting him on the shoulder to show his appreciation. "I can't imagine getting a gift that will be more meaningful than this. Thank you!" He reached out to shake Fritz's hand.

Fritz's face flushed in embarrassment as Kelly said, "Lean down here, I want to give you a kiss." He bent over and Kelly gave him a warm hug in addition to a kiss on his cheek.

"You know, it's funny how things work out," Fritz said, smiling. "Maybe, just maybe, what happened today was meant to. When I first realized I'd been tricked, I have to confess one of my first thoughts was that the two of you may have orchestrated it. The fact Mike had come out with that framed photo of the waitress's just as Mark and I were about to leave, and verified what Mark was telling me he'd discovered in the trunk, seemed to support my belief. Stuart and the others told me you hadn't been involved or even privy to what was going on. And Stuart wasn't, either. But all three of you, probably more than any of the others, would have been justified in arranging a pay-back for the way I treated you. I am so sorry. I know change is difficult, but I'm going to do my damnedest to change."

Kelly and Mike glanced at one another as Fritz continued. There was no hint of anger as he assumed the full blame for what had transpired, and apologized again. They were both having difficulty accepting the personality change they were witnessing.

"I didn't intend to get so emotional," Fritz said. He then laughed. "But don't think this is all an act to weasel an invite to the wedding. You make a hell of a couple, and I'll be there in spirit. I just hope that I'll be as fortunate someday as you are Mike, in finding a girl who comes close to measuring up to Kelly."

Glancing at his watch, he concluded by saying, "I don't want to keep Mark waiting. I just hope our paths will cross again someday."

Chapter 63

Kelly and Mike sat staring at each other for the next few moments after Fritz had left.

"I think he's sincere," Mike commented.

"I do, too. I never imagined I'd ever be saying this, but I hope we'll cross paths again with him someday, too."

"What a transformation, almost a religious experience," Mike said with a grin.

"That's maybe stretching it a bit," Kelly replied, returning his grin. "This painting is marvelous, I'm sure we'll treasure it for the rest of our lives."

"Always remembering how we came about getting it, too," Mike added. "Something we'll be able to tell our children about."

"Maybe even our grandchildren," Kelly said. "I haven't even told you what David had to say. Nothing new as far as finding McConnell, but they've figured out how he disappeared. Not really magic, just his amazing luck."

For the next few minutes, Kelly related all she learned from David. "I think he was a little embarrassed at one point," Kelly explained, smiling. "Guess he wanted to shield me from some of the words he had to use to provide a full picture of what happened. He even asked if he could talk to you rather than me."

Mike smiled. "And you said . . .?"

Kelly laughed. "Actually, you were in the bathroom at the time. I didn't tell him that, though. I just told him I thought I could handle anything he had to say and I could communicate it to you."

"And you have, I think every detail," Mike replied.

Kelly smiled again. "No, I left out one thing. I told him we'd be heading back to Ann Arbor early in the morning. He didn't suggest another time-table—just asked us to stop in at headquarters as soon as we arrive."

"Do you feel up to giving me a tour of Harbor Springs this evening?" Mike asked. "Maybe we could call for dinner reservations at The Pier."

"Sounds good to me," Kelly answered. "I should probably call my parents, they were expecting us back tonight."

"Why don't you go ahead and call them while I'm looking up the number for The Pier," Mike suggested.

Her parents weren't home, but the answering machine was on. She left a brief message saying they'd decided to stay an extra day and she'd probably see them tomorrow afternoon or evening. She also said that they had a tentative date for the wedding, August 24th.

"They're probably out to dinner at Paesano's," Kelly said. Mike knew her parents ate there quite often. She didn't say anything to Mike, but she did feel a little anxiety over not finding her parents at home. It hadn't crossed her mind earlier, but it was possible McConnell might use her parents to get to her. He'd done it once before. He knew where they lived, he'd even been in the house. I'll call again tonight, she thought as she pondered over the best way to communicate her concern without unduly alarming them.

•

Mike was able to get a reservation for seven-thirty. "They had a cancellation. It must be a popular spot, I didn't think there'd be any problem on a Monday night."

"It is," Kelly said. "I think they have the best whitefish in this area." She smiled. "I already know what I'm going to order. I think you'll enjoy the atmosphere, too. It's located on the harbor, right by the main pier. I'm sure there will be an impressive array of boats there, they're always fun to see. If we leave soon we'll have time to take a stroll on the pier before dinner."

"Part of my personal tour," Mike said with a smile. "I can be ready in ten minutes. Do you want to be the first one in the bathroom?"

•

They were on their way by six-fifteen. As they passed the State Park on their left, Kelly suggested they take the next main road to their left.

"It's a beautiful, scenic drive. It will take us down by the lake where you'll be able to see the backs of dozens of impressive waterfront cottages. We pass them on the way to that stretch of beautiful old Victorian homes I told you about. The road runs in front of them. No, not here, it's the next left. That's L'Arbre Croche, it means 'crooked tree'. It's a conclave of homes and condos in a natural environment, really the ultimate. My parents rented a place there one summer for a couple of weeks. I'll always remember it, great tennis courts surrounded by towering pines. This is where you turn."

•

Even with the advance billing from Kelly, which led to high expectations, Mike was impressed by Harbor Springs. Nearly every home lining the waterfront appeared to have been given a fresh coat of paint for the summer. There were literally thousands of geraniums in varying colors lining the front walks of the homes. Their huge porches appeared so inviting. Mike saw the yacht harbor ahead on the left.

"The restaurant is right there at the foot of the pier," Kelly explained. "We still have over half an hour before our reservation. Why don't we drive past the restaurant and you'll be able to see some of the waterfront homes on the other end of town. They go on for miles, one more impressive than the next. We won't be able to see the homes on the Pointe very well, you can't drive past those. It's sort of a miniature Mackinac Island—no cars allowed. You'll be able to get an idea of the type of homes there from the end of the pier. Maybe we'll still have time to do that before dinner. If not, we'll do it after dinner."

•

They drove a couple miles past town and then turned around and came back along Main Street.

"They erect a huge Christmas tree in front of this church, right in the middle of the street," Kelly said. "And all these stores are decorated. I think Harbor Springs is as charming in the winter as it is in the summer."

Mike was reveling in Kelly's enthusiasm. It was similar to when they'd first arrived on Mackinac. It was hard to imagine that had been only four days ago.

"We should probably turn here Mike, and head to the restaurant. It's about twenty after. You don't have to bother dropping me off in front. We can just park anywhere in that lot facing the yacht harbor. I'll use the wheelchair, we'll have it then for later when we go out on the pier.

•

"Why don't you go in and check on our reservation, Mike. Sometimes they get a little behind. If they are, we can take a look at the boats now."

"Fine, I'll just put you over here by the foot of the dock. Which way do you want to face?"

"Doesn't really matter, I guess," she replied. "Why don't you turn me around, though, so I'm facing the main entrance. I don't like to have you out of my sight," she added with a wink.

Mike grinned back and started to say, "The feeling's—" as a man spoke to him.

"Excuse me, but I saw you getting out of that Explorer. Are you aware you left one of your windows down? I've heard a storm's moving in tonight, you might want to put it up."

Mike was surprised, he was fairly certain he'd put his windows up before pushing the button on his key chain to lock the doors. "No, I hadn't realized we'd left one down. That's nice of you to tell us, thank you."

The tall, middle-aged man looked familiar, but Kelly couldn't recall from where. He smiled down at her as Mike told her he'd just be a minute. The lot had been crowded and the parking space they'd found was at the opposite end from where they were.

"I hope that's not too serious," the man said, pointing to her foot.

She assured him it wasn't, that she could actually walk on it, but using the wheelchair would hopefully speed up the healing process.

"It was only a slight fracture, surgery wasn't necessary."

"Stay right where you are, Kelly. I have a gun with a silencer aimed at your back."

She immediately recognized the voice. She twisted her neck around to see Webb's face.

"Careful now," he said, a trace of a smile appearing.

There was also a hint of a smile on the face of the other man as he walked behind her and grabbed the handles of the wheelchair. The open window had been a hoax.

"I'm sorry, Kelly, but we thought we had a deal," Webb said. "Your friends are the ones who are breaking it. Things didn't go quite the way we planned this morning—you were supposed to disappear with the Millers. We had more leverage when we had you."

The other man had turned her wheelchair around and was pushing her out onto the pier. Webb walked beside her. His hand was in the pocket of the windbreaker he wore, supposedly pointing a gun at her. The dock was fairly crowded and Kelly glanced at people, hoping they'd notice the look of alarm on her face and realize something was wrong. But they all seemed to look away as they passed, seemingly not wanting to embarrass her by their stares.

"We don't want you to be hurt, Kelly," Webb cautioned her. "But don't provoke me. I'm the one on the carpet for switching off the arming device prematurely. Maybe you're not responsible, but that's when all hell broke loose with the FBI going all-out to undo what we believed was a done deal. By the way, how's your ankle?"

Kelly remained tight-lipped. The audacity of this man! Here she was being kidnapped and he was acting nonchalant, as if this was a minor inconvenience. Where were they taking her? Was one of these boats theirs? Had they been following her and Mike?

His comment about me disappearing with the Millers doesn't make sense, she thought. Martha was the one who suggested that Mike and I go outside. Roy directed us up the street. Maybe the two of them hadn't bought into the idea of kidnapping her again.

"So, you don't think we're really concerned about your welfare?" Webb asked, laughing. "I can tell your mind's racing. Just don't get any ideas that you can rescue yourself by attracting attention. Your ankle would be the least of your worries, besides the fact a number of innocent people would probably be hurt. Just cooperate, we kept our word before. The fact you're having to relive the nightmare is your friends' fault, not ours."

The other man was pushing her faster now. There were several extensions to the pier branching off to their left, with boats berthed on both sides. The man turned down the third one they came to as Kelly's mind continued to whirl. What were her options? Was it safest to just follow their instructions, or had she just been lucky the previous time? Would her luck hold out?

Chapter 64

Mike glanced again; all the windows appeared to be up. He quickly looked over his shoulder to where he'd left Kelly minutes ago. He couldn't see her. He turned and broke into a run, his concern mounting, his heart pounding.

•

Kelly noticed the various names on the boats they passed, along with their cities of origin—Sea Breeze from Milwaukee, Escape from Fort Lauderdale. Her eyes widened as the man brought her wheelchair to a halt next to a boat with the name, 'Webb's Warriors, Chicago'.

"Here we are," Webb said. "You tell us the best way we can help you get aboard. Maybe I can carry you piggyback."

Kelly shook her head. "I'm not incapacitated, I think I can manage if you can just help me stand." She extended her arms to enable him to pull her to her feet. As he did so, she smiled and remarked, "So you call yourselves Webb's Warriors."

He was taken aback for a moment, before he realized how Kelly had drawn that conclusion. He smiled and was nodding his head, unprepared for the vicious kick to his groin.

Standing on her injured ankle, Kelly had gathered all the strength and willpower she could muster, to swing her left leg back and launch the kick. She'd immediately dropped back into the wheelchair and raised both legs, bending her knees. Webb had doubled over in pain and was just beginning to right himself as Kelly moved the wheelchair toward him. She extended her legs into his chest, sending him reeling off the pier into the gap between the boat and the dock. He frantically grabbed for something to hold onto and succeeded in gripping the roping on the boat deck with one hand. He dangled precariously, his feet just out of the water, as Kelly rose from the chair and swung around to face the other man.

He had a shocked expression, the scene had unfolded in front of him in a matter of seconds.

"Oh, no you don't," he said, advancing towards her. She spun the chair around and charged at him. The foot pedals hit him in the shins and the man tumbled forward into the chair. With a surge of effort, she twisted the chair around and shoved it off the dock with the man clinging to it.

At the sound of the splash, she'd already started limping back toward the main pier. The pain was excruciating. She almost toppled as she struggled to maintain her balance and put distance between herself and the boat.

She spotted a young couple ahead of her on the main pier, strolling hand-in-hand. She saw them notice her.

"I need help," she gasped, continuing to stagger forward. They ran toward her and together were able to catch her as she fell forward. "I need to get away," Kelly mumbled. "Can you help me get to the restaurant?"

•

Mike was questioning people, frantically trying to find someone who'd seen Kelly. As he spoke to one couple, a young girl, who appeared to be about ten years of age, overheard him.

"I saw her," she blurted out to Mike and her parents at the same time. "There were two men with her, one was pushing her."

"Where did you see them?"

"Back there," the girl said, turning and pointing. "They passed us when we were looking at that boat where all those people were having a party," she explained to her parents.

Her father nodded and said to Mike, "If she's right, it's that large one on the left, about halfway down the pier."

Mike thanked them and started running in that direction. His eyes widened in a combination of horror and relief as he saw Kelly, her arms around the shoulders of a young couple, limping in his direction.

•

The pain was so intense, Kelly closed her eyes so she could concentrate on keeping her feet moving forward. The couple was almost carrying her, she could hardly place any weight on her right ankle. She opened her eyes and saw Mike darting towards her, a look of alarm on his face.

"She's my fiancée," Mike explained to the couple. "Thank you, I think I can carry her."

He bent down and picked Kelly up, noticing the tears in her eyes. "I'm sorry," he told her. "Can you two run up ahead and call for an ambulance?"

The couple nodded as the young man asked, "Sure I can't help you carry her?"

Mike shook his head. "Thanks, I think I can manage. Tell them to hurry."

Kelly still hadn't said a word. He stared at her, assuring her everything was going to be fine. People on the pier moved aside to let them pass. Mike could hear their hushed voices, asking one another what had happened. Kelly was trying to catch her breath, as if she'd just been hit in the stomach. She was struggling to say something.

"They tried to take me hostage again, the same man, Webb."

"I understand, but first we need to—"

Kelly pulled on his sleeve. "They may be coming after us," she managed to say. "I pushed them in the water."

Mike nodded, envisioning what must have happened, an attempt to get her aboard one of these boats, he thought. He glanced over his shoulder to see if he could spot anyone following them. There didn't seem to be.

"Need to tell Stu," Kelly gasped. "Boat's name is Webb's Warriors, Chicago."

"I understand," Mike answered. He paused a moment to adjust her in his arms, before starting forward again. "We're almost there."

Kelly smiled as she said, "I'm heavy."

Mike bent down and kissed her on the forehead, a lump in his throat. She was going to be fine, he assured himself.

•

The couple came to greet them as they reached the foot of the dock. "They're sending an EMS unit," the woman informed them.

"Should be just a few minutes," her companion quickly added.

"Maybe you can help me carry her into The Pier," Mike said to him. "I need to phone someone."

•

The vestibule area of The Pier was fairly crowded. People stepped aside as Mike and the young man carried Kelly towards the hostess stand.

"I need to use your phone," Mike explained to the middle-aged woman standing there. Another younger woman, just behind her, was on the phone, probably taking a reservation.

"They just called for an ambulance," the woman said, nodding toward the couple.

"I know, I need to make another call."

"I can get a chair for her," she replied, referring to Kelly. "There are some pay phones just down the stairs from our bar, over there."

Mike shook his head. "No, she's staying with me. Where's the manager's office?"

"That's quite a ways, clear on the other side of this building. I'm sorry, we need this phone for our customers, otherwise—"

Mike removed his billfold and flipped it open. "This is police business and this is an emergency."

The woman's eyes widened. "Oh, I'm sorry, we thought she'd had an accident. Was she assaulted? On the pier?" She saw the glare in Mike's eyes as he nodded, and she turned and said, "Beverly, this man's with the police, we need to clear the phone for him." The young woman was just hanging up.

"Would you happen to know the number for the Perry Hotel?" Mike asked.

"Certainly," the hostess answered. "We're under the same ownership. It's 347–6405."

Kelly was settled in a chair, attracting the stares of those waiting to be seated, as Mike phoned The Perry. He couldn't remember if he'd placed the number for Stuart's portable phone in his billfold or not. There was no answer in Stuart's room. He asked the operator if by chance, Mr. Kreicheff was in the dining room or the bar. She said she'd put him on hold and check.

Mike explained it was an emergency and she said she'd hurry.

"The EMS unit just arrived," the man who'd helped Mike, whispered. "Should I have them come in? Use a stretcher?"

Mike nodded. "I'll be right with you."

The young woman came back on the line. "I don't see him. I don't see any of the people in his party, either. Would you care to leave a message?"

It was a simple question, but Mike wasn't sure how to answer it. He'd be leaving with Kelly in a matter of minutes, they couldn't contact him here. Maybe he should be staying, though, watching to see if anyone he recognized was attempting to leave the pier. Maybe they already had, while he'd been here inside, using the phone. No, they wouldn't leave one of those $100,000-plus boats behind. Maybe they were leaving in the boat. Should he contact the Coast Guard on his own?

"Did you hear me, sir? Would you care to leave a message for him?"

"Yes, I'm sorry. For him, or anyone in his party. Have them contact Mike Cummings at the hospital. As soon as they can."

•

Kelly was being loaded into the EMS vehicle as Mike came out the restaurant door. He introduced himself to the two-person team, a man and a woman. He explained he had his car in the parking lot and would follow them. "I'll just explain that to her," he said, climbing into the back of the vehicle.

"I heard you," Kelly said. "Shouldn't you be staying here, waiting for Stuart and the others?"

"I couldn't contact Stuart," Mike replied. "Nor any of the others. I'm going to keep trying on our car phone while I'm following you, maybe contact the Coast Guard, too. The boat was named Webb's Warriors, out of Chicago?"

Kelly nodded. "But shouldn't you wait here and watch to see if any of them try to leave the pier?"

Mike shook his head. "I'll be damned if I'm going to leave your side again. There's nobody else I can really ask to do that though, no one who'd know who to look for."

"I'll be fine on my own, Mike. You just be careful and come when you can. I think you can tell, I'm much better already." The wince as she experienced some pain, counteracted her statement.

"I want to be with you," Mike said. "This is all so confused anyway, I'm not sure if anything's lost if I don't stay here."

"Think of Mr. Woodbridge, Mike. Think of Chandler. And Anderson, too, though we hardly knew him. Please stay, you can accomplish far more here than if you were just holding my hand. Promise me you will?"

Mike nodded and squeezed her hand. "I'll be there just as soon as I can, though."

As Mike climbed out of the back of the vehicle, he explained to the woman, who'd been standing outside waiting, the change of plans. He wouldn't be following them after all.

Chapter 65

The reason Mike hadn't been able to reach Stuart or any other agent was because they were all at the Harbor Springs Airport. A plane had been flown in by the Bureau to fly several of the agents out. Mary, Mitch, Rick and Stuart were staying on for another day, but the rest were leaving. They'd driven three cars from Petoskey in order to accommodate everyone and their luggage.

"We might as well leave two of the cars here," Stuart suggested. "We'll be coming right past here on our way back from dinner."

"Good idea," Rick said. "Would you like me to drive?"

Stuart nodded. "Our reservation at The Pier is for eight. Our timing should be perfect."

"I don't think we should go there," Mary said. "Kelly and Mike are having dinner there. They need some time alone. It's a chance for them to try and distance themselves from all that's been happening, at least for a couple hours. If we march in there—"

"I'm with you," Mitch said, interrupting her. "The Pier has another restaurant in the same building. I think it's called the Chart Room, a little less formal. Same good food, but it's around the side in the basement."

Stuart smiled, appreciative of the sensitivity of Mary and Mitch. "Suits me, how about you, Rick?" he asked.

Rick nodded, also smiling as he opened the car door for Mary.

As this was happening, the EMS vehicle with Kelly on board was passing the airport on its way to Petoskey.

•

Mike was chatting with the young couple who'd come to Kelly's aid. He learned their names were Heather Pomeroy and Jim Dowling, both in graduate school at Michigan State in East Lansing. He explained to them that he and Kelly were from Ann Arbor. The three of them joked about the rivalry between Michigan State and the University of Michigan. He thanked them for all they'd done.

Mike could tell they wanted to ask him some questions. He'd noticed their surprised expressions earlier when he identified himself to the hostess as a police officer. They were probably curious over why he hadn't accompanied Kelly to the hospital.

"Can we be of any further help?" Jim asked. "Keep you company when you go out there to investigate what happened?" he continued, gesturing toward the pier.

"I appreciate the offer, but no, I'm planning to wait until some of my . . . friends arrive before doing that. Thanks anyway, though."

"We don't know what happened out there," Heather said, "but your fiancée was terrified when we first saw her. Right, Jim?"

He nodded as Mike explained, "I wish I had the time and could tell you what this is all about. I just can't, maybe another day."

"Will we be reading about it in the papers?" Heather asked.

Mike shook his head. "That might not be the case, either. I'm sure you kept her from being even more seriously injured, though. We'll be forever grateful."

•

Mike had positioned himself on a bench in the park area to the left of the foot of the pier. From that vantage point he was able to scan the faces of those coming off the pier. He was pretending to read a newspaper he'd retrieved from a nearby trash container to conceal his face.

He knew he should be getting a message to Stuart as to where he was, word that he hadn't gone to the hospital. He cursed himself for not having thought of asking the young couple to make the phone call for him. That would have been the best bet. If he were to go inside the restaurant now to call, he might miss out on seeing one of the people he was watching for as they came off the dock.

Another option would be to use his car phone. There were several empty parking spaces near the restaurant now. It might be wise to move his car closer so that he'd be ready to follow someone if need be. It would only take a minute or two to get the car. He could call Stuart or leave a message after he'd driven up closer to the pier. He could watch while he called.

Most of the people strolling the pier were now clustered around a boat on which a man was playing a banjo, entertaining them. Now's a good time to get the car, he thought as he jumped up and began jogging toward his car.

•

"Mine's delicious!" Mary exclaimed. "I don't know how the food could be any better upstairs."

The others were in agreement, raving about their entrees as well.

"I still can't get Fritz out of my mind," Mitch said. "I think we were all surprised over how well we orchestrated the hoax. I still can't fathom his reaction, actually being the one apologizing. I know you were upset, Stuart, but you certainly can't fault the end result."

Stuart nodded. The others even noticed a hint of a smile.

"I just hope everyone, including me, learned something from this incident," Stuart said. "I hope I never see anything similar to this occur again. But you're right, Mitch. In this instance there was a happy ending."

"None of us have spoken to Kelly and Mike yet about the painting Fritz bought for them," Rick said. "When we leave, why don't we stop by upstairs and see if they're still there."

"I'm for that," Mitch agreed. "I'd like to have a look at the main dining room and see the view, anyway."

•

Mike was fortunate to find a parking place next to the handicapped spaces, as close to the foot of the pier as he could wish for. He was able to clearly see people as they strolled by him after sightseeing on the pier.

Stuart still wasn't in. This time, he left a far more lengthy message with the Perry Hotel operator, including the number of his car phone.

As he sat in the Explorer continuing to watch people, he wondered if he should be venturing out onto the pier to see if he could locate the boat they'd tried to get Kelly aboard. If he were to find the boat was gone, should he be contacting the Coast Guard on his own without first clearing it with Stuart?

The sky had darkened and the wind velocity was starting to pick up. Maybe I should venture out there now, before it starts to rain, he thought. There was still considerable activity on the dock and he didn't feel at all fearful about being out there, even though he wasn't armed. He didn't want to risk missing a call from Stuart, though. He continued to watch people as he pondered over what he should do.

•

Mike was elated as he saw two policemen approaching him. Maybe

Kelly had the EMS team contact the Harbor Springs Police Department on their way to Petoskey. He'd have help to look for the boat, possibly have one of them wait for Stuart's call. He climbed out of the Explorer and extended his hand to greet them.

One of the officers asked if he was Michael Cummings. Neither was offering to shake his hand as Mike nodded his head.

"Would you please come with us, sir? We're parked over there."

"How much do you know about what's happened?" Mike asked as he accompanied the two officers.

They glanced at one another before the older of the two replied, "Enough, I think."

"I've been on my car phone, trying to reach the FBI agent in charge," Mike explained.

The two officers smiled and exchanged looks again. They drew abreast of the police car and the younger officer said, "I'm afraid we'll have to put these on you, Mr. Cummings," as he removed a pair of handcuffs from his belt. "You should be aware that's mandatory. We need to read you your rights, too."

Mike stared at the two in wide-eyed amazement. He stepped back a few paces as he said, "There's a problem here. You seem to know me, what's this all about?"

"Please turn around and place your hands behind your back, Mr. Cummings." The one officer had his hand on his gun as the other snapped the cuffs on. "I think you're well aware what this is all about. Assaulting your girlfriend, Kelly Travis. We know she's on her way to the hospital now, for the second time in two days."

"I know, the same people are responsible," Mike replied. "I head up the investigative division for the Ann Arbor Police Department."

"We're aware of that. Would you please get in the car?"

Mike realized they thought he was responsible for Kelly's injuries. Either he was being set up or there had inadvertently been an erroneous communication, from the EMS team or someone at the Northern Michigan Hospital, Mike thought. Authorities had to be immediately notified in cases where physical abuse was suspected.

"Who made the charge?" Mike asked. "I know it wasn't Kelly. This is all a mistake. We have to contact Stuart Kreicheff, he's with the FBI. He can get this straightened out in short order."

There were smirks on the faces of the two officers as they glanced at each other, nodding their heads.

"I can't believe this," Mike said, raising his voice in frustration. "This is ridiculous, it will just take one call."

"You're entitled to that, as you know," the officer climbing into the driver's seat replied. "It'll have to wait until we get to the office, though."

•

Glancing around, none of them saw Kelly and Mike in the dining room. "It's a beautiful room, isn't it?" Mitch commented. "Do you see those artifacts on the ceiling? My grandfather had a boat similar to that one."

"Maybe they've already left," Mary suggested. "I'll check with the hostess and see if they had a reservation."

The three men waited off to the side while Mary inquired. The woman nodded as she heard the question. She turned to look at the three others, who she correctly assumed were with Mary, before she replied.

"They had to cancel their reservation."

Maybe they just decided to have dinner in Petoskey, at the Perry again, Mary thought.

"Well, they missed a treat," Mary told the hostess. "We had dinner downstairs in the Chart Room, it was wonderful."

"They couldn't help it," the woman explained. "There was an accident out on the pier. Quite serious, they had to take Mrs. Cummings to the hospital in Petoskey."

Mary looked over her shoulder—the others had overheard the hostess. Stuart quickly joined her.

"Anything else you can tell us?" he asked.

The woman hesitated. Stuart quickly pulled out his ID and showed it to her.

"Her husband was also a policeman," she responded. "Do you know him?"

Stuart nodded as she continued. "He used our phone."

"To call for an ambulance?" Mary asked, thinking Kelly must have been seriously injured. She may have tried to put too much weight on her injured ankle and fallen.

"No, one had already been called. He was trying to reach someone else. I don't think he was successful, I think he left a message."

"Could I use your phone?" Stuart asked.

The evening was winding down, everyone was seated who had reservations for tonight. The woman didn't hesitate. "Certainly, help yourself."

•

They still hadn't allowed Mike to call Stuart. To his consternation, they were methodically going through all the proper procedures beforehand, listing an inventory of all his valuables, taking his fingerprints and completing forms. They simply ignored his complaints and pleas to make the call, despite his threats that they were going to be responsible for the real culprits having time to escape.

"And who are they, Mr. Cummings?" the younger officer asked, smiling.

"I don't know their names, I just know some of them by looks. They killed one man, an FBI agent, and tortured two other people. They were trying to kidnap Kelly; she's my fiancée."

The two officers again exchanged looks. Mike was totally frustrated. He realized the two men were probably having difficulty comprehending him—things such as he'd described didn't happen in the quaint town of Harbor Springs.

"Please, let me make the call," he pleaded again.

Finally, he was invited to sit down at the desk and provided a phone. The two officers started to step outside the office to allow him some privacy.

"No, I want you to stay. I want him to tell you that this has all been a mistake."

Stuart was still not there. The hotel operator explained that Mr. Kreichoff had called in for his messages less than ten minutes ago. She'd given him Mike's messages.

"Listen carefully, this is very important," Mike told her. "I need you to call the Northern Michigan Hospital." He continued on, telling her to speak with Kelly Travis or, if she wasn't available, to the person in charge. "Tell them Mr. Kreicheff will be arriving shortly and he needs to immediately call the Harbor Springs Police Department. What's the number here?" he asked the two officers. He relayed it on to the operator and again stressed how important it was that she immediately relay the message.

As Mike was hanging up he glanced at the paperwork to his left. He gasped as he saw the names of Roy and Martha Miller.

"That's how this all happened," Mike said, looking up at the two officers. "The Millers are two of the people the FBI are after. Those aren't their real names. They're involved with the group I've been trying to tell you about, those responsible for a broad range of criminal acts—from kidnapping to murder. They conned you, and they set me up."

"The two people I spoke with, met with, don't fit with what you're telling us, Mr. Cummings," the older of the two officers replied. "I'm a pretty fair judge of people. They aren't out to get you, to the contrary, they feel sorry for you. They just want to protect your girlfriend. They hope you can get some treatment—they stressed they don't think you belong in jail."

Mike sat in despair as the officer spoke. *The Millers conned us. They've conned these men, too. Nothing I can say right now is going to alter their beliefs. I just have to hope that Stuart gets the message and calls back soon.*

Chapter 66

The EMS team had called ahead, and the same doctor who'd seen Kelly the previous night was there to greet her. They wasted little time—Kelly was undergoing surgery in less than forty-five minutes. The x-rays showed the minor ankle fracture was now a major one. She'd also broken a toe. The doctor had carefully detailed to Kelly what he thought was necessary. He was confident she'd have no permanent injury.

They'd brought Kelly up to her room a few minutes ago. She was somewhat surprised Mike wasn't there, she thought that he'd have joined her by now. She was anxious to hear what had happened. She asked the nurse if any messages had come in for her and was told there hadn't been any. As the minutes passed, her concern mounted. She hoped Mike was okay.

•

Stuart related Mike's messages to the others and all four went outside to look for him. They immediately noticed his Explorer, but there was no sign of Mike. They went out on the pier, splitting up as they looked for him. Still no luck. They left a note on his windshield, indicating they were heading to the hospital. Stuart jotted down the time.

Rick stopped by the Harbor Springs Airport so they could pick up the other two cars as they headed back to Petoskey. They dropped one off at The

Perry, not even taking time to go inside, and then drove directly to the hospital. Stuart and Mary were in the lead car with Rick and Mitch following.

The four entered the hospital through the emergency area. They identified themselves and the nurse quickly updated them on Kelly's surgery and gave them her room number.

"We'd been told to be on the lookout for you," the nurse added. "I have a message for you, Mr. Kreicheff, from a Mike Cummings. He wants you to call him at the Harbor Springs Police Department as soon as you can. Here's the number."

"Mike must have recruited them to assist him," Stuart said to the others. "I'll use one of the pay phones, I think they're down that corridor."

The nurse nodded, indicating he was right. The other three accompanied Stuart as he headed down the hall.

"If the Harbor Springs Police Department is anything like Mackinac Island's, that might not be many people," Mitch joked. "And I would expect that to be the case."

•

They could hear Stuart's end of the conversation. He was becoming very upset. "Everything he told you is true," he said. "They've conned you. They're pros—they had us fooled, too." After listening for a few seconds, Stuart blew his top.

"You'll have a fax from the Director herself. You get him out of that cell and put him on the line. We'll be over there with our identification in about forty-five minutes. Don't you dare put him back in a cell. This is a very sensitive case, I don't have time to give you all the details. I'll just tell you one more time, you've been duped. We can understand how it happened, but you know better now. Cummings is working with us, and so is Kelly Travis, his fiancée. We need your cooperation, now put him on the line."

•

Mike was relieved to hear Stuart's voice. His first question was to ask about Kelly. Stuart explained that they hadn't seen her yet, that he'd gotten Mike's message as soon as they arrived at the hospital and immediately called.

"Everything we've been told is positive though, Mike. The surgery was successful. We'll check on her before we head out to see you. Now, bring me up to date. The only thing we know is what you related in your messages. What happened?"

Mike quickly told Stuart what had transpired. "I didn't venture out on the pier to see if the boat was still there. My guess is, they probably left after Kelly escaped. I don't know if the Millers—the man and woman who impersonated the Millers—were on the boat or not when they attempted to kidnap Kelly. The police indicate they met with them when they filed the complaint. They could have strolled off the pier when I was inside the restaurant, trying to reach you. Kelly was inside with me."

"It'll probably be over half an hour before we're there, Mike," Stuart said. "We want to see Kelly first, hear what she has to say. Did the police take your gun?"

"No, I left it at The Perry," Mike replied. I thought—"

"I understand," Stuart said, interrupting. "Maybe I can convince the officer I was just talking with to provide you with a gun and accompany you out on the pier to check and see if the boat's still there. I'm not sure what we should do if it isn't. But if it is, you should keep it under surveillance until we arrive. I'll give you my cellular phone number so you'll be able to notify me about what you discover. It's 670–4470. As I already said, I'm still not sure if we should contact the Coast Guard in case you find the boat's gone. That might prompt too many questions. We still need to be extremely careful not to attract the attention of the news media.

"We'll be able to tell you about Kelly when you call. Be extremely careful, Mike. Now put that officer back on, I'll see how good a salesman I am. And remember, we don't expect or want you or them to take any action on your own. Just determine if the boat's still there."

•

Kelly was just dozing off as Stuart, Mary and Mitch entered her room. Rick had stayed behind to call the Perry Hotel to check for any additional messages. He'd join them as soon as he could.

Coming awake immediately, Kelly greeted them with a smile.

"You look good!" Stuart said. "We really didn't know what to expect. Mike didn't have much of an opportunity to provide us with many details."

"Where is he?" Kelly asked. "I expected to hear from him by now.

Were you able to apprehend anyone?"

"In answer to your first question, Mike's been in a jail cell for the past hour. Your friends—the Millers, or whoever they are—are the ones responsible. They convinced the Harbor Springs police to take immediate steps to stop Mike's physical abuse of you. They prepped them well, explaining he was with the Ann Arbor Police Department and that he might concoct a story about being involved with the FBI in a highly-confidential matter. They warned them that Mike could be very convincing in trying to shift the blame for your recent injuries to someone else."

Kelly's eyes bulged in surprise. "You have to be kidding! But you aren't, are you?"

"No. I just spoke to Mike and we're heading back to Harbor Springs as soon as we leave here. In answer to your second question, no one other than Mike has been apprehended. We were having dinner downstairs in the Chart Room, thinking you and Mike were dining upstairs."

"We didn't get that far," Kelly replied. "Did Mike explain to you about the man who told us we'd left one of the Explorer's windows down?"

Stuart nodded. "He did. And he also mentioned that the man who took you hostage yesterday was also involved. That's about all he told me, very few details. You can probably provide more."

Starting from the moment Mike had left her to check on the window, Kelly described what had taken place. She explained about being told the plans had called for her to disappear along with the Millers.

"That doesn't jive with what took place, though. You'd signaled us with the pagers, but it was actually the woman impersonating Mrs. Miller who suggested Mike and I wait outside. I don't understand why she'd have done that if they were planning on taking me with them. They could have attempted some deception to just get Mike out of the store."

Stuart nodded. "After surveying the scene inside Gattle's, she may have concluded they wouldn't be able to pull that part off," he suggested.

"Perhaps." Kelly replied. "But the man posing as Mr. Miller backed her up. He's the one who suggested that Mike and I head down the block, window-shopping, and they'd catch up."

"Maybe the two hadn't bought into the plan to take you hostage again," Stuart said. "That's a possibility."

Kelly went on to tell them about the two men wheeling her onto the pier, finally stopping next to one of the boats. "I'm still not sure what actually provoked me to take the risk I did, perhaps it was seeing the name on the boat, Webb's Warriors." A slight smile surfaced as she said, "Maybe I wanted to show them I could be a warrior, too. Who knows?"

Stuart, Mary and Mitch all grimaced, identifying with the pain Kelly must have experienced as she described kicking Webb and ramming the wheelchair into the other man. They observed the look in Kelly's eyes as she relived the experience, describing how she'd staggered along the pier, fearing that any second a bullet might rip into her spine.

Chapter 67

"If we aren't back in twenty minutes, Roy, you should call Billy and Keith and bring them in," the officer who was going to accompany Mike directed the other. "I'm hoping we'll be back before that FBI contingent arrives. The one in charge is named Kreicheff, Stuart Kreicheff."

"Should I have them wait?" Roy asked. "Or should I have them come join you?"

"They'll want to do the latter, I'm sure. But there's no telling where we'll be or what we'll actually be doing." Turning to Mike for input as he continued, he said, "We could both be hidden somewhere, watching them preparing to set sail, who knows? They could inadvertently foul things up by attracting attention, by even calling us. I think it would be best if they waited here. I'll call you on my cellular phone and let you know what we discover."

Mike nodded. "I think you're right. Remember, we're only supposed to see if the boat's still there. Chances are, it isn't. As you've indicated, it shouldn't take long. We should know long before they're here."

•

The weather had taken a dramatic turn for the worse during the past hour. The temperature had dropped into the fifties and the sky looked ominous, as if a storm was brewing.

"If they haven't already left, this weather could scare them off from leaving now," the officer accompanying Mike suggested.

As they started out onto the pier, Mike said, "Wouldn't it be a good idea if you told me your name?"

The officer grinned. "You're indicating I haven't been too friendly, is that what you're saying? Suggesting Roy and I should have introduced ourselves?"

Mike couldn't help but smile as he nodded. Even following his lengthy conversation with Stuart, the officer had remained suspicious of Mike. There was no way he was going to equip Mike with a gun. The jury was still out as far as he was concerned. The Millers had planted the hook very solidly and he still wasn't convinced where the truth lay.

"It's Rupert Elkington, but I'm known as Rupe." He still didn't volunteer to shake Mike's hand. "I want you staying right beside me though, son. You shouldn't have any need to call out to me."

Make the best of it, Mike thought. At least Stuart had been able to convince him to immediately investigate whether the boat was still here. For a while, it had appeared that the search would be delayed until Stuart's arrival.

The large yacht looming ahead on Mike's left was the one the father of the young girl had pointed out. It was the boat his family had been viewing when Kelly had been wheeled past them. As they passed it, Mike observed an extension of the pier jutting off to the left, a few feet beyond it.

He turned to Rupe and whispered, "I think the yacht we're looking for might be berthed off this section."

Five or six boats were tied up on each side of the portion of the pier he'd referred to. As they started out on the extension, it appeared to Mike that all the slips to their right were filled. However, on their left, maybe thirty yards ahead, it looked as if there was an empty one. They checked the names on the boats as they walked past them. They'd previously discussed the possibility of the name, Webb's Warriors, being changed. Thus, they were also looking for signs of fresh paint. In a couple instances, in the growing darkness, Mike had made good use of the flashlight Rupe had given him earlier.

Standing in front of the empty slip, the two noticed lights on in the cruiser tied up just beyond the vacant space. The boat they'd just passed was completely dark.

"Our choices are pretty limited," Rupe said, looking over his shoulder at the opposite side of the dock. Only two boats had lights on and both were in slips closer to the main pier. "Guess this one's our first option," he said, pointing to the cruiser ahead of them. "I'll do all the talking, I don't want anyone getting unduly alarmed."

•

The man who responded to Rupe's shout asking if anyone was there, was startled to see a policeman standing on the dock. It was apparent he'd been drinking. His words were slurred as he asked what the problem was.

"We're trying to locate a boat," Rupe explained. "We're wondering if you can tell us if there was one docked here next to you earlier this evening."

The man grinned, nodding his head, seemingly pleased he'd been asked a question he could readily answer. "Sure can, yeah, a cabin cruiser out of Chicago. Just left, maybe half an hour or so ago."

Mike was elated to hear Chicago mentioned as the boat's home port. He hoped Rupe's next question would be to pinpoint the boat's name.

But instead, he asked for the man's name. It was Madison, Jim Madison, from Grand Haven. Rupe next asked for a description of the people Madison had seen onboard the cabin cruiser. Mike held his tongue as Rupe made notes.

The initial person Madison described closely matched the description Kelly had given of Webb. The second could be the one who'd told him he'd left his window open, Mike thought. Mike couldn't contain his smile when the overweight couple in their fifties was described. Rupe glanced over at him, also picking up on who they probably were.

"Now, how about a description of the boat?" Rupe asked. "You mentioned it was out of Chicago. Do you remember seeing a name?"

Madison nodded and put his palm on his forehead, trying to recall. "It began with a W, two words."

Mike felt like calling out bingo, it definitely was the boat they'd been looking for.

"Wave, that's it, Wave Runner," Madison said smiling, delighted it had come to him.

Rupe glanced at Mike, as surprised to hear the name as he could see Mike was.

"You're certain of that?" Rupe asked.

Madison nodded, and there appeared to be no doubt in his mind.

"Jim, are you all right? What's going on?" It was a woman's voice from inside the cabin of the cruiser.

"I'm fine, honey. There are a couple of gentlemen here asking questions about our former slip mates."

The woman opened the door of the cabin and poked her head out. She glanced at Mike and Rupe, taking in the latter's police uniform.

"You're asking questions about the accident?" she asked. "My husband wasn't here when it happened, maybe I'm the best one to answer them."

They both nodded as Rupe asked, "Can you tell us about it, Mrs. Madison?"

"It's Molly, I'm sorry, maybe I misled you. I didn't see how it happened. I was inside at the time, when I heard something bounce off the side of their boat and the splash."

Rupe glanced at Mike again. It was apparent he was finally giving credence to Mike's story.

"When I came out onto the deck, a man was floundering in the water between the pilings and their cruiser, trying to grasp onto something. He had a hand on a wheelchair, trying to keep afloat, but it was sinking. I thought he might be crippled and wondered whether I should throw him a life preserver. Another man was pulling himself up from where he'd been dangling off the side of their boat. He saw me staring at him as he swung his legs onto the deck. He was gasping for air, but managed to say they'd just had a stupid accident. He stood up and quickly grabbed a rope and threw it to the other man, telling him to tie it under his armpits. He hauled the other man up out of the water, thanking me in the process for my concern, saying they had everything under control."

Wondering if she'd made herself clear, Mrs. Madison looked from Rupe to Mike and back again, anticipating questions.

"Did either of them say anything further, explain the accident?" Mike asked.

"Not much. The man who'd hauled the other one from the lake smiled and asked me if I was much of a diver, pointing to where the wheelchair had sunk. As I was shaking my head, a man and woman came out of the cabin and asked what had happened. The man who'd been talking to me gestured for them to go back inside. He followed them in. The man who'd been pulled out of the water also went in the cabin. I remember wondering which of the two had needed the wheelchair, neither was limping or looked as if they needed one. About five or ten minutes later the couple left, heading toward the main pier."

"That's the couple I described to you earlier," her husband explained. "Middle-aged, overweight, they came back as the others were preparing the boat for departure."

"Did you tell these men that they just motored out there a quarter of a mile or so and appeared to drop anchor?" Mrs. Madison asked her husband.

He shook his head. "I haven't had time, honey. I was planning to. You can't see their boat now, it's way too dark. Besides, they might not still be there. But we were able to watch their boat lights and saw them stop out there, to the left of the main channel. They doused their lights a couple minutes later."

"Let's have a look," Rupe suggested, leading Mike out to the end of the section of pier they were on. Even with the benefit of their flashlights, their vision was limited in the darkness. They couldn't see if a boat was still there.

"You can't imagine how sorry I am about all this, Mr. Cummings," Rupe said. "That couple was so convincing. If I'd listened to you, we might have been able to stop them before they took off."

"That's behind us now Rupe, and you can call me Mike. The important thing now is to call Roy and tell him what we've found out. We can see if Stuart and the others have arrived, but I doubt it."

Rupe nodded and reached for his cellular phone. He had difficulty getting it to work.

"Damn it, I've been having trouble with this for over a week. Maybe that couple has a phone we could use."

Mike nodded and they headed back along the pier. The Madisons were still standing on the deck of their boat.

"Could you tell if they're still there?" Jim asked.

"No, we couldn't see a thing," Rupe replied. "We're wondering if you have a phone we could use?"

They both nodded, Molly gesturing for them to come aboard.

"It's just inside the cabin door to the right," she said.

While Rupe went inside to call, Mike conversed with the couple.

"Your husband says the name on the boat was 'Wave Runner'. Is that the same name you recall?" he asked.

Mrs. Madison nodded. "Yes, from Chicago."

Everything ties in except that, Mike thought, as he went on to ask, "Does the name 'Webb's Warriors' mean anything to either of you?"

The question resulted in blank stares to begin with, but as her husband shook his head, Mrs. Madison's face suddenly lit up.

"That's right!" she exclaimed. "That's the name I saw when I came out on deck to see what had happened, after I heard the splash and the sound I guess of the wheelchair striking the side of their boat. It was on a plaque, hanging down over the other name. I thought it was strange, but I completely forgot, with everything else that was happening."

Seeing the smile on Mike's face, she turned to her husband and said, "I guess that was important. I'm sorry I didn't mention it sooner."

Rupe came out of the cabin door and walked over next to Mike.

"I got through to Roy, your friends haven't arrived yet. I told him what we'd learned and said we were on our way back. We'd be there in a few minutes."

"I think I should call Stuart on his cell phone," Mike said. "While you were on the phone with Roy, I did learn something more. Mrs. Madison remembers seeing the name 'Webb's Warriors.' She can fill you in while I call Stuart. Is it all right if I use your phone?"

The Madisons both nodded.

Chapter 68

"He looked familiar, but you still haven't been able to place him?" Stuart asked.

Kelly nodded, picturing in her mind the face of the man who'd told them their car window was down. Maybe after she had a chance to talk to Mike, it might jog her memory.

As Stuart was continuing to question Kelly, following her detailed description of what had happened, Mary leaned over and whispered to Mitch.

"We need to get some flowers, a bouquet or at least a plant for her."

Mitch nodded. Stuart noticed and said, "You two are probably thinking the same thing I am. We need to arrange for some type of security for Kelly. It's probably not likely, but those people might pay her a visit while we're in Harbor Springs."

Mary indicated with a nod of her head that she agreed with Stuart. "But you're a step ahead of us, we were hoping we could arrange to get some flowers for her."

Stuart smiled as Kelly said, "Oh please, don't worry about flowers, I don't plan to be here very long. Besides, apprehending those people is the important issue now. I've taken too much of your time as it is, you should be leaving to join Mike."

"We'll be on our way in a minute," Stuart replied. "Mary, I'm thinking you should stay here with Kelly. We're limited in the number of people who might recognize—"

Stuart was interrupted by the ring of his portable phone. As he began to talk, he indicated it was Mike. After listening for a moment or two he asked, "But you haven't actually seen it?" And then a few seconds later he replied, "I understand, we're just leaving. I'll put Kelly on. If she's feeling as good as she looks, there's nothing to worry about."

He handed the phone to Kelly as he conferred with Mary and Mitch.

•

Kelly limited her conversation with Mike, realizing Stuart was anxious to leave and would want to take the phone with him. As she handed it back to him she said, "It's probably more important that Mary be with you, rather than staying behind with me. You could just tell the staff to make my room off-limits to anyone but them. They might even be able to lock the door."

"No," Mary said. "I'd love to accompany them, but Stuart's right, I should stay with you. You need some sleep, Kelly. My being here will hopefully take some worry off your mind. Locks don't hinder us much, and I'm sure those people are probably pretty adept at getting past them, too. I can get a chair to sit on outside your door. I'm wide awake now and I'm sure you'll be able to get me spelled within the next few hours, right Stuart?"

He nodded and wished both of them well as he headed out the door, followed by Mitch.

Chapter 69

Rick met Stuart and Mitch as they came down the corridor.

"Bad news," he said. "I've just been on the phone with Fritz. Their car, the Lincoln, has been stolen."

Stuart and Mitch stared at him in amazement as Rick explained. "They pulled off the freeway in Flint to grab a bite to eat. They chose a Wendy's right near the exit ramp. Mark was driving and they waited a minute or two to get a parking place where they'd be able to watch the car as they ate. They both washed up in the men's room and Fritz told Mark what he wanted and then went to get a table next to the window. The car was gone."

Stuart was familiar with Flint, an hour or so drive north of Detroit, maybe a three-and-a-half to four-hour drive from Petoskey.

"Of course, anyone could have stolen it," Rick continued. "Car jackers waiting in the parking lot and quickly seizing an opportunity. Fritz doesn't believe that's the case, he's sure they must have been followed. He also thinks there may have been a sensor device on the Lincoln. The state police arrived as I was talking to him, an alert's been put out on the vehicle."

Stuart didn't believe in coincidences anymore than Fritz did. This meant the people they were attempting to identify had regained possession of what was perhaps the best evidence which may have enabled them to do so. They also had the letters and the remainder of the money.

"There was also a phone message for you," Rick said. "It was a threat from Roy Miller, 'Back off or this will blow up in your faces'."

Stuart nodded. "It probably means that if we're fortunate enough to locate the Lincoln, we'll probably find it's been destroyed. Useless for obtaining any prints or other evidence."

"Should we go back and tell Mary and Kelly?" Mitch asked Stuart.

"Let's wait," he replied. "Mike's waiting and we need to make a few phone calls. We have to arrange for a couple of speedboats, hopefully equipped with search lights. We'll require some additional people and added firepower. I'll also need to clear this with Washington. When I tell them about the missing car, they might reconsider authorizing us to proceed. I doubt if Fritz has informed them yet."

"I doubt it, too," Mitch said. "He's had one hell of a day, hasn't he? Guess that goes for all of us, though."

Stuart nodded as the three of them hurried down the corridor. He couldn't help but remember how elated he'd been a few hours ago. Even with the Millers' disappearance, there had been some bright spots. It was difficult to see any now.

•

"I should be letting you rest," Mary said. She and Kelly had been chatting for the past twenty minutes or so. In addition to discussing the day's events, Kelly had taken the opportunity to get Mary's input on some of the wedding plans.

"I've really enjoyed talking to you, Mary. This has been such a hectic few days. I probably haven't been making much sense, I'm getting a little groggy."

"I'm amazed you're as alert as you are. I don't know too many details, but Stuart shared with us at dinner the fact that the man, who you and Mike were so instrumental in apprehending last fall, escaped. And he also told us how elated you'd been earlier in learning he was finally going to go to trial. Between that and this, you have to be exhausted, similar to being on two roller coasters with all the ups and downs. I'll leave in a minute, but there's one more thing I wanted to mention.

"It just dawned on me why your description of the man, the one who told you about the car window being down, sounded familiar. It's similar to the description witnesses gave of the man who posed as a Dr. Overbeck, the one who suddenly appeared on the scene after Mr. Woodbridge's supposed accident. I wonder if Mr. Woodbridge is still awake. I can probably get him on the phone and have him describe the man to you, see if you think it's the same man."

"It would mean one less person to track down," Kelly replied. "I told you the man looked familiar, but of course, I never saw the man who posed as the doctor. Maybe I did at some other time though, not realizing who I was seeing."

•

Rick adjusted the windshield wipers up a notch. The rain was heavier now. Despite the nasty weather, they'd been able to make good time during the drive to Harbor Springs. Stuart had been on the phone for almost the entire period. The State Police and the speedboats should be waiting for them.

"Was that a deer?" Mitch asked.

"I think it was," Rick replied. The glare off the wet pavement had marred their visibility. Rick slowed down slightly as he said, "We should be there in about ten minutes."

Washington had not been happy. The missing letters, rather than the money, had been their concern, as Stuart knew they would be. Though he'd been given a go-ahead, Stuart was nervous. The concession was far from an endorsement. He and his people would really be on their own, knowing there would be many second-guesses if things went awry. The three men were silent as they mulled over what lay in store for them. The silence was broken by the ring of Stuart's phone.

"This might be Mike again," he said as he answered. But instead of

Mike, it was Mark.

"We found the Lincoln," Mark began, "in the middle of a field about six miles from the Wendy's. It's been torched, totally gutted. It appears they emptied everything out first. Fritz is still going over the car with a couple of the State policemen. There's not much left of it, I doubt if they'll come up with anything. Fritz was able to find a woman who saw a man entering the Lincoln. Her description seems to match one of those men in the photo Anderson took from the boat."

Mark also informed Stuart that there had been no witnesses to the torching of the car, and no lead to the make or model of the other car which had to have been used. Stuart brought Mark up to date on developments at their end, and was given the phone number at the State Police post where Fritz and Mark could be reached.

"Just stay where you are," Stuart said. "I'll try to call in the next hour or two and let you know how we've made out."

"Good luck, we'll keep our fingers crossed," Mark said before hanging up.

•

"I'm sure we have an extra raincoat at the station I can loan you," Rupe said to Mike. "I should probably just give it to you, try to make up for my goof. I'm really sorry, Mike."

"Forget it," Mike replied. "I told you, I'd been conned by them, too."

They were just coming off the pier as Mike exclaimed, "Look, my car's gone!"

The Explorer had been there when they'd passed it going out on the pier a few minutes before.

"I can't believe it!" Rupe exclaimed, glancing around the now-near deserted parking lot. "I'll put out an alert. I can't believe all this is happening."

•

Following Mike's suggestions, after returning to the office, Rupe called the Harbor Master. He lived just outside of town and promised he'd come meet them at the pier in less than fifteen minutes. He'd be able to check and see under whose name the Wave Runner had been registered, and also let them borrow two pairs of binoculars with a night-time lens feature.

•

From their vantage point beneath the overhang of the restaurant, Rupe and Mike had an excellent view of the pier. There were only a handful of yachts and cabin cruisers with their lights still on. Rupe had found a raincoat in his car for Mike. Through the downpour they were able to see two speed-boats approaching the shoreline to the left of the pier. Mike stepped out from under the overhang and signaled them with his flashlight.

As the boats neared the shore, Mike glanced at his watch. Stuart and the others should be arriving any minute.

•

Mary had checked with a nurse and learned Mr. Woodbridge was asleep. Verification of her hunch would have to wait until morning. His room was only seven doors down from Kelly's. Mary had carried a chair from Kelly's room into the hallway, positioning herself next to the door. A nurse had supplied her with some reading material, a copy of *People* maga-zine was currently laying in her lap.

Though the main hall lights were off, the glow from the night lights was more than sufficient to give her a view of both ends of the corridor and the nurses' station. One of the nurses had just completed her round, check-ing on patients. The present silence was very conducive to dozing off. She checked her watch as she stood up and stretched. It was nearly eleven-thirty.

•

Mike was able to recognize Stuart and the other two men as they drove up. He walked over to greet them as they parked. After the exchange of greetings, he took them over to meet Rupe and the others. Four State Police officers had arrived on the speedboats. An additional three had ar-rived by car a few minutes ago.

"We're just waiting for direction from you," Mike said to Stuart. "You can see they're almost set." He'd pointed to the two officers who were stand-ing in one of the boats dressed in wet suits. They were in the process of checking out their gear.

Stuart nodded as he scanned the two speedboats, pleased to see the automatic weapons, sets of night goggles, the spotlights, bullhorns and other gear. He'd been able to devise a game plan during the drive from Petoskey and began to spell it out to the others.

"Feel free to make suggestions or ask questions," Stuart explained. "Many of our decisions will have to be made on the fly, depending on what we discover. We aren't sure if we'll find their boat where it was last seen. They may have moved on. Mike says you didn't notice it when you came through the channel. But I realize you were keeping your distance to avoid alerting them. We hope we can surprise them and apprehend those on board without anyone being injured, them or us. I want to caution everyone though, that they could be planning a surprise for us. We still don't know why they've done what they have, anchoring their boat near the channel rather than proceeding on into Lake Michigan. Of course, the weather could have something to do with it, but personally, I'm suspicious more than that's involved."

During the time Stuart had been talking, the rain had increased and was now coming down in torrents. Though all were in rain gear of some type, those officers in wet-suits were the only ones adequately prepared for this type of storm. The whitecaps were growing in size as the boats docked at the pier rocked, their flags flapping in the stiff breeze. Stuart realized he needed to cut this short as he eyed his listeners, they were turning up their collars and jamming their hands deeper into their pockets.

"We received a message in the past hour, a threat that if we continue our pursuit of these people, it might blow up in our faces. There's already been one incident in which this has happened."

Mike glanced up at Stuart in alarm. Had something happened at the hospital? Was Kelly safe?

"A vehicle has been torched. We were using it to transport evidence to a lab in Detroit, evidence which would hopefully lead to the identity of those on the cabin cruiser and possibly others. The destruction of the car could have been what the threat referred to. But it also could mean they have an arsenal on board the cabin cruiser with plans to blow these boats out of the water," Stuart said, pointing to the two speedboats. "Or it could mean they've planted explosives on their boat. I don't think they're suicidal. They could have rigged the boat and abandoned it. The point is, I want all of us to be aware of the potential risks, that we need to be cautious. We don't want to walk into a trap."

Mike was wondering if Fritz and Mark had escaped injury. He was anxious for Stuart to wind up so he could find out.

"We don't have room in these boats for everyone, and that's just as well," Stuart continued. "I think the two of you should wait on the pier," he said to Mike and Rupe. "If something does go dreadfully wrong, you two might have to literally pick up the pieces."

•

Mary shifted in the chair before standing up and stretching. She'd looked in on Kelly a few minutes ago and was pleased to see she appeared to be sleeping. As she glanced down the hallway, she saw one of the nurses seated at a desk in the nurses' station. I think I'll ask her to keep an eye on Kelly's room while I visit the restroom, she thought. The nurse looked up with a smile as she heard Mary's footsteps approaching.

•

Mary exited the ladies' room and nodded to the nurse she'd spoken to earlier. They'd had a pleasant conversation. It was a quiet night and the attractive young woman had appeared to enjoy the interruption.

"I just discovered this note," the nurse said, holding up a slip of paper. "I wasn't aware of it when we were talking earlier. Vivian, the other nurse, took a phone message for Ms. Travis. She went off dirty a short time ago and must have forgotten to tell me. I just noticed it on her desk. It's from her doctor in Ann Arbor. He called to see how she was doing. Do you want to take it down to her?"

Mary nodded and thanked the nurse as she took the note. She glanced at the message, 'Sorry about the accident. You should be more careful. Hope to see you soon.' The name the caller had given along with the message was Dr. George Overbeck."

Alarmed, she looked up at the nurse. This was the man she and Kelly had just been talking about.

"Is something wrong?" the nurse asked, a look of confusion on her face. She'd probably read the note, Mary thought. She doesn't understand why I'm so concerned.

"No one's been near Ms. Travis' room, have they?"

"Only you," the nurse replied, smiling again, waiting for Mary's answer to her earlier question.

Mary wasn't sure what she could say without going into a lengthy explanation. Maybe a little white lie would be best.

"I'd thought Dr. Overbeck was deceased. But I guess he must not be. Do you have any idea when the call came in?"

"She usually notes the time in the upper left-hand corner," the nurse replied. Sure enough, it was, eleven-twenty p.m. Less than half an hour ago.

"It is, I should have looked closer," Mary said. "I'll make sure she gets this."

Mary hurried down the hall and opened the door to Kelly's room. It was the same scene as earlier—Kelly appeared to be sleeping. Mary placed the note on the tray table and went back out into the corridor. She reached inside her pocket to assure herself her gun was readily available, before sitting down. She should be hearing from Stuart soon, it had been over an hour since they'd left to meet Mike. He'll be interested in hearing about the message. They all will be.

•

Stuart drew Mike off to the side for a moment prior to boarding one of the speedboats. He quickly briefed him on the theft of the Lincoln, including the fact Fritz and Mark had been inside the Wendy's and hadn't been injured. He also told Mike of the go-ahead they'd received from Washington.

"This will probably be the final time we'll get clearance for continuing our pursuit of these people. The Director realizes she's gone out on a limb with us, the go-ahead was far from a unanimous decision. You probably won't be able to see all that much from the pier. I'm sorry we don't have an extra pair of night goggles to leave with you."

"Rupe called the Harbor Master," Mike explained. "He's supposed to be here in another few minutes with some night binoculars."

"Perfect," Stuart said, nodding to the men already in the boat, indicating he was ready to join them. Mike held out his arm so Stuart could balance himself as he stepped into the boat. He thanked Mike and told him to keep his fingers crossed.

As the two boats backed away, Mike and Rupe heard the sound of a vehicle behind them and turned to see a Chevy pick-up truck.

"It's Bob, the fella who manages the pier," Rupe explained as a young, red-haired, slender man was exiting from the cab of the vehicle. Bob leaned back inside the cab and retrieved a set of binoculars.

"What the hell's going on, Rupe?" he asked. "Does this have something to do with the woman who was injured earlier? I was leaving just as the EMS team arrived."

"I'm afraid so," Rupe replied. "First off though, this is Mike Cummings. He's engaged to the woman who was injured. This is Bob Irish, Mike."

The two men shook hands as Rupe continued. "We think the people who were responsible are out there in the harbor, on a boat anchored next to the harbor channel."

Bob's expression conveyed how dangerous he thought that was, in the raging storm. "Do you know the name of the boat?" he asked.

"The Wave Runner, out of Chicago," Rupe replied. "But they also used the name Webb's Warriors."

Bob nodded. "The Wave Runner just arrived today, mid-afternoon. The girl I spoke to said they were headed back to Chicago, they'd spent the weekend at Mackinac Island. We'd had a reservation cancellation, otherwise we wouldn't have had room for them."

"Can you describe the girl?" Mike asked.

"Sure, maybe about five-seven, slender, dark hair, dark-complected. Her hair was braided, tied in a ponytail. Want to know what she was wearing?"

"No, that's not necessary, thank you," Mike replied.

Bob's description matched Mr. Woodbridge's sketch and Kelly's description of Sandy, the young woman they'd both encountered.

"As a matter of fact, I may have passed her on my way here. A man was driving the car, they were headed towards Petoskey. I'm not certain it was her. With both our wipers going, I didn't get that good a look. But I remember at the time thinking she looked familiar and then recalling where I'd seen her. We'd both had to slow down to nearly a stop as we drove through a huge puddle. That's the only reason I had a chance to recognize her."

If that's true it means she's no longer on the boat, Mike thought.

"This is probably too much to hope for, but could you describe the man who was driving?" Mike asked.

Bob shook his head. "Oh boy, that's tough. I really can't. I think the car they were in was a Ford Explorer, if that's any help."

"It is," Mike answered, thinking it was no doubt his.

"I'll notify Roy," Rupe suggested, removing the cell phone from his raincoat pocket. "I can call while we're heading out to the end of the pier."

Mike didn't appear to hear him, his mind was preoccupied with the thought that the couple Bob had seen could be headed to the Northern Michigan Hospital. Stuart had just informed him that Mary had remained there purposely to keep an eye on Kelly. He'd forgotten to tell Stuart his car was missing. He needed to call Mary, needed to warn her and Kelly.

Rupe was shaking his head as he said, "Damn, I'm still having problems with this phone."

"I need to make a call, too," Mike said. "The phone in your car is working, isn't it?"

Rupe nodded as he replied, "Yes, but if we take time now, we're apt to miss out on things. Here's my keys. Bob and I'll go on ahead, you can call Roy, too."

Mike nodded, maybe he was overreacting. Would these people be so bold as to try and kidnap Kelly from the hospital? Bob isn't even certain it was the same woman. They're dozens of Ford Explorers around here. It won't take long for Stuart and the others to verify whether the cabin cruiser is still there. Rupe and I better get in position now, the calls will have to wait. Rupe was holding out his hand with the car keys. Mike waved his hand, indicating he should keep them.

"We need to get out there now, we'll make the calls later."

•

The cabin cruiser was slowly coming into view. It has to be them, Stuart thought, raising his arm and motioning for the other speedboat to join them. There was no sign of activity on the boat, all was dark as it rocked in the waves. He considered whether to utilize the men in the wet suits. No, he decided, it would make more sense to confront them by turning on the spots, ordering them to surrender over the bullhorn. The other speedboat was now beside them. He directed them to circle and position themselves on the other side of the cabin cruiser.

"Turn on your spotlight in exactly eight minutes, at twelve-eleven a.m. Take cover and have those weapons ready. Be sure to keep a safe distance.

The men in the other boat nodded as they moved off.

"What if there's no response?" Mitch asked.

"We'll face that question if we have to," Stuart replied. He had an uneasy feeling they could be headed into a trap. "This is about as close as we want to get," he said to the man driving the boat. "Maybe over to the right about twenty yards, though."

The officer nodded as he turned the wheel.

•

Rupe had slipped on the wet pier and would have fallen if it hadn't been for Bob. Bob had asked to join them and Mike was now glad they'd said yes, as he assisted him in righting Rupe.

"That was dumb," Rupe said, shaken and chagrined over the fact he'd nearly sprawled onto the wet planks. Mike tried to conceal a smile. Rupe had resembled a beginner skater, waving his hands as he bobbed and weaved, trying to maintain his balance. It had been almost slow motion. Thank heavens Bob had been able to catch him.

"If you want to go on ahead, I can catch up," Rupe suggested as he shuffled along, taking care not to slip again.

"No problem," Mike said. "We haven't far to go. That could have happened to any of us." Checking his watch, Mike saw it was just past midnight.

•

"One minute," Stuart informed the officer who already had his hand on the searchlight switch, holding one of the automatic weapons in his other. The rest of them were kneeling in the boat, positioning their firearms.

"Ten seconds," Stuart said. The spots came on, fully illuminating the cabin cruiser. Raising the megaphone to his lips, Stuart shouted, "This is the FBI and Michigan State Police. We have you surrounded. Come out on deck with your hands on your heads. You have—"

The roar was deafening as an explosion blew the cabin cruiser apart, catapulting pieces of the boat high into the air. Even at this distance, the impact from the blast had knocked them all off balance. Stuart reached for the side of the boat to pull himself up. How lucky they'd been that one or more of the guns hadn't accidentally discharged, he thought. Flames and smoke were rising in the air. Everyone was raising their hands to shield their faces from the heat as the officer at the wheel shifted the boat into reverse.

"That was awesome!" one of the officers said, his eyes bugged in amazement.

"Is everyone okay?" Stuart asked, relieved they hadn't elected to use the officers in the wet suits. They would have surely been killed. He wondered whether the explosion had been triggered by the sound of his voice. More likely, it had been set off with a remote device. Someone could have been watching them from another boat, possibly from the shore, they might still be. There's the possibility a timer was used, Stuart thought. But the timing was too perfect, it had to have been triggered by his voice or a remote device.

•

Mike and the other two men gazed in horror, watching as flames shot into the air. The burnt smell of smoke was already filling their nostrils. Lights were quickly coming on in the nearby yachts and cabin cruisers. A number of people saw the three of them, with Mike training the binoculars on the burning boat, and began shouting questions.

"Can I have those keys?" Mike asked Rupe. "I'll meet you on shore. See if you can play this down with these people."

Rupe nodded as he handed him the keys. It had been an amazing turn of events for him in the past hour or so. What he and his partner had assumed was a routine case of spousal abuse had proved to be far more complex.

As Mike raced off he heard Rupe's voice boom out, "Calm down, there's no danger."

There were already dozens of people on the decks of their boats, confused, wondering what had occurred. Lights were continuing to come on. Rupe glanced at Bob, who was still spellbound.

"We need to get the word circulated that this is an isolated incident and that there's no need for panic. That we suspect arson."

Rupe turned to meet the group of people who were approaching him. I hope I'm being honest with them, he thought.

Chapter 70

The nurse informed Mike that Kelly was sleeping, but that she'd get

Mary Zuckerman on the phone. It would just take a minute. He nervously drummed his fingers on the steering wheel as he waited. He hoped that no one had been injured or worse in the explosion. The warning that things could blow up in their faces hadn't been an empty threat. This—

"Hi Mike, what's happened?"

"First off, are you in a spot where you can still keep an eye on Kelly's room?" Mike asked.

"I am, her door's about a hundred feet from where I'm standing. She's fine, Mike. She managed to fall asleep an hour or so ago. I just checked on her, I have a chair outside her room."

Mike breathed a sigh of relief and began to tell Mary what had taken place in Harbor Springs.

"It surpassed any Fourth of July fireworks finale I've ever seen. The noise was deafening, flames shooting into the air. I didn't wait to see if anyone was injured. I was anxious to call you as soon as I could. They carried through on the warning in their message."

"What message, Mike? A recent one?"

"Oh, I'm sorry, I assumed you knew. Stuart must have received it after he'd seen you. You know about Fritz and Mark, don't you?"

"No, what about them?" Mary replied. "I haven't spoken to Stuart since he left us. That was over an hour ago. Kelly also received a message I've been waiting to tell you and Stuart about."

"What was hers?" Mike asked, realizing he still hadn't explained the most important reason for his call.

Mary related the message and how it was signed. "He's the—"

"I know," Mike replied, remembering how Kelly had tried to track down a Dr. George Overbeck in Ann Arbor. His fears were mounting as he warned Mary about the possibility the couple who'd taken Kelly hostage previously might be headed to the hospital or might already be there.

"Can you alert the main desk, the hospital's security personnel? I'm going to try to get there just as quickly as I can."

"I will Mike, and I have a gun. Don't worry, I was primed before and now I'll be even more so, ready for anything. I'll see if I can get one of the security people positioned outside Kelly's door so I can be in the room with her. Don't worry, we'll be ready if anyone does show. We certainly won't be taken by surprise. Now, what's this about Fritz and Mark?"

•

Kelly woke with a start. She sensed someone was in the room. Her eyes gradually adjusted to the darkness. She saw no one. Someone could be hiding in the bathroom or the closet, though. Maybe even under her bed. She checked her watch, twelve-thirty a.m. She'd been asleep for over an hour. With the myriad of thoughts going through her mind, she was amazed she'd been able to drift off to sleep. She wondered what had happened while she'd been dozing. Her door was ajar and she called out.

"Mary, are you out there? Have you heard anything from Mike or Stuart?"

There was just silence. She could be using the restroom, maybe on the phone talking to one of them now, Kelly thought. She reached for the control and switched on the light. She strained her ears for any sound.

I could buzz for the nurse, she thought. She decided to wait a few minutes; Mary might be back soon. Maybe she woke me while she was looking in on me before leaving to use the restroom, or the phone. That's probably what made me think someone was here in the room with me.

As Kelly laid there waiting, numerous thoughts went through her mind. She hadn't called her parents back; she hoped they were okay. She wondered if there had been any sighting of McConnell. She wondered when she'd be seeing Mike, when she'd be back in Ann Arbor and her own bed.

"Mary, are you there?" Still no answer.

•

Stuart and Rick spotted Mike as he exited from the Harbor Springs police car. He came toward them as they were climbing out of the speedboat. Stuart turned to Mitch, who was still in the boat.

"I wouldn't waste too much time out there. Chances are we'll have more success in the morning, as the storm subsides and in the daylight."

Mitch nodded. The men in the other speedboat had remained at the site of the explosion. Mitch and the two State Police officers were going back to join them. Stuart had asked to be brought ashore so he could confer in private with Washington. As the speedboat backed away, Stuart and Rick turned to greet Mike.

Mike saw the looks of despair on the two men's faces.

"I guess they've made their point, haven't they?" Stuart said to Mike.

Nodding in assent, Mike replied, "I need to fill you in on some other developments. I want to get to the hospital as soon as I can."

Mike quickly told the two men about the phone call from Dr. Overbeck and the message left for Kelly. Before they could even digest that piece of news he told them of his more major concern, the fact that the couple who'd held Kelly hostage yesterday might be headed to the hospital.

"But . . . what did you say his name was, Bob Irish?"

Mike nodded his head in answer to Stuart's question.

"You say he's not certain it was the same woman?"

"No, and it's just speculation as to where they were headed. Nonetheless, I'd like to get there as soon as I can."

"Understood," Stuart answered. "Rick, let's give him our car. I'm sure between the State Police and the Harbor Springs Police, we'll be able to get to Petoskey."

Rick handed Mike the keys as he pointed out their car. Stuart reached into his pocket for his revolver and handed it to Mike.

"Let's hope not, but you may need this. Good luck, we should be there with you in less than an hour."

●

Mary noticed that the door to Kelly's room was ajar as she came down the hallway. She definitely remembered closing it after she'd looked in on her a short time ago. She reached inside her jacket for her gun and made certain the safety was off.

She'd called downstairs and spoken to the security people. They'd been anxious to cooperate and said they'd be sending one of their people up right away. She wondered if she should wait before going in Kelly's room. Why delay, she thought. Positioning her body against the wall, she pushed the door open.

Kelly jumped as the door swung open. She glimpsed Mary's face peering around the door casing. A second or two later, Mary charged into the room, clutching a gun in her hands. She quickly turned in a circle, her gaze taking in the entire room. She glanced under the bed and then moved to the door leading to the bathroom as Kelly watched. Something must have occurred to prompt Mary's actions, she realized.

The bathroom and clothes closet were empty. Mary smiled at Kelly as she replaced the gun in her pocket.

"Lots has happened while you were sleeping," she explained. "I was sure I'd closed your door, for one thing. But first off, Mike's fine. He's on his way now, he should be here in the next half-hour."

Mary then proceeded to tell Kelly about the call from the man identifying himself as Dr. George Overbeck and the message for her. As Kelly mulled over that news, Mary went on to tell her of Mike's concern, the fact the two people who'd held her hostage yesterday could be headed to the hospital.

"One of the hospital's security people should be here in a minute or two. I'm going to have him position himself outside your door while I'm here in the room with you."

Kelly nodded, now understanding Mary's earlier actions and concern.

"And believe it or not, I haven't told you some of the major things that have occurred," Mary continued. "The cabin cruiser they were trying to get you on was blown up in the harbor. The Lincoln was stolen and torched."

Kelly shook her head as Mary talked, providing details on her two latest revelations.

•

Mike had been able to make good time. The combination of the hour and the storm resulted in scant traffic; he'd seen only three or four cars. He saw the stoplight up ahead at the main highway, which would take him into Petoskey. The parking lot of the Mexican restaurant on his right was vacant, it had been jammed with cars when he and Kelly had passed it on their way to dinner. With no cars in sight, he was able to turn on the red light.

He was praying that Kelly was safe, he'd be with her in another ten minutes or so. Knowing he was exceeding the speed limit, he kept an eye on the rearview mirror. Stuart had been very depressed when he'd left him just now. Mike wondered what the reaction of the Bureau would be. He empathized with Stuart's having to relate the details of this latest development, so soon after reporting the Lincoln had been stolen. The fact they'd been able to recover the letters and a portion of the money had taken part of the sting out of the Millers' disappearance. But now they were out of their hands again. There was no way anyone could put a positive spin on what had occurred.

He thought of Kelly again. Good and bad things frequently happened in threes. Mike hoped that the Millers' disappearance, the theft of the Lincoln and the attention-drawing destruction of the cabin cruiser had completed the cycle, that something happening to Kelly wouldn't be a third disaster. He felt his heart pounding as his foot pressed the accelerator pedal a little closer to the floor.

•

Kelly and Mary looked up at the door at the sound of the knock.

"Security," a woman's voice called out.

Mary held up her hand, afraid Kelly was about to say 'come in.' "I'm going to ask her to slip some identification under the door," Mary said as she started toward the door.

There was another knock as the woman called out again, "Hospital Security." The door knob began to turn before Mary had a chance to say anything. Kelly watched as Mary dashed to position herself so she'd be behind the door as it opened, her gun drawn. A young woman's smiling face peeked in at Kelly as the door opened.

"Hi, I'm Karen Steiner. I—" The woman's eyes bulged in surprise as she caught sight of Mary.

"Do you have some identification?" Mary asked. Regaining her composure, the woman pointed to her name badge as she also reached into her pants pocket. Mary quickly scanned her ID, thanking the woman as she handed it back to her.

"I'm sorry," Mary explained as she returned the gun to her jacket pocket. "But I've learned it pays to be cautious. I'm Mary Zuckerman, and this is Kelly Travis."

"I was told that much," Karen said, nodding at them. "But not much more. You took me by surprise, this is serious business, isn't it?"

Mary nodded. She hoped the rest of the security people realized how serious, that Kelly could be in extreme danger.

"We aren't sure, but we think one or more persons might attempt to kidnap her," Mary explained, pointing to Kelly. "They're probably armed. We need you to stand guard outside this door, get word to your people if anyone attempts to enter this room. Can you give her a description of the couple we think may make an appearance, Kelly?"

Kelly nodded and quickly described Sandy and Webb, the two who'd taken her hostage yesterday. Actually two days ago, Kelly thought. It was already Tuesday.

"I should also tell you about another couple," Kelly continued as she went on to describe the man and woman who posed as the Millers. "They've deceived a number of us already, appearing as a very naïve, innocent twosome. But don't be taken in by them."

"I'm thinking we should get you up to one of the C.P. rooms," Karen said. "I don't think either of them are currently occupied." Seeing the lack of understanding on Mary's and Kelly's faces she went on to explain. "We have two small suites upstairs, they're used for celebrities or other VIPs. We can control access very easily, keep the news media away. They're large enough so another person besides the patient can stay in the room. One big difference from a normal room is the fact you can lock the doors from the inside."

"What does C. P. stand for?" Mary asked.

"You know, I'm not really sure," Karen replied and she grinned. "There's lots of jokes—Costly Penthouse, Celebrity Privacy, Customer Pays—but I actually don't know."

Mary felt sure the Bureau would pick up the cost difference for one of the rooms for Kelly. Mike would be arriving shortly, it sounded perfect if he should spend the night and she was sure he'd want to.

"Can you get on this phone, Karen, and start making the necessary arrangements? It really sounds ideal for our needs."

•

Mike yanked the door open and raced into the hospital. The two men seated at a desk just to the left of the entrance glanced up.

"You must be Mr. Cummings. Mary Zuckerman told us to be expecting you," the uniformed one said.

Mike nodded as he showed them his driver's license.

"Everything's been pretty quiet here," the man continued. "I'll take you up to Ms. Travis' room."

As the two hurried up the stairway, the security guard once again explained to Mike that none of the people they'd been cautioned about had made an appearance.

"There's actually been much less activity than normal, probably due to the weather. The handful of people we've seen all checked out."

As he quickly led Mike down the corridor, he looked back over his shoulder and said, "Her room's just a few doors down here on the right."

The door was standing open with the light off. It was empty, even the bed was gone. With a lump in his throat, Mike nervously asked, "Are you sure this is the right room?"

"Positive," the guard said as he backed out of the room, looking toward the nurses' station, another fifty feet down the corridor. No one was there. Mike's imagination was going wild, he was too late. As the two men pondered their next move, a nurse came out of a room a couple doors from the nurses' station.

As they approached her she smiled and said, "We've just moved her, up to CP2, Charlie. You must be Mr. Cummings. Your fiancée is doing fine. As Charlie knows, there's far better security upstairs. Even though we've had no problems, it was decided it would be best to move her as soon as we could."

Mike returned her smile as he thanked her. "I was terrified when we saw the room was empty." Turning to the guard, Mike asked, "I'm sure you know the quickest way to get to her new room?"

He nodded and smiled, also clearly relieved to hear about the change in rooms.

•

"Is there anything else I can do for you?" the nurse asked. "Do you need any additional pain medication? All this activity, it might be advised. You tell me, how are you feeling?"

"Actually, quite good," Kelly replied with a smile, glancing around, viewing the new room. "I feel as if I just moved into a luxury resort hotel." She laughed. "I was so anxious to be out of here, now you might have a problem getting rid of me."

Mary, Karen and the nurse all laughed as Mary glanced at her watch. "Mike should be here soon, he's going to be surprised."

No sooner than the words were out of her mouth than Mike appeared in the doorway. He immediately rushed to the side of the bed and leaned down and kissed Kelly.

"Maybe I should leave," the nurse said, laughing again. "Maybe we all should."

Charlie was still standing in the doorway, smiling and perhaps having the same thought. Kelly and Mike were blushing.

"No, don't think you have to leave on our account," Kelly said. "What do you think of this room, Mike? I just said they might have trouble getting me to leave."

"It's really awesome, isn't it?" Mike replied. "There's almost the same amount of room in here as in your apartment. Charlie tells me in addition to a door that locks, there's a hot tub."

"True," Kelly said. "But I'm not going to be able to use it for a while, with this cast. Maybe you can, though."

Mike had immediately realized his mistake as he mentioned the hot tub. As Kelly was speaking, it dawned on him that he still hadn't asked about her injuries.

"I'm sorry, I don't know what I was thinking. How are you feeling? I heard you had surgery."

Kelly nodded. "Not bad, considering. The doctor tells me he was very pleased with the results. Want to take a look?" she asked, pointing toward her foot, which was propped up on a couple pillows.

"Is this supposed to be some kind of joke?" he asked, his face flushing in anger.

"What do you mean?" Kelly asked in confusion.

"This signature on your cast." He read it to her. "Hope this is our final visit. Speedy recovery, Martha and Roy."

Kelly was attempting to lift her head to see for herself. From her expression, Mike could tell this was news to her. Mary and Karen were crowding next to him to look.

"That has to have been done in the past hour or so," the nurse said. "It wasn't signed when I last had a look at it."

"I woke up, sensing someone was in my room," Kelly said. "You were away from the door then, Mary."

Mike frowned at Mary. She noticed and could read his mind. "I was on the phone with you, and then I called the security people. I thought I was keeping an eye on Kelly's door the whole time. I guess I wasn't."

Mike moved to Kelly's side and reached out to take her hand.

"Who are Martha and Roy?" Karen asked. Mike glanced up at her. He was aware from her uniform that she was one of the hospital's security guards.

"This is Karen Steiner, Mike," Kelly said. "She's the one who came up with the idea of moving me up to this room. Martha and Roy are the middle-aged couple I told you about, Karen. Ones we wanted you to be on the look out for, in addition to the younger man and woman I described."

Karen nodded. "I told Charlie and the others about them. I also informed the other nurses."

Charlie and the nurse nodded, acknowledging she had.

"The fact their names are on the cast doesn't necessarily mean they were the ones who were here," Mary said.

"You're right," Mike responded. "It could have been anyone, any of them."

"I guess I should be happy all they did was sign my cast," Kelly said. Turning to Mike, she continued. "The message suggests they're going to back off until they see if they're going to continue to be pursued. Isn't that the way you interpret it?"

"It's the way they want us to," Mike replied. "But it could also be an attempt to get us all to relax, lower our guard. I'm going to be staying here with you tonight, regardless." He squeezed Kelly's hand. "Except for being on the alert for any strangers or suspicious doings, the rest of you can probably get back to your regular routines. We should be able to handle things for the remainder of the night, shouldn't we, Mary?"

She nodded as she replied, "Three others should be here soon, too. We should have things covered. But thanks for all you've done."

"I echo that," Kelly said, a smile appearing on her face. "I feel very secure with all of you involved."

"We're glad we could help, though we really haven't done much," Karen said. "I still find it hard to believe someone was able to get into your room without anyone seeing him. Or her, I guess. I'll ask some questions and let you know if I find out anything. We'll also be here if we're needed."

As the three started out of the room, Mike said, "One more thing. This might be a little melodramatic, but in case any of you or other security personnel or nurses have need to come back to this room, let's have a code. If someone's holding a gun on you, using you to gain entry to this room, use the word 'just'. Rather than saying, 'it's me,' you'd say, 'it's just me'."

Charlie smiled. "That's even simple enough for me to understand." Karen and the nurse smiled and nodded in agreement, assuring Mike they'd inform the rest of the staff.

Chapter 71

The downpour hadn't let up. The State Police car slowed as it drove through a large puddle. Stuart, Mitch and Rick were in the rear seat. Stuart had been filling the other two men in on his recent phone calls.

"So Fritz and Mark are coming back up here?" Mitch asked.

"They should already be in the air," Stuart replied. "Two of the state troopers will be waiting for them at the Harbor Springs Airport. They'll transport them to The Perry."

"But from what you've said, there's really nothing that they can do, is there?" Rick asked. "All our hands have been tied, haven't they?"

Stuart nodded. Washington had made it clear that their involvement had ended. With the letters now out of their hands, a number of people were very nervous, to say the least. Paranoid or panicked would be better words to describe their concerns. The message had been loud and clear, direct from the White House—immediately cease and desist.

"Does that mean we won't be involved in any additional search of the wreckage site in the morning?" Rick asked.

Again Stuart nodded. "Nor will anyone else," he answered. "The State Police have also been notified and a communiqué from the Bureau is on its way to Rupert." He shrugged his shoulders, clearly discouraged.

"So what do we do?" Mitch asked. "Besides apologizing to that waitress for losing the photo of her family. Besides telling the Millers their car's been destroyed."

"Besides viewing the past few days as a huge nightmare," Rick added.

Stuart shook his head. "I wish I had an answer other than nothing. Your questions are the same ones Fritz raised. I tried to persuade him to just head back to Washington. But probably like the rest of us, he's hoping some freak thing may happen, a miracle of sorts. Something such as those two who posed as the Millers being in a car accident. I've hesitated calling the hospital to let them know we're on our way. I didn't want to wake Kelly, but I guess I'm also hoping something has occurred there that changes the picture. I find it hard to imagine they'd actually target Kelly again, try to take her hostage again. It would make no sense. They must realize they're in the driver's seat, even without knowing we've been grounded. On the other hand, I'm hoping someone might have appeared at the hospital and been taken into custody. A farfetched thought, I know. That's why I haven't called. I'm afraid of finding out that hasn't happened, having my last glimmer of hope extinguished. I'm fairly sure they would have gotten word to us, called me on my cell phone, if there was news of some kind."

Mitch patted his hand on Stuart's knee, realizing his own mood of dejection was probably minuscule compared with Stuart's. It shouldn't, but this episode could spell dire consequences in regards to Stuart's future with the Bureau. Searching his mind for something to say, he glanced at Rick. Mitch could tell he was having similar thoughts. The police cruiser turned onto the main highway leading into Petoskey.

"Another ten minutes," the officer in the passenger seat said as he turned and viewed the three of them sitting in silence, all deep in thought.

•

Though it was nearly two a.m., Kelly and Mike were wide awake, anxiously awaiting Stuart's arrival, hoping he'd have some good news to share with them.

"Why don't I turn on Headline News," Mike suggested.

"Good idea," Kelly said. "It might put things into perspective. The world's going to continue on regardless of what happens here."

"We've pretty well exhausted ourselves on this subject anyway," Mary said. "But maybe you want to talk about what's happened in Ann Arbor."

Mike and Kelly both smiled. "I think we'll forego that for now," Mike said. "There will be plenty of time for that in the morning."

The three of them had spent the last twenty minutes or so discussing the 'Mackinac Mess' as Mary described it. They'd finally all agreed that the best thing that could happen would be for the Canadians to quickly come to an agreement as a result of the preliminary discussions begun on Mackinac. Mike had compared it to a hole-in-one in golf. All the previous mistakes and errors would be quickly forgotten. They were all aware of the fragile nature of the talks, however. Mary had commented that they, too, could blow up in people's faces.

One of the nurses had come in to check on Kelly shortly after Mike turned on the TV. She'd been amazed over how well Kelly was handling the surgery. She told Kelly to buzz her if she was having any difficulty getting to sleep.

A few minutes after the nurse had left, the phone rang. Mike answered, it was Karen informing them that Mr. Kreicheff and two others were on the way to Kelly's room.

•

It was nearly two-thirty. Stuart realized Kelly needed to get some rest. He'd tried to be as quick as possible as he filled them in on the details of everything that had transpired since he'd last seen them. Mary had asked several questions while Kelly and Mike mainly listened. When it came their turn to reciprocate, Mary, Mike and Kelly had an attentive audience. The three men were fascinated as Kelly showed them the signing on her cast.

"I'm truly surprised," Stuart said. "I don't think any of us thought they'd risk further contact with you, Kelly. Of course, they don't know we've been ordered to stop all further moves to identify or apprehend them. Still, in light of what's happened, you'd assume they'd wait to see if we had been."

"You say none of the staff noticed anyone entering your room?" Mitch asked Kelly.

"That's right," she replied. "But even more concerning is the fact no one saw anyone even entering the hospital who may have been involved, no one who came close to matching the descriptions I gave them. Everyone, all the security personnel and the nurses, had been alerted on who to watch for."

"Well, no one's going to be able to get up to this room without being seen," Rick said. "I don't know how you arranged for it, but this is a super layout."

They all joked about sharing the hot tub with Mike as they prepared to leave. Mary was able to convince Stuart that she should stay at the hospital with Kelly and Mike.

"I know all the people involved, the nurses, the security personnel. I'm also probably less exhausted than the three of you are. I'll be downstairs at the nurses' station, where I can watch the stairway and elevator access to this floor. If anything occurs, we can contact you at The Perry. You're less than ten minutes away."

•

Mike wasted no time after their company had left. First, propping the pillows so Kelly could sit up, he then climbed onto the bed. He maneuvered so he could put his arms around her. For the next few minutes they hugged and kissed like two love-struck teenagers, who'd been parted for a month or two while both were at summer camp.

"You need to get to sleep," Mike said, coming up for air. Kelly laughed as she replied, "I'm sure this is better medicine than sleep would be. But you must be exhausted too. I was so worried about you."

Mike propped himself up on his arm, staring down at her with a twinkle in his eyes. "You worried about me? I was completely undone wondering if you were safe."

"Well, we both are," Kelly said. "And I think you should really try out that hot tub. Even though this room leaves little to be desired, I hope I'll be discharged tomorrow and we can get back to Ann Arbor. Tonight might be your last chance."

As Kelly was talking, Mike had left the bed and walked over to the door, making sure again he'd locked it.

"I think I'll pass, tempting as it sounds. I'll stretch out on this couch. Yell if you need anything. And you might have to actually yell, I could be dead to the world. I didn't realize how tired I was until now."

•

Mike had been right in his assumption. Minutes after Kelly had switched off the lights, he had dozed off. Kelly was a little envious as she lay there listening to his relaxed breathing. The combination of the brief catnap and the thoughts racing through her mind left her still wide awake a half-hour after Mike had fallen asleep.

There was a knock at the door. Mike had heard it, too, and was starting to sit up.

"It's just me – Mary."

Mike waved at Kelly and pointed to the bathroom. She nodded, quickly comprehending his message.

"Just a minute, Mary, Mike's soaking in the hot tub. I'll let him know you're here. Give him a minute or two."

As Kelly was saying this in a raised voice, Mike had dashed to the phone.

"Hello, is this Karen? Mary Zuckerman is outside Kelly's door. She used the code word we agreed on. I'm certain it wasn't by accident, she's much too sharp for that."

After listening for a moment or two, Mike hung up and whispered to Kelly, "They're on their way, we need to stall." He'd no sooner said that when there was another series of knocks on the door.

"It's important that I talk to you right away," Mary called out.

"Mike's toweling himself now," Kelly shouted. "Give him a minute to slip on some clothes. He's putting on his pants now."

Mike circled his fingers in an 'okay' sign and moved across the room to the side of the door, the revolver now in his hand. Kelly and he both jumped at the sound of a gunshot, the noise reverberating just beyond the door. Mike reached for the door lock.

"Wait, Mike!" Kelly shouted. "Maybe that's what they're hoping our reaction will be."

He nodded in agreement and pressed his ear to the door. He flipped his hands, holding his palms out, indicating he wasn't hearing anything.

"Can you reach the phone, Kelly? Call security."

She grabbed the phone and placed it in her lap, quickly dialing the number. "The line's busy, I'll call the nurses' station."

Mike still hadn't heard any sound of activity outside the door.

"There's no answer," Kelly said. Both were dreading what may have happened. "I'll try security again."

The line was clear and Kelly recognized the voice of the guard she knew as Charlie as he answered the phone.

"This is Kelly, what's happened?"

•

Mike waited nervously as Kelly listened on the phone. She flashed him a thumbs-up sign as she asked, "Should Mike and I notify Stuart Kreicheff?" She listened for a moment or two and then smiled as she replied, "Okay, we'll be here."

As she hung up, she explained to Mike, "Karen Steiner is on her way up to fill us in on the details of what's happened. Sandy has been shot. It's not life-threatening. They're treating her now, she may require surgery. From the little they know, they're quite sure she was acting on her own. She drugged one of the nurses and used a gun to force Mary to try to gain entry to this room. Karen was on the phone talking to Stuart when I was speaking to Charlie. They tried to reach us, but our line was busy. It was probably when I was waiting for an answer when I called the nurses' station."

"Was Mary injured?" Mike asked.

Kelly shook her head. "Luckily, no. She made a move to wrestle the gun from Sandy as they were waiting for you to open the door. That's the shot we heard. The gun fell to the floor and Mary chased her down the stairs. It was one of the security guards who fired the shot that injured Sandy."

There was a knock at the door and a voice called out, "It's Karen."

Mike immediately went to the door and unlocked it, opening it so she could come in. She smiled as she said, "I can't believe this, we've had more excitement in the past few hours than in all the years I've worked here."

Mike motioned to a chair, wondering if she wanted to sit as she briefed them.

"No. Thank you anyway, though. I'm not going to be long. I just wanted to tell you what we know, but that's not much. First off, that girl's going to be fine, it's not a serious wound, no vital organs were hit. On the basis of what she told Mary and what I've overheard, it appears she was acting on her own. She blames you, Ms. Travis, she—"

Kelly's eyebrows had arched over this last remark. She interrupted Karen to say it was all right to skip the formalities and to call her Kelly. Karen smiled and continued from where she'd left off.

"That girl says her boyfriend has become infatuated with you, Kelly. His affection and admiration for you was only heightened by how you handled things when he and that other man were trying to get you aboard their boat. Telling her how beautiful you looked when he signed your cast was the final straw. She mentioned some other things that had also set her off, but I really didn't catch on to what she was saying. Something about his decision to let you off the hook too soon and vetoing the earlier plans to take you hostage."

Kelly and Mike exchanged looks, fully aware of what the young woman had referred to.

"She planned to get into this room and put both of you out with some type of drug. She was carrying half a dozen syringes; she used one on the nurse who was with Ms. Zuckerman. They'd both been at the nurses' station downstairs when the girl confronted them. The way she evaded us was by posing as one of the maintenance people. The public areas of the hospital are cleaned in the wee hours of the morning. She'd disguised herself with a wig to hide her braid and used padding to make her look fifty pounds heavier. She was also wearing thick eyeglasses. We have frequent turnover among the maintenance personnel. By avoiding contact with the other maintenance staff, she was able to deceive the rest of us. We think she planned to get you into the large container on her service cart and out of the hospital some way. She's angry and real talkative right now. If that doesn't change, they should be able to learn a great deal more."

The phone rang and Kelly answered it. It was Stuart, he was elated. He was still in the process of questioning Sandy with help from Mitch and Mary. He said he'd be up to see them in about ten minutes. Sandy was scheduled for surgery. Hanging up, Kelly informed Mike and Karen of what Stuart had said.

"I'm sure he'll have far more information, better answers to your questions, than I can provide," Karen said.

•

Stuart looked relieved. There was a sparkle in his eyes as he explained what they'd learned during the questioning of Sandy.

"You were the one who triggered this, Kelly. Sandy felt compelled to do something to counteract the impact you'd made on Webb. She's in love with him. I think she wanted to impress him, like a cat venturing out and capturing a mouse or a chipmunk and dragging it home and leaving it on the door stoop in expectation of praise from its master."

Kelly and Mike flinched in reaction to Stuart's comparison.

"I didn't get the impression when they took me hostage that the two were romantically involved," Kelly said. "Actually the reverse—they appeared to be at odds with one another."

Stuart nodded. "I don't know what their relationship had been, whether or not they had a mutual thing going. All she alluded to was the fact that after you appeared on the scene, their relationship changed. She did say Webb was angry over her failure to get Mr. Woodbridge to cancel the meetings. Though she didn't actually verbalize it, I think he'd let her know how disgusted he was over how Woodbridge and Chandler had been handled. He had probably already begun to tune her out when you first saw them together. But she blamed you and was furious at him for having become so captivated by you.

"Having bungled this, she's now retaliating by telling us everything she knows. In the car coming from Harbor Springs, I told Mitch and Rick it would take a miracle to salvage anything positive out of this affair. Thanks to you, to Sandy, our prayers are answered.

"The man who wore the hood heads up a fairly large, loose-knit organization. Their specialty is industrial espionage, from pirating technology to actual sabotage. He's a former high-ranking military leader who was ousted from the service. It was a heavily publicized, controversial case. His picture was in all the news media at the time. Hence, his disguise—the hood.

"She says he has some leverage over Webb, the couple who impersonated the Millers, too, for that matter. Webb comes from a wealthy family. He did something which could result in his possibly ending up in prison. I don't think Sandy knows the details. I suspect it could have been drug-related. Regardless, it's being used as a club, so to speak, to coerce Webb's involvement. The same holds true for the couple who posed as the Millers. They're professional con artists and Sandy says the man's threatened to expose their role in an elaborate pyramid scheme. The fact that those three were coerced into this fiasco helps explain some of the things that have occurred. Maybe I should say some of the things that didn't."

Stuart smiled. "One interesting thing we learned was the ringleader's code name. It's Spider. The switch in names on the boat was a stunt the Millers pulled off, by the way. It came as a surprise to Webb, according to Sandy. Suffice it to say, we've learned a hell of a lot from her. We should be able to identify everyone involved. That was our main goal. So we can keep them under surveillance, take action if they cause added trouble or renege on their promise not to release any details of the Mackinac Island meetings to the media.

"Sandy says some Canadians paid them a substantial sum of money, no actual knowledge of just how much. There appears to be some truth to their contention that they'd asked us for money to enable them to give it back in light of having failed to get the meetings canceled or postponed. I think we've learned everything we're going to from her. My gut feeling is that she's going to be clamming up, feeling remorse over what she's done. But as far as we're concerned, it couldn't have played out better. As I've already said, Kelly, we have you to thank. I'm not surprised you wowed Webb and I'm sure Mike's not, either."

Stuart glanced at his watch as he continued. "The two of you know more details than they do in Washington. I need to call them back; they've been rounding up people for a conference call. I'm sure they'll have plenty of questions. Unless you have one or two I can answer quickly, I need to excuse myself. Besides, you both could use some sleep. You've both been wonderful. I just hope things work out as well in regard to that fellow, McConnell, in Ann Arbor.

"Oh, I almost forgot. Here are your keys, Mike. Your car's out in the visitor's parking area. Sandy wasn't able to tell us how it got there. She claims it wasn't her or Webb. It's probably one of the questions, one of the mysteries, we might never have an answer to."

"There's one question I have that's puzzled me," Kelly said. "Why did Roy let you get your hands on that photograph of those two men on the dock? Why did he get the film developed? It's one of the reasons I had so much trouble accepting the fact the two who impersonated the Millers were involved."

Stuart smiled, shaking his head. "Good point, Kelly. I should start out by saying I had a terrible time convincing him we should pick up the photos. He may have had plans to switch photos. When he learned Anderson was dead, he may have assumed the risk of others seeing it was minimal. When I told him I thought you might be able to recognize who Anderson was photographing, he may have concluded there was a greater risk in switching the photo than not. They could have blown their cover if you claimed it wasn't the photo Anderson took. I guess I really don't have a satisfactory answer, though.

"But before I leave, I just want to say if either of you ever want to join the Bureau, coming back in your case, Kelly, you'd both get a glowing reference from me."

Kelly and Mike smiled. "You're not going to get away without our offering congratulations to you, Stuart," Kelly said.

Mike reached out to shake Stuart's hand as he added, "Now, let's hope the Canadians can quickly find a solution so your efforts will be truly rewarded."

Chapter 72

Kelly and Mike were surprised to see it was so late when they were awakened by one of the nurses at ten-fifteen a.m.

"We decided to let you sleep in," she said with a smile. "That's VIP treatment, it doesn't happen very often around here. In fact, I can't remember it ever occurring before. But that's true for most of what took place last night. The doctor has you scheduled for an x-ray at eleven, Kelly. If it comes out as he expects it will, it looks as if you'll be free to go."

"That would be great," Kelly replied, grinning at Mike and the nurse. "I need to call Mom and Dad, Mike. But I guess it would be best if we waited until after my x-ray so I can give them an idea of when we'll definitely be back in Ann Arbor."

"I think I'll call David right now, though," Mike said. "See if there's been any new developments. Have there been any messages for us?" he asked the nurse.

She shook her head. "But I have breakfast just outside the door for both of you. You might want to use the bathroom to freshen up, while I'm helping Kelly. I can get a razor and shaving cream for you if you'd like."

•

Mike placed a call to David a few minutes later as they were having breakfast. He was out, expected back within the hour. His secretary had hesitated when Mike had asked if there were any new developments as far as McConnell was concerned.

"No one's seen him, but he's still in the area, at least he was last night. I think David would prefer filling you in himself."

Mike relayed the conversation to Kelly after hanging up.

"What do you think that means?" she asked. "Something's happened." She wondered if it involved her parents.

"We'll know soon enough, I told her I'd call back by noon. That we'd know by then what our plans were in terms of getting back to Ann Arbor."

"We still have a few minutes before I'll be going down for the x-ray. I've changed my mind, I think I'll call my parents now. We'll be able to find out if that tentative wedding date works out for them."

•

Kelly's mother was delighted to hear from her. There had been some concern when they hadn't been able to reach her at her condo last night.

"Your father's out running a few errands, I expect him back any minute. He'll be disappointed not to have been able to talk to you."

Kelly enthusiastically filled her mother in on all the wedding details, including Mr. Woodbridge's offer to pick up the bulk of the wedding reception expenses.

"That date you mentioned on the answering machine is fine for us," her mother said. "It all sounds wonderful. But you tell Mr. Woodbridge that your father and I want to be hosting and paying for the reception. You'll tell him?"

Kelly laughed and said, "We'll have plenty of time to discuss it, Mom. But I also need to explain why we've been delayed getting home. I had a nasty fall and broke my ankle. I've had surgery and the doctor tells me I'm going to be fine. He wants another set of x-rays taken, actually in just a couple minutes, before he discharges me. I'll call and advise you. Dad may be home by then."

"I'm sure he will be. How did the injury occur, Kelly?"

She knew her parents would be asking and had a little white lie prepared. "We had a terrific rainstorm last night and I slipped on the wet pier in Harbor Springs. As I said, the doctor thinks I'm going to be fine, no permanent injuries."

The conversation ended with her mother saying she hoped the x-ray results would be good news and telling Kelly to take care.

Chapter 73

The six people were seated at the same table they'd used just over a week ago. The senior member of the group had just finished telling the others about the call he'd received last night from the leader of Canada's ruling party.

"He wants to meet with me and anyone else I choose to bring at four o'clock this afternoon. He says he has some ideas he wants to get our opinion on."

"Did he mention the Mackinac Island meetings?" one of the men asked.

"Not in that context, all he said was a number of people had met and developed a scenario of sorts for coming up with a solution on the secession issue."

"Do you think he knows we tried to derail the meetings?" another asked.

"He gave no indication of that, he was upbeat, positive. Said he thought we'd like to hear the ideas, that he was hopeful we'd lend our support to them."

"We should listen, but I'm not optimistic," John said. "Why the change of heart? I think they're setting you up, us up. They're probably aware of the role we played, threatening to expose us if we don't buy into their thinking."

"Have you heard anything more from those people you made arrangements with?" Marie asked, alarmed over his comment. "Is there something you haven't told us? Were they apprehended?"

John shook his head. "At least I'm not aware of it. But I'm not as sure we're going to be getting all our money back as I was. You don't need the details, but I was called this morning and told they'd had some losses they'd be deducting."

"So we'd still have a difficult time explaining the missing money in case there's an audit?" the youngest man said.

"Damn it, I just said I'm not sure how much of our investment we'd be getting back," John exclaimed.

Marie put a finger to her lips, cautioning him to hold his voice down.

The senior member of the group spoke again. "None of us are blaming you, John, for the fact they weren't successful. We all agreed it was worth a try. But there will be hell to pay if we're connected to those people. That should be our worry now, not the dollars. Hell, I can confess to embezzling the money if it would protect the cause. I'm suggesting that you accompany me this afternoon, Marie."

Viewing the others, he continued. "Don't worry, we won't be making any binding commitments. We'll tell them we have to obtain our Executive Committee's input and approval before we can. Who knows, maybe this is the way it was supposed to work out. We could have more influence now due to having been left out of those meetings than if we'd been invited initially. Let's hope that's the case."

Chapter 74

"Everything looks good," the doctor said, standing at the foot of Kelly's bed with the x-rays in his hand. "I want you to pace yourself though, baby yourself for a while. I'm sure Mike's not going to mind waiting on you for a few days. You can leave as soon as you're ready. Your insurance covers almost everything and Mr. Kreicheff made arrangements to be billed directly for anything that isn't, this room for example."

Kelly thanked him and had him answer a few questions before he left.

"Guess as soon as you've called your parents and we call David, we can be on our way," Mike said. Grinning as she vigorously nodded her head, Kelly reached for the phone.

"Hi Dad, we just spoke with the doctor. He says the x-rays look good and I'm free to go. I'll call after we're back in town, probably around eight or eight-thirty."

"I'm delighted, your mother will be, too. We've just been talking, wondering if you'd want to move in with us for a few days. It would be a treat for us and I think we could be of help to you."

"It might not be a bad idea, Dad," Kelly replied. "I'll think about it on the drive down, okay?"

"Fine, honey, whatever you decide. We'd love to be of help if we can be. Your mother and I are excited about the wedding plans. She's already starting to put some names down of people you might want to invite. I'm going to go to the other phone in the den, there's a letter I want to go over with you on your car insurance."

"Can it wait, Dad? I'll probably be seeing you tonight or tomorrow."

"It'll just take a minute, hold on."

Kelly winked at Mike as she waited. "I should just be another minute or two."

"That's fine, no hurry," Mike said as he continued to pack Kelly's things in a carry bag the nurse had given him.

•

"There's not a letter on car insurance, Kelly. I didn't want your mother to hear me, it's about something I saw this morning. You know the big rock on the corner of Hill and Washtenaw?"

Kelly did, it was an Ann Arbor tradition to paint the rock for someone's birthday, anniversary or whatever. Maybe just to say, 'Beat Ohio State' or 'Christ Has Risen' on Easter morning.

"I passed it today. It has yours and Mike's names painted on it along with that tentative date you've decided on for your wedding."

Kelly smiled, wondering who would have done that. Who knew the date?

"The problem is your names are on a tombstone with a painting of a broken heart, ripped in half, with an actual bloody knife stuck to the rock. I'm sure it's red paint."

Kelly glanced up at Mike as she realized who the painter had to have been. Her anger was tempered by her growing fear as she considered the implications of the message.

"Oh, Dad, you're right not to alarm Mother. Don't worry, I'm sure you realize who's responsible. I'm certain he'll be behind bars soon." She cringed, thinking how McConnell had learned of the wedding date. He must have broken in and heard her phone message.

"I think I'll be taking you up on your offer to move in for a few days."

•

Mike frowned in concern as Kelly told him the news, his face flushing in anger. "I'll call David, see if he's aware. Have him put your parents' house under surveillance."

David came on the line immediately. "There's been no sighting of McConnell yet, Mike, but I was just about to call you. I've just come from supervising the painting of the rock on the corner of Hill and Washtenaw."

"Kelly and I know all about it," Mike replied. "Her father saw it this morning."

"Don't worry, we're going to nail that son-of-a-bitch for good this time, Mike. We're checking the knife for prints. Not that we need to. There were half a dozen or so Payday candy bars scattered around the base of the rock. The good news is it means he's still here in town. Or at least he was last night or very early this morning."

Mike explained that Kelly was being discharged and that they were ready to head back to Ann Arbor. He also explained how they thought McConnell gained knowledge of their wedding date.

"I want you to notify me the second you arrive," David said. "Better yet, come right here to the station, I'll wait for you. In the meantime, we'll be doing everything possible to hopefully capture him before you're even here."

•

Mike had gone to the Perry Hotel to gather their belongings while Kelly visited with Mr. Woodbridge and Chandler. Kelly was still chatting with Mr. Woodbridge when Mike returned. He greeted Kelly with a kiss, explaining he was ready to leave for Ann Arbor anytime she was.

Mr. Woodbridge's eyes were twinkling as he said, "That's right, you just continue to romance her, Mike. You have a jewel here. Of course, you know that already."

Kelly blushed as she said, "Mr. Woodbridge has some great suggestions for the wedding. He's going to provide us with a carriage decorated with fresh flowers, for one thing."

"Kelly's told me about all the excitement I missed yesterday and last night. I'm happy you two can get back to Ann Arbor for a little relaxation."

Kelly glanced at Mike and took his hand as she said, "Hopefully so, hopefully so."

Chapter 75

"We're over halfway," Mike said. "How's the ankle? Would you like to stop so you can stretch a bit? We can pull off at the next rest stop or stop off for some food if you're getting hungry."

"I'm feeling fine, Mike. I really am. I'd just as soon keep going unless you want to."

"No, I'm set. We should be in Ann Arbor about seven p.m."

•

A short time later as they drove past the Bay City exit, the car phone rang.

"I'll get it," Kelly said, reaching for the phone. "Hello."

"Hi, Kelly, it's me, David. You two were right, your parents' phone is bugged."

"I assumed so, that seemed to be the only logical explanation," Kelly replied, as she mouthed to Mike that it was David calling.

"Except for the rock painting and the bug on the phone, there's been no sign of McConnell. I was hopeful we'd have him in custody again by the time you and Mike arrived. But that's probably not going to be the case. I have some ideas I'd like to get your input on, though. After we've talked, you can run them past Mike and get back to me."

"Sounds good," Kelly said. "You've spoken to my parents, I take it."

"Yes. They're aware of the phone being bugged. We also checked out the house to make sure he didn't leave any other surprises—listening devices, explosives, notes, or what-have-you. We're fairly certain he hasn't.

"It appears clear he's targeted you, Kelly. Mike, too, for that matter. He's had months to think about it, plan what he wants to do. I'm not suggesting either of you are in immediate danger, and I don't think your parents are, either. But we've taken several precautions. We have two people in the house across the street from your parents. The family is away on vacation and we were able to contact them to get permission to use their home. Your parents' neighbors have been extremely cooperative. We have someone at the homes on both sides of your parents, too. They've been dressed in gardening clothes this afternoon, puttering around the yards. Tonight they'll be hidden in the shrubbery, equipped with night goggles. I'm getting ahead of myself, though. Let me explain what we have in mind."

"That's fine, David," Kelly responded, "but I should let you know in advance I'm very hesitant about my parents being involved, exposing them to any added risks. I'd like to avoid it if possible."

"I understand, Kelly, and I wish we had more options. But hear what I have in mind. I want you to call your parents if the two of you buy into my plan, and let them know you'd like to take them up on their offer to stay with them a few days while you recuperate. My initial thinking was to get your parents out of the house. But my fear is McConnell may be watching the house and see them leave. I'm afraid he'll get suspicious if he realizes you're there alone. We don't want him frightened off. Even if he didn't see them leave, he'd easily be able to determine they're not there. With a telephone call, for example. I suppose you could say they'd turned in early and you'd relay the message, but if they were to take the call and act as if everything was normal, it might lull him into thinking the coast was clear. I'm only proposing that we do this for a couple days, tonight and tomorrow night. If he hasn't made an appearance by then, I'm suggesting we get both you and your parents out of town."

"Are you planning to have anyone in the house with us, possibly Mike?" Kelly asked.

"No. Again, I don't want to risk scaring him off. I think it's best if Mike gets you situated at your parents' and then drives to his house. That's not to say he won't be involved. I'm thinking Mike and I should position ourselves in the house across the street. He will probably argue the closer the better, suggesting he hide in the shrubbery of one of the yards abutting your parents'. I don't foresee McConnell making any moves until after midnight. That will give Mike time to drive home, pretend to turn in for the night, and then sneak out a short time later. We'll have someone waiting for him a few blocks away who'll chauffeur him back to your parents' neighborhood."

"I can see you've given it considerable thought," Kelly said. "We can make sure all the doors are locked and set the alarm. Only the doors are wired, but it's better than nothing. I'll need my gun, of course, and a cell phone so you can keep us apprised."

"Definitely. And as I indicated earlier, I'm thinking the risk is minimal compared to the reward of apprehending him. I don't think we need to worry about a drive-by shooting or McConnell tossing an explosive device through a window. I don't think he's out to injure you . . . or worse, at least not yet. I think he's out to terrorize you for a few days first, to make it a game."

"I agree," Kelly replied. "That's more his style. But as you indicated, he's had several months to brood over this, in all likelihood building his anger. I guess I'm not as confident as you are that he will want to string this out. Still, I'm the one—Mike and I are the ones—he appears to have focused on. Hopefully that doesn't mean my parents, too. Give Mike and me a chance to discuss this."

"I want that, he's apt to have some suggestions," David replied. "Remember, we'll have nearly a dozen people whose priority will be the safety of you and your parents. That won't change even if Martians were to land on the opposite side of town. He's not going to trick us into relaxing our guard. Take as much time as you need to, I'll be waiting here for your call."

Chapter 76

Kelly could sense Mike's concerns as she explained David's plan. She held up her hand to delay his questions and comments until she'd voiced her opinion, thinking it would be best for him to know her comfort level first.

"You seem to have already pretty much made up your mind," Mike said. "I—"

Kelly shook her head as she replied. "That's not true, I just thought you'd want to hear my thoughts. I could tell by your expressions you're not overjoyed about me or my parents placing ourselves at risk."

"That's true," Mike said. "I guess my major concern—major fear—is underestimating McConnell. We know he's no dummy. After the rock painting, he has to realize we'd take some precautions. I wouldn't be at all surprised if he assumes we know about the phone bug, that we figured out that had to be the way he learned of our wedding date. I think we'd be foolish to assume this is going to go smoothly, that he'll just blindly walk into our hands.

"That said, I think we should go along with David's plan. It doesn't mean my concerns are any less in regards to you, more because I agree there aren't many options."

"Good, I'm glad you agree," Kelly said, smiling. "Then I'll call David."

Mike also smiled as he reminded her she'd also asked him for his suggestions.

"I have a couple. First off, I think it would be a good idea for us to orchestrate a call to your parents after I've dropped you off, from a friend or a relative. It would let him know your parents are there, for one thing. If they just act as if they haven't a care in the world, it might lull him into believing we're not expecting him to pay you a visit tonight. Think about who we should have make the call.

"It's also in our best interests if he makes his move tonight, while everyone's fresh, mentally and physically alert. I think I might be able to precipitate that by phoning you after I'm back at my house. I'd tell you that I was going to be late in getting over to your parents' in the morning to see you, to bring bagels or sweet rolls. That David wants to see me first, to tell me his ideas for immediately implementing a plan to intensify the search for McConnell."

Kelly nodded. "It might work, prompt him to make an appearance tonight rather than waiting. But if he suspects we know about the bug, he could think he's being set up. I think the risk is worth it, though. He's so sure of himself, so confident he can outsmart us, he'd still go ahead."

"I agree, but there's another risk you've probably thought of, too. The phone call could backfire if it motivates him to accelerate his plans. To not waste time terrorizing you over a period of time. To instead collapse his timetable into hours rather than days. I think what he initially has in mind is something to make us all realize how vulnerable you are, to frighten everyone. I don't want to risk doing something that would make him change that thinking."

"It's a good idea, Mike. Both of your suggestions are. Anything more, before we call David?"

"Just one additional thought. I want to make sure I'll be equipped the same way as those officers positioned in the neighbors' yards. Dark clothing, a ski mask, gloves, night goggles, black sport shoes—the works. David can get everything together ahead of time. He's probably already done so, way ahead of me. But what I especially wanted to mention is that I'm going to try and convince him to let me sneak into your parents' house so I can be there with you, maybe through a basement window. I agree with him that McConnell will probably wait until after midnight before making his appearance. I can be inside by that time."

Kelly grinned. "And I'd love to have you with me," she replied. "But we don't want to risk him seeing you. That could blow everything. Your phone call would have led him to believe you were home, tucked in bed. Let's see what David's reaction is."

Chapter 77

Kelly's parents were delighted to see them. They'd said they'd be there around eight p.m., and they were even a few minutes early. Her mother had the lights turned on in Kelly's room, with a fresh bouquet of flowers on the dresser. She'd rounded up plenty of extra pillows so Kelly could make herself comfortable. The covers were turned back, the bed looked very inviting. Kelly wondered how much sleep was in store for her tonight, however.

•

The four of them gathered around the table in the family room as Kelly excitedly told her parents about the wedding plans. Kelly's father and Mike made hot fudge sundaes for everyone, while Kelly and her mother discussed the list of things they'd have to start working on, the decisions they'd have to make over the next few weeks.

•

"That was great, Dad!" Kelly exclaimed. "You know ice cream is one of my favorite things."

"Are you sure I can't convince either of you to have a cookie?" her mother asked. "They're fresh. Your father and I picked them up when we drove over to the real estate office to meet the police chief."

Kelly and Mike both smiled as they shook their heads. David had told them he'd met with Kelly's parents in the late afternoon. He'd had them drive over to the Charles Reinhart Company branch office nearby. He hadn't wanted to talk on the phone, nor did he want to be seen visiting them or have them seen stopping by headquarters. He'd arranged to use an empty office. He called a neighbor and had her go over to the Travis's with the message he wanted to see them.

Mike glanced at Kelly and pointed to his watch as he started to gather the dishes.

"Oh, please just leave those, Mike," Kelly's mother said. "It'll just take me a minute or two to rinse those and get them in the dishwasher."

"I know, but I can be doing that while Kelly reviews what might be in store for the three of you tonight. We know you spoke to David, but we thought you might have some questions."

Kelly and Mike were surprised to see how relaxed her parents appeared to be. Her father reviewed what David had told them, including his request they call Kelly's aunt and uncle in Grand Rapids tonight to tell them about Kelly's wedding plans. David had suggested this in place of arranging for someone to call them. Kelly provided her parents with a few more details, in addition to assuring them that many people—including Mike—would be nearby to insure they weren't harmed.

•

Mike excused himself a few minutes later and Kelly accompanied him to the door. They embraced and exchanged several kisses before Kelly broke away and stepped back, giggling.

"My parents are going to be wondering if McConnell's kidnapped us. I better get back and let them know I'm okay."

"And you're going to be," Mike said, with the smile that Kelly had come to love on his face. "Sweet dreams, and remember, I love you."

Kelly leaned over and kissed him again. She then replied, "A lot, if it compares to how much I love you."

•

Her mother was on the phone when Kelly came back into the family room. "She's right here, why don't I let you tell her," her mother was saying. "It's your aunt."

Kelly smiled as her mother handed her the portable phone.

Chapter 78

Mike arrived home shortly after ten. He puttered around for ten or fifteen minutes, looking over his mail and glancing at the newspaper, turning off the lights before heading upstairs with his suitcase.

He pulled the shades before opening the suitcase and laying out on the bed the gear David had provided. He'd had everything ready when he and Kelly had stopped by headquarters. There had been plenty of room in Mike's suitcase for all of it.

A cold shower would wake him up a little and prepare him for what might be a long night, Mike thought as he began to undress. Before heading into the bathroom, he placed the call to Kelly.

•

After slipping the ski mask over his head, Mike stepped over to the full-length mirror on the back of the bedroom door. He laughed to himself. His image almost frightened him. I hope I don't run into anyone while I'm sneaking through the neighborhood, he thought. He glanced at his watch before turning out the lights.

In a little less than half an hour, he'd be hiking over to a pre-arranged spot a couple blocks from his house. An officer in an unmarked car would be waiting to drive him back to Kelly's parents' neighborhood. He'd be dropped off and approach the house across the street from Kelly's parents' from the back. David would be there, along with several other officers.

He reached up to his ear to make sure the listening device was securely in place. He also checked his pockets, reviewing where each object had been placed—his gun, the cell phone, the flashlight, the night goggles, gloves, and the key to Kelly's parents' house. Now it's just a matter of waiting, he thought as he sat down on the edge of the bed. He wondered if McConnell was outside, watching him.

Chapter 79

"Hadn't you better call it a night?" Caroline Margolis' mother shouted down from the head of the stairs. "It's nearly one o'clock. If you don't get some sleep, you aren't going to be in shape to make the presentation, regardless of how good it is."

Her daughter shook her head and laughed. "It's a good thing you weren't around at college, Mom, I'm used to this. But I just finished. I'm going out and put it in my car now. I'll be up in a minute or two."

Caroline pushed the garage door button and turned on the outside light before walking out into the driveway. Catching a movement out of the corner of her eye, she turned and looked into the backyard. There appeared to be a large animal in the bushes to her left, maybe twenty yards from where she was standing. Stepping forward a few steps as she squinted her eyes, she realized a person was crouched there. Whoever it was suddenly stood and darted across the yard into the neighbors' yard. She retreated back inside the house and went to the foot of the stairs, calling up to her mother.

"Mom, there's a prowler in our backyard."

Mrs. Margolis came to the head of the stairs and said, "It's probably one of the neighbor children, maybe one of the Smith boys."

"I don't think so, it looked like a man. Real eerie, dressed in black. I mean completely—a ski mask, gloves. He, at least I think it was a man, was carrying a small carryall bag."

"I suppose we better call the police, Caroline."

•

David's phone rang. It was Lisa Rotweiler, the 911 operator supervisor.

"We just had a call reporting a prowler. I thought I should notify you before we sent someone to investigate. It was on Heatherway, not far from the house you're staking out. I thought it could have been one of our people, maybe even McConnell."

"You did the right thing," David answered, referring to Heatherway on the map laid out on the desk in front of him. "What's the address?"

She related it and he thanked her, explaining he'd handle it at his end. He lifted the small microphone to his lips to notify the two men in the yards bordering the Travis home. Three, actually; Mike would also be in place by now and would be hearing him.

He'd vetoed Mike's suggestion to sneak into the house. Instead, Mike was going to position himself in the shrubbery cover on the north side of the house, not far from Keith Bartel, where he could view the front of the house in addition to the side. Glen Stevens was on the south side. Mike had left through the back door over half an hour ago, taking a circuitous route to avoid being seen.

•

Keith had just acknowledged hearing David when he saw someone come dashing out of the backyard and flop onto his stomach in the ground cover next to the side of the house. Keith immediately stood, switching on his flashlight with his left hand as he aimed the gun with his right.

"Freeze! Police!" he shouted.

In the beam of light he saw the person was already halfway into a basement window, sliding in feet first. It had to be McConnell. The man had reached out to grab the small black bag on the ground in front of him and tossed it into the air toward Keith and the flashlight beam.

Keith's gun was targeted at the man's head. He hesitated a second, wishing he could merely wound the man. The opportunity was lost; the man had disappeared through the window. Keith turned and saw Mike approaching from the left. He appeared to have seen what had occurred.

"Watch the window, check out that bag," Mike instructed. "I'm going inside."

Mike dialed Kelly's phone as he dashed toward the rear of the house. He hoped Keith would be careful when he opened McConnell's bag. I should have warned him, he thought.

•

Kelly immediately reached for the phone. Still fully dressed, she was stretched out on the bed.

"He's inside, through a basement window," she heard Mike say. "I'm on my way in through the back door. Go to your parents' room, try to barricade the door."

Kelly reached over and switched on the lamp. She reached for her crutches as she swung her legs off the bed. Moving quickly out of the door to her room, she reached for the hall switch to turn on the light. As she was halfway down the hall, the lights went out.

Reaching her parents' open door, she saw her pajama-clad father coming toward her. Slamming the door behind her, she wedged the handle of one of her crutches under the door knob. Understanding what she was attempting to do, her father had reached for the small bookcase in the vestibule entry and began turning it. Kelly grabbed the other end. With one end of the bookcase flush to the wall and the base of the crutch positioned against the other end, it should hold the door closed.

"Get Mother under the bed. You too, Dad," Kelly said as she saw the knob turn and heard McConnell as he attempted to force the door open.

•

"You've heard what's happened?" Mike said as he approached the back door.

"We did," David replied. "Your mike is working fine. We're on our way out the door. I'll leave someone in the front yard and we'll follow you through the back door."

As Mike was inserting the key in the lock, Glen Stevens joined him. Both noticed the lights go off upstairs. He must have thrown the master switch, they surmised as they stepped inside.

Mike entered the security code to turn off the alarm as he explained to Glen, "Only the doors are wired. I'm familiar with the house. Have your gun ready and just follow me. Kelly should be upstairs in her parents' bedroom."

The two men cautiously moved through the kitchen. Mike pointed to the open door leading to the basement.

"He's probably had time to get upstairs," Mike said. "Don't hesitate to use that," he added, nodding toward Glen's gun. "I'm sure he's armed."

•

Wood splintered as bullets penetrated the door. There were pinging sounds as shots ricocheted off the door knob. McConnell was using a gun with a silencer and Kelly wasn't certain how many bullets had been fired. Trying to move out of the way, she nearly tumbled. McConnell was now forcing the door open.

"I have a gun, too," Kelly screamed as a gloved hand reached through the opening. His hand gripped the crutch and he attempted to pull it aside.

Kelly stepped forward, pressing her shoulder against the door, placing weight on her left foot for leverage. Her father had been assisting her mother in getting under the bed and saw what was happening. He raced toward Kelly, following her lead, charging against the door with his shoulder.

McConnell screamed. Another shot ripped through the door, narrowly missing her father. A large splinter struck him in the cheek, only an inch or two under his eye. As he pulled it out, blood gushed from the wound.

The door was being forced open again. Relieved, Kelly saw he was withdrawing his hand.

•

From the foot of the stairs, Mike and Glen heard the sound of bullets shattering the door and striking the door lock. Seconds later, as they were halfway up the stairs, they heard McConnell's scream and the sound of the door splintering again.

Reaching the head of the stairs, Mike looked to the right, toward Kelly's parents' bedroom, just as the door across the hall was being slammed shut.

"It's me, Kelly," Mike shouted as he and Glen arrived at the door to her parents' bedroom. "I think he's gone into the room across the hall. Is everyone okay in there?"

Kelly struggled to get the door open as she shouted, "Yes!" She'd removed the crutch, but the shattered door knob presented a problem. As the door edged open, Mike saw the blood streaming down Kelly's father's cheek. He and Glen cringed before quickly realizing it was only a small, superficial wound. Pushing the door open, Mike was relieved to see Kelly, apparently unharmed.

"There's a door to the attic off that room, Mike," Kelly hurriedly explained. "There's another at the rear of the closet in my bedroom."

Mike nodded, understanding what she was saying.

"You watch this door, Glen. I'll go down to Kelly's room. The others should be getting—" He stopped in mid-sentence as they saw David, followed by four or five officers, reaching the top of the stairs.

Mike motioned to David to follow him as he explained, "Kelly and her parents are fine. McConnell's gone into that bedroom across the hall from them. There's an attic that runs the full length of the house. There's an entrance door to it in Kelly's room in addition to the one in the room he's in."

Before heading after Mike, David told two of the officers to stay with Glen and watch the door. "Don't attempt to go in after him just yet. See if Kelly or her parents need help."

Calling to Mike, he asked, "How about windows in that room?"

"Two," Mike shouted. "One next to the outside chimney, the other to the north of the front door. That's the one to watch. He could climb out onto the roof and just have a one-story drop."

David nodded as he raised the small mike in his hand to his lips, relating the information to the officers outside.

●

Mike was pushing aside the clothes hanging in Kelly's closet as David and another officer joined him.

"Let's get some of these out of here," Mike said, grabbing a batch of the hanging garments and handing them to the officer with David. "Just put them on the bed or drape them over that chair."

"I'm sorry, Mike, someone screwed up," David said. "McConnell must have unlocked that basement window when he bugged the phone. We should have discovered it."

Mike nodded as he replied, "We can't do anything about that now. Did Keith check out McConnell's bag?"

"He did. Some surprises. There was no rope, handcuffs, tape or weapons of any kind. There were a couple small canisters of tear gas and a mask, a bottle of chloroform with a rag, and a bag of candy. Those small conversation hearts you see around Valentine's Day."

"That's all?" Mike asked.

David nodded. "It's just conjecture on my part, but I think all he intended to do was scatter those candies around on Kelly's bed while she was asleep. The chloroform was probably a safeguard in case she happened to wake up while he was there in the bedroom with her or she wasn't asleep when he arrived."

"You thought he'd want to play some mind games with her," Mike said. "It appears you were right. An attempt to terrorize her, frighten all of us."

David nodded. "I haven't even told you about the messages on the conversation hearts. Keith says they'd been carefully chosen, not just run-of-the-mill. Threatening messages. One was 'It's Over 4 U.' The for was the number four and the you was simply the letter U. Others had the message 'Drop Dead' on them. Another expression was—"

David held up his hand, pointing to the miniature receiver in his ear. After listening for a moment or two, he started to share what he'd heard with Mike just as Kelly was coming into the room on her crutches.

"Anything happening down there?" Mike asked.

Kelly shook her head. "Glen hasn't been able to hear anything through the door, either. I think I interrupted you, David, just as you were about to say something to Mike."

David nodded. "I just heard from Sue, she's in the front yard. McConnell opened the dormer window and started to climb out on the roof and then abruptly changed his mind."

"Does she think he saw her?" Mike asked. "That she frightened him off?"

"No. She said it appeared he was having a problem trying to get a grip on the window casing."

"I think I know why," Kelly said with a hint of a smile. "I think my dad and I crushed his hand in the door."

Mike smiled. "That's why we heard him howl, isn't it? I should have guessed."

•

During the past few minutes, David had been using a mike to amplify his voice, pleading with McConnell to surrender. He'd stood outside the door to the room McConnell had entered and also at the attic door in the back of Kelly's closet. There'd been no response.

"I'm going to give him one more chance before we go in," David said. "This time I'll announce our intentions to use tear gas."

"He'll know you're not bluffing," Mike said. "That we could even use those two canisters he had in the bag."

David smiled and nodded as he announced, "This is your final opportunity, Joe. You have three minutes to come out with your hands on your head. Don't be a fool, we can all avoid any bloodshed."

•

"There's a possibility he's taken his own life. With the silencer, we may not have heard the shot," Kelly said.

"We'll soon see if that's the way he's decided to end this," David replied. "You know the plan," he said to the two officers poised outside the door. "The rest of us need to get back out of their way."

•

The room was empty. The curtains were flapping in the breeze coming through the open window. The door leading into the attic was shut. There was a sheet of paper with writing on it on the floor in front of it. One of the officers picked it up and called out to David.

"He's left us a note."

David entered the room and the officer handed the sheet of paper to him. Kelly and Mike had followed him and were now glancing over his shoulder. The note was difficult to read, a hardly-legible scrawl that one might expect from a very elderly person. It was fairly short and David read it aloud.

"'I'll surrender if you promise. One, to immediately get me to a hospital so I can have my hand looked after. Two, to give me a private cell. Three, to arrange an interview with the press.'"

"He's got a hell of a lot of gall to think he can make demands," Glen commented. "My advice, for what it's worth, is to tell him to shove it."

"I don't buy into any conditions either," David said. "But with the first two, he's not requesting anything we wouldn't plan on doing anyway. But I'll be damned if we're going to give him the opportunity to try his case in the media. No way. But it's tempting to agree to the other two, end this without bloodshed."

"I think Mike and I might have a solution, David," Kelly volunteered. "When we were at Mackinac Island, we met the publisher of the local weekly newspaper and his daughter. They expressed interest in writing a book about this case. The daughter had followed the news accounts at the time of McConnell's arrest and we happened to be with them when we learned he was finally going to trial."

"The neat thing is that an interview by them would meet his demand, yet it would be something we could control," Mike said. "Don't you feel confident, Kelly, that we could get them to promise not to publish a thing until after the trial?"

Kelly was nodding. "I'm certain we could."

David was smiling. "Seems too easy. Are you certain you'll be able to get them to agree to that and also not to do a story for another paper until the trial's over? They could be tempted. I've been disappointed in the past over assurances from the media."

"I'm sure that's true," Kelly replied. "But you'll have to trust us on this one, David. Do you have any doubts about being able to rely on their word, Mike?"

"I'm one-hundred percent certain," Mike replied. "And I've been burned before, too. I think it's a unique opportunity."

David still wasn't convinced. There must be something Kelly and Mike knew that they weren't communicating, he thought.

"I don't doubt you could get their assurances," David said. "I'm sure they would honestly think they'd never betray them. I'm just worried that if this trial becomes a major story, the pressures on them could be enormous. It's a highly competitive business, a news scoop converts to big dollars. I'm still hesitant."

"But what do we have to lose?" Glen said. "The media's not around now. We don't necessarily have to honor what we promise this creep after we have him in custody. You can meet that man and his daughter on your own, Chief, make a decision then."

David glared at Glen. "That's not the way I do business, and not the way this department should do business."

Kelly and Mike exchanged glances, both with similar thoughts. How refreshing to hear David voice this philosophy in light of the experience they'd just been through.

David pondered for a moment or two more before saying, "I think the risk is worth taking. I can tell you two are convinced it is." He raised the microphone to his mouth.

"We're going to open this door a few inches so you'll be sure to hear us, Joe. We're going to honor all your requests." He repeated the message after the door had been opened, telling McConnell to come out with his hands on his head.

"Call out if you can hear me."

"I hear you," McConnell shouted from the recesses of the attic. "Put the future Mister and Mrs. on that mike. If they make the same assurances, we have a deal."

Chapter 80

They could hear McConnell moving through the attic, the sound of boxes and pieces of luggage being shoved aside as he neared the door. He was on his hands and knees when he finally appeared in the doorway. He'd removed the ski mask, it was clutched in his left hand. He had a grin as he placed his hands on his head and started to stand.

"Turn around," Glen instructed. "Put your hands behind your back."

"Careful now," McConnell said as Glen slipped the handcuffs on. The grin disappeared and he winced as Glen clicked them shut.

"We're going to be taking you to University Hospital," David said. "We've already notified them you'd be coming, we called while you were on your way out."

"Thank you," McConnell replied. "What are the chances of me using the john before we head out?"

He's amazing, Kelly thought. She could almost envision him now, sweet-talking the jury. A master con artist, reacting as if he'd just been found by friends in a game of hide-and-seek.

"No problem," David replied. "But you're going to have a large audience. The games are over. Don't try our patience, Joe."

McConnell appeared surprised by David's retort, but he smiled as he glanced at Kelly and Mike.

"Let's hope I'm acquitted by the time of your wedding."

They couldn't help but smile as they shook their heads. "No way," Mike said. "Maybe you'll be out in time to meet our grandchildren."

McConnell grinned as he replied, "Maybe I'll bring them some candy."